Time, Swords & Blood

Hannah Manders

Time, Swords, and Blood

First edition paperback edition October 2024

Book cover design by Kaillie Simms

ISBN 978-1-0688999-0-4 (paperback)

Published by Hannah Manders
www.hannahmanders.com

For Matt
You can read it now.

Name Pronunciation

Listed below are *some* of the character names which have different
pronunciations than their spelling:

Nerice pronounced 'nair-reece' (French-Canadian)
Theone pronounced 'theo-knee' (UK English)
Vice pronounced 'VEE-chay' (Latin)
Caoimhe pronounced 'qee-va' (Irish)
Saoirse pronounced 'SHEER-sha' (Irish)
Pirc pronounced 'peertz' (Slovenian)

Content Warning:

This book contains religious themes, war, descriptions of gore,
general violence, swearing, sexual content, death and a main
character who experiences anxiety and panic attacks.

Chapter One
Day One

I was falling.

Bright lights rained down from red, twisting clouds in the night. A storm raged above me with lighting cutting into the air in sharp bursts. Wind blew my hair around, obscuring my view, and I scratched at it to get it out of my face, terrified. In the distance, echoing all around me, I heard screaming, *so* much screaming. Terror rung out from numerous frightened voices, but the sound was dulled by the air whistling past my ears as I continued to plummet. This could not be real. I wanted this to be a dream. A large ball of fire sped through the sky beside me, its sparks shooting dangerously close to my eyes, its heat brushing my skin.

I was awake.

I remember volunteering at the hospital in the café and the smell of coffee there. I stood in the back, loading coffeemakers, and staring at the floor, debating if I wanted to put another batch of pastries in the oven. I was still young, and the roasted scent of coffee engrained itself into my brain, reminding me of a time in my life that was so much simpler. The smell always calmed me after I had volunteered there.

I remember pausing during dinner service while I worked on the line at a diner and, with the absolute conviction of someone who never had anything bad happen to them, I screamed as hard as I could. Everyone stopped working to look at me, shocked by my outburst. Even silence hung in the dining area for a few moments. I had never done anything like it before, but I was committed to the act until I ran out of breath. My chest heaved and while everyone continued to watch me, I simply returned to grilling burgers. Nobody brought it up afterwards.

I remember going out on a date with a nice girl I had met at my cousin's wedding. We instantly hit it off and were caught in the bathroom while she pinned me against the sink and her hand was under my bridesmaid dress. While I was waiting for the train to pick me up after our first date, the very next day, she pulled me to her and kissed me softly as the snow fell on our hair. The date was pleasant. She brought me to a comedy club for dinner and afterwards we went on a walk along the pier. Though we did not progress into a relationship due to the distance it would have to endure, it was always a fond memory to look back to.

I also remember being inclined to take note of the large letters on the front page of the newspaper this morning, before getting ready to leave.

MISSING: THIRD TRAVELLER IN SIX MONTHS; COINCIDENCE?

"Another one. You never know who's next," the elderly gentleman who delivered the newspaper sighed. His demeaner seemed changed from what I usually received from him. I nodded, agreeing. He sighed again before wishing me a nice day, tipping his sun hat in farewell and slowly walked back up the path to the main road with his old wire trolly full of papers.

A missing Traveller was not unheard of. The Machines were not perfect and on average one in every hundred malfunctioned, its driver never heard from again. The general rule was a Traveller had up to six months to check in. Missing Travellers were getting more common since the beginning of the decade, a disturbing statistic considering time travel had only been figured out a little over fifty years ago. It was a frightening possibility to never return to the modern era and many people stopped using their Machines. According to the latest data, sixty percent of Travellers had halted with the hope that if they waited long enough, engineers would figure out why others were not checking in anymore. The whole situation made a lot of people nervous.

There were theories that some Travellers simply did not want to come back, but counter speculators pointed out people who wanted to travel back in time and stay there did not purchase

Machines; they simply paid top dollar to be left behind by regular Travellers. The Machines could not last hundreds of years unmanned. People were just gone.

Admittedly, I was getting nervous about Travelling even though I never used my Machine to go through time.

I never asked for the newspaper, but every Sunday the paper would show up anyway despite calling the service to end its delivery. It was one of the only newspapers left in circulation and I suppose they pushed it because there were still people who refused to use computers for everything. The elderly man who delivered them would knock, smile at me when I opened the door, and held the paper out asking how my morning had been going or if I was planning anything exciting for the week ahead. He always appeared happy to see me. This morning, he nodded to the paper with his brows slightly raised as if to provoke curiosity in me before he left in a more somber mood.

I leafed through the newspaper after closing the door until I found the page that addressed the latest missing Traveller. This one's name was Cifarelli Salvatore, the latest of many who had gone missing. This name stirred memories of clips on news channels. He was in his late fifties and had been CEO of the Salvatore Corporation and had been attempting to run for prime minister. The provincial police had sent out an arrest alert and his mother commented on details of the circumstances leading to his disappearance.

Months ago, he was all over television screens and internet articles for some scandal that arose during his political campaign. He lost everything thanks to a whistleblower at his company. His money only got him so far in his campaign and many people did not like him, despite his efforts to pay them off. He was never going to win. I was almost happy he disappeared.

His mother said in the newspaper interview that Cifarelli was supposed to have checked in by now, having lied six months ago that he was just going on a little vacation before he had to self-surrender to prison. The problem was he never gave a location to where he was supposed to be going, and the Machine was stolen from a former business partner, the whistleblower to his scandal. Security footage showed Cifarelli had beaten his former business partner within inches of his life then dragged his bloodied body onto the Machine, abducting him. Reporters suggested Cifarelli went on the run since he had missed several court dates, his self-surrender, and now had a warrant out for his arrest, without bail. His mother stated she missed him and was disappointed she had raised a man so filled with greed.

The article listed the Machines serial number for other Travellers to locate it if they happened by him and showed a picture of him along with a written description of what he looked like. It was his first time Travelling when he disappeared. He was untrained.

I was not a first time Traveller. For four years I had used my Machine. By no means was I an expert, but I knew more than an angry rich man.

A new owner was officially trained *once*. The woman who sold me my Machine had taught me how to run it, gave me tips on simple repairs and stressed that if anything drastic happened, I could refer to the manual and *pray*. She brought me to Salem Massachusetts in the 1980's where we had our fortunes told, stayed one night and promptly returned. The old owner had walked me through everything, having me control the Machine, only cuing me when I needed help, confident in my training from school. I had found her after a year of searching for a used Machine. She had confessed she was selling because she feared getting lost like the others, but she showed confidence and composure beyond her years when we Travelled together.

"This here," she pointed to a small blue button covered in a plastic case on the control panel. Her model was old, having belonged to her dad when Machine's first started rolling out to the public for purchase. The panel had years of dirt and stain on its keys and switches, but the blue button and its case was pristine. "If you don't think you can get out of something, that button will make sure history won't change because of you."

I nodded. The self-destruct button had since blended into

the controls, unnoticed and forgotten about since she pointed it out to me.

I used my Machine for vacationing in different countries. It was a safer Travelling method in case of a Machine malfunction compared to getting stuck Travelling through time. Many couples and families used them as vacation homes and rented land in foreign places to park. I had often stayed on my cousin's farm in Germany or camped lavishly in the Appalachians.

My Machine doubled as a small, single floor home, which was a selling point to me when I had seen it listed in the newspaper four years ago. It had one bedroom, a control room that I also used to stash my book overflow, a kitchen, a living space and dining area, and a bathroom with a stand-in shower.

I rented a half acre of land from an old couple, though not quite the age of the newspaper delivery man, at a very modest eight hundred and fifty dollars a month, so long as I took care of their gardens, as they were unable to handle them on their own anymore.

Paintings of forests, castles, and old villages I bought off the previous owner littered most of the pale-yellow walls. I had several bookcases, overflowing with books and tarot card collections I would take out when I had friends over.

The exterior looked like an old stone cottage *that could pass for anything from fifteenth century to twenty-second century design*, as the advertisement had said when I first saw it printed. It had a thick, heavy wooden door and old round stone around every exterior wall with a gabbled wooden roof.

It was home.

Needing to be prepared for my trip, I went over my usual TO-DO List, newspaper still in hand. I was still in my pajamas after a rough night full of dreams of dark monsters and sharp weapons. My Machine would not care if I was not dressed for the day ahead.

The Machine cell was operational and there was enough energy to last a year without solar power, as was mandatory. Enough canned food to feed me for up to six months filled my cupboards and my fridge was full of fresh produce and meat. The computer was syncing with my flight plan, and I was ready to leave for a long-awaited holiday.

At twenty-nine, I was amongst the youngest solo Travellers on Earth, which made travelling both easier, since I had a younger mind and understood technology better than older Travellers, but more dangerous since I had less experience in actual Travelling. Many Travellers started their schooling at thirty and invested in five to six additional years of Machine programing and engineering on top of the education I completed. Having undergone four years of extensive schooling in world history, geography, Machine engineering, horticulture, languages, and First Aid and CPR, I completed the minimum requirement of four years knowledge and training to drive a Machine. A lot of people involved were in their forties through sixties, a few in their seventies having started when the Machines were first brought to the public. Despite my youth, I had faith I understood my Machine as much as I felt It understood me.

My life was preoccupied by two part-time jobs when I did not Travel. I would wake up to get to my first job as a baker at a patisserie. I would work there late night through early morning making bread, pastries, and chocolates for the opener, and sometimes even stew and stocks for the café it was attached to. Then I hauled ass across the city to the local radio tower hosting an oldies station where I had a three-hour slot during morning commutes. I would play my favourite songs, talk about the different vacations I had as a Traveller, tell jokes and stories I saw on the internet and take a twenty-minute power nap during the commercial and music breaks before the traffic report. It was a repetitive lifestyle, but I loved baking, and I loved music. Despite the schooling I had, I almost preferred that life was simple. Almost. Sometimes I felt I was missing out on something. Perhaps that was why I screamed on the line at the diner: just to feel something.

I had scheduled the next two weeks off months ago and I had planned to spend my time on a farm in southern Europe. I looked forward to stepping away from my daily life for just a little while.

My parents, who had been given my itinerary in case of trouble, were travelling the world themselves, just the old-fashioned way. I had told them where I was going and would message them when I arrived and when I returned to my rented plot safe and sound. The last time I got a message from them, they had been touring castles in the United Kingdom. In the years I had Travelled, I had yet to see a castle in person. Maybe, for my next vacation, I would book a castle stay.

With preparation completed I went to the control panel and typed in the serial number for the stolen Machine. The screen blinked *Not Found* and would continue to do so unless I came across the right time of the lost Machine. I opened my Machine's manual to the back of the book and penned the number there too, adding it to many other names and numbers of missing Travellers and Machines printed there. I took a deep breath, reminding myself that I could *relax*. It was hard to do sometimes. Between my two jobs, my mind was always occupied, *mostly* keeping my anxiety at bay. Anxiety about money, about dating, just life in general would plague my mind on a regular basis. There had been several incidents that were so bad I had to go home from one of my jobs because I was throwing up. Even though life was simple, taking vacations always gave me a hard reset. The next two weeks would give me some reprieve from my anxiety where I could pretend regular life did not exist and I would carry that feeling when I returned, for at least for a month or so. I turned on my stereo to tune out the remnants of my strange dream, the music wrapping around me like a warm blanket.

It was strange, the feeling of the world changing around me.

The pre-procedure of my Machine was starting. The walls gently vibrated with life as it woke up and disengaged from the water hookup and city electricity. The destination was locked in, no piloting needed. My Machine would simply go when it was finished booting up because I was Travelling through space, not time.

I walked to my kitchen, discarding the newspaper to my

dining table so I could lock the cabinets in case Travelling was rough.

But something *changed.*

Something felt *wrong.*

I paused, my hands hovering by first cabinet, unable to proceed with an unnerving feeling growing strong in the back of my mind.

A bright red light leaked in from the windows and I winced away to cover my eyes, the light stinging if I tried to locate its source. My Machine began to tremble in a way I knew was dangerous. I turned, attempting to keep my eyes shielded from the red light as it shined in. I could hear as the plates and glasses in my cupboards rattled with more force than there should be. I heard books tumble from shelves.

I hurried, the red light blinding me as I stumbled into the control room, trying to read my Machine and find out what was going wrong. The Machine was screaming, and lights flashed warnings all over the control panel screens. Every sound that could go off went off in a deafening manner, blocking out the music. It shook more and more, as if the earth was quaking beneath it, waiting to crack open to swallow me up. I could not look at anything for more than a second at a time, the light too bright to bare and everything covered in a haze of disorienting red.

I felt as something wrapped itself around my body. Whatever force it was gripped, hard, and I almost lost my footing as it attempted to yank me from the control panel. I shielded my face with one arm. Pushing forward, my feet slowly dragged back as I struggled against whatever restrained me. I needed to read the panel, something had to be malfunctioning. I had to stop it. I had to cancel the mission.

I was scared.

Was this what happened to the Travellers who disappeared?

Did they die?

I gripped the edge of my control panel with one hand and tried to plant my feet there as I heard things crash to the floor in other parts of my home. The force still pulled on me, squeezing me tighter, the light becoming brighter the more I tried to resist it. I thought, I hoped, the Machine was making some sort of detour; it could happen because of bad weather or a low internet connection, but then I felt the control panel disappear from under my fingers and suddenly the force let go of me.

Everything was still and quiet.

Cool air brushed against my bare legs and the soles of my feet burned from standing on a frozen floor. I moved my arm from shielding my eyes and I was somewhere else.

I stood within a dimly lit corridor, no longer within the walls of my home. Sandstone walls were built high, and tapestries depicting stories of battles, small groups of people hunting, and dragons flying in the sky were nailed to the walls. Dirt and moisture were tracked in around me, and cobwebs hung from old carved beams supporting the tall ceiling. The air smelt stale and thick, like walking into an undiscovered castle or cave. Faintly the smell of incense and copper carried in the air. Torches and candles were the only source of light in the hall.

"What the fuck," I whispered.

I pulled my sweater tightly around me.

A green sweater and my pajamas were the only clothes on my body, making the cold in the air set in quickly. The soles of my feet and toes started to freeze from the cold stone floor and the deep feeling of a winter's night sunk itself into my bones. A chill ran down my spine.

This place looked medieval.

The Machine had to have malfunctioned. I could not think of any other way I would have ended up here. Then again, I should have still been within my Machine, not starting to freeze outside of it.

I looked around and there was no sign of anything familiar. Only long, shadowy corridors that flickering in the torch light and…bodies laying in pools of blood that slowly crept towards the carpet.

I felt sick and my heart slammed against my chest at the sight.

"What the actual fuck," I whispered again.

I stepped carefully down the hall, unable to completely avoid the blood as it squelched between the cold carpet and my toes. The blood was still warm. My stomach churned until I felt drawn to something down another hall, a thick trail of bodies leading down it. Bodies that wore medieval amour. Bodies that wore religious robes.

"Holy shit."

The word "No!" echoed towards me from a loud, defiant feminine voice. Absentmindedly, I walked down the hallway, the images of the massacred bodies drifting from my mind as whatever drew me to it put me in a small trance. Muffled voices in the distance grew louder by my approach and with every step whatever the *pull* was grew stronger and the voices angrier. The was a loud, frightened scream.

Red light shimmered from under a set of intricately carved wooden doors and beckoning me. The colour was the same as the light that shined in from the windows of my Machine, but this time it did not blind me. It whispered of a thousand different futures, promises yet to be made. It tugged and pulled on my mind, begging me to make a decision. There was a part of me that wanted to run the other way, afraid, but as I looked at the warm red light and heard the sobs of a woman beyond it, I felt called for a greater purpose. Before I could think twice about it, I opened the doors. They were heavy, and it took everything in me to push them open.

As I stepped through them into a dark corridor, a woman collided into me within moments.

The fear in her eyes left as she caught herself from ricocheting off me. Her dark hair was a mess around her face, and she wore a red chasuble. She panted from the full sprint she had been in.

In her arms was a huge sapphire, the biggest I had ever seen rivaling the size of a volleyball. I stared at it. It hummed with the strange red glow that had called to me under the door and I felt its pull even stronger now.

The woman looked me over with golden eyes, shiny with tears, as a decision of her own was being made in her mind.

It happened fast.

She pushed gem into my arms.

As I caught it, pain took hold of me.

I screamed, holding it in one hand clutched against my belly. I tried to release it but could not move. Pain crept up through my arm, stinging like hot oil on flesh. Then, abruptly, the glowing gem disappeared into dust leaving behind the ache it had given me.

I looked at the woman and brimmed with tears as I trembled to the ground, unable to stand the burning sensation shooting through me.

The woman ran behind me and hooked her hands under my arms. She dragged me back through the doors. She moved quickly, pulling me over muck and blood until she was satisfied with where she put me around a corner. In the distance I could hear running footsteps approach, and her head shot in their direction. She looked back at me, leaning over to kiss me on the head.

I sat crumpled up against a cold wall, shaking as the pain stretched out over my body. My ears rung and my arm radiated with pain as it crept into my shoulder, then my chest, and up my neck. Whatever hungered inside me clawed up into my face and my skull throbbed behind my left eye. A pounding headache took hold of me, my head feeling as if it was going to explode. The woman plucked a ruby ring from her fingers then slid it onto one of mine. I lacked the strength to pull away from her.

"Give this to my *otrok*. I will make sure you have time to get out," she whispered.

"I don't know-"

"Flee, now!" she demanded before running back in the direction we came.

Doors hissed shut.

The *pain*.

"People who seek power never get it in the end!" the woman yelled. "You will never have it now!"

A corrupt, inhuman sound echoed throughout the hallways.

I do not remember getting up, but I was running, the world around me even stranger than before.

Something chased me, and my feet hurt against the rough, sharp stones on the ground. Strange and terrifying screeches echoed around me, and claws stretched out grazing my flesh. I remembered telling myself to not look back, to just keep pushing forward, through the pain, through the fear. A warm liquid leaked out of my eye and the burning in my upper body and face numbed with the adrenaline that now pumped through my veins, pushing me forward. The terrifying sounds screamed out, hurting my ears, and bounced around. Whatever made the sounds were on the cusp of finally catching me. I was nauseous, and tears streamed down my face beside whatever leaked from my eye as I ran. I had to keep going because if I stopped, I *knew* I would be dead.

I heard a loud *boom*, and walls crumbled as if reality itself was falling apart. I narrowly missed being crushed under the rubble as I scrambled my way forward, ducking around corners, weaving through hallways and over countless bodies, a wild heat on my tail. Fire was suddenly everywhere and where it had come from, I did not know. Just as whatever was behind me screamed to devour me, I turned a corner and stood before another woman clad in armour. She was surrounded by red, warm light. The horrific monstrous screams had stopped, and her hand stretched out to meet mine.

My chest heaved as I tried to catch my breath, and I looked around for some sign of what was happening. Nothing. Just the light and the woman. I got the impression she had been patiently waiting for me all this time and my breath returned to me as I took her hand. She gripped me tightly, a sense of serenity enveloping her and extending out to me. I forget about the horrors I had been running from. The pain in my body subsided and cool sensations flowed through my arm and up into my face.

"You will be alright," she cooed reassuringly, a smile forming on her lips.

There was another loud explosion causing my ears to ring. I

felt her let go of my hand and watched her fade into the light. Fear rose inside my chest again as my body became weightless, floating. I scrambled for something to hold on to, searching for her grasp again, to feel safe. I could not feel ground beneath my feet or see walls around me.

Just as soon as I was floating, I felt the sensation of falling.

I tried to focus, tried to see what was happening around me.

I was falling through the night sky.

I pushed my hair from my face again and again, trying to look around. The lights, the raging balls of fire shooting down from the clouds were in the hundreds, thousands. Falling stars crashed to the earth below and I watched as the sky above cracked open like splintering wood.

I whimpered, closed my eyes, and hit water.

My eyes shot open from the impact to my back against the waves. I clawed at the cold water, trying to find the surface.

An eternity passed me by as I choked, searching for air. As the panic set in, the possibility I might drown looming in my mind, a hand plunged into the water and yanked me up from above the surface. I gasped above the angry waves, coughing out the brine in my mouth, the taste of lake water sticking to my tongue. An angry wave hit me, and I struggled against the storming current to stay above the water. I tried to focus on my surroundings again, but the night was black. A violent red storm curled and covered the break in the sky as it continued to rip open, constellations bursting at the seems within it. Crimson lighting struck again and again, filling the heavens like creeping vines, and meteors showered down to the earth below. I saw something aflame in the far distance, the smokestack reaching into the storm and the base aglow with heat. With each new falling star, the clap of thunder rung out, louder than any noise I had ever heard before. The tremors of the storm shook even the water.

I searched for who had pulled me up, but there was no one there. I looked for land with no avail.

"Hello!" I cried.

Nothing, only the violent meteor shower; only the loud

thunder; only the angry skies and waters around me; only the *screaming*. Another violent wave hit me, and the air was pushed from my lungs as my body collided face first into something solid.

I gasped, coughing, my lungs burning from inhaling too much water. I was no longer in the lake. Everything was still. Everything was quiet. I lay prone on blackened earth, feeling over-encumbered. The sun tried to make itself known beyond the deep-set shadows of night. I experienced an inviting tiredness and the urge to close my eyes. Sleep was powerful despite the fear still pumping through my heart. I tried to push myself up but collapsed over my arms.

The last thing I saw were the silhouettes of people running towards me against the rising sun. I heard voices, though I was not coherent enough through the ringing in my ears to understand all the words they said. I felt a pair of arms wedge themselves under me, turning my body face up.

Gasps sounded.

Somebody lifted me from the ground.

"Breath of Krix, be careful!"

"Does anyone recognize her?"

It so warm in these arms.

Chapter Two
Five Days Later

Blurred glimpses of moments marked time passing as I blinked in and out of consciousness.

A candle lit room and shadows mumbling about what I wore.

The warm rim of a cup pressing to my lips, with the gentle command of "Drink".

When I awoke I, at first, was relieved. I was chilled in the moments it took me to take in my surroundings fully. I lay under layers of blankets in a cold room. The floor was a dirty stone, cracked and gnarled by time and disrepair. I sat up quickly, a fur blanket falling from my body. The disorientation from just waking up lingered in the back of my mind.

Where was I?

Torches lit three walls and a large iron-bound door with a small window was guarded by two men in chain and leather armour. They stood on the opposite wall of where I sat. I went to rub the sleep from my eyes and was met with bandages over my left. I removed it, seeing it stained with dried blood and my heart pinched with fear.

I touched my eye, winced, and jerked my hand away from the tender tissue around it. It felt like it was severely bruised.

My breath began to speed up in sync with my heart. The men tensed and took a step forward as I looked at them, both moving their hands to their waist ready to draw a weapon.

"What the fuck!" I cried, my words practically tripping over one another.

The guards drew their swords at the sound of my voice. They pointed their blades towards me, sharp massive weapons with the promise of death on their tips. My heart slammed against my chest, and I put my shaking hands up in defence.

Fuck, fuck, fuck.

My eyes widened, and my stomach was in my throat. I tried

to collect myself as I stared at them. As my brain caught up with the rest of my body, I realized my left hand stung, the tenderness that of burning it badly off a handle of a hot steel pan. Glancing over to examine it, I saw it too was wrapped in linen, the yellow and brown discharge of a wound seeping through the bandages. I felt my body begin to vibrate, my anxiety bubbling up and threatening to boil over. My head *hurt*. It throbbed behind the eye that had been covered, and I went to touch it again, wondering why it was so tender.

My sleeve.

I was not wearing my clothes.

In their place was a linen tunic and trousers. A weathered leather jacket with a fur hood was draped over the end of the bed I had been laying on. The cold really started to settle into my body.

I moved slowly from under the fur blanket, my hands still held in the air, sliding my feet to the floor. When I looked down to them, I saw they too were wrapped in stained bandages. One of the guards spoke, though his eyes stayed locked on me like predator to its prey.

"Tell the Colonel and Mother Nerice that she's awake."

The other guard lingered, the eye contact he made with me intense and uncomfortable. Slowly the door creaked open, and the first guard disappeared behind it. He moved clumsily, his armour clanking against the iron. A few moments passed. My breath puffed into the air and the remaining guard watched me intently, still holding his sword ready for a fight.

Several long minutes passed before heavy footsteps stomped down a hallway beyond the door. The door it slammed open. A person clothed in elegant plated armour with short black hair and a scarred face burst through it practically knocking the guard watching me over with their strength. The armour they wore held small intricate details along the edges of it, tiny engravings of deer and dragons danced where each piece joined together.

The person came right up to me, their eyes two piercing daffodils, glaring at me with aggravation and the need to understand. "Tell me what happened!" they demanded.

I scrambled back on the wooden platform, clutching my hands to my chest, trying to make myself as small as possible. A collection of swearwords riddled my mind as my panic choked me.

Though this person's face had soft, feminine features, they had a robust body, with thick thighs and large shoulders. A lot of muscles clearly hid beneath their armour, and they were in the prime of their life, a living weapon. Their eyes were blackened with makeup making the yellow within them pop in a terrifying way. Their expression threatened something dangerous.

My heart hit my chest, hard. My breath shortened and it was hard to find it. My eyes welled and the headache behind my sore eye worsened. I felt instantly sick, and my stomach twisted, now threatening me too.

"Was it you? Did you do it?!" they accused.

I felt the first of my tears escape and run down my checks, the only real warmth on my exposed skin in this room for the torches were too far to grant any heat. I wanted to pull the furs back over me and use them both for warmth and to keep something between me and the interrogator, though rationally it would not protect me from them. I remained silent as I tried not to fall completely apart in a room full of armed strangers.

I was never trained for this.

Where was my Machine?

Something had gone terribly wrong, that was clear.

A woman sauntered into the room. She watched from afar while I trembled with fear. This woman did not wear armour, but a regal navy duster with a hood covering most of her ear-length ginger hair and large ears. The leather belt around her hip donned a single scabbard holding a dagger. Her lips were plump on her scarless skin, and her eyes were…*red.*

When our eyes connected, her brows rose, and I watched her expression shift. She watched me, taking something about me in. The woman stood exceptionally tall, the ceiling mere centimeters from grazing the top of her head. Embroidered with gold beading over her heart was an owl grasping a feather in its talons. She seemed terrifying in her silence, her red eyes disturbing.

I swallowed not knowing what to do. The interrogator grabbed my tunic and pulled my attention back to them, our faces so close I could feel their breath on my flesh.

"Explain yourself!" they demanded.

I tried, with no avail, to compose myself before them. I really did. When I spoke, my voice trembled, and I felt I was going to burst out sobbing. More tears fell down my face. I was positive whoever this was could feel me shake beneath their grasp.

"I…can't," I said as my voice wabbled, fear surely evident.

The two exchanged looks and the armoured person gently let go of me. "What do you mean you can't?" they said through their teeth; trying calm their tone.

"I don't know what's happening or how I got here!" I blurted out. I tried to catch their eyes with mine in hopes I could convey the truth to them. They refused to look at me directly and my sore eye stung as the realization that I was officially in trouble settled in. I tried to bite back the vomit that threatened to rise. The last thing I wanted was to throw up on armed strangers.

"You're lying!" The interrogator lunged back at me, grabbing me and pulling me up into a stand, away from the safety of the wall. They completely supported my weight, and my toes dangled over the frozen floor below.

I tensed, whimpering. "Please," I croaked.

The ginger woman stepped in and calmly put her hand on the interrogators shoulder. "*Look* at her, Colonel," she said.

I tried to change my focus for just a moment, to distract the bile churning inside me. The ginger haired woman had called the other *Colonel*. I struggled to remember what the guards had said before these two entered.

Colonel and Mother Nerice.

If the interrogator was the Colonel, then maybe the woman was Mother Nerice.

The ginger woman looked nothing like clergy.

The Colonel closed their eyes as Mother Nerice removed her

hand. Slowly and gently, they placed me back down to the floor, releasing the fabric of my clothes. The Colonel took a step away from me.

"I'm so confused!" I sobbed collapsing to my knees. I hinged forward, cradling my face in my hands trying to make myself small and be away from anyone's clutches.

Mother Nerice spoke again, her voice controlled and even. "Do you remember what happened to you? To the Temple?" she asked.

"What Temple?" I whimpered into the floor. "I don't know what's going on or where I am." I peaked back up at them so lost, pleading. I felt pathetic; *what a lovely first impression.*

The Colonel and Mother Nerice exchanged looks again before Mother Nerice nodded to the remaining guard in the room, an instruction to leave. The Colonel seemed less hostile once he left, and the door latched behind him. Mother Nerice lowered her hood. Her ears were not only large, but pointed at the end, like an elf. She moved in front of the little window on the door, blocking the possibility of anyone looking in.

The Colonel knelt before me, their voice calmer and gentler than before. They hinged forward, trying to come to my level with me on the floor. "Do you really not know where you are?" they asked.

I shook my head as tears continued rolling down my cheeks, the salt from them getting on my lips. I felt my hands trembling and wiped at my nose with the cuff of my sleeve. "I have no idea, I swear! I'm really scared, please don't kill me," I begged.

The Colonel sat back up and looked at Mother Nerice again, who came closer at the Colonel's expression. They briefly spoke in a language I did not understand with hushed voices.

"You are near Blackwick of Brawm," Mother Nerice said, her words chosen carefully, her tone suggesting she was trying to jog some sort of memory in me. I stared up at her from the ground, still clearly lost. "We found you unconscious and soaking wet at what remains of Andreja's Temple just a few kilometres north of here. Everyone who was there is gone or dead, except you." Mother Nerice knelt beside the Colonel, and my building anxiety eased slightly. "Perhaps what happened has made you a touch delirious, but we need to know of anything you can recall."

I concentrated.

This was hard, considering the pressure I felt. I preferred the anxiety of a hot, understaffed kitchen with a line out the door. I preferred any anxiety over this. I searched my mind for any answer.

Nothing.

I shook my head. Whatever had happened was gone. All that remained was being in my Machine and then waking up here after drifting in and out of consciousness.

I could not tell them about my Machine.

The two huffed in unison.

"What are your thoughts on making it to the refugee camp?" the Colonel asked.

Mother Nerice nodded. "Let me go ahead alone through the game trail. You bring her on the main path and look for the lieutenant," she replied simply.

The Colonel nodded, their expression calculating. "Gods willing, he is still out there."

As Mother Nerice left, the Colonel stood and held their hand out to me. It was outfitted in a shiny gauntlet. The only skin exposed was their face, that looked down at me skeptically. It took a lot to not let my sobbing overcome me. I took a few upset breaths, thankful the Colonel gave me a several moments to collect myself before pulling me up. Their eyes watched me curiously as I looked at my clothes and around the room. I looked at my feet which, without counting the bandages, were bare.

"Can I ask what's happening?" I asked quietly.

The Colonel motioned to underneath the wooden platform, and I saw a pair of boots there when I looked under it. I slipped them on and fumbled with the laces as I swallowed and sniffed, trying to resist crying more. I felt like a fool and slipped the leather jacket on.

"Aside from the usual? You will see," the Colonel said frankly, continuing to watch me. The boots were tight, and my feet ached inside them. When I stood the Colonel stepped forward, their eyes turning threatening again.

"You make one misstep, and you're dead. Do you understand?" Their voice had a dark tinge to it, and I paled at their words, nodding, obedient.

The Colonel led me out of the room and through a small dug-out passage. Old support beams held the ceiling low and flat rocks made an uneven path to brittle wooden stairs that ascended into the unknown. I followed behind them, tripping a couple times, awkward in the boots.

"We can get you different footwear at the refugee camp. We don't have a lot of supplies here and everything is running low. We were not prepared to be held nearly a week," the Colonel said climbing the stairs.

The air was dry and smelt of mold. The cold stung the throat when inhaled. Cobwebs gently swayed in a draft that came from in front of us. I tripped again climbing the steep stairs. When the Colonel reached the top, they opened the door to outside.

I gasped looking at the landscape. Snowy mountains and coniferous trees stretched on endlessly. The structure we exited was barely holding itself up. The only surviving element of what it used to be was the cellar we had left. Several small tents were set up sporadically around ruins of an old stone building, pieces of it crumbled or covered with snow. What I could only assume were soldiers sat around firepits making small talk, exhaustion clear on their faces. The air was fresh, and my lungs felt free inhaling it. The cold rushed down my shirt and snow melted in my hair as it fell softly from the sky and dampened my boots.

Something tugged at my mind, the direction unclear, seemingly everywhere.

I clutched my arms to my chest as the winter chill set further into my body. Thunder boomed out and everyone in the camp cringed from the sound. I watched as the snow clouds puffed out like a ripple in water. My left eye throbbed more sharply with my headache and a ball of fire ripped through the clouds, shooting down to the earth in the distance.

"Have you heard the story of Shamira's Avowal?" the Colonel turned around to face me, noticing I had stopped following them, enthralled by the meteor rather than fearful like everyone else in the camp.

"No."

"Oh." The Colonel contemplated for a few moments then tried again. "After our loss at Temple Samu last year, we thought it was the end of days. Andreja's Temple suffered a worse fate than Samu's, its destruction heard all over the mountains. Then the sky opened up and spit out thousands of stars. When we made it to the ruins of the Temple, all we found was you. You, the only survivor after two tragedies. Then the demons attacked. Demons have been plaguing us for years, but since the explosion at the Temple five days ago, their onslaught has increased at an overwhelming rate. We have been trapped here since. If we cannot make it back to our village, we fear the worst for our people."

My mind took a while to catch up to what I was hearing. "Wait," I choked. "Five days ago? You found me five days ago?"

The Colonel nodded and continued to speak, but as they did, thunder rocked across the mountains again, louder than before. It was as if it was right next to us. People walking around jumped in fear, those sitting ducked in cover, some even covered their heads expecting the worst. As the echo eased, their faces looked up to the sky as if waiting for it to fall upon them.

My eye pounded in response this time. Pain shot through my body, and I collapsed to my knees, screaming out, clutching at my face. When the pain subsided, I looked at my hand and blood soaked into the bandages over my palm.

"What the fuck?!" I screamed. The headache pressed on. I felt as more liquid leaked from my eye, and I wiped at it with the cuff of my shirt. Blood stained it. "What is happening to me?!" I looked up at the Colonel, pleading for an answer. Onlookers whispered to each other, eyes watching from small groups huddled together in the cold, as I panicked

The Colonel crouched beside me. "Each time the storm cries out, your eye bleeds," they said. The Colonel focused on the eye that was bleeding, that burned inside my skull. They sighed, as if having trouble grasping something I had yet to discover. "You have been *gifted* something magnificent. None of us thought we'd have a sign such as this." The Colonel seemed to want to say more but did not elaborate. Their words only confused me further.

I doubled over as another shock of pain reverberated through my skull and the sky lit up with lightning. The wind picked up and the snow fell heavier. I tried to breathe.

I felt so many eyes on me now. I wanted to disappear back into the cell I had stumbled from. The Colonel continued speaking, pressing a dirty piece of cloth to my cheek and wiping the blood from my face. People hurried by, giving a large berth between themselves and us. "You woke up screaming many times over the last few days. We tried to help soothe the pain. I apologize for my brash behavior earlier, but as I said, we must make it back to our village. I worry for them. Discovering you were awake and not screaming has been nothing less than a miracle."

"I'm so confused," I whimpered. I looked at my hand again where the blood stained my soiled bandages.

Why was my eye bleeding?

I continued to whimper for a minute, maybe longer. Everything hurt so badly, and I was overwhelmed. I could barely catch my breath. I worried I would dizzy from the dread that hung heavy in my chest. I knew I could not have my usual recovery time from an attack like this. I would not get an hour or two to calm down and look at things rationally. I closed my eyes and, again, took a deep breath. I closed out everything. All the panic, the blood, how I had apparently been in some state of unconsciousness for nearly a week, and whatever impending doom that loomed ahead was all shoved down. I had to compose myself now, not later. Deep, even breaths would have to be my relief. If I could not handle this, I could pretend that I could. I thought of an old song. Lyrics about the disconnection from being social, wanting nothing and thinking of nothing but the anticipation of my own personal dessert filling my head. For a few blissful moments, reality did not exist. I opened my eyes and met the Colonel's gaze, tears still running down the sides of my face. The Colonel wiped at my face again then pocketed the cloth in a satchel at their hip, hidden by the cloak they wore over their armour.

"How do I help?" I asked, doing my very best to keep my voice even, actively, desperately, ignoring my eye swelling and aching in my skull. "Just tell me what I need to do. Whatever it is, I'll do it."

A small spark inside me hoped that cooperating would lead to me to a solution of my own. Perhaps something messed up the calibrations of my flight and that was how I ended up here. I needed to find my Machine, wherever it was. I swallowed, trying to gather myself further.

The Colonel pulled me up and motioned for me to follow them. They led me past the camp to a small opening in the forest. Soldiers and small families slowed their activities to watch me as we passed. There were roaming chickens shooed from our path, goats on ties pulled closer to tents. People whacking the snow from the roofs of their temporary homes slowed and gawked. It was intimidating feeling all the eyes on me. All the different, strange faces in medieval styled clothing staring at me. My stomach threatened to turn again, and I continued to breathe as deeply as my body would allow moving forward. Lyrics still hummed in my mind. The snow slowed.

"For now, pray we find Lieutenant Hawke and his entourage," The Colonel explained, noticing me watch people as we walked. They led me down a small path through the opening in the woods, the sounds of the camp slowly quieting the deeper we went into the trees.

"I am sorry to say we mourn for High Priestess Katerina now as well. A temporary truce was supposed to be called. My mother intended to bring leaders together, discuss options after years of destruction, but now all that planning is for naught. Thank the gods most of the Order did not make the journey, or else the Temples would be in a more disastrous state than they are now," the Colonel went on.

Time moved slowly. The Colonel became silent after a while since I did not engage in the conversation. Maybe they had hoped to trigger my memory, but I knew I did not have the answers they were seeking.

The forest was thick with enormous trees, the underbrush overgrown and tall around the path. Long creeping shadows stretched out over the snow, and it seemed quieter than it should in a forest like this. No birds sang, the wind did not whistle through the twisted branches. The Colonel tensed up the further we walked.

I had clearly been pulled back in time, though, if this was my world, if this was Earth, in all the history I studied, I did not recognize what laid out before me. I had never known of any *High Priestess Katerina*; no *Andreja's Temple*; no *Samu's Temple*. The time walking in silence let my mind race away from my earworm. If this was Earth, I would still be in my Machine. I was sure of it.

Where was I?

I had to keep myself preoccupied, letting my mind wander to the actual situation stressed me further. I tried to summon songs back into my mind to no avail. Maybe I should have tried to hold a conversation with the Colonel, asked questions, but I was unsure how to not raise any suspicions in them.

The sounds of the camp behind us were now silent. I had been experiencing the feeling of being watched as we walked, and I had become increasingly on edge over our surroundings. Every sudden shadow, every snap of a twig in the distance made my blood run cold. We were alone together, and I was relieved when the Colonel broke the silence.

"You will go to trial. There are suspicions behind you being the only survivor, but you will be able to speak for yourself. Prove your innocence perhaps." They seemed less tense when they spoke.

I forced my breathing to stay even, swallowing down my panic. The cold combined with my continued tears made my face stiff. I felt overstimulated between my headache, the frigid temperature, and the crunching of my uncomfortable boots into the thick snow. There was a snap of a branch somewhere in the forest and it made me scurry closer to the Colonel.

"Where are we going?" I asked.

"A scholar within our ranks has proposed some theories, we must test if he is correct. Earlier one of our lieutenants went out with him and a small party to attempt clearing a path between our camp and another but," the Colonel paused, collecting themselves before they continued to speak. "It was unknown when, if ever, you would awaken. We must find them."

The Colonel led me down another trail where the forest opened up and became a little less eerie. A sharp edge dropped down abruptly several feet from where the trail led and a wide, frozen river awaited the spring thaw at its base. A clap of thunder sounded. More blood leaked from my eye and another shock of pain shot down through my bones. I crumbled to the icy path, screaming out, trying to clutch at my eye, stop it from bleeding, but the gesture only caused it to hurt more. The Colonel halted at the sound of my cries and lugged me back up, holding me steady until I bore my own weight. I strongly preferred this side of them; the one who did not grab me to scream in my face and instead held onto me acting as support.

They continued forward. "I'm sorry. I know this must be hard," they said.

We had started jogging, the Colonel seemingly impatient with the time we were making. It was tiring trying to keep their pace while my body ached and eye stung. I was discombobulated, but aware enough to realize I had to keep up. I already lagged behind them by several feet when we walked. If I did not jog too, I would certainly loose them on the path.

We descended the side of a mountain, keeping close to the river. Eventually, slowing, we met a small stone bridge, worn by years of weathering and cracked by the cold. Half of it was gone. I looked back up the path we had been following, seeing the steep angles of the mountainside, the grey, snow-covered forest asleep for the winter. High in the hills I watched streams of smoke rising into snowy skies, marking where the camp was and how far we had travelled.

Another loud thunder clash reverberated and my eye pulsed,

a threat for more pain, for *something*. I cried out, unable go further and hunched over clutching at my face. The Colonel turned around on their heal, realizing how far behind I was.

"Are you okay?"

I nodded, lying, tears still streaming down my eyes, mixing with the blood and cold. The Colonel's hand held my arm, waiting for me to be ready to move forward. "I have a splitting headache," I said to them. "I'm so tired."

The Colonel was silent for a few moments before they spoke. "We must keep going before it gets dark. Just keep pushing forward."

I was unmotivated. It was hard to find my breath. I felt dizzy from the headache and the anxiety. I was tired from the trek down the mountain. I did not understand how I was expected to move so far after being unconscious for five days. I slowly rose. "Let's go," I breathed.

With their free hand the Colonel pulled another dirty looking cloth from the pouch on their hip and passed it to me.

Blood already crusted to my cheeks from the cold, and I tried to be careful around my eye as I wiped it. When I finished, I attempted to hand the cloth back, but the Colonel shook their head and lead me forward, carefully stepping down the banks for the frozen river to cross it. Following them, I immediately lost my footing and slid down to the hard ice. I slid a few feet from the bank before I was able to get up.

This was going to be a long day.

Several hundred meters down the river there was a massive hole in the ice. Black pieces of debris littered the area around it and cut into the ice, sticking out like shattered pieces of glass. The Colonel helped me up the other side of the river once we crossed it. I tried not to notice the wagon that was tipped over at the riverside. Crates had tumbled out onto the snow and cracked open overspilling goods. Bloodied corpses lay mutilated beside the wagon, innards frozen in the snow around them.

What had happened here?

"Stay on the trail," the Colonel said, bringing my attention back to them

I followed them further through the mountains. I saw more bodies lacing the trail, some looking as if they had laid there for a while and others fresh, maybe dead only a few hours, a mix of armoured individuals and commonfolk. Some people seemed to have simply collapsed from exhaustion, no signs of a struggle on them, but others were gutted or had missing limbs. It was a disturbing sight, but the Colonel seemed indifferent to it all.

We walked for a while. The sun was high in the sky, trying to force its past the snow clouds when we had left the original camp. Now it dipped low, threatening to hide behind the trees and mountains. The trees got more eerie the longer we walked. I kept my attention to the Colonel, afraid to look away from my guide.

Eventually we reached a pair of men, and I could not comprehend the creature they battled. The area where they fought was flattened, the trees around it either gone or pushed outward from the collision site of whatever crashed there. Large sheets of blackened metal lay strewn around the ground half buried by a fresh sheet of snow. Huge, jagged pieces of metal stuck sharply from the earth. Pipes and inactive wiring singed to a point of uselessness lay scattered throughout the debris. My stomach dropped.

I knew what this wreckage was.

A massive white monster with long limbs and exposed bones lurched around the battleground, spitting up black, sticky ooze from its mouth. Its jaw was dislodged, and its eyes held onto its skull by threads as greenish, sickly flesh melted from its body leaving the thin desiccated muscles beneath. When it screamed, it sounded painfully unholy. I froze in horror.

I could hear the Colonel cuss under their breath when we arrived at the scene. Unworldly sounds echoed around us coming from the trees, closing in. The Colonel pulled a sword from the scabbard at their side and snatched a small shield from their other hip.

"Stay behind me!" they commanded, running towards the

creature, their sword igniting in flame.

I obeyed attempting to keep up with them, but at a safe distance.

The deep crunch of heavy weight stepped into the snow nearby, my attention drawn away from the battle before me. I forgot myself, looking into the trees where I heard the sound and watched as black monster, different from the one the others attacked, crawled its way into view. The body was that of a primate with spiked wings uncurling from its back as if the creature was hiding them to stay small and hidden. Long, razor-sharp fingers scraped against the snow, readying to pounce, and its flesh actively decayed off its body. It bared its large, mangled set of teeth and black ooze dripped from its lips like drool from a hungry animal. Its eyes were locked on me and then it shrieked, the sound high and bird-like. All my senses went on high alert.

These did not exist on Earth.

I screamed as it charged me.

Scrambling backwards, trying to flee, I immediately tripped over something. I only had a moment to realize it was another body; that of a soldier. A large, dented shield lay snug beside her, and a short sword was still grasped in her fist. There was only had a second to think. I knew how to cut up dead animals and poultry to cook them, not how to kill. I grabbed the shield. I could not try to fight, but I could try to defend myself.

I unsuccessfully kept the creature off me and was pinned between the frozen earth and the shield very soon. The twisted monster was heavy and agile. It made another dreadful screech, wanting me, my death. My ears rung from the proximity of it while I tried to hold it off me with the shield. I attempted to push it away, to give me some reprieve to get back up to run for the Colonel. I hoped if I could lead the creature closer to an actual skilled fighter, I would have a better chance of surviving. The black ooze dripped more from its mouth, pouring over the shield and into my hair. It smelt of rot and fungus. Bile threatened to come up from my belly.

"Help!" I screamed, trying to thrust the monster off me

again. Temporarily it retreated from the shield, and I put the shield in front of me, peaking over the top of it to watch the creature as I knelt. It hissed and spat at me before it rushed me. The sound of its claws scraping against the shield was coarse, like the sound of nails on chalkboard. I screamed desperately for help.

Had the other creature won the battle?

Was I alone?

Fear flowed through me now more than before. I could no longer feel the aches within my body or my feet stinging within the boots. My eyes were only on this *thing*, if they left it, I would die. I struggled to force myself up to a standing position but tripped on the poor soldier's body a second time, nearly falling again. Heat blistered off the monster and its claws cut into my arms from around the edges of the shield. It was strong and I was running out of energy fast. I looked back at the soldier, seeing a dagger on her hip. I chanced taking the dagger from the corpse. The creature's inky rotting body crawled desperately over the shield to reach me, its claws reaching out, a sharp nail scraping over my face. When its monstrous face screeched in triumph, I shoved the blade up through its jaw. It shrieked, and I winced from the piercing sound.

Then it was gone.

A flaming blade went clean through its neck, beheading it mid-shriek. The second its head was severed it disappeared into the air, like smoke off a candle, and the Colonel's burning sword hung in the air where the creature once stood.

The other monster was gone, and the Colonel had rescued me. Their hair was slick with sweat and black ooze was splattered over their armour.

"Thank you…" I said relieved, slowly standing back up and lowering the shield, glad I did not have to bear the weight of it or the creature anymore.

The Colonel advanced with their sword, still alit with fire, still at the ready, as if to attack me. "Drop your weapon, now!" they demanded.

I panicked, my eyes widening, but not before dropping the

dagger and shield at my feet. "I'm sorry!" I yelped, stepping away from both items and backing away from them with my hands in the air. I was shaking, my breath short. "That creature it- I'm sorry! I don't want to die! Please don't kill me!" I continued to feel my heartbeat in my head and tears once again ran down my face. I wanted to wipe at them, I wanted to clean my face, everything was sore, but we were in the middle of the mountains.

My *eye.*

The Colonel looked surprised by my response, at my complete cooperation and crying. They lowered their sword, and their stance became less on the offence.

A man suddenly rushed me. He had large, pointed ears like Mother Nerice and braided black hair. He looked determined, serious, and he grabbed my bandaged hand to pull me toward the metal debris. He refused to let me go as I tried to escape him. Small fires were now alit, and he pulled me away from the corpse of the soldier and the weapons I discarded. I could see my blood staining his exposed fingers through the bandages, having not realized I had irritated the wound on my palm. When he was pleased with where we stood, he pointed at his eyes, grabbing my attention as we stood amongst the flames and metal. He then indicated the carnage.

"Look at the torment. Want peace. Claim it. Repeat after me," the man instructed. His bright, blood red eyes caught mine and I swallowed, frightened, nodding that I understood his command and stopped struggling against his hold.

He began to chant in the language I had heard earlier, and I struggled to say it back to him, mispronouncing words. When I failed to say them correctly, he eyed me, assessing his next move. His grip loosened on my hand.

"I will say it slower. Repeat after me." He spoke slower, calmer, articulating the words and I followed his instruction. My eyes gazed over the blood and fire, catching the shiny and singed metal sticking from the ground. As the words left my lips something like a ripple in reality opened up, engulfing the scene. It swelled and wind picked up around us. I felt as my aching eye began to leak again.

More creatures like the ones who attacked us were dragged by some unseen force from the trees, towards the rupture. The monsters struggled against it, red light shining out as each one was swallowed up. When the last disappeared, it exploded into nothing, a wave of air thrusting outwards, the fires blown out leaving black ashes to mark where the flames once flickered. As remnants of the rupture glittered down to the snow, the man let my hand go and wiped my blood on his hand off with a part of his thick cloak.

I looked at him, shocked.

His hair was pulled into a thick braid that sat over his shoulder. Several piercings hung in his large ears and left eyebrow. His skin was nearly flawless of any blemish. His unsettling red eyes gave the impression he was older beyond what his young face presented. He only seemed a few years older than I was, if at all. His height towered over me; his body lean and covered in layers of leathers and furs. His pointed ears really threw me off and I stared at them a little too long.

"What was that?" I asked.

"A cleansing spell," he replied matter-of-factly eyeing his hand. Something crossed his expression when he noticed a little blood he missed then he met my gaze while wiping his hand on his cloak once more. "Despite being out of practice with Bygone Speech, you did a decent job with it."

"What? You mean I did that?" I asked, looking back over the scene, over the metal and blood and ash. The were no signs of monsters anymore; no corpses either.

"We have been having trouble cleansing the mountains since the sky fell. No number of swords or spells were enough, but…" He analyzed me more, a million thoughts crossing over his eyes as he watched me. "I, like many of us, want to believe the gods have not completely forsaken us. It seems they sent you to remind us they are still here."

This man had a stoic and educated way about him. He stood very straight and cocked a brow when I continued to stare at his ears. I shook my head, returning my attention to his words. I vaguely remembered the mention of a scholar. *Was this him?*

"Does this mean she's…?" the Colonel left a question in the air, their voice hopeful.

"It's possible," the man said, his eyes continuing to assess me. He wore a dull red, embroidered tunic and thick leathers underneath his cloak. The embroidery matched the details that the Colonel had on their armour. A belt with many bottles filled with glittering liquids hung around his hips caught my eye. He carried no weapons.

I took a deep breath, trying to hold back more tears threatening the rims of my eyes. Responsibility was hanging all around me, responsibility that I had to have.

He had to be kidding.

I was not sent by gods to remind people their gods had not forgotten about them.

All I could focus on was the pain in my eye. I was sore. I wanted to lie down and wake up in my own bed. I wanted to *eat*. I wanted my eye to stop aching and bleeding.

"Good to know there could be a solution! Just when I thought I'd be turned into monster shit," a friendly male voice said sarcastically. I looked behind me. A small, burly man with a long bow stood from picking up the dagger I had use just minutes before. He was splattered in black rot.

"Lieutenant!" The Colonel said excitedly. They rushed past the other man and I, straight to the short man. The Colonel grabbed his arm, squeezing it tight as he looked up at them with a dashing smile.

"Hello Theone," he said.

The Colonel dipped their neck, being almost a full foot taller than him, and leaned their forehead on his. A relieved expression crossed over their face, making them look softer, vulnerable. The small man closed his eyes while the Colonel leaned their forehead to his, continuing to smile until they released him.

"I was worried," the Colonel said.

"Aye, don't worry about me." The small man smiled again at

the Colonel, before looking past them to me. He slid the dagger into his own belt. "My name's Durin Hawke: skilled bowman and this one's lieutenant," he winked at the Colonel and walked over to me, holding his hand out to shake. My heart warmed at his presence; my anxiety easing slightly. It was nice to see such a friendly face after everything that happened.

I liked him immediately.

Durin kept his sandy, shoulder-length hair in a bun. Several small braids hung freely from the right side of his face tied with beads. He had loads of piercings in his cartilage and his face looked unshaven for several days. His eyes were a deep, mossy green that reminded me of my sweater, the one I swore I had been wearing before waking up; they shined brightly against the darkening skies around us. He had a thick and short stature with strong shoulders. He seemed around my height; and I was not very tall to begin with.

"I'm Delilah Golding: very confused cook and music lover." I shook his hand.

Durin smiled fondly as I heard the Colonel mumble something behind me. Durin had a strong grip. When he let go, it occurred to me that these people had no idea of who I was until this very moment. Then again, no one had asked my name or introduced themselves to me until Durin did.

The Colonel stepped forward. "Lieutenant. Are the two of you the only ones left?"

"They were everywhere, Theone. We received an owl from the Commander. His soldiers can barely hold control. We need to make it back to Blackwick, or we will not survive another week."

The Colonel let out a tired sigh, knowing something I obviously did not. Silence hung for a moment as they seemed to plan something in their mind.

Durin leaned in close and in a quiet tone he said, "Don't address me as *Lieutenant*, I don't go out much and I bet you can see why." He leaned away and patted my back.

The tall, large-eared man now held a long walking stick in his hand and tuned to me after having studied the situation. I had not noticed him move away or come back. "My name is Vice. I am pleased you woke up." He looked me over and made a face. "Though, let me give you something until we can get you to a proper healer."

"He was one of the people who made sure you didn't bleed out while you were unconscious, in case you were wondering,'" Durin explained to me.

Yes, I definitely like him.

I gulped, trying not to dwell on the fact that my eye bled so much they thought I would die from it. And the Colonel had said I would wake up *screaming*? I brought my mind back to the present and looked at Vice.

Vice waved a hand over my face, his eyes focused. A pleasant tingle ran down my spine and my body ached a little less; enough to ease the nausea.

"Thank you," I said quietly.

More magic.

It was nice to not feel like I was going to fall apart.

"Thank me when the war is over, and you are not dead." Vice turned his attention back to the Colonel. "Colonel, you should know the magic involved here is unlike any I have seen. Perhaps no one has seen this kind of magic, not for a long time. We have been given grace with Miss Golding. Though I find it difficult to imagine having such power at birth, not unless someone were the child of the gods or," Vice's gaze met mine again, concentrating on the eye that hurt before he handed me one of the glittering bottles on his hip. "Well, you know."

I scowled at the glass vial.

Durin caught my attention as Vice and the Colonel continued to talk. When I looked at him, he made a drinking motion with his hand. I nodded and downed the contents of the bottle. It was thick like syrup and tasted like bog water. I gagged, but I felt better after the taste went away. The aches dulled fully, my stomach stopped pinching.

"Perhaps the Commander can help you with the gash on

your face, he is a very talented mage, from my understanding," Vice said to me.

"We know a lot of very talented people," Durin bragged.

The Colonel nodded then said, "We must make it to the refugee camp immediately. This is too many demons encounters for one day. The refugees cannot defend themselves if demons make their way to the village, if they have not already. With the spell working we might be able to clear a path on the roads now," they glanced at me and the other two nodded in agreement.

We moved on. The path was easier with two extra people. I wondered what they meant by *demons*. They could not be serious, but the more I thought about it the more I realized there was no other word to describe what we encountered. I wanted to ask about what else may be in the woods, it could not have only been the demons that I sensed nor what made the Colonel so tense during our hike. I bit my tongue on the matter. No matter what I was sensing, I knew I feared finding out what it was. I knew enough to not ask questions, not in the woods and not with night approaching.

Durin slowed his pace to stay beside me as I practically dragged myself behind the Colonel and Vice. My tiredness continued to grow like a looming cloud, my hunger squeezed my stomach. I had no idea how long I had been out here, but surely, we were going to reach our destination soon.

"I'm sorry about the rest of your party," I said to Durin. The silence on the path made me uncomfortable. Vice and Theone were quiet, and I was still on high alert from the battle despite my growing exhaustion.

"We've been trying to clear these roads since before the explosion. Clearing them would make it easier for refugees to come and our troops to go, but then the stars fell." Durin shrugged. "We've been stuck in this area almost a week and nearly didn't make it to our camps once we investigated the Temple. We were lucky that you two showed up when you did. Theone is a force to be reckoned with."

I could not help but agree, though I could see the sadness in Durin's eyes that he and Vice were the only two who survived the days patrol.

I could smell them before I saw them; the putrid scent of decay hitting me and twisting my insides just before the sounds of battle came within earshot.

We hiked through a steep path, wild brush scratching against me and snagging on the rips in my clothing. Where some areas were wide for many to cross, others were thin, only large enough to pass in single file. The sun barely held onto the sky and slinked behind the mountains eager for slumber. Shadows in the surrounding wood seemed to bend and creep sinisterly towards us. Durin tried to keep my attention as the Colonel and Vice marched ahead of us, clearly sensing my unease. Vice's walking stick glowed bright as the sun disappeared, an enchanted staff. The Colonel drew their sword, giving it a single shake, flame igniting, brightening up the creeping shadows.

It was quiet, save for the sound of swords clashing and terrible, unearthly screams.

As the stench hit me, I observed more metal debris; more charred and scattered pieces of Machine littered across the darkening landscape. There was too much here to be just one Machine.

Many had crashed across these mountains.

We reached an area where a deep crater festered with demons. Soldiers, like the ones at the first camp, fought in font of a gate with tall, spiked logs pointing defensively outward in front of a flat red mountain face. The soldiers appeared to have everything mostly under control, though they were clearly tiring.

"Commander!" the Colonel shouted as they joined the battle.

Everyone worked together. At the edges of the crater stood pairs of soldiers, one holding a torch and another with a sword and shield or some various weaponry to hold off any demons that may approach them. The center of the crater was scattered with burnt metal jutting out, broken and dead in the snow and a dozen demons swarmed the soldiers.

I wondered if there was anyone on Earth that were alive today who would cooperate with one another like the people did before me, but my heart sunk remembering the horrors that the people of Earth could also commit. The selfishness and greed. Yet here these people moved as a team and relied on and protected one another without a second thought.

I watched as the Colonel leapt from the craters edge and landed on a winged creature, its legs collapsing beneath it as the Colonel jammed their flaming sword down through the demons skull. It had been coming up behind another soldier. The soldier had not known it was there.

Vice shouted at me. I looked at him, frightened.

"Hurry! Use the spell!" Vice commanded as he ran towards me. He pointed at the battle, for me to bring my concentration to the demons; my thoughts focusing on them, their destruction. Once Vice reached me, he began to articulate the words of the spell. When I did not immediately chant them, Vice slowed his voice. I repeated his words, watching him, tense. He brought two fingers to his eyes then moved them to point at the demons again. He continued saying the spell, is voice low, ethereal. My eye begun to sting as I moved my attention from Vice's gaze to the monsters. I felt it leak.

How could I keep going like this?

I reached out my hand towards the monsters, pretending whatever magic I could apparently wield with a spell was an extension of myself, just like a knife in the kitchen. I repeated the chant, and another rupture breathed to life in the middle of the battle. I spoke more forcefully, and the demons shrieked in defiance. A headache worsened within my skull.

Just as I thought my head would burst, all the creatures were sucked into the portal behind them, and another rush of wind shot out around the crater.

The mountains were quiet.

The soldiers relished in the silence.

Blood seeped down my face. I was exhausted. Everything hurt. Everything was frightening. My stomach gurgled, both hungry and nauseous from the smell the demons left behind and fatigue. I was beginning to forget what it felt like to not feel this way. I stepped one foot forward to catch my balance but felt the will to stay standing leave me.

Vice caught me, discarding his staff in the process as I collapsed. Blackness clouded my vision, and I struggled to find my footing beneath me.

"The demons are gone! Open the gate!" a mans voice shouted from the crater.

The gate clanked and creaked open, old wood slowly lowered to the ground in front of us while Durin jogged to our side. He fanned my face with his hand.

"The green vial," Vice hissed at Durin. "Give that to her." His arms were hooked under my armpits, and I wiped at my face with my sleeve, now long soiled by my blood leaking through the bandages on my palm and from wiping at my eye. Durin clumsily moved between us, searching Vice's belt for a few moments before I heard a cork pop and Vice lowered me slightly so Durin could reach my mouth without completely crowding me.

When I swallowed the first sip, I coughed but drank the rest when Durin cooed, "It's okay, Shorty," at me. My light-headedness eased and I could feel my legs again. Vice gently lifted me upright and both he and Durin kept a hand on my arms until I waved them off.

"I'm sorry," I said. "I'm just so fucking tired."

Durin laughed and patted my back with a strong hand. "We all are, lets get inside the gate."

"Colonel Ward, you came to my rescue! It's good to see you!" The same voice that shouted for the gate. It was a warm, strong voice. My heart pumped excitedly as if I had smelt my favourite meal before I saw it. I saw a soldier approach, dressed differently from the others.

He was a very handsome man. Dirty blonde hair, closely cut to his head, his once closely groomed jaw, now grown wild without having the luxuries of home to keep up with the growth. He had a large burn scar stretching from his left ear, along his jaw to the corner of his lips and down his neck below where furs and armour covered his skin. His eyes were the prettiest, pale green I had ever seen. I stared at him. He looked like he was a fit man, the bulk of his armour showed that much.

Damn.

The Colonel hauled themselves up over the craters edge near us. "We could not have made it this far without her magic," they said standing. "You said your name was Delilah Golding, correct?"

I nodded, still staring at the man.

He was so *beautiful.*

"Is that so?" He came to a halt in front of us and smiled. "Good to see you're up and well."

I enjoyed the way his cheeks creased with his smile; how playful his expression was despite the massacre that we went though just minutes before. He sheathed his sword before his attention returned to the Colonel who came up behind him.

I felt like I was going to melt. Durin elbowed me and I stopped staring.

"Thank you," I whispered.

Durin chuckled. "You're polite, you know that?"

I bit my lip and shrugged, trying to do anything other than ogle the literal model in armour. I looked over the soldiers who were still in the crater. Some leaned over their legs to catch their breath, others flopped into the dirt, panting. The pairs along the edges of the crater where it met the treeline, switched positions. Those on the defence took the torch and sat carefully to the snow while the ones with the torches took arms and watched the darkness beyond.

What was in the forest?

"Who is that?" I asked Durin in a hushed voice, looking back to the soldier talking to the Colonel.

"Our Commander," Durin replied.

Oh my.

Durin still had his hand on my arm, and he motioned towards the gate. "We should get inside," he said.

As I started to move with Durin, Vice waved the Commander over, indicating me with his staff having picked it back up. "If you have a moment, Commander, could you lend healing to

Miss Golding? She has not had a favourable day."

I blushed as the Commander looked at me again, his eyes scanning over me in a slow, almost savoury manner. He had been talking to the Colonel in the language I did not understand. "We all experience days like that, do we not?" He moved to face me and gently took my arm from Durin. "May I?"

I nodded. "Yeah."

Durin stifled a laugh as he stepped away to give the Commander some space for whatever he was about to do. Both he and Vice moved towards the gate as other soldiers started to file towards it, but the pairs with the torches remained stationary.

I did not see a medical kit or small glass bottles like Vice had on the Commander. Just layers of plate armour and furs and a belt to put his sword on. The Commander raised my arm with one hand to examine it as he tugged the leather glove on his free hand off with his teeth. After he let the glove fall to the snow, he held his free hand over the gashes on the arm, looking up at me through long eyelashes. I felt my heart flutter. His hand began to glow in the darkness, and my arm felt warm and tingled. He gradually moved his hand up from my wrist to my shoulder and back down over the tares in my jacket. I had been actively not looking at the aftermath of my first demon encounter.

When the Commander finished, the pain in my hand and arm had subsided. He then carefully put my arm down and lifted the other to do the same gesture. Once finished he clenched and unclenched his fist as the glow disappeared from his hand.

This world kept getting more magical.

"There is one cut just here," he lightly put his hand near one of the cuts in my sleeve. "It was very deep, perhaps if I was more skilled in the art of healing, you would not be able to tell. I hope a scar is alright with you?"

"More than fine, thank you," I practically squeaked.

"Your hand needs a little longer to not break open again. I've always believed healing naturally is the best for the body, but I gave it a little push."

"I appreciate the help," I said.

The Commander smirked. "Happy to help." He crouched and looked at the blood-crusted fabric on my thigh, another cut that had apparently gone unnoticed or ignored by me. "This one may be a little too difficult. You might still feel some soreness if I heal it for you. The surgeon in Blackwick would be better suited for this, if you would rather wait. I can clean it for you instead?"

I looked down at him as he knelt before me, his eyes meeting mine. I gulped. "Whatever you think is best," I said.

The Commander nodded then held his hand by the wound making a soft motion, grabbing onto something invisible in front of it. Slowly he pulled his hand away and black and red vapor floated away from my thigh. He flicked his hand, and the liquid splattered into the snow like ink. "There we are," the Commander said grabbing his glove from the ground. "Clean and free of infection." He put his glove back on and stood up.

"Thank you," I said quietly.

We went through the gates, the pairs with torches the last to file through. The chains of the gate clanked together as it began to close and when I looked over to watch it, I swore I saw a set of glowing eyes in the darkness staring straight at me. My heart hit my chest, and I looked forward.

Another camp was set up next to a deep cavern that had been hidden by the huge fence line. The cavern was carved so deeply into the earth that all I saw below was darkness. The only thing keeping anyone from tumbling into it was a small stone wall no higher than my knees. Torches flickered in stands welded to the wall. More torches were set up encircling the camp, lighting up any shadow that may creep into it.

Most of the camp was made of scattered fire pits and soldiers, similar to the camp I had woke up in, except there appeared to be more commonfolk than soldiers here. Murmurs followed me as I walked through it, eyes on my back.

I spotted Mother Nerice standing next to an animated older

man wearing navy robes, like the ones she wore, though more modest. It was impressive Mother Nerice made it here unscathed. I looked back at the others. The Commander had been met with Durin, who shook his head at him, his expression sober. The Commander put a hand on Durin's shoulder and patted it in a soothing manner. Vice stood by a few crates, taking inventory of the bottles on his belt.

The man with Mother Nerice seemed more frantic when the Colonel came beside them. His voice echoed through the camp louder than any other, but when he spotted me over the Colonel's shoulder, he pushed by them and approached me with hostility. His billowing navy fabrics had gold and cream coloured embroidery covering everything but his head; which was almost clean shaven. About a week's worth of hair growth and stubble suggested he had not had the chance to groom himself in a few days. His jaw was sharp, and he had a small gold, braided ring in his septum. He seemed older than a lot of the others around. I tensed at his approach.

The torches dotting the stone wall gave me a better look at Mother Nerice's outfit too. It was agile and elegant. Less flowing than the mans, Mother Nerice's piece clung to her body and was sewn in a way as if to act as both ritualistic and practical, ready to fight and defend at any moment. Her hood was up, covering her ears and shadowing the upper half of her face. Nerice slowly followed behind the man, her hands in pockets.

"Ah, look who's here," the man said, sounding irritated.

"Deacon Adder, this is-"

"I know who *she* is," the Deacon interrupted the Colonel who had turned and followed him and Mother Nerice. He had a blackened eye that looked mere hours fresh. "As *Grand* Deacon of Temple Samu, I hereby order you to take this criminal to Zaanthru and face execution."

My nausea wrenched on my insides. *Execution?*

"Order me?" the Colonel's voice hitched from professional to something more challenging, reminding me of the Colonel I met earlier. Their eyes had a feral look to them, wide and ready to attack.

"You are a thug, who supposedly serves the Temples, and you must listen to your betters. Your mother isn't here to defend you anymore!" the Deacon snarled.

"We all serve the Gods, *Deacon*," The Colonel's eyes shined, and I could sense their temptation to give Deacon Adder a matching pair of black eyes. The Colonel took a step closer to him.

"Katerina is dead! We must elect a replacement and obey *their* orders on the matter! This *girl* is unknown and thus a danger!"

My emotions overwhelmed me, panic seized my throat, and I practically shrieked, "I'm not a danger to anybody!" For a moment across the camp everything was silent.

Deacon Adder spat to the ice by my feet and stuck an accusatory finger in my face. "You shouldn't even be here!" he boomed at me. His eyes darted between the three of us. "Our position is hopeless. It's only a matter of time before Blackwick is taken, like all the other villages in the mountains. Brawn is long dead. We were lucky to hold this many people as it is!"

The Colonel's fists clenching at their sides, their fingers hungry to have a sword in them. I watched their black painted lips twitch, measuring their next words before saying them. Before they spoke, Mother Nerice stepped in between the deacon and colonel, holding her hand up to the Deacon's face.

"Seel your lips for a moment, *Adder*, we need to work together, and your voice is," Mother Nerice turned her head to look at him, a sneer on her lips as her eyes went over his face. "*So irritating.*"

I felt my mouth fall agape, not just for Mother Nerice's words or that she held a flat palm almost directly against the deacon's face, but at his complete and total compliance to her words. His face was red with anger, but he held his tongue, and his finger dropped out of my personal space.

"Did she handle the demons?" Mother Nerice asked, her head turning to look at the Colonel.

"Yes, Sir Vice was correct," said the Colonel.

"Thank the gods!" Mother Nerice nodded approvingly to me

then returned her attention to the Colonel. "Do you believe we can make it back to village?" she asked, continuing to hold her hand out to the deacon's face, her hand was the only thing keeping him from speaking.

"Yes, I'm confident of it," the Colonel replied.

Mother Nerice dropped her hand and glanced at Deacon Adder, daring him to interrupt the conversation. "We'll move out within the hour then," she said.

"Listen to me. Abandon this now before more lives are lost!" Deacon Adder begged.

Mother Nerice glared back at Deacon Adder, pointing a finger to him just as he had to me. Her nails were filed into sharp points and the Deacon flinched at her movement. "Did I stutter?" she hissed.

Deacon Adder looked down in shame, his lip curling before he crossed his arms like a small child in trouble.

Thunder pulsed again, a huge crackling noise echoed through the sky making many people along the bridge cringe or duck for cover. My eye stung in response, though not has terribly as it had earlier in the day. My legs still wobbled below me, and the nausea increased with the pain. I shakily went to wipe the blood I felt once again leaking from my eye. Deacon Adder's eyes widened as he watched me.

Durin, Vice and the Commander joined us, Duin presenting an embroidered silk cloth to me as he looked over my face. The embroidery showed four initials: *D.H* and *T.W*. I looked at him, my hand on my cheek in attempt to hide my blood and he smiled softly, encouragingly, motioning for me to take the handkerchief from his leathered fingers. I took it graciously, seeing a hawk stitched into the fabric on another corner of the cloth. I hissed as it connected with my eye and another wave of nausea washed through me.

I saw the rips in my trousers and sleeves. The dried blood crusted to the fabric and the evening chill inched into my skin through the tares. When I had wiped my face, I felt the layer of dried blood laying over my cheeks.

How much blood was leaking out over the course of the day?

I looked between everyone. I could do this. Just hold it together until I was alone. That's *all* I had to do. Hold it together until I was alone, then cry. That was two things. I could do two things.

Deacon Adder's attention was caught by Vice, the sneer on his face returning. "Ah, I see that *this* was where you ran off to, hmm?"

"I had a higher calling than your toys," Vice quipped.

"A shame," Adder sneered

"You must excuse the *Grand* Deacon," Nerice said to me through gritted teeth. "He is probably overwhelmed with his new position and responsibilities. How are the mages doing? I trust you're taking care of them? Or is your successor doing all the work for you?"

Everything had begun to blacken around me. I felt my body waver underneath me and Durin put a hand on my arm. I heard voices continue to snap and hiss at each other.

"Shorty, are you doing alright?" he asked softly as the others continued to argue. I nodded, but I was not confident it convinced him because Durin stepped in front of me, his expression concerned. "Shorty?"

"Alright, bring everyone left in camp. Everyone," the Colonel ordered. "The path is clear between here and the old mill camp. We can make our way back there where our numbers will be greater. Perhaps we can even push back to the village. Tonight."

"Consequences be damned, Colonel!" Deacon Adder hissed.

Mother Nerice jerked her body forward at him, as if to lunge, and Deacon Adder jumped in fear as a result. "Get out of here. Take some scouts with you back to the old mill camp ahead of us. You may be able to sleep in your old bed again, thanks to this woman you want to damn. Unless, of course, you want your head served to the forest instead?"

The deacon grimaced. "Sorry, your Holiness," he said in defeat, before turning and walking in the direction we entered from.

Mother Nerice nodded to two women who wore similar

outfits as her nearby. They had been standing there, waiting on orders. At her movement they flanked the deacon, who crossed his arms again as he turned his head and noticed them. He stood up straight, trying to walk proudly.

"I, um," my voice cracked. I could not form a solid thought. I sensed more eyes on me as Durin snapped his fingers in front of my eyes.

A sick feeling swelled inside of me. It had been an exceptionally long day and all the pain from it was starting to resurface despite Vice's potions and the Commander's healing. I stumbled more and Durin grabbed me with his other hand.

I collapsed to the snow, Durin's arms guiding me down gently. Footsteps moved around me and voices murmured. Someone moved my hair from my face.

I looked up at the sky, where snow fell down onto my face.

"We don't know when the last time she's eaten," Vice's voice. He must have seen me go down. "She could be starved more than we are."

"Allow me." The Commander?

I closed my eyes as Durin handed me over to someone else. I did not feel the cold anymore.

Chapter Three
Day Eight

I lay buried within warm blankets and furs, curled into a ball. As consciousness settled in and the aches in my body woke up, I was reminded of everything that had happened. I peeked out from beyond the covers and looked around, afraid I was back in a cold cell.

This place was nicer. Stone walls surrounded me on three sides and a wooden wall on the fourth held the door. Yellow curtains covered an open window that blew in a cool breeze and on the opposite wall of the window was a roaring fire in a large hearth. I sat up looking at the soft wooden bed beneath me and then two chairs by the door with folded clothing on them. Animal skins covered the floor and the large wooden door with iron hinges stood cracked open on the opposite end of where I had been sleeping. I was in a long night dress the same colour as the curtains and my stomach growled for food.

"Hello?" I squeaked.

The door groaned open revealing a woman with yellow and white robes. She had a large hood over her hair and a hoop in her nose. Her face was gentle and regarded me as she stepped inside the room. She leaned back into whatever space was behind her and spoke softly, though I missed what she was saying. When she looked back at me, she picked up a pile of clothing from one of the chairs beside the door and took a step closer. She spoke to me, but her words did not make sense. We stared at each other awkwardly.

I pulled the blankets up a little as the cold breeze from outside found its way to my skin. "I'm sorry, I don't understand.," I said.

She approached me tentatively and held the clothing out when she reached the bedside. "My name is Captain Florence Pirc. You have met my superiors, Mother Nerice and Colonel Ward. You have been asleep for some time. If it is alright with you, I have sent someone to notify them that you are awake."

I took the clothes from her hands. Her nails were filed sharp, like Mother Nerice's were. "Yes, that's alright…" I said quietly.

She smiled and stepped back towards the door. "A laity volunteer will have some nourishment for you in a few minutes. You must be starving."

I nodded. "I am." As those words left my lips, I felt as if I could cry. My stomach was tight and cramped with hunger. My body was sore and ached from running around a mountain, being attacked by demons.

I paled, remembering the dark creatures. Their distorted faces, their smell, and the thick black ooze that dripped from their mouths unnoticed by them, all of it flooded my memory. Anxiety fluttered in my chest.

Captain Florance gave me a sympathetic look. "The Council will be in shortly. You should have time to dress, if you choose to." She closed the door behind her.

I looked at the folded clothing in my hands. They were made of linen and were soft against my skin. I set them beside me and lifted one piece, unfolding it as I looked over it. The shirt was a corn yellow wrap top, which took me a few minutes to figure out. The pants were a dull white and took me some time to figure out how to put on as well. By the time I finally had them positioned correctly, there was a quiet knock at the door, and I held the pants tightly around my waist before I said, "Yes? Hello?"

I furrowed my brows, looking back at my pants to see where I missed something, its ties limp in my hands, then back to the door. "Hello?" I said again.

Another woman with the same robes as Captain Florence popped in with a tray of food in hand. She had deep orange hair so lovely it seemed artificial. It was tied behind her head, though a single thick curl escaped and hung over face, obscuring one of her eyes. She smiled an absolutely stunning smile at me and set a tray on the chair next to the door. She left as quickly as she arrived.

The smell of mushrooms, dill and paprika filled the room and my stomach grumbled in response, wanting it. I eyed the tray seeing a creamy soup sitting on it with a cup of tea and a thick slice of buttered, toasted herb bread. I felt my mouth water just seeing it. I let the pants slip off my legs and stumbled over the fabric to the tray. A drizzle of fresh cream made a wispy design over the thick broth, and I gaped at the food excited to have something to eat.

I brought the tray over to the bed and dipped the bread into the soup eagerly, scooping it up with pieces of wild mushrooms on it. The bite was satisfyingly flavourful. What a relief to have something to eat. The demons soon left my mind and only thoughts of foragers soup and tea filled my mind. I picked up a ceramic cup of tea and sniffed it, camomile. I took another bite of soup-dipped bread just as there was another knock at the door. I wiped my mouth, standing again, fumbling with the pants as I heard the door creak back open before I could say anything with a mouth full of food. I tightened the pants around my legs again, holding them up as four people entered the room, and regretted not staying in the nightgown.

I blushed immediately and coughed down my bread.

The first to enter the room was the Commander, who took several long strides inside before sliding to a stop, noticing me struggle with the pants. His brows rose with surprise and his eyes ran over my body. "Apologies!" His abrupt stop caused the Colonel to almost walk right into him.

"Oh!" Colonel Ward said, narrowly mission the collision. They looked past the Commanders shoulders and their eyes widened, seeing me hold the pants up. "Do you need assistance?" they asked.

I nodded, feeling my cheeks grow redder.

As Vice walked in the Colonel spun him around to face away from me and Mother Nerice dodged around him, looking at me. I could have sworn she smirked before moving to stand in front of the Commander, matching his height, and speaking to him in another language, obscuring his view. I thought I caught the Commander look at me again before my attention went to the Colonel.

They marched over clad in amor, now clean and shiny, and knelt before me. They held their palms flat out. "Ties please," they said.

I obliged and the Colonel expertly moved the fabric around my waist and through my legs, tying the pants. They stood after a few moments then walked back to the chair where more folded clothes were. There was a long robe, resembling what Captain Florence wore, and a shawl. The Colonel handed them to me, and I slid them on, tying the robe at the waist and wrapping the shawl several times around my neck.

"Thank you," I whispered.

They nodded to me. "Alright Commander, Sir Vice, she is decent."

The Commander peeked around Mother Nerice's head before she turned around and Vice stepped around the two of them. Mother Nerice approached, dragging the now free chair with her after closing the door.

When she reached the Colonel and I, she spun the chair around, its back to me, and straddled it, leaning forward as she looked me up and down.

The Colonel motioned with their hand for me to sit back on the bed. I did so and took the tray back to my lap. "Can I eat?" I asked.

"Of course!" the Commander said. He went to the door and grabbed the other chair there, putting it behind the Colonel who sat down on it after the Commander put his hand on their shoulder to indicate something was there. He stood behind them and looked at me, as everyone else did.

I felt embarrassed to eat but took a tentative sip of the tea.

"So," the Commander said. "Colonel Ward and Mother Nerice have told me you were having some memory troubles."

I took another sip of tea and nodded. "Yes, I don't..." I had to be careful with how I phrased everything. "I don't know how I got here...I was home and then...I wasn't."

"How peculiar," Vice sad.

The Commander made a face and looked at Mother Nerice then Colonel Ward. They made similar faces at him.

"I see. Well, Miss Golding, we are hoping to assist you with recovering your memory. Are you open to some spellwork?" The Commander asked.

"Excuse me?" I replied.

Vice coughed and looked at the Commander. "If I may, Commander."

The Commander held his hand in a way to say *go ahead*.

Vice approached me from around Mother Nerice and Colonel Ward then indicated the bed. "May I?" he asked.

I nodded and took a bite of the bread before finally grabbing the wooden spoon and taking a spoonful of the soup. I was trying desperately not to ravage the tray.

Vice sat beside me.

"The Commander and I are mages. Though not as powerful on our own, we can work together to cast more advanced spells. We were hoping you would be amenable for a memory spell. I believe it should work, especially with your talent for old spells."

"I am not a mage," I said after swallowing another spoonful of soup. The pinching in my stomach began to subside and my anxiety began to fade as fast as it had troubled me. The soup hit the spot just right in my stomach.

"Yes, but anyone can become one with practise," Mother Nerice said matter-of-factly. "And considering your gift, I imagine we can all agree you will be a talented mage at that."

My gift?

"May we have your permission to do this? It is easier when the person is willing," the Commander said.

"Am I able to finish my meal first?" I asked.

"Aye!" The Commander said. "Take your time."

He looked at Colonel Ward and Mother Nerice, his voice lowered, not to hide it from me, but to show me his attention was elsewhere. He spoke in the same language Captain Florence had earlier. I took another sip of the tea and glanced at Vice who was watching me, his ruby red eyes shining in the hearth light, reflecting like an animal in the night. I remembered the eyes that stared at me beyond the gate in the night, the glow, the uneasiness it left me. I shivered.

I felt self-conscious finishing the soup and bread. The others murmured together and when I set the tray back beside me, I held the cup of tea in my hands, using the residual heat to warm my hands.

"I'm ready, I guess," I said.

"Alright," the Commander said. He took his gloves off while he knelt in front me, sitting on his heels. Holding his hands out for me to take, I noticed more burn scars over the top of one of his hands. I could feel my heart speed up with the anticipation of touching him. "All you need to do is concentrate on the time before you woke up at the old mill camp. Focus on the Temple."

"I'm sorry, but I don't remember the Temple," I said.

The Commander tapped his fingers to his palms, encouraging me to hold them. "That's fine, just," he glanced at Vice, "concentrate on our words and be open to them."

I nodded, setting my teacup back to the tray and took his hands. They were warm and welcoming, calloused. He held my hands firmly.

"Turn your back to me please," Vice instructed.

I did so, but as I felt hands settle on my hair I jerked, surprised, and the hands disappeared.

"My apologies, I need to have a connection to you as well," Vice explained.

"Okay."

"The Commander and Vice know what they're doing," Mother Nerice said. "They studied vigorously for the last few days in preparation. Just relax and breathe."

I took a deep breath and closed my eyes, shutting out everything around me. I suspected that whatever the two of them were about to do would be like the spell Vice had taught me in the mountains. Words I could not understand, commanded in an almost lyrical way, would soon surround me and I would pretend I was listening to music. "I'm ready," I said, continuing to take concentrated breaths.

"Good," the Commander said. My heart tried to jump out of

my throat, and I squeezed my eyes tighter at his voice.

Vice adjusted behind me, and his hands gently settled on the sides of my head.

"Breathe," Mother Nerice said.

I let out a long breath as the two men began to chant softly. Soon I felt my hands tingling, the sensation working its way up my arms. The crown of my head began to feel the way it did when I was drunk, my inhibitions lowering. I tried to concentrate on my breathing and shifted uncomfortably as the tingling faded from my body and the sensation of weightlessness overcame me. Only the Commander and Vice kept me grounded, holding my body from floating away. The air in the room shifted, became colder, and everything silenced within its walls.

A dark voice sounded around us. I could hear metal shift from Colonel Ward's direction and the Commander softly shushed them. The dark voice was vaguely familiar, something picking at the edge of my mind.

"*No! You are a blight to this world!*" a woman hissed. Her voice was forceful, a tone reminding me of the Colonel's, but older.

My eyes shot open, startled, and I looked around expecting someone else to be in the room with us. The Commander was within a couple feet of me, his green eyes focused on mine, and the smell of fresh coffee wafting off him pleasantly. "It's alright, your mind opening up," he said reassuringly.

"That was my-"

"Colonel," the Commander said sternly. His gaze did not leave mine.

A memory scratched closer to the surface of my consciousness. I could feel my left eye begin to sting and I knew blood had started to seep down my cheek. I whimpered.

Colonel Ward stood from their chair, and leaned over the Commander with a cloth, wiping at my face. I groaned at the pain, sucking in a sharp breath at the building pressure behind my eye. The Commander tried to calm me again, his gaze soft, understanding. "Concentrate," he said.

"Holy shit."

That was *my* voice, though I knew I did not speak. My eyes widened. My body felt hot, electric. Everyone seemed less phased than I was.

Reality boiled around us like an invisible bubble within the room was about to pop. The five of us looked around in anticipation. A transparent scene burst out surrounding us, bringing forth a moment trapped in time. A lost memory from when I arrived here.

I felt the Commanders hands tighten around mine as he sensed my tension.

A woman collided with me in a dark hallway.

She handed me something shiny.

I screamed out.

She dragged me to a corner as I cried.

"Give this to my otrok. *I will make sure you have time to get out,"* she whispered.

There was a new pretty ring on my finger.

"I don't know-"

"Flee, now!" she demanded before running away.

A door hissed shut.

"People who seek power never get it in the end!" the woman yelled. *"You will never have it now!"*

We watched as I struggled to stand up. I followed the sounds of screaming.

We watched the same woman struggle, pinned between two men. The image became something more beautiful, intricate, *holy*. No longer was it translucent and no longer were we sitting in the cozy room, but we were transported to a courtyard. My form stood in a large doorway, my eyes wide in horror and staring at the huge, twisted creature in front of the woman.

"Is that a demon?!" Colonel Ward gasped. Our eyes connected and their face softened, their voice lowering as they stared at me in disbelief. "My mother trusted you..."

Our attention returned to the creature, gnarled and angry as it moved around the woman, its guards still struggling to hold her as she fought against them. "*We missed one...Kill her*," it growled, pointing at me with jagged fingers.

The woman looked at the dark entity before her, and we watched as flames ignited on her arms where enemy soldiers restrained her. They cried out, releasing her as the fire somehow caught flame on their armour. The fire ran up her arms and the woman began to scream out, not in pain. she was releasing something after holding it in for a long time. The louder she got, the more the flames consumed her. The soldiers rolled on the ground of the sanctuary, trying to snuff out the flames on themselves, but it only encouraged the fire further. The dark entity whirled away into the air, gone.

I turned and ran so fast I could not believe it was me we were watching. More armoured solders rushed towards me, their bodies melting into demonic forms, their flesh melting off their figure in wet piles. My form ran through us, disappearing, sending chills through my body, my head pounding. I felt as more blood trickled from my eye, but we all were too involved with the memory around us to bother with cleaning my cheek.

The woman detonated with the intensity of a nuclear bomb and the Temple around her exploded outward. Every soldier who was there, every dead body, gone instantaneously. The scene flickered away as if it was a glitch in time and space.

I was crying.

All eyes settled on me, and I tore my hands away from the Commanders, my hands shakily wiping the blood from my face and swatting at Vice's hands still on my scalp.

How did I survive an explosion?

"Do you know who attacked? What did we just see?" Colonel Ward's voice bombarded me.

I shook my head. "I don't remember any of this!" I cried. I kept wiping at my eye, the blood would not stop running and my heartbeat pounded in my skull. The blood stained the fresh bandage over my palm.

I could hear Vice let out a long breath behind me and his

weight left the bed. The Commander tried to console me, looking pained by my tears. I felt like my grip on reality was slipping. The Commanders hand patted my leg as he fished for something on his belt with the other.

"Echoes of what happened plague you. This must have been very traumatic. Your spirit blocks it out; perhaps a few more sessions and some meditation can help work through this," Vice suggested. I felt like I would crumble. I sucked in a hard breath, choking on my crying.

The Commander handed me a silk to wipe my face, his other hand gave a comforting squeeze to my leg. His eyes searched over my expression. "So many deaths can leave a mark like this, *perhaps* we wait before we try again. Our *guest* has been through a lot in a short time," the Commander said. He stood, the absence of his hand on my thigh leaving an ache somewhere within me and I felt a little bit of myself coming back.

"We know she is innocent in this. Our next step to convince the rest of the Temples of this knowledge," the Commander continued. His gaze caught mine, and I was able to find my breath. My mind drifted to song lyrics, and I yearned to blast music in a dark room until I felt like a human being again.

"That vestige; it looked like the Eye of Andreja. A holy relic we thought lost when we retrieved you from the ruins. It appears Andreja picked you and the High Priestess knew you were to be trusted. Perhaps your memory was barred until this point, to keep you safe, in case you ended up in the hands of people less hospitable than us," the Commander said, his tone low and palatable to the ears.

The Commander put his gloves back on. He nodded to Vice who quickly exited the room. Mother Nerice and Colonel Ward stood from their chairs, ready to leave.

"We have a lot to discuss," the Commander said. He returned his attention back to me as the others left. "Thank you. You can return to resting for now. Do you need anything?"

I was still shaking, trying to wrap my head around what happened and my lost memories as lyrics still swirled in my mind;

familiar in a world so strange. I looked at my tray on the floor, what was left of my tea now cold. "May I have some more tea?" I asked.

"You may," the Commander said, and he left me alone in the room.

A few moments of quiet passed. The Commanders handkerchief was still balled up in my hand, stained with tears and blood. I wiped at my face again, the silk cold and damp, a hint of coffee scent lingering on it. I let out a shaky breath and a knock at the door brought me back to the present.

Captain Florence, accompanied by the red-headed woman, stepped inside. The other woman held a new tray in her hands, this time with a steaming pot on it and a small cookie. They both approached me. I went to stand, but Captain Florence held her hand out to stop me.

"If you feel inclined, the Council will see you down the hall when you are ready," she said.

The red-haired woman put the tray she held down on my bed and put the cup from my old tray on it. She poured tea then picked up the old tray from the floor before smiling at me again. With her being so close, I noticed the eye her hair covered. The eye was pale and blind. She left the room quietly.

"We have procured a larger chamber for you," Florence said. "It has been outfitted with clothes and anything else your heart may desire. If you need anything else, please let a member of our laity know, and we will abide by your wishes."

I took the teacup into my hand. Holding it, feeling the warmth in my hands, made me feel a little better. "Uhm…okay," I said. "That's very generous."

Why was everyone suddenly so nice?

"When you'd like to go to it, Gwen can show you where your room is and will give you the key. Just find any of the sisters and they will notify her for you."

I nodded and took sip of tea. "Is my face clean?" I asked as the captain moved to leave. My eyes stung with the promise of more tears, and I intensified my concentration on the music in my head.

Florence looked over my face. "Well…" She was trying to be polite and find the right words. "I can have some hot water brought to you?"

"You don't have to," I said.

"It is no burden," she said then left me with the pot of tea and cookie.

The cookie was made of oats and warm spices and if I closed my eyes, I could almost pretend everything was normal as I ate it.

*

When I was on my last cup of tea and after Florence had returned with some lemon-scented hot water and a linen towel to wash my face with, I decided I should go to the others, like Florence had suggested. I clutched the cup of tea, got up from the bed and crept to the door. I knew I could not stay in this room forever, but the last time I left a room here, there were demons, and a lot of walking involved and that made me apprehensive to leave again.

Beside the door was a pair of wooden sandals and I slipped my bandaged feet into them. When I opened the door, I saw several women in similar garb as Florance standing in a wide hall. They were talking amongst each other and one peaked at me briefly. Her voice lowered before the whole gaggle looked at me with wonder. I scurried past them.

To the left down the hallway there was a grand door. It was carved with images of people gathered around a great fire, some of the people were crying, others seeming relieved. When I concentrated on it, I noticed there was a person laying in the middle of the flames. A funeral pyre.

The rest of the hallway greeted me with art, yellow silks on the walls and the sound of arguing muffled behind a door at the far end of it. I followed the voices.

Old wood boards, cracked and darkened with decades of weathering soaking into their bones, lined the walls at the front of the building. Walking deeper into it, the wood was replaced by solid stone. Doors leading to other rooms or halls were bolted directly to rock with rusting hinges. Candles lit alters carved into the rock walls and torch light flickered in a cool draft. Worn mustard-coloured carpets lined the floor straight to the door I suspected the voices were leading me. It was a massive space, and I wondered how much more of it was built behind at least a dozen different doors I had passed.

Incense wafted through the air with a soothing smell that seemed to help ease my ever-present anxiety. The stone walls, painted a soft yellow, had white lacey floral patterns with dragons and bats flying in clouds and I was momentarily enthralled by the designs. As I reached the far door, I heard Colonel Ward's disgruntled tone speaking. I knocked tentatively and when no one answered, I entered the room.

Two guards stood at each side of the doorway. I recognized them as the two who had been guarding me when I woke up in the cell. I felt like a child amongst giants here and I turned to leave, immediately regretting my decision to enter, even though I knew they were expecting me. Deacon Adder's eyes instantly found me, and rage bubbled and boiled beneath his red face. "Chain her! She's a witch!" *There it was.* "I want her prepared for travel to the capital with me immediately!" he hissed.

"Ignore that and leave us. Tell the Commander and Colonel Vale to come here as soon as they're able," Colonel Ward demanded, their eyes focusing on the two guards.

Mother Nerice stood with her arms crossed on the far end of a table that resembled a large slice out of a massive tree. She waved at the guards, in agreement with Colonel Ward, and both guards eyed me as I stepped aside to let them through the door.

The deacon, now completely clean shaven, including the top of his head, looked more than irritated with his yellowing black eye. "Do you think I will not report your insubordination to the Temples, Colonel?" he growled.

"The mountains are safer thanks to *her*. Do you think the Temples will ignore that fact?" Colonel Ward replied through gritted teeth. "Imagine the potential across the province!"

I questioned why they even wanted me here. I felt dazed,

albeit curious, and I did not care for the deacon's attitude.

"So, I'm still a suspect? Even after being completely compliant? I have done everything you have asked of me. Why would someone guilty of heinous crimes be so cooperative?" I asked, glaring at the deacon, the words leaving my mouth before I even realized.

"You absolutely are still a suspect," the Deacon glared back.

"No, she is not," Colonel Ward said firmly.

Mother Nerice uncrossed her arms and looked at Deacon Adder. "High Priestess Katerina was behind the explosion at the forum. We saw it in the vision that the Commander and Sir Vice pulled from her mind. Someone infiltrated and killed many before Miss Golding appeared. Our Divine knew she could be trusted and sacrificed herself with the hope of destroying the evil within her home. Obviously, this creature, this *thing*, has allies who yet live otherwise the war would have concluded when demons started dropping out of the fucking sky." She cocked a brow at the deacon.

"You're accusing *me* as a suspect?!" the deacon said, appalled.

"Yes," Mother Nerice replied firmly.

"But not this witch?!" the deacon asked in disbelief.

"Katerina gave her the *ring* with instruction to give it to *me*," Colonel Ward growled. "We will oblige your need for a trial and soon everyone will see the truth. Owls have already been sent to Zaanthru. Rest assured; *someone* will pay for this."

"You?!" Deacon Adder hissed. "Unbelievable! And not one of you believe her survival is suspicious? Heretics! All of you!"

"The gods sent her to us when we needed her most," Colonel Ward looked at me, almost fondly. "My mother knew she could help us".

"You think I was sent here?" I asked in disbelief.

"Absolutely," Colonel Ward said. They did not elaborate.

Not the gods again.

"You have the power to cleanse our land and magic demons back to the Other, a true gift after you held the Eye of Andreja; something that is never to be held, aside from the chosen few. This evidence is our only hope at ending this war, and I will bet my birds you were given this gift for that exact purpose," Mother Nerice added.

"This is not for you to decide," the deacon growled at them. "Perhaps Colonel Ward is blinded for they mourn for their mother!"

The Colonel slammed their fists down to the table, staring the deacon down with sharp, yellow eyes. "Do you not grasp the situation, Adder?" they asked. "High Priestess Katerina granted us authority. *We* were given permission to rally armies after centuries of destruction because *my mother* and the other High Priestess's of the Holy Order agreed there was no other way for this war to end. Right after we were granted this permission, *she* held a forum to discuss a possible conclusion to this chaos and invited those forsaken vagabonds from the Southern Province in an act of peace. As a result, someone tried to kill her and steal a holy relic." Colonel Ward approached the deacon, closing in on him like a hungry lion, their eyes wide with determination as Deacon Adder who, despite his own angry face, receded into himself as they backed him against a wall. "We will send those demons back to the Other. We will find who is responsible, *and* we will restore order, with or without your approval. The trial will prove a waste of time, just you wait."

There was a long moment of silence as the electricity buzzed between the two of them. Colonel Ward held their ground and after a long moment the deacon, defeated, stormed from the room, pushing passed me through the door even though there was room to spare.

Colonel Ward growled angrily as the door slammed shut behind the deacon. They shook their head, closing their eyes and massaging the bridge of their nose.

Mother Nerice appeared less rigid once the deacon was gone. She tried to ease the Colonel's obvious tension when she addressed them. "We will end this war, but we aren't ready. We do not have the numbers right now. By the time the deacon is through with us any Temple support will be adjourned. We must go to trial and prove there is other ways to finish this."

"We have no choice," Colonel Ward said, opening their eyes and setting their hands to their hips. "We must act now, with you at our side." The Colonel looked at me.

"What *exactly* is going on?" I asked.

Mother Nerice and Colonel Ward exchanged looks with each other.

"You mean aside from the war?" the Colonel asked, their tone concerned. I remember a similar brief conversation when we were moving through the mountain. *Aside from the usual,* was the reply I had received.

Oh, fuck.

Mother Nerice's blood-red eyes connected with mine and I was again unsettled by their colour, the tales they held within them. "You poor creature, your memory must be in shambles," she said to me.

I avoided her eye contact and felt as I shrunk into myself a little, embarrassed. I did not know how I was supposed to explain myself to them, what questions were okay to ask without causing suspicion. I let out a long breath, calculating what I should say.

"The night of the forum, when the sky began to fall apart, demons crashed all over the Northwestern Province. Our world has been run tired with centuries of bloodshed and now it has been made worse," Mother Nerice explained.

"My mother knew something would happen; I know she did. And those imbeciles in the South Province have not helped this war at all." The Colonel rolled their eyes, exasperated, probably from years of trying to find a solution. "Many believe they are the ones who started it. Even some history texts have it written that way, and I would not be surprised if they did, considering it has been them verses the rest of the world for a long time. Where their numbers and power came from, I will never understand." They looked at me. I could feel their empathy towards me, their eyes tired and concerned, wondering how my confusion was so strong.

"So, you're trying to restore order?" I asked. "In a war."

"Aye, *trying,*" Mother Nerice said.

"Help us rectify centuries of mistakes, before it's too late." Colonel Ward held their hand out to me; it was the first time I saw it without an armoured gauntlet and the armour they wore appeared more of a statement piece than practical. Flowing red fabrics hung at their hips and a hooded cloak draped over their shoulders. They still carried a sword and small hand shield on their belt, but the urgency and need for protection was lessoned. Their short hair was combed back behind their ears and the dark make up was clean, making their eyes and lips more striking.

Mother Nerice's eyes were on me, waiting for my next move; her hood on, shadowing her features, her high cheekbones elevated in the torch light of the room.

I took Colonel Ward's hand in mine, and they squeezed tightly, a deal made. I returned the squeeze and watched as all the anger they had been holding from arguing with the deacon left their expression, relief replacing it.

I knew I was agreeing to help them. I knew that what they were doing must be a good cause since all they wanted was end a war. What I did not know was how I was supposed help. I was an ordinary person. I knew how to escape attackers in city alleyways, not how to fight against an opposing army or demons. I was just a woman. I was not the key to salvation by any means. Whatever magic I had apparently been given I did not know how to use.

How was I supposed to be of any use to them?

Mother Nerice and the Colonel began another discussion and a soldier came in, speaking in hushed tones, occasionally glancing over at me, almost gawking to the point of making me further embarrassed. Eventually Mother Nerice noticed and put her hand to his chin, moving it to look at her.

Around thirty minutes passed. I had felt too awkward to sneak back to the little room I had been in before or find a laity member to be shown my apparent new room. When the soldier finally left, a hand full of papers, I thought that would be my opportunity to leave too. As I faced the door to leave, the Commander walked through it. He was accompanied by a beautiful woman wearing elegant leather armour and a turquoise duster. Her silky long black hair hung over her shoulders with gold chairs threaded through it like a delicate crown and her face lit up when she saw me.

"Commander, Colonel Vale, thank you for coming," Colonel Ward greeted. "How about some proper introductions with Miss Golding before we return to our work." They turned to me and moved their hand as if presenting the Commander. "You've met Commander Lachlan Blackwick, the Champion of the Gods Wall and the leader of our forces and people here."

"I am but one of their advisors," The Commander said, a very handsome smile on his lips.

"How humble," Mother Nerice snickered.

Commander Lachlan held his hand out for me to shake formally. When I reached out to take it, the Commander gripped my wrist in his hand, aligning my palm with his forearm as he shook it with one firm shake. I gripped his wrist, trying to match his strength and felt a finger sweep over my forearm, as if checking for something. He smiled pleasantly as he let go. I remembered the feel of his skin from this morning, and I almost missed it through his leather gloves.

"I am Colonel Theone Ward. I had an opportunity to train as a monk and Mother of Andreja's Temple, thanks to my own mothers standing, but I chose to be outside it's walls as a Keeper and soon thereafter Commander Lachlan's Second. If he were to die in battle, I am to take over as his replacement," the Colonel explained.

"And you would do a marvelous job at it, Colonel Theone," The Commander said proudly.

Theone, what a pretty name. Others had said it in passing. I wondered if the Colonel did not mind being on a first name basis with people who were closer to them.

The Colonel nodded to the Commander, a hint of pride in their expression, then moved to present the ray of sunshine that was Colonel Vale. "This is Colonel Bellamy Vale, a duchess from the Northeastern Province and our ambassador. She has graciously funded much of our endeavours over the last few months since the

Temples have been able to lend us little aid. We had hoped to relieve her of that generosity after the conclave, but with another Temple in ruins and another High Priestess gone we have no opportunity for increased approved aid until after your trial." My stomach pinched at the mention of the trial. I did not know how their judicial system worked, nor how I would make it out of it alive. "Luckily Colonel Vale is charismatic and that has come in helpful in past discussions with the Temples and Dukes across the Province. She is Mother Nerice's Second."

"You flatter me, Theone," Colonel Bellamy turned to me and held her hand out in a delicate way, beautiful jewels on her fingers. "It's a pleasure to meet you. Please simply call me Bellamy." she said pleasantly. I shook her hand. She had a good grip, despite her delicate frame and billowing, richly coloured turquoise clothes under her goldleaf leathers. She wore more layers than the Commander did.

"Of course you've met Mother Nerice," Colonel Theone continued.

"I am the Spymaster here," Mother Nerice said, a smug look on her face. Her ruby eyes went over me briefly and I almost thought she was checking me out.

"Her rank is equal to that of our Commander. If I cannot answer a question for you and Commander Lachlan is busy, Mother Nerice will have the answer," the Colonel clarified

"It's a pleasure," I said nodding to everyone. I felt small next to them, most having to be at least ten years my senior. Colonel Theone had a younger face beneath the hardness of their expression. Maybe I was not the youngest here, but I was still naïve to everyone's obvious skills and the goings on in their world. Yet I was treated with unexpected respect, especially being a stranger to them. When I went to shake Mother Nerice's hand, her grip was the same as the Commanders. Her eyes locked with mine until I let go, her long, sharp nails skimming my skin *almost* threateningly. I swallowed, my heart pumping and stomach squeezing with anxiety.

"Now that we have that settled, we were discussing the acquisition of mages from the Temples," Colonel Theone explained.

"Which means we must plead for support from them at the trail in the Stills," Mother Nerice said.

"Why not directly ask for Keepers to assist?" Commander Lachlan asked.

Colonel Theone sighed. "We need *magic*, Commander. Most Keepers, while talented, do not have magic. The Temple will have a list of mages we can contact-"

"Keepers have charms that could enhance our defences-"

"This is with the assumption the charms are powerful enough," Mother Nerice interrupted.

I suddenly got the undeniable impression that when these four were together, a lot of their discussions were instead heated debates. The Commander, Colonel Theone and Mother Nerice all had a similar tick in their jaws that appeared as their conversation went on. While the Colonel and Commander seemed engaged, Mother Nerice appeared to be unperturbed by a rather common occurrence, biding her time to strike with calculated words. Bellamy leaned over the large table with parchment and a quill in hand, writing something down rather quickly, though her ears pricked at certain moments.

"I was a Keeper. Colonel Theone is a Keeper. We know what they're capable of," Commander Lachlan said sternly.

"Unfortunately, we need to have the trial *first*," Bellamy stated. "The Temple's do not recognize us officially without Katerina and have denounced Miss Golding." She looked right at me then returned her eyes to the parchment. "Until the trial where they can make their own conclusions on the matter, we must be patient and present what we can to them. We will make our decisions on who we need after."

"How do they think I caused this?" I jumped in.

"That is not the entirety of it," Bellamy corrected. "Some have begun calling you 'Seer', while others say you are an omen to tell us the end of this world is nigh. That frightens the Temples. Many of the remaining clergy have declared you a blasphemy, and we heretics for..." Bellamy stood from leaning over the table and pushed her dark hair behind her shoulder. Her eyes were the colour of sand shining brightly in contrast to her tanned skin, and they searched my face for a moment. "Sheltering you," she finished.

"Deacon Adder's doing," Colonel Theone hissed, saying the man's name as if he was a blight on the land.

"Mother Nerice has sent her sigil declaring you nonhostile but because there are two conflicting statements within the Temples, no decisions can be made until the trail. High Priestess Katerina was one of the last of the remaining Divines that held onto the old ways. Every other Temple has either young masters becoming their heads or angry heads, mourning their fallen Sisters. They cannot be reasoned with at this time," Bellamy huffed. "The Temples have gone through a lot of reformation in the last few decades and Katerina had held what was left of tradition afloat," she went on. Her eyes did not leave me, and I was inclined to believe Bellamy was informed of my *memory issues*. An infliction in her tone suggested hope that additional details would trigger more memories from me in a less aggressive way than the spell Vice and Commander Lachlan had preformed.

"The fact is our options are limited. There is too much warring in the Stills below the mountain for us to move through safely in large groups; unless we want to have the bloodshed focused to us. We must also cleanse the rest of the demon centers being reported," Bellamy said, her concentration returning to the parchment she had been writing on.

"Seer? What does that even mean?" I interrupted. A Seer was someone who can see the future; I certainly did not. I could see the curiosity on everyone's faces when the question left my lips. If I had exposed myself as an alien, my day was about to get a lot worse. "I'm sorry," I said, quickly as the silence went on a little too long. "Where I'm from, we just don't have a lot of the customs as you do here. I just want to understand."

"Many know you were the only survivor of Andreja's Temple. A miracle since no one survived Samu's Temple last year. They know how you were able to cleanse two areas of demons where others could not. People have *seen* your face and your gift. They know

High Priestess Katerina must have trusted you with the Eye of Andreja," Bellamy explained, rolling her eyes as she spoke again, her hand a little heavier on the parchment as she wrote. "Damn guards can't keep their mouths shut." She huffed and continued. "Regardless, everyone is talking about you and hope has sparked that the old gods have not left us yet. A Seer is the highest honour in the Temples, even more than the High Priesthood. A connection, directly to the gods. A Seer to the gods themselves and to us."

"How do you feel about being called such?" Commander Lachlan asked. He had a smile on his lips, suggesting he was amongst those who believed what the people were saying about me.

"I don't know. Uncomfortable, I guess," I said. I had to assume Andreja was another holy figure since she had a Temple dedicated to her. But *me?*

The Commander chuckled. "I'm sure the Temples are as well."

"People have been desperate for a sign and then you fell out of the sky with the stars. A blessed spirit among demons," Colonel Theone said.

"So, would it be easier for things to move along if I wasn't here?" I asked.

"This moment has been many years in the making, and you were the cog in the wheel to get everything moving in the right direction," Commander Lachlan said. "Meanwhile, there are other matters to attend to, if you are inclined to help us further," he continued. "My Third, Major Cathal Vale, is trapped in the Stills on his ship the Titan. While you move through the province to retrieve him, you can cleanse any areas you pass then turn back once he is safe. Owls have brought news of a large population of demons on the beach there and his crew cannot get through it on their own."

"Vale? Is he related to you?" I asked looking at Bellamy.

She smirked, nodding. "My uncle. He enjoys the sea's much more than I, I'm afraid. Hence why he is trapped on his ship, and I am safe within the cold mountains." Whatever Bellamy had been writing became satisfactory to her and she moved two smooth stones onto the top and bottom to keep the rolled parchment flat and let the ink dry. She turned. "Anyway, word is beginning to spread and if you can make it to the Stills, word could go further when more people see you for themselves. More lives could be saved from this war. While there, you can also get comfortable with the area as it will lay host to your trial."

"Of course, we won't make you do this alone, Miss Golding," Colonel Theone interjected. "You are a 'miss', correct? If I am missing a title, I do apologize."

I shook my head. "No, you were right, just *Miss*. Also, you all don't need to address me so formally," I said. Everyone looked at me with inquisitive eyes, the only clue to their thoughts with otherwise composed expressions. The only one who showed no surprise was Bellamy, who had already requested I address her informally. "I mean, well, you all know my name. Honestly, I'm adjusting to all this, and I'd rather hear my name over anything else."

"Understandable," Commander Lachlan said with a nod. The way he spoke and held eye contact made my heart skip, and I knew I was blushing.

It had been a large effort not to stare at him during the whole conversation, but Bellamy had made a good substitute, and she had a lot to say. Maybe my gawking was not as obvious when I had been concentrating on her.

Colonel Theone and Mother Nerice eyed me for a moment before the Colonel spoke.

"Nevertheless, *Delilah*," I could tell Colonel Theone was having trouble addressing me informally in a professional setting, "you must begin your training as soon as possible."

When everyone left the room, I followed them back through the building and out into the open air like a lost puppy, unsure of what else to do. Through listening, I learnt of their preparation for upcoming missions off the mountain and tried to remember everything I could, so there was no need for repeating later.

For a moment we stood on a plateau that overlooked a small

village. On either side of us, steep staircases descended towards several dozen buildings with footpaths winding between them like roots and rivers. At the far end was a large log fence, seemingly the only line of defence. Beyond that, were mountains and forests as far as the eye could see, smothered in glittering snow.

"Welcome to Blackwick," Mother Nerice said before returning to a conversation with Bellamy.

I followed them down the left stairs, dreading the climb back up.

I spotted Vice as I shadowed Colonel Theone, who eventually noticed my uncertainty with the situation and detached us from the others, deciding to give me a tour of the town. Vice watched me with puzzled and glowing eyes while we passed him outside a bunkhouse in the darkening evening. He sat in a wooden chair that hung low to the cold earth. In his hand he read a tattered book by oil lamp light with an orange cat asleep on his lap, tucked lovingly into blankets he had draped over his legs. His hair was down over his shoulders and unbraided from the style he had worn it earlier that day.

Durin looked like he felt sorry for me when we walked by him. Deeper into the village, on larger roads that had stones to line them and not frozen dirt, there were tents set up in groups of up to four encircling large fires. Barrels of water sat close enough to the fires to keep from freezing, but not so close that the wood containing the water would burn. Families occupied the tents, refugees of war.

Sitting on an old log beside a communal firepit, Durin poked at an iron pot hanging over the flames. He gave me small salute with his fingers, before his gaze shifted over to the Colonel. He winked at them, and Colonel Theone quickened their pace.

Those who were still awake and walking the streets appeared awestruck by my presence and some occasionally bowed as I passed. In the lamplight, I spotted more painted designs resembling the ones I saw on the walls of the building we had left. The images were scattered on the sides of homes and over doorways, as if to brighten up a war-ravaged world and bringing colour to the dark wood and grey stone that the buildings were made of. I wondered how colourful the village was in the daytime and how rich it would be without the overcast.

I continued following Colonel Theone, feeling an atmospheric shift in everything around me. A shiver went down my spine and I looked up at angry twisting clouds, waiting to let loose a blizzard. A memory of a meteor flying through the clouds arose in my mind. A flicker of many falling in the dark skies around me. The wreckage of Machine's in soiled snow. I looked away from the clouds, anxious.

Eventually Colonel Theone led me back to the building at the top of the village. Through a door off the main hall was another hallway, which was much quieter. I panted from our stair climb as Colonel Theone unlocked the door, having acquired a key from one of the laity members within the building. They explained if I lost the key anyone in the Tabernacle could make me a new one from the collection in Mother Nerice's office.

I had learned, through my tour of Blackwick, that this building, called the Tabernacle, acted as a church to its people. Its acting Mother had gone to the forum at Andreja's Temple. After the explosion, Mother Nerice was named the acting Mother because of her position as Priestess under Samu's banner and her position within the army here. Deacon Adder was soured by this, and Mother Nerice was exceptionally indifferent, encouraging the search for an official Mother as soon as the Council had more resources.

When the Colonel opened the door, it complained from being locked and the smell of old wood and fresh earth wafted out into the hall. The smallest hint of coffee lingered in the air before disappearing. Colonel Theone stepped aside to let me in first.

"Your new chamber," they said.

This room was a large space, able to comfortably sleep at least six people though only one bed was placed inside. The room I had woken up in was snug and, unless people wanted to trip over one another, was only large enough for one person. I thought about the people on the streets of the village, my heart distressed for them. Surely, if this place was a church, they could house the people. Surely, I did not need such a large room.

A small desk with parchment and ink on it sat a few feet from the door, a chair tucked underneath it. Neatly folded clothes were on top of a chest that looked like treasure would be inside. Upon closer inspection, the clothes were stitched with exquisite embroidery and had adjustable strings along the outer side of the pant legs, suggesting I could tighten or loosen them to my desired snugness. An embroidered owl and dragon stitched over the heart of the shirt, and I wondered if there was a significance to them or if someone had seen my back tattoo throughout all the chaos. A pair of fur boots that looked more comfortable and welcoming than the sandals I had on, leaned against the chest. The leather jacket I remembered, now mended from the battle scars, hung on a set of antlers bound to the wall on the other side of the door. There was a tray with a glass pitcher and two cups on a barrel next to a large wooden bed layered in fur blankets and linen sheets. A warm fire blazed in a hearth.

Inside this room everything was safe, and, though it made me uncomfortable to do so, I knew could call it my own.

"Why move me to this room?" I asked. "The smaller room was fine."

"This room was occupied, but-" Colonel Theone's caught themselves from saying something. "The person who had this room volunteered to take the small one if that meant *you* could be more comfortable."

I imagined trying to make this room home, but I was not sure how I could. I yearned for my Machine and Earth. I did not own anything anymore. I was alone.

"I was fine in the small room," I insisted. I sat on the bed, and it sunk comfortably into the frame.

There were two windows on the opposite wall from the door and I imagined a view of a cotton-candy coloured sunset in the mountains. I had seen a rich sunset trying to take over the skies, but the snow clouds still twisted, dominating the heavens. Shadows of the mountains darkened the village, but fires and oil lamps lit the walking paths. Smoke drifted from chimney stacks. The smell of roasted meat and warm cider lingered on the wind and a piece of it followed us inside before Colonel Theone closed the door behind them, locking us in with the incense and old wood smell of the Tabernacle. Whispers of the living brought the village to life under the horror of war.

The people who were still awake on the village paths had made me incredibly self-conscious. I had tried to smile politely at them, but I was not reciprocated with a smile back or a wave. Soldiers froze and stood at attention when they saw me and I walked through them warily, a feeling of embarrassment threatening to bubble up to my chest. Some townsfolk bowed, the refugees overflowing from tents gaped and held out their hands as if I would reach back to touch their palms. I did not know what I found more uncomfortable.

"We insist," the Colonel said.

Colonel Theone stayed with me for a little while. Their voice was soft, calming, even though they talked business with me. They told me what to expect in the coming weeks and the Council schedule should I wish to join them at any time. Mealtimes were listed, only breakfast and dinner, and noteworthy rooms that the Colonel thought I would benefit from within the Tabernacle were mentioned. There were several chapels within for prayer and song, a meditation chamber if I needed somewhere quiet to reflect. All I had to do was ask a laity member to take me.

I perked up at the thought of finding a kitchen, baking bread and pastries. Maybe someone would show me the kitchens and I could feel useful there.

The Colonel inquired about my poor fighting skill while I ran my fingers through the furs on the bed; the fibers much softer than expected. I admitted to never having fought before with any sort of weapon in my life. "I'm skilled with a blade, but not a blade like a sword or dagger. Give me a chicken or a pig and I will clean it, cut it and cook it, but I really was frantically trying to stay alive," I confessed. We sat in my room, a fire lit in a stone hearth, and I realized I was hungry again. Nearly ravenous. My stomach made itself known while our conversation went on.

The Colonel's laugh was unexpectedly reassuring. "I could tell. I'm personally seeing that you are trained and versed in the art of wielding a weapon —or two," they said. "I am surprised your parents never trained you. The world has been this way for so long, it is rare to meet anyone who doesn't know how to defend themselves. I will be back at first light to bring you to a mentor for training. I'll also find the surgeon to check your eye again. The Commander thinks you'll be okay, but let's be safe."

A large animal skin acted as a rug on the ground and books and bottles laced old wooden shelves on the walls. Pale yellow curtains hung over the windows like the room I had awoken in, but they were pushed back behind hooks on the wall beside the glass. A lantern hung in the middle of the room from the dusty rafters and a large beeswax candle hung lit inside.

"Do I need to train? I know I would be better help in the kitchens rather than on the field," I said, hopeful.

Before Colonel Theone could reply, the door opened, distracting them. A fit, young woman with red hair walked through it and I recognized her from earlier in the day when she was with Captain Florence. She was dressed differently now, in armour. In her hands she held a wooden crate. Upon seeing me look at her, she grinned and hauled the crate onto the desk by the door.

"Colonel," she nodded to Colonel Theone then to me. "You are all anyone has talked about for the last three days, it's nice to see you well," the girl continued.

"Three days?" I repeated. I had lost over a week to wherever this place was.

"Aye."

I made a face, my mind racing.

"Private, would you be so kind to get a dinner plate for us?" the Colonel asked.

The woman nodded cheerfully. "Certainly Colonel Ward."

"Thank you."

The woman disappeared, closing the door behind her.

I heard Colonel Ward laugh to themself then they moved to leave. "She will be back with enough meat and bread for two, maybe some cheese and preserves. I imagine you must be very hungry."

I nodded as the Colonel put their hand on the door to open it.

"Colonel Theone?" I said softly.

They stopped and turned to face me again, their hand still on the lever to open the door. The Colonel's brows raised, waiting for me to continue, an intrigue in their eyes from me addressing them by name.

"High Priestess Katerina was your mother?"

They nodded.

"My condolences. I can't imagine the pain you must feel," I said.

The Colonel nodded to me, their features softening more and the rough exterior falling away to reveal just another person who was a product of a world at war. "I will meet her again, when it is my time to join her in the After. Thank you for your words. I will see you at first light." They left and I had my answer for working in the kitchens. I sighed.

It was so quiet in this room. I could not hear anything beyond the door, but it felt late, and people were settling in for the night when we had come back inside. I waited for the laity girls return and it was about ten minutes before a hard rap sounded on the door. When I opened it, a tray with a thick slice of pâté, more toasted herb bread, pickled cucumber, pickled onions and red jam sat on a small stool to be off the floor; the girl was nowhere in sight.

I picked up the tray and stool and went back inside the room. I set the tray on the desk next to the crate and left the stool next to the door. Taking a small bite of the pâté on the toast, my stomach pinched with excitement.

Finally, I had that moment. The moment where I knew I

would not be disturbed, and I was alone with my thoughts and my dinner.

Everything I had experienced until now flooded my mind.

I was not on Earth.

I was lost.

Strangers thought I was a solution to great horrors.

I could cry in peace.

I sat down slowly to my new bed and took a long, deep breath. Gradually, I slid out of the sandals and robe, the fire warming the room enough that I did not feel cold without them. I poured myself a cup of water and looked across the cabin to the fireplace, where the fire continued to roar with life. I looked at my plate of food still on the desk. I closed my eyes and took another deep breath, wanting to eat.

I fell apart.

Tears streamed down my face. I tugged off the bandages on my feet, thankful to see the only small scabs on the soles, no signs of recent bleeding. I unwrapped the linen over my hand and dark pink wrinkled, fresh skin in the shape a handprint was burnt into my flesh. I felt sick and sucked in a breath, trying to hold back a howl. No matter how upset I was, crying was not a long-term solution, and I knew that, but I was scared. It was relieving to have a private space, so no one could see me cry.

I hugged a pillow, quietly weeping into it for hours until my eyes stung. My face felt stiff with dried, salty tears, and whatever wound was on my face stung. I gave myself a pounding migraine by the time I was ready to stop. The fire in the hearth had faded to glowing embers.

I went over and over how I could have gotten here. It did not make any sense. I *knew* our space travel capabilities were still very weak compared to being able to travel through time. We had barely made it to Mars a few years before I was born and that was a whole different planet. The colony there had long since lost contact with Earth and probes showed they had disappeared without a trace.

This was a whole different *planet*. I felt it deep within my bones.

It was the beginning of my vacation. It had been a completely normal day; routine by the book. No one would even know I was gone for another week. I would not return. My parents and my cousin would try to contact me for a check in. My friends would wonder why I had not posted any photos of my holiday. Both my bosses would call, looking for me. My landlords would not get their rent on time and their gardens would overgrow.

I wondered if I had really been brought here by this world's gods as these people said. Of all the people on Earth and in this world, why was *I* pulled here and given an apparent gift by one of *their* gods?

I wanted to be *home*.

I had nothing here. My Machine was probably destroyed in the explosion if it even made it here with me. Just like the debris of others' Machine's I had seen around the mountain, it was gone. My family and friends would never know what happened to me. They would mourn me, and I would never be able to see them again.

I was just another missing Traveller.

I squeezed my tear-soaked pillow tighter; it smelt of hay and old linen. I missed my things.

Even if by some miracle I found my Machine intact, I was on another world; I would not be able to send a note for help. If by another miracle I did somehow return to Earth, I was at a loss with how I could explain this ordeal to anyone. People would want to know how I got here, the coordinates so they could see. It was all so far out of reach.

The fact was, I had no one here, nothing. I was a part of this world whether I liked it or not.

I continued to sob until the candle in the lantern melted away and the coals in the hearth cooled. I knew without a doubt that no matter how tired I was, it would still be hours before I could find a restful sleep. I could already sense the glow of the early morning sun, birds beginning to sing as they awoke.

I slowly sat up from the bed, chilled by the winter air that had sunk its teeth into the room since I did not keep the fire fed. My legs wobbled underneath me, and I slipped the sandals and rob back on so I could collect the tray on the desk to finish the plate of food. I noticed a little dried flower had been placed on the plate. It looked like thyme. The bread was now stale, but still flavourful, especially when I piled pickled vegetables and pâté on it. I ravished the plate quickly and after I had a drink of water, my lids felt heavy with exhaustion.

Chapter Four
Day Nine

At some point I had drifted to that state of tiredness that was on the cusp of sleep. While the morning light grew brighter and the sounds of townsfolk and laity starting their day became more prominent, I would jerk awake with visions of the demons haunting my mind. I dreamt of running scared and their claws digging into my back. I dreamt of the menacing voice from my memory ordering soldiers dripping with black ooze to kill me. I could not relax.

A knock at the door woke me fully. I sat up gasping, startled, the sound of my quickened heartbeat slowly fading from my ears and the images of my dreams disappearing. The room was cool, cutting into my bare skin. The door creaked open.

Colonel Theone walked in, smoothly pushing it shut behind them with their foot to block out the morning hustle of laity. The crate that the woman had left the day before still sat on the desk and the Colonel clocked it before picking it up and walking it over to me. I pushed the blankets off; rubbing my eyes of the excessive sleep build up that always accompanied a night of crying. The cold helped wake me, despite the fatigue that hung heavily over me from a night of not sleeping.

"Good morning," I croaked.

"*Dobro jutro.* You said your name was Delilah Golding?" Colonel Theone said.

I nodded and yawned. "Yes." I eyed the crate in their hands, picking the crust built up in the eye that was not sore.

"Golding sounds highly regarded, are you hiding nobility?" A hint of embarrassment crossed their expression, a sudden youth came into their face as if this was something they should know and hoped they were not overstepping. I recalled the day before, when they had asked about a title in front of the rest of the Council. I could only guess they sensed my unease with revealing anything about myself and thought I would be more open in private. "I apologize for my curiosity, I mean no disrespect, but no one has heard of that family name, at least not here in Blackwick." Colonel Theone explained.

"I swear I'm not a noble. My family are just average, everyday people. We live well, but no way do I or them live in luxury," I told them.

"Where are you from?"

"Far away."

The Colonel did not seem satisfied by my reply, but they did not press on. "You know, we found you with nothing. No armour, barely any clothes. You weren't even cold when we picked you up and brought you back to camp. You were just wet." Colonel Theone patted the crate and handed it to me. "Have you taken a look inside?"

"No, I was distracted last night," I admitted. I had figured it was just some supplies, like more clothes or blankets. I had not even investigated the chest or books on the shelves. It was just me and the bed last night.

"These are the items we found you in at the Temple. We hadn't seen anything like quite like them before. You are truly unique." Colonel Theone popped open the crate and inside was pure joy.

"My pajamas!" I squealed in excitement, reaching in and grabbing my green sweater; it had been cleaned. Tears welled in my eyes again. Hugging it against me, I was grateful just to have a piece of my life back. How I wished I had checked the crate sooner. Last night might have been more bearable wearing my own pajamas.

Underneath the sweater was my night shirt with a fairy printed on the front and a small leather pouch. When I pulled the pouch out and opened it, inside were my earrings, rings, and toe ring; they had left my nose ring on my face. I had felt so naked without wearing them. There was an additional ring inside, the ruby ring, surrounded by diamonds like a flower petals. I remembered the memory, where a woman told me to give it to her *otrok*.

"*Otrok* means child, right?" I asked.

The Colonel nodded, their eyes looking at the ring almost longingly.

I held the ring out to them. "Then this is yours."

It took them a few moments, but they carefully took it from my fingers. "What if I'm not ready?" Colonel Theone asked me.

I was unsure what they meant. Already hurriedly putting my own jewellery back on and staring at the rings on my fingers. They looked shinier than I remembered. The normalcy of having them eased my unease of being somewhere so foreign a little further.

"She told me to give it to you."

"Usually there is ceremony."

I looked at Theone, who still looked at the ring, now in their own grasp. Their gaze suggested their thoughts were far away.

"A Temple exploded. When would there be time for a ceremony?" I asked a logical question, but the Colonel seemed satisfied with the answer. They removed a glove then slipped it on, treasuring the moment. After a few more moments of looking at the ring on their finger, Colonel Theone looked at me.

"Mother Nerice and Sir Vice studied your things for a few days. I hope that is alright. None of Nerice's scouts could find information on their smiths. Vice analyzed them, but he did not give us any answers either. We were hoping to find the name of your tailor or jeweler so we could figure out where you came from, make contact your family, but no leads." The Colonel tapped their finger to the image of the fairy on my pajama shirt. "This was particularly interesting. Who do you know with such skill to stitch such clean art on cloth?"

"I thought these were gone," I said. "Thank you for bringing these back to me."

"Happy to." Colonel Theone said. "We are still in awe of your survival, let alone these garments. Sir Vice speculated that because of your clothes connection to you, that is what saved them from the fire. There is no other explanation that you or these fabrics should have come out unscathed."

I cradled my sleeping shirt against me with my sweater. I never would have thought I would treasure my clothes in this way. I sniffed them, but the smell of home was gone. In its place was a just a fresh scent. I set them down on my pillow and Colonel Theone put the empty crate to the floor after putting a glove back over their hand.

"Thank you so much Colonel, this means a lot to me."

The Colonel nodded. "It was the least we could do, returning your clothes to you. Thanks to your blessings against the demons, we can move more freely throughout the mountain. Many were close to perishing from exposure before you awoke and we hope you will be able to cleanse more area's when you are healed. Now dress and come with me. You must officially meet your mentor and begin training."

Colonel Theone strode to the door.

I fumbled from-the bed and pulled on the embroidered pants and jacket that lay on the chair by the desk. "Honestly, I didn't really sleep last night, Colonel. I don't think I'm rested enough to train properly."

"We are all unrested, I'm sure you will be fine." The Colonel waited for me to finish dressing then led me from my room in the Tabernacle.

Colonel Theone spoke in a casual manner as we navigated through the long halls. The smell of incense and fresh bread was strong, bringing musty corridors to life. The people within were preoccupied with morning chores, sweeping the carpets, dusting small alters on the walls and lighting new candles to warm up the dark corners. I heard what I could only assume was prayer behind closed doors and those who we passed did not gawk.

"We are presently obtaining armour for you, but until we can get you fitted, what you're wearing will have to do. Resources are slim at this time, as I'm sure you're aware."

I nodded, knowing that I had zero clue about anything going on in this world, but could fake my way through a few small lies and conversations. I looked down at my embroidered pants and fur boots, the patched leather jacket. The fabrics would barely protect me if I fell and scarped my knee on a rock. The anxiety that had eased with having a few of my own belongings again spread back through my skin and I tensed, thinking about trying to train with weapons.

Reaching the door I knew led to the main hall, a man in a dirty tunic and thick leather apron stood from a bench seeing us approach. He came up to us hurriedly. His hands were grimy, and he bowed briefly before he stepped closer to me, his eyes scanning my face and landing on my eye. There was a nervousness around him that I could not place.

"Is it still troubling you?" he asked.

"Not right now. I just want to know why it bleeds."

Who I expected was the surgeon and Colonel Theone exchanged looks before he nodded to me, dismissing himself. "What's important is that has been relatively stable. No severe bleeds are good." He bowed again, this time formally, and opened the door, hurrying into the main hall and leaving it open for us. The exchange felt rushed, and I could tell the Colonel was not impressed with it. They sighed and then continued leading me into the main hall.

As soon as I turned out of the smaller hall and into the main one, I spotted Commander Lachlan standing at the grand doors to outside. My heart sped up and I swallowed, trying to gather myself as we approached.

Colonel Theone greeted him with a boisterous tone and stood very straight as they came beside him. "Commander, you said you have someone ready to train?" they asked.

The Commander nodded. The smell of coffee floated from him like he had just finished a fresh pot, but his eyes were still sleepy, and he yawned before saying "I do. Please follow me, we'd like you to begin as soon as possible." He nodded towards the door. "Colonel, I'll meet you back in the Council Chambers."

The Colonel nodded and turned, leaving us alone together, their footsteps louder in the hall then anyone else's.

The Commander opened the massive door with ease, letting me through before him. He walked with less urgency than the Colonel. When we got to the steep staircase he paused to look down, a heavy sigh puffed out into the cold air and then he began to descend it. I stepped carefully behind him, watching him move at random to different parts of the stairs, avoiding black ice.

"Colonel Theone said they thought you'd do well with duel-wield training. I don't have many in my forces who specialize there, and Major Vale is stuck at the Stills until we can retrieve him, but I did find one I believe has the skill to teach you to be a mastered swordsperson," the Commander explained once we reached the bottom of the staircase.

The village was awake. Just like the laity within the Tabernacle many moved around with the beginning of their daily chores. As we moved down through the streets, I watched villagers let out goats and chickens from small shacks attached to houses. Children peeled potatoes, parsnips and beets in large groups, the skins going into one barrel and the peeled vegetables in another. The smash of a hammer against an anvil echoed in the distance, the whinny of horses carried on the wind. Soldiers marched through both narrow and wide footpaths, only occasionally glancing in my direction. A few people foraged on path edges, plucking what looked like kale and leeks from the sides of common buildings.

I brought my attention back to the Commander. He mindfully kept my pace, leading me towards the fence line of massive logs with pointed tops.

"If Mother Nerice did not always have her scouts out doing errands, I'm sure one of them would be happy to assist with training, but I suppose I'm lucky that a scout decided to join the frontline several months ago."

"I appreciate the help," I lied. How I wished I did not have to do this or be here.

Commander Lachlan smiled. He looked at me with his eyes then looked forward again as we made it to the big defensive wall around the front of the village. "*Seer*, it is the least *we* can do to help *you*," he said.

The large wooden gates at the front of the village were open wide with the tracks of many coming and going between them. Past the fence several outer buildings stood with newer materials than the homes and shops within the village, the wood less weathered and no white and yellow designs painted on their walls. A large chimney puffed thick, metallic smelling smoke in the air and one of the buildings was the source of hammering sound. A large field was cleared for several acres to house canvas tents of various sizes. The air, though cold with the scent of coniferous trees carrying in it, had an undeniable hint of coal fire and sweat.

Further out from the scattered tents, a sparring yard appeared to be our destination. Soldiers practiced fighting straw combatants, and it began to snow as we got closer to them.

"I know you must still be healing, but time is of the essence. If our walls are ever breached, we cannot afford to protect you, nor loose you, so having the ability to defend yourself is of the outmost importance."

"I barely slept last night," I told the Commander. He continued to lead me through the soldiers and nodded, acknowledging me. "I'm not confident I can retain any lessons today, let alone stand and fight."

"I understand your concern, but as I said, unfortunately time is not a luxury we have.

"Private Gwen," Commander Lachlan's voice was lifted over the grunts of soldiers and the clashes of blades and shields as he came to stop, calling out into a group.

One of the soldiers stopped sparring and immediately jogged over to us.

"Commander Blackwick," she greeted. Her voice had a thick accent, my mind pricked with memory at it.

"Meet, Miss Delilah Golding, our *Seer*. As discussed earlier, you will be training her in duel-wielding daggers with short swords," the Commander said.

He was *definitely* amongst believers.

The private saluted Commander Lachlan with two fingers to the forehead of her helmet, which completely obscured her face. She had blended into the rest of the troops, most of them wearing full plate armour as they sparred, but now as she stood before us, I noted the differences in her armour compared to theirs.

"Yes, Commander!" she said.

Commander Lachlan nodded to her and then to me. "Very good. Enjoy your training." He turned and walked to a nearby line of troops, making rounds to watch them.

I looked to the private. She was taller than me and her armour was mostly leather and chainmail with the exception of a single plate pauldron. Scout armour.

"Seer," Gwen greeted me.

"Hello," I said uncomfortably.

"Do you have weapons?"

"No, I tried to hide behind a shield last time and Colonel Theone assigned me dueling swords or something."

The private nodded. "Right." She looked over her shoulder and then back to me, removing her helmet. Bright red curls fell from within her helmet to frame her face. Her beautiful skin was warm, flushed from sparring, and one eye, which was pale and blind in its socket, made her other blue eye, more vibrant in the morning light. She smiled fondly, catching my gaze.

Gwen was the laity member who had brought me food and my crate yesterday.

"You're laity," I blurted out.

She nodded enthusiastically. "Aye, I volunteer there often. How about we go somewhere quieter? That way others won't see you getting schooled." She smirked. We'll begin with hand-to-hand combat and move on from there."

I did not know how to respond to her, but I followed her away, her helmet held between her arm and her hip as she walked. Upon closer inspection of her armour, I noticed a dragon stitched into the leather of one of her bracers, the design similar to the one that was stitched on my tunic next to owl. She had a thinner, toned build like Bellamy and Mother Nerice appeared to have and Gwen had an almost salacious gate to her steps.

"I am a follower of Andreja," Gwen said, catching me looking at the dragon. "Though I was raised under Samu's teachings, and this Tabernacle is dedicated to Manoach, Andreja just spoke to me. I transferred here five years ago to be closer to her Temple and was a scout until earlier this year. I would ask which god is your favourite, but it appears one has chosen you instead."

I moved my eyes forward, embarrassed, and attempted a change in subject.

"I should mention that I didn't sleep last night. I have no idea how I'm standing," I said.

The private smirked. "Oh, aye, I have been there myself. Don't worry. I won't be too hard on you."

Gwen looked around. I had followed her down a small trail towards an area with more tree coverage. We could still hear the clangs of swords colliding together and the grunts of soldiers as they tried to grapple, but I did not see anyone anymore. A chilled breeze stirred, and my hair whipped around in my face.

Gwen tossed her helmet into the snow and looked me up and down as she pulled a ribbon from a pouch on her hip. She tied her curls behind her head, trying to contain the mane of hair she had.

We stared at each other for a moment. As I continued to try to push my hair out of my face, the wind growing stronger, Gwen pulled another ribbon from the pouch and held it out for me. I took it and fought my hair into submission, braiding it tightly to my skelp. Stray hairs still came for my eyes, but it was better than all my hair in my face. When I finished, Gwen took a stance, as if she was about to pounce, her fingers primed for grabbing.

"Do you have any war experience?" she asked.

"I have minor self-defence and combat training. *Very* minor." I hoped kickboxing videos online and a women's self-defence class counted.

Gwen nodded. "Let's see what you have." She lunged at me, and I was tackled into the snow before I could even react to her, the wind leaving my lungs harshly. Everything hurt and the collision with the ground made my bones vibrate.

I struggled against her grip, but she was strong. I gasped for air then thrust my hips up as soon as I could think. The private fell forward over me, though she still gripped my arms, pinning them to the cold ground. She could think much faster than I. I spun my wrists towards her thumbs, breaking free of her grip and forced my way out from under her. I turned to crawl away, but just as soon as I was free, she grabbed my legs and yanked me back into the snow.

When I was back on the ground, my face covered in snow and clothes dampening, Gwen crawled over me, pinning my arm behind my back like a chicken wing. I groaned and could feel my eyes sting with the threat of tears.

Gwen laughed. "That was better than I expected, but you would have been dead if this was actual combat."

"I figured," I whimpered.

She laughed again then rolled off me and helped me to my feet. When she saw my expression, her face softened, and her smile dropped. "Are you alright?"

I wiped at my eyes, trying not to let the tears escape. "I'm just in a lot of pain," I said, swallowing, trying to gather myself. "And I'm *so* tired."

"I know you have been through a lot over the last week-"

"*But time is not a luxury we have*," I said, disappointed. I lightly touched my face to check the scabbing there. A tear slipped out. "I understand. I'm not used to this."

Gwen rubbed my arm. "Let's try again. This time, you attack me, and we can practise a little more gently until you are completely healed, deal?"

I brushed the snow off myself. The sun had just barely rose above the horizon when Colonel Theone had woken me. I had not eaten. The day already felt long, and I yearned for the half-eaten food I left in my room. I thought about trying to bolt back up through the village to hide, but something told me my effort would prove fruitless.

I nodded to her, raised my fists to protect my face and lunged, quickly dropping my arms to grab her. I aimed for her hips, wrapping my arms around her waist, as my shoulder snagged hold of the chainmail there. Her legs lifted and I used my momentum to push her down into the ground. I was surprised it worked, but now my shoulder hurt from the connection with the metal and bone.

Gwen grunted as she hit the ground, but I was in the snow with her. She coiled around my body with ease and switched our positions quickly. We scrimmaged on the ground for a few moments, ending with me being pinned again. I hissed from the stinging on my limbs, completely beaten.

"I'll give you this much, Seer: I sense fight in you, but, again, you died."

"I know," I said, defeated.

Gwen laughed, thoroughly amused, and freed me to help me to my feet. "Again," she instructed.

The dance continued for hours. The sun worked its way high into the sky, though the cloud cover kept it from warming the cold earth. Gwen had my face buried in the snow, pinned down by her knee against the back of my head.

How was this *going easy on me?*

The day began to curve into dusk, and I had barely managed to flip her over my shoulder when she grabbed me from behind. The second she landed in the snow Gwen swept my feet from under me and I landed hard to the ground.

The private easily won every round, by no surprise of mine. By the time we finally stopped not a single part of my body was unscathed. I lay in the dirt and snow, a headache probing at the edges of my mind, my chest heaving from exhaustion in attempt to give me any sort of air. I felt my body longing to fall sleep as I lay staring up at the approaching night.

Most of the snow had warred away where we brawled, and my clothes were smothered in dirt and soaked with melted snow. I breathed hard, forcing myself to watch as stars began to blink to life in the clearing sky, the fear of falling unconscious outside strong. Two small moons floated behind lingering clouds, one larger than the other.

This place had two moons.

I sniffled, searching for something that would let the unease of being so displaced and uncomfortable go. I could hear Gwen moving, almost pacing, around me. The evening approached with an extra bite of frost and as I continued to search, I found that I felt magic surrounding me.

It was the kind of magic that accompanied the view after a long hike through a national park, a beyond satisfyingly delicious taste of an expensive dish at a restaurant. That feeling that could only be grasped for a moment that said everything in the world was good, a restoration in humanity after watching a person do a selfless deed. The kind of magic that felt safe washed over me for a split second before it fleeted.

Gwen stopped moving and held her hand out to me. She seemed unmarred by a day of kicking my ass and showed no signs of tiredness. "I know it doesn't feel like it, but you did good work today, Seer. It's getting dark so we'll stop until tomorrow. You can eat and rest for the night."

I waved at her hand, part of me wanting to remain laying there and become one with the forest floor beside us. Something whispered inside my mind telling me it would be peaceful in the soil, quiet, and the worries of this world would not bother me there. "I feel weak," I said.

Gwen knelt then pulled me into a sitting position, whatever called out to me disappeared and I got the overwhelming feeling that I should not stray my attention from my new mentor until I was back within the safety of the village. Gwen waited as I collected myself then helped me to stand.

I brushed the rubble off my clothes the best I could, but I was still filthy. I closed my eyes and took a deep breath. Gwen's hand stayed on my arm for an extra moment, making sure I would stay standing, then let go when I opened my eyes. I remembered Vice and Durin doing the same thing, the concern evident in her eyes just as it had been in theirs. I could still feel my heartbeat in every sore spot and craved *my* bed, not the one waiting for me in the Tabernacle.

Gwen picked up her helmet and put it back on, shoving the

hair that stuck out up behind the metal. She pointed to where the other soldiers were. "Get back into the village. I'm going to report to the Commander of your training today. Make sure you don't stray outside of the camp before you're through the gates."

"Are you going to tell him that I suck?"

"Pardon me?"

Whoops. I needed to watch my language. This world did not have the slang I was used to. Thank goodness they at least spoke English. Mostly.

"Are you going to tell him I'm terrible in combat?" I corrected.

"I wouldn't use the world *terrible*," she replied, a teasing tone to her voice.

"Thanks," I said as we hiked up the side of the hill and reached the other soldiers.

"I will see you at first light, Seer," Gwen confirmed, a hand going to my back to steer my in the direction of Blackwick's gates.

I groaned my displeasure before walking that way and Gwen laughed as she strayed towards the Commander. When I reached the gate, I looked back over the camp. I watched as soldiers secured string around pegs in the ground. Bells hung on the string and the pegs were topped with metal plates that held candles. Small teams unravelled the bell strings while others lit the candles as shadows reached out around the tents. Hundreds of people must have lived within the camp, hundreds of soldiers. Some canvas tents could hold dozens of people where others were barely large enough for one person. Barely any snow covered the earth with the amount of foot traffic waring it away. Snow drifts surrounded the camp, along with men made of straw and archery targets. I saw Gwen walking over to the Commander and salute him, before he turned to greet her. I watched their exchange and saw as Commander Lachlan looked past Gwen and to me. I blushed as his eyes connected with mine across the field and a close-lipped smile settled on his face. I turned, embarrassed he had noticed me watching them and hurried into the village.

When I returned to my room in the Tabernacle, after some confusing navigation within the halls, I noticed a small bouquet of dried primroses in a short clay pot on the desk. Maybe they were put there to bring some character into the room by one of the laity. Next to the flowers was a bowl of red soup with potatoes, sausages, beans and cabbage floating in it. When I took a sip to test it, the undeniable taste of sauerkraut, spiced sausage and turnip hit my tongue and my belly cheered, excited to be fed. I set the spoon back down, carefully removing my jacket. One of the cuts on my leg stung and I placed the jacket over the chair, angling it towards the fire to dry. A new roaring fire warmed the room, and I had almost forgotten what it was like to be thawed out.

I looked down at my aching legs and pushed my pants off to assess them. The bandages had some light stains on them, but not as much as I thought there would be. Some of the stains matched the mud on my pants, though one on my thigh was coloured suspiciously like dried blood.

I sighed and slowly unravelled the bandages on my legs and feet. Underneath, my legs were marked with healing scratches and scabs. A large cut on my upper thigh had definitely been bleeding earlier in the day but was now dry. Considering the memories I had of my encounters with the demons, the marks did not look as bad as I thought they would. The claws had been unexpectedly jagged, like a dull knife, but whatever the Commander had done in the mountains had helped them look less awful.

Had he really pulled out possible infection with magic? It was hard to grasp.

What made me uneasy was the amount of bruising.

I breathed, trying to suck back another crying session. A tear ran down my cheek.

I knew I was a crier, but I had never sobbed to this extent in such a short amount of time. It was exhausting, overwhelming. I scratched at the edges of my mind to find music to distract myself with, try to sing the words, but was unsuccessful. More warm tears ran down my face.

At least my eye did not bleed today.

I let myself explore the room a little, in an effort of distraction. I went to the chest and opened it, seeing fresh bandages, some changes of clothes, hair ribbons, soap, and herbs that I was unsure of what their usage was. I sniffed the herbs. One smelt like stinky cheese, and the other was a breed of lavender. I picked the lavender up and sniffed it again. The uneasiness that I carried in my chest since I got here lifted a little bit. I picked up the clean bandages then walked over to the desk and chair, setting the items there before retrieving the pitcher of water by my bedside. The water was cold as I poured it over my legs. Dirt and grime beaded in the water and streaked over my bruised skin. I stunk.

I dabbed my legs dry with the wrap shirt I had been wearing the past two days then began wrapping the leg that had the ugly healing gash on the thigh. I wondered if there was any alcohol in camp, and if I could get my hands on it to clean the wound on my thigh more thoroughly. Once the bandages were tucked securely around my leg, I grabbed the lavender again to place under my pillow. I sat on the bed, staring at the fireplace for a few minutes before putting my pajama shirt and sweater on. Feeling better with their familiarity, though they felt slightly stiffer with whatever washing method was used to clean them, I ushered myself back to the bowl of soup. It smelled hearty and I was excited to have something to eat after another long day. I took a comforting bite and hoped I would sleep better tonight.

First light came quickly. After I had eaten and lay my head down, having fallen asleep immediately. I was given a rude awakening, however, when I did not show up to the sparring yard by myself, having depression slept through the rising sun. It was Gwen, not Colonel Theone thankfully, who burst into my room and ripped the covers from me. "Arise from your slumber, Seer! You have a world to save!" she exclaimed.

I groaned rubbing my eyes, then flinched, remembering the

one might hurt, but when I realized it did not pang with the sensitivity of a bruise, I relaxed.

"Where I am from, I worked in a kitchen. I slept until midday then worked nights making pastries and bread," I yawned sitting up. "I would be better use in the kitchens here than I would be as a soldier." I was hopeful that Gwen would take pity on me, that she would give me the chance to show how useful I could be and then I would not have to leave the safety of these walls.

"You're in our forces now, Seer. Your old ways are no longer the custom," Gwen handed me a bowl of stew. It smelled of pickles and dill and chunks of potatoes floated in the milky broth.

I spent several long minutes begging Gwen to allow me to rest for the day. I asked her repeatedly to show me where the kitchen was, saying I would show her my skills were better there. I cried, frustrated that every day I had been awake in between starving unconsciously under their care, I was pushed to my wits end. I cried about how my eye bled and ached when there was thunder or I was involved in a magic spell.

I was animated and throwing my hands in the air as I sobbed, stalking around the room. I vented and practically screamed for a break. I had no time to myself. No time to process what was happening to me. Gwen reached her hand out to me, and I quieted finally realizing she had not said a thing during my whole breakdown. I slipped my hand into hers and she led me back to the bed, coaxing me to sit as she sat there too.

Once I was quiet Gwen, thankfully, took pity on me. She watched me fall apart in front of her and understood the toll that everything had taken on me.

Gwen left me, with the promise of coming back tomorrow, and a pat on the back.

I ate my soup and then curled up under the covers of the bed.

Chapter Five
Twenty-Three Days Since Arrival

People on Earth would know I was missing by now. Since I finally stopped passing out for days at a time, I had spent most of my evenings crying. I yearned to return home without any option to do so. Around day fifteen I had cried the hardest, knowing that my parents, my friends, my landlords, and my bosses would figure out something was wrong.

On the day Gwen left me to rest in the Tabernacle, Mother Nerice had come to my room in the late morning. She did not knock and just let herself. The Mother loudly closed the door to announce her presence, and I had heard her walk over to the fireplace from under the covers. The fire roared back to life quickly and Mother Nerice moved around the room tidying it.

I snuck glances from beyond the furs, seeing her pick up my dirty bandages and pants and top, balling them up and tossing them by the door. She collected my soup bowl, placing it on top of the pile she made. Mother Nerice opened the curtains to let the sun in and went to the to the chest, riffling around in it until she pulled out an iron kettle. She filled it with the water left on my desk then hung it on a hook at the top of the hearth to boil.

Back to the chest she went, pulling out fresh clothes and the herb that wreaked of cheese. I felt the weight of the clothes on me as she tossed them to the bed and then she popped the lid up on the kettle before dumping the herb inside it.

Her weight sunk the bed deep, and she patted my hip, giving me the courtesy of pretending I had been sleeping the entire time she was moving around the room.

"Do you have the lavender hiding somewhere?" she asked.

I pulled the furs down from around my head. "Under my pillow," I said.

Mother Nerice leaned close to me. I could smell spiced cider on her skin mixing pleasantly with the lavender under my pillow. She pulled a fistful out then stood and tossed the lavender in the kettle. She moved to the door as I sat up and she knocked on it. It creaked open and she whispered something before hands reached in from close to the floor and grabbed the pile there. The door closed and Mother Nerice dragged the chair from where I had angled it over to the bed where she straddled it, leaning forward over the back.

"Gwen told me about this morning." She was giving me an option to speak openly to her.

"I don't know what else to say to explain myself," I replied.

Her brow cocked, unsatisfied with my response. "I spoke with the council, and we decided if you need to work in a kitchen to feel *useful*, you can. However, we have conditions."

"Conditions?" I almost hissed. "I have been doing whatever has been asked of me every conscious moment I've had in the last week, and I am being given conditions?"

Mother Nerice smirked at my tone, unscathed by talking back to her, as if she had expected me to snap back from the start.

I defused.

"You know you are the only one who can successfully cleanse the influx of demon activity. You also know our resources are thin in this war. Ignoring it is not an option we have. We need you, but you also need us, Seer. If you require a kitchen to feel sane, we need you trained and ready to be utilized for this war. If you make no effort, we cannot guarantee your safety at the trial, even with your memory as evidence. A Seer would not do nothing."

Mother Nerice's eyes were penetrating, analyzing my reaction to her words. The red staring back at me held truth in them and I felt guilty for my actions earlier. I knew it was okay to be selfish sometimes, but this was not one of those instances.

"I do not feel like a Seer, Mother," I admitted.

"You can drop the formality and call me Nerice, if you want. I did not want to be a *Mother* here, but the only other option was stupid Adder, so I was voted in." Nerice huffed, made a face then continued. "But we all do what we must, for our people. You may go to the kitchens in the morning, work with the laity there. Once breakfast is served, you are to spend time in either prayer or meditation for an hour. I will join you in one of the choir chambers or in your room if you wish to be more private. Gwen will bring you to training in the afternoon and you will learn and practice your combat skills like everyone else does until dusk. When you return, Bellamy or I will do more meditation or prayers with you and guide you through some healing stretches. If you are still in pain, I will summon Sir Vice or Commander Lachlan to help ease it. The rest of the evening will belong to you, and this is how your days will be until we believe you can retrieve Major Vale from the Stills with a small team. Do you understand?"

I felt like a child who just went though a scolding. I nodded as the kettle whistled at the fireplace and Nerice stood, taking the kettle from the hearth.

As Nerice set the kettle to the stone around the fire, the door knocked. Nerice answered, keeping the door only open wide enough that she could look out, but no one could see in. A tray was passed to her, and she walked over to the hearth setting the tray down. On it there were two large cups with herbs and dried fruit in them beside a plate with a small mountain of spiced oat cookies.

Nerice kicked off her shoes, flinging them towards the door and hunched over, pouring the liquid from the kettle into the cups. She shoved a whole cookie into her mouth and spoke through the food as she flopped to the floor.

"Come," she said, her mouth full. "Just drink tea and eat a treat with me. Watch the flames and pretend only they exist." Nerice patted the floor beside her.

I slowly rolled from the bed then slugged over to her.

"What's in the tea?" I asked.

"Apple, orange peel, lavender, chamomile. That stinky shit in your chest is valerian root. It's good for sleep. The fruit will hide the smell in tea." She nudged the cup closer to me but did not look at me. Her concentration was on the fire.

I stared at her.

Nerice was not what I expected when a priestess came to mind. She looked young, but something told me she was not, just like Vice. Her pointed ears twitched at every small sound in the hall beyond the room. She wore a leather gorget and pauldron over navy clothes stitched with gold thread, another variation of the outfits I had seen her sporting each time I saw her. Her toenails were filed sharp like her fingers.

"I've never met or known of a religious figure quite like you," I said taking the cup into my hands.

Nerice let out an entertained breath and swallowed what was in her mouth. "What were they like where you are from?" she asked.

"Saintly, humble, modest. At least in public. What church do you serve?"

Nerice shrugged. "As a priestess you are supposed to serve all the Temples, but I was an island girl. I grew up under Samu's Temple and my love for birds grew strong. Amaranthine's make up a large flock of Manoach and the Tabernacle here offered a nice balance of Andreja's and Manoach's teachings. Samu's relationship with the god of death and rest has always been a good one, so it made sense to me to transfer here four decades ago." She shoved another cookie in her mouth.

"Four *decades* ago?" I repeated.

Nerice winked at me. "I look good for my age, don't I?" she teased through a mouth full of cookie. She did not look older than twenty-eight at best.

When we had finished the tea and cookies Nerice assured me I would be still granted today to myself. She would have someone show me the kitchens in the evening so I could find my way there tomorrow.

And so, the days moved on as Nerice said they would.

The kitchens were deep within the depths of the Tabernacle. A narrow stairwell led to another branch of hallways where I learned more laity slept. At the far end of the hall was the kitchen. A thick iron door was held open by a large bucket full of green apples. The ceiling was lower than the hallway outside, as if building the kitchen had been an after thought to whoever had built this place. Wooden beams on the ceiling had onions, garlic and other various dried herbs hanging on string and nails. There was a whole wall dedicated to shelves of pickled vegetables. There were many stone ovens and a hearth so large three people could walk in and fit comfortably.

At the center of the kitchen, there was a large basin full of water and an even larger butcher's block.

When I first entered the kitchen two people were mixing herbs with ground meat, and another person was chopping potatoes. Above them hung an iron rack where many small skillets dangled on hooks with yet more herbs around them. A larger man was hauling a cauldron of water with oats floating near the rim into the hearth. The cooks, all dressed in laity garb and dirty aprons, looked at me in unison when I showed up. I quickly found my place amongst them.

We would serve breakfast, eat our own together, and Nerice would magically appear at the kitchen door to retrieve me for meditation and prayer.

I sheepishly followed her into choir chambers where others meditated. Sometimes there were people there, sometimes it was just Nerice and I. Nerice led me through breathing techniques, guided visualization, and I would do my best to follow her. Sometimes she would just ask me to listen to the other laity members as they sung harmoniously ancient love songs to their gods. It was oddly soothing. After an hour Nerice would then free me to Gwen, who would hand my ass to me on a silver platter.

The end of each day left me sore, but I felt like I was catching on to the routine, the fight, the skill.

The moment I was released from training with Gwen, I was met with Nerice or Bellamy and they would walk with me back to the room they gave me where Bellamy would happily guide me through some relaxing standing stretches reminiscent of yoga or Nerice would talk me into a pretzel without me realizing it.

When they finished with me, I would occasionally wander through the streets of Blackwick, smelling the meals villagers were cooking or taking my time looking at the murals on homes. Often, I would find Durin, and he would share dinner with me and several others from the tents scattered around the streets. On those evenings, I actively tried to pretend I belonged. Other evenings I would remain in the room and the second I was left alone, and I would burst into tears.

I longed to invite my friends over for tea, I longed for modern comforts like music at my fingertips or a shower. Instead, I knew my loved ones were worrying. The news would announce another missing Traveller, the world would speculate my disappearance for a week before my name would just be listed on the Missing Traveller's Registry. More Travellers would stop exploring and the world would go on without me. I mourned for my family and friends; how concerned they must still be. I had no way of telling them I was alright, that I was safe, at least for now.

In the afternoon I pleaded for breaks while training. The muscle pain had increased to a point that every movement hurt, my body feeling twice as heavy. Gwen had tried to get me to enact spells from a book she borrowed from the Tabernacle, an additional task given to me by the Council to help me prepare for opening ruptures on the field. She told me about mage light and shadow magic, a practice long neglected. Yet any time I tried a simple spell between sparring, my eye would bleed, my head would ache, and I would crumble from the pain.

Gwen would attempt to encourage me, but when I puked from exhaustion and pain one afternoon after trying another spell, she changed her approach to meet my needs and decided spells would be best dealt with by actual mages, not herself. She would give me a snack of nuts and dried mango when the sun was at its highest, and every few hours she would refill her canteen and share some water; the process of which giving me ten minutes to sit and catch my breath. The day I puked, Vice had appeared at my door when Bellamy was leading me back through the Tabernacle and gave me a flask that tasted like ginger, lemon and alcohol.

Eventually my wounds stopped opening back up and stinging after each training session and soon I did not have to wear the bandages, just see small shiny scars in their place.

The days passed in a blur and my thoughts numbed as I kept telling myself I just had to do two things every day: finish my daily schedule and cry when I was alone. My only marker of how much time passed was the sheet of parchment I ticked off days with on the desk in the room where I slept. I was not sure if it was a good or bad thing to do so, but it was *something* for me to do other than cry.

When I realized I needed some semblance of normalcy, that I was craving socialization, I tried to get to know the people I saw the most. I needed to keep myself from completely falling apart every day and the urge to refuse to leave the Tabernacle was strong.

Just go out for them, I told myself. It was better than isolation. After a lot of discussion, I convinced Nerice of a variation to my schedule. Once every week I would do a full day of training, if Gwen agreed to have a slow morning with me before we went out to train.

Gwen was thrilled by the proposal and Nerice said the rest of the Council was glad I was taking the training more seriously.

Together we ate boiled eggs and stale bread or stew from the night before in my assigned room. It gave me an opportunity to get to know her.

I took a chance with Gwen and admitted I missed my home but did not believe I would ever see it again. Gwen gave me a rather friendly and sympathetic hug, something I had unknowingly craved for weeks.

"You're allowed to miss home," Gwen told me, rubbing my back. She smelled like citrus and cinnamon and for the first time in weeks I was allowed to be human in a place I thought I could not be. Gwen then told me about her home, her favourite meals as a child, her friends, an attempt to distract my sad heart from my circumstances.

On the twenty-third night, I sat at Durin's fire, watching him stir a pot that smelled spicy with sweet potatoes and chicken floating in thick yellow broth. Most nights I sat with him after refugees were served, they would scurry away to their tents. I had always thought they were cold, but when Durin saw me watch a woman usher her child back down the street to their little camp, he spoke up.

"To her you are the holiest thing she or her son will ever meet, save in the After when they see the gods," Durin pointed out. "They don't know how to be in your presence."

He saw how uncomfortable that statement made me and risked a question I felt the rest of the Council were itching to ask. "Are you still confused from the explosion?" he asked.

I almost choked on my food. I had been declining the Commander's offers to come assess me over the last couple weeks. Though I knew everyone who worked with me were reporting back to him on my progress or lack thereof, I had only agreed to take the beverage Vice had showed up with. Nerice and Colonel Theone kept telling me the Commander could help, but I was too chicken to admit that I was afraid of talking to him because I was sure I would make a fool of myself. It was hard enough biting my tongue with Bellamy, my mind occasionally slipping from where I was and just focusing on her beauty, her radiating happy aura, the delicate curve of her neck or pretty hands. Everyone in my immediate social circle were all gorgeous, especially Bellamy and the Commander. I had a hard time understanding how anyone could get work done around each other.

After swallowing, I nodded. "Very confused. I have no idea how I got here. I am *very* far from home."

Durin nodded and dipped some bread in his stew. "I don't blame you, Shorty. The mind can be strange and sometimes the gods hide details from us, so we don't hurt further."

My heart ached at his words. Though I knew I had no idea how I got here, I was still lying to these people about my origins. It was getting hard not to say anything, especially to people who showed their sympathy and trust towards me.

Silence hung in the air for a long moment, and I looked in my bowl absentmindedly. Durin and I usually talked about our days and what we did with them. We talked about music and Durin would enthusiastically regale tales from his life in the Southern Province. That was where his flavour profile originated from, consisting of strong flavours of paprika, cayenne, garlic, oregano, thyme and black pepper. I was undoubtably grateful that the food here was almost the same as on Earth.

I risked a question back to him. "Do you believe me to be your Seer, Durin?" I asked, my voice only loud enough for him to catch it.

Durin looked up, thinking about his answer. I could see the smallest lift in his lips as he stirred the stew pot then scooped himself a second portion before sitting on the worn log beside me.

"I do," he said. "Having you here makes everything more magical, and it's been a long time since I felt the world that way."

*

One afternoon, about a month and a half into my training, I noticed a pair of swords strapped Gwen's back. A pair of short swords hung in scabbards fastened to a belt on a low tree branch, clearly waiting for my hands to hold them. A wave of nausea hit me as I was overcome with nervousness. Gwen had not mentioned we were changing our routine, and I had gotten used to sparring in hand-to-hand combat.

"Seer, I trust you slept well?" Gwen asked. She greeted me with a hand to my wrist as she did most days. I had only seen Commander Lachlan from afar for the last few weeks, but each time made my heart flutter, especially when he happened to notice me looking and smirked before returning his attention to what he was doing prior.

I nodded, squeezing Gwen's wrist. "I typically sleep well after the day with you. You're exhausting," I teased, still staring at the swords on the tree. It was the truth, despite my nightly cries, I had begun to sleep better, getting too tired from all the exercise to stay awake long.

Gwen howled with laughter. "My family used to tell me that!"

Her gaze followed my own and she immediately figured out my distraction. "You've been developing the skill, Seer. It may not feel like it, but it's time we begin the training I was assigned to you for." Gwen motioned to the short swords hanging on the tree branch, a prompt to grab them. My stomach dropped further.

When I did not move to retrieve them, Gwen took the swords from their scabbards and presented them to me. "I had the blacksmith make them special for you. They are lightweight and sharp. Perfect for a novice, but also for a skilled swordsperson. It's okay to be nervous if you feel that way. I know this isn't exactly your element, but I believe it can be!"

The swords were very pretty, for deadly weapons. I took them into my hands to examine closer. They seemed like large daggers. Daggers were *basically* knives. I knew knives. I would pretend they were daggers.

"You know, when I first entered the culinary industry, my friends were surprised anyone hired me to be near sharp things and fire because I had been so clumsy as a kid, but it turned out to be one of my greatest talents," I said as I moved the blades in my hands, holding them like I did a chef's knife. Each pommel had owl heads carved into them, expertly detailed.

"Culinary industry?" Gwen repeated.

"I worked in kitchens, remember? That's why I like doing so here." I really had started to enjoy my mornings in the kitchens. Nerice would sometimes join me before our morning meditations to make bread with me and the other cooks. Recently she had let us skip our morning ritual, just so she could watch me move around the kitchen and make a late brunch for the other cooks. They would talk to each other a lot in Bygone Speech but were clearly happy to have the extra set of hands. The laity would make me a spiced tea with milk and sugar while I made bread with honey and thyme with fried eggs and bacon. Nerice took a plate when I finished and told me to head over to Gwen when I was ready.

"You worked in a tavern, right!" Gwen said, amused. "Remind me to ask you where you're from so when this war is over, I can visit. I'll be surrounded by a culture that allows you to 'play with fire and sharp things' and not demand you to know how defend yourself with them. It must be so disconnected from the war, how relaxing!"

I brushed her statement away, continuing to look at the daggers. I traced my fingers over one of the blades. Each dagger had a serrated side and a sharp hook at the point.

Gwen pointed to the blade's hooks. "I thought you would benefit from these. They do more damage and will rip up the insides up when you pull the blade out. If the person lives, a healer will have more trouble repairing them than a clean cutting blade." She looked at me seriously. "But they also require more strength. If you were to shove the dagger through your aggressor, pulling it out will not be as easy."

As she continued to explain the daggers, and demonstrate different stances in front of me, I believed Gwen thought I was stronger than I ever thought I could be. Gwen believed in me, and it dawned on me that others truly did too.

Nerice, Bellamy, Colonel Theone, and Commander Lachlan had all urged for me to train.

The people here in Blackwick believed I was sent from their heavens.

Gwen and Durin treated me as a companion, despite their belief that I was part of a higher purpose.

I had made *friends* here.

I smiled wide, staring at the blades. For the first time in a month and a half, I felt happy, and it lifted a weight I was unknowingly holding from my shoulders.

"Hurry up and teach me, Gwen. Nerice hinted that the others on the Council want me to leave to the Stills and collect Major Vale soon. I'm sure the faster I can hold my own, the earlier I can leave." Though the thought of leaving the safety of the village scared me, I also had to admit to myself that something curious stirred when thinking about the world beyond the mountains.

"Aye, it has been a long wait, but they could not send you without *some* survival skill," Gwen teased. "Those you travel with cannot always protect you and the Stills will be at least a fortnights journey. The world waited one thousand years for you to save it. It can wait until you are skilled enough to not need backup." Gwen walked close to me and adjusted my grip on the hilt of each weapon. "You need to hold them like this during combat, you are not in a kitchen. I'm confident you'll be ready for adventuring in seven sols week, maybe fourteen, if we continue to practice as we have."

I nodded, still nervous. I sweat at the thought of using a weapon skillfully in two weeks, in one. I reminded myself that I learned to use a knife that fast in a dive bar. I could try to apply the same confidence with daggers.

"You can do this," Gwen said encouragingly. She drew her two short swords from the scabbards on her back, holding them to block. "This is the easiest way to block an attack. Take this stance." Gwen moved into a ready stance.

I echoed her.

"Good." She moved a bit, showing another position. "Now take this stance."

I followed her orders.

"Good. Now defend yourself." She attacked.

The day ended early with a slice on my upper arm, my blood splattered on the fresh sheet of snow, and a trip to an herbalist who whined about having to act as a healer. The surgeon in town had become overwhelmed with a recent group of refugees and the herbalist had a shorter wait for medical attention. It was rare for the Commander to be approached about healing matters, according to Durin, since the Commander had a lot more on his plate than the sick and wounded. Vice apparently could not be found if anyone tried to seek him for remedies, except when I had been sick, and with Major Vale and his team gone there were no other medics in the village.

"I have enough problems with the soldiers, now this?" The

herbalist asked when I entered his apothecary with Gwen, holding the handkerchief the Commander had given me weeks ago to the wound on my upper arm. I had been using it to wipe my face any time my eye acted up or when I had a crying fit at night. I had washed it a few times, intending to give it back to him, but I was still too nervous to approach him.

I tried not to look at the wound and I did not like the attention, but Gwen insisted I see the herbalist. "Does it need stitches?" I asked. "If not just give me some alcohol and be done with me."

"This is no time for a drink, Seer," he said crossly.

"It isn't for a drink; it's for cleaning the cut."

The herbalist gave me cross look and I could feel Gwen's eyes on me too.

"Please?"

I had already cleaned it before Gwen forced me up to the apothecary. Gwen did not have the patience to scold me while I sat at the well pump rinsing my arm with the water and a bar of lye soap. I had left a dripping trail up from the soldier's camp to the Tabernacle and a nun gave me a bar of soap before I could get far in the building to get my own.

The well was on the opposite side of the Tabernacle that the latrines were, next to an old trebuchet. and water had been running pink with my blood when Gwen hauled me up and over her shoulder. She had been done arguing with me the second we reached the well. She walked towards the apothecary for about ten yards while I attempted escape, before I gave in, and she set me down. Gwen was *uncannily* strong.

Colonel Theone burst into the apothecary shop, the door wheezing like it was going to fall from the hinges. "You *cut* the Seer?!" they growled at Gwen. "She just finished healing from when we trekked down the mountain!"

Onlookers had watched our ascent into the village. Gwen yelled to a patrolling scout next to the Tabernacle to inform the Council of what happened, all of which were in a meeting about plans for the coming weeks. I had still been on her shoulder then, growling with defiance.

Commander Lachlan was not far behind the Colonel, and he rolled his eyes at them. "Colonel, she is training. The Seer is bound to get worse injuries on the field, and she will not have easy access to healers there like she does here."

"It doesn't need stitches," the herbalist said, his voice a little more on the defence with two high ranking officials in his apothecary.

The bleeding had finally stopped, the herbalist having applied pressure to it the second he could assess it. This cut was nothing compared to the ones I had received from the demons, and the blade was sharp, leaving a clean cut. The herbalist got me to hold a fresh cloth while he popped a cork out of a leather bottle. The Commanders handkerchief was balled in my free hand, and I squeezed it tight at sight of him.

When the herbalist returned to my side, he poured some alcohol over the wound, and I hissed at the stinging that came with it. The alcohol caused it to act up and bleed again.

Colonel Theone grumbled. "Well, be careful soldier . You're supposed to hone her skills, not injure her."

"Yes, Colonel," Gwen said.

"Don't be mad, it was my fault anyway. I blocked wrong. I'm tired and clumsy," I said, trying to defend Gwen. I could feel Colonel Theone calm at my words.

The herbalist wrapped clean bandaging around my arm before letting me get off the table I had sat on, and Gwen helped me back into my jacket. I had disposed of it at the well to clean my arm. She must have grabbed it right before she picked me up.

"How is our Seer doing, private? You are the only one I haven't received a report from this week," the Commander said.

I shoved his handkerchief into the sleeve of my jacket and actively tried not looking at him. I hoped my cheeks were only pink because of the cold air outside.

"Her defensive skills in hand-to-hand combat have improved. We *obviously* started her on the blade today, but she shows spirit," Gwen commented.

Colonel Theone nodded approvingly.

Commander Lachlan managed to catch my eyeline and gave me a small smile. "I've noticed," he said.

"You've been watching us?" I asked, self-conscious, red definitely flooding my cheeks. I was foolish to think he never noticed me sneaking looks at him in the afternoon when I arrived or in the evening when I left. His eyes caught mine one too many times for me to kid myself now as he looked at me. What a treat it was every day for me to see him; a light to the impending darkness that I felt every night before I slept.

"The Commander has said the same things to me while reporting your progress, Seer. Spirit, eagerness to improve," Colonel Theone added.

I smiled shyly. "I'm doing a good job?" I could feel myself flushing more, feeling the Commanders eyes still on me even though I looked at Colonel Theone instead. I had not believed I was making much progress until today.

"You are," the three of them said in unison. I felt reassured and the flush from my cheeks started to fade.

We all left the apothecary together. I fondled the hilt of one of my new daggers sitting on my hips. I thought about how right they felt in my hands. I had thought I would just be given weapons available from the armoury, but knowing Gwen had them made for me was so much more special.

Gwen was sent to retire for the day after Colonel Theone apologized for their outburst to her. The Commander, Colonel Theone and I wandered back down to the sparring grounds, watching troops practice on each other until the sun was just about to disappear beyond the horizon. The two of them discussed plans for leaving to the Stills and updated me on other subjects they had discussed since I started my training. Colonel Theone eventually excused themselves to make arrangements with Nerice's scouts. Word would be sent to Major Vale that I would be finally coming to help after weeks of waiting.

Commander Lachlan and I walked in silence for a few long minutes, my heart speeding up the second Colonel Theone walked away leaving us alone together. He steered us back up towards the village.

"So, you noticed my spirit?" I asked. I felt anxious, being alone with him. He was the leader of an army, he had more important things to do than have small talk with me.

The Commander ran a hand through his blonde hair and laughed, almost, nervously. "Yes, I, umm, need to make sure Gwen is training you properly. I watch everyone."

"I suppose you have to, being Commander."

"Ha, ha, aye, you're right. Also, if I don't bring proper reports to Theone every evening they get —well, you've seen how the Colonel gets." Commander Lachlan grinned, entertained by his own words.

I smiled. I did not know what kind man he was, but it was nice to slowly find out.

It occurred to me that perhaps Gwen and Durin were not the only friends I made here. I recalled a couple nights when I was ready to settle down, Colonel Theone would show up at my door to inspect me and ask me questions, as if the reports they were getting were never enough for them. We would chat and they would tell me about their day and sometimes even gossip about things they noticed around Blackwick. They offered a wonderful distraction from thinking about home. In fact, on the nights they would come by, I would almost fall asleep to their chatting and when they noticed me drifting, they would help me get comfortable and blow out the candle hanging from the ceiling before leaving.

"I was under the impression you led us, Commander, yet Colonel Theone acts as if they do," I said, teasing, testing the waters.

The Commander chuckled. "Yes, well, before I arrived Colonel Theone, Mother Nerice and Colonel Bellamy held this place together. I took Theone as my Second because I saw their potential and it's better to have a whole council at the hands of an army than just a single person making all the decisions, don't you agree?" He had a point.

Commander Lachlan had ended up walking me to the Tabernacle without me noticing. The sun was about to disappear behind the mountains and the sky leaked a deep orange and pink showing a beauty I had not observed in this world yet.

I looked up, seeing stars dotting the heavens. I feared making eye contact with the Commander would cause me to be lost in his gaze. Always so exhausted from the days schedule, I never really took the time to appreciate the strange sky above me. As the sun settled in for the night, the stars decorated the sky more beautifully than I had ever seen any night sky before it. I felt I could see whole constellations, galaxies even. I was stunned, loosing myself there instead of the Commander. A moment breathed through me, allowing this world to be just a little more bearable.

"I love the stars," Commander Lachlan said thoughtfully. I regarded him. He too was looking up, admiring stars and was standing *very* close. "They're so lovely this time of year. Too bad the clouds have been in the damned way so much this season."

"I love the stars too," I said.

The Commander looked down to meet my gaze just for a moment before clearing his throat and looking every direction but me. My heart felt as if it would leap out of my throat from just meeting his eyes with mine. He opened the Tabernacle doors and indicated for me to go inside.

We quietly walked through the halls back to my room. I opened the door, and it swung all the way to the wall behind it, giving a full view inside. Commander Lachlan's attention momentarily settled on the dried primroses still sitting on the desk. I had not removed them, liking the way they brightened up the space.

"Primroses are usually a spring flower, but some people grow them in greenhouses," the Commander said. "They are a sign of new beginnings…a declaration of love." The Commander took a deep breath, and our eyes met again. He smirked a little. "Those demons scratched you up, but it looks like the surgeon took good care of your marks. If you like, I could help with the one on your face. I could perhaps encourage it to be barely noticeable. Only if the sun catches it, would anyone know it was there."

I ran my fingers over the scarred tissue on my face. I suppose my expression changed because the Commander hurriedly spat out "Not that you look terrible, Seer! You are…" His voice lowered slightly and slowed when I looked back to him "very pleasing to look at. I just thought I would offer…if you wanted me to."

He thought I was *pretty*.

"That would be really nice. I'm fond of the way my face looked before the demons ruined it, not that I get to ever see it anymore. I don't think I've looked in the mirror since before the explosion," I said. It was strange not to see my face for so long. Even windows were too frosted from the cold to show my reflection.

The Commander took a step closer, his armour nearly pressing against the front of my body. He removed one of his gloves. "I wouldn't say the demons ruined it."

I swallowed as the Commander gently placed a finger on the beginning of my scar and carefully traced over it. I felt my skin tingle under the feeling of his finger and in the dim light of the Tabernacle hallway, it hummed with light. I could smell coffee on his breath. Our eyes met briefly while he slowly traced the mark and when he was finished, he put his glove back on.

"There we are, I hope that is adequate for you," the Commander said.

"I'm sure your work is more than adequate, Commander," I replied.

We smiled softly at each other for a long moment before Commander Lachlan ran his hands through his hair and bit at his lip, looking away. "Well, keep up the good work, Seer," he said simply. He seemed a little uncomfortable, trying to say goodbye. He nodded at me before turning to leave.

"You can call me Delilah, you know. I was addressing all four of you when I said it in the Council Room, and no one really calls me by my name. I would really like it if you did."

Commander Lachlan paused when he heard my voice, and he looked over his shoulder at me with a slightly hopeful expression crossing his face. "Only when I am in your company shall I call you as such, *Delilah*." He carried on back the way we came. My heart fluttered rapidly with the memory of his voice saying my name, of his skin on mine.

I waited until he was completely out of sight before going into my room and dancing a little bit in excitement on the other side of the door.

He had *touched* me. He said I was *very pleasing to look at.*

"Holy shit!" I squeaked excitedly.

I felt it again.

That moment.

Something of normalcy crossing my mind, a weight lifted. It almost felt as if things would be okay.

I did not cry to sleep that night.

Chapter Six
Day Forty-Six.

I had read the few books that sat on the shelves of my room. There were books on poisonous plants, some fairytales, a history book talking about what was known of the war, which had gone on for many generations. When Gwen had told me the people had waited a thousand years for me, she was not exaggerating. It was *The History of the Tabernacle* and the *Legend of Andreja* that stuck out to me the most and were the first I went through. Andreja was a *goddess*. One of nine. Everything that people were saying to me was making more sense.

The chance of these books being here were no coincidence and I suspected someone put them in my room on purpose. All the books were common knowledge amongst most of, if not all, the homes in this world. These subjects I had no familiarity with, not until I finished reading about them. These books would help me fit in without asking an obscene number of questions about things I should already know. These books that would help me hide.

It had become very clear. Someone *knew* I was an alien and was trying to help. I tried not to let this realization get to me. The fact this person was helping me learn about this world and not telling anyone had to be a good thing.

I set a book of prayers back to one of the shelves, next to where I had been collecting shiny rocks I liked and jars of spices and herbs I had been gifted or traded for. I wished I had something to make this room feel more like home, colourful paint like the murals on the buildings in the village, or pretty curtains and blankets.

The worry of someone knowing my secret plagued the back of my mind.

It had been a couple weeks since I had a good dinner conversation with Durin, and I had not spoken to Vice since his brief "Take this," when he handed me his stomach tonic weeks before. I would spend a lot of nights at the campfire with Durin, but we rarely spoke outside topics of the day or an epic retelling of something Durin did before joining the army.

My body was growing stronger, and my combat skills begun to hone. With that in mind my desperation for a day off, away from the training and meditation and prayer or whatever it was that Nerice and Bellamy had me doing, only grew stronger.

A day to just exist and come out of the shell I had put myself into was needed.

If I was going to be stuck here, I wanted to discover who I could be even though many had already assigned that to me; Seer.

I stared at the fresh cut on my arm, scabs forming over it and the skin pink and irritated from sleeping on it. I knew it would heal better if I did not stress it for at least a day. If I had the day off, perhaps I could get to know Durin and Vice a little better. Through listening to Colonel Theone and the Commander I had discovered the two would be accompanying me with the Colonel on the mission to retrieve Major Vale. I wanted to know who my travelling companions were.

I wrote small note to Gwen and slid it into her tent early in the morning saying I would be resting today and if she got into trouble, she could tell Colonel Theone and the Commander to speak with me. I was sure she would respect my decision, considering how patient and understanding she had been.

I still found myself in the kitchens, baking bread and oat cakes flavoured with jam. When Nerice came to retrieve me for prayers, I told her I wanted to spend the day getting to know my companions for my journey to the Stills. I assured her I would pick up the usual routine tomorrow and she appeared content not to argue with me.

Nerice took an oat cake into her hand, still warm and leaking raspberry juices then left me to the kitchen.

Once I was finished there, I brought Durin breakfast. Still covered in flour, I had asked the laity cooks for some eggs in exchange for the recipe of my honey and thyme bread. Its smell had been a hit amongst them, and they had been having me make it regularly since I joined them.

I carried a small loaf, a pouch of eggs and other cooking accessories with me as I approached Durin's tent. Durin stood, barely awake, stirring a pot above a fresh fire.

"Durin Hawke!" I said enthusiastically, waving with the loaf of warm bread in my hands.

He turned to me and gave me a big, warm smile. A gold tooth shined at me that I had not noticed before. "Shorty, come to take more of my stew?" His smile turned playful. "Oh, wait, or do I call you *Seer*?"

The mornings were livelier than the nights. Parents corralled their children to follow them to the market area of Blackwick for trading cheese and dried meat or textiles. Tradespeople brought their fires to life, the sound of metal clanking and wood chopping echoing throughout the streets. Soldiers patrolled more actively with the sun in the sky and nuns held sermons scattered throughout the town, praying for the war to end, praying for safe travels for the refugees, praying for a simple commoners life for the village children so they did not have to go to war when they got older.

I handed Durin the loaf of bread, the smell of it wafting in around us.

"Oh, please call me Delilah; all this *Seer* formality is weird. I don't see the future, why would I be labeled as such?"

Durin laughed, "You got it, Shorty," and tapped his spoon on the edge of the pot. He eyed the skillet and pouch in my free hand. "What other presents do you have there?" he asked.

"I brought breakfast! Though if you'd rather have your stew..." I smirked at him.

Durin looked at his pot, obviously disappointed with it. "It's just potato stew. I lost a bet the other night and forfeited my vegetables and venison. I'm more interested in what you were thinking of making. You said you were a cook, right?"

I set the iron skillet I borrowed down over the hot coals and opened the pouch in front of Durin. "Yes! I am!" I said triumphantly.

Durin peered inside the pouch, seeing the blue eggs inside.

"Mm, EGGciting!" Durin said wiggling his eyebrows for more encouragement.

"That was bad," I laughed.

"Aye, well, I don't get enough practise anymore." Durin thumped onto his bench and watched me cook. I cracked the eggs into the skillet, frying them in some animal fat I took from a jar in the kitchens ice box.

"Durin, how have you been?" I asked as I pushed at the eggs with Durin's spoon.

"No different than I was last night. I'm relaxing until our quest with Sir Serious and Theone. How is training with Blondie's soldier? How's Blondie?" Durin smiled knowingly at me and pointed a finger to my face, his elbow leaning on his knee. It was sunny out. I blushed.

How did he know it was the Commander who healed the scar?

"I slipped up trying to handle duel-wielding yesterday. Is Sir. Serious supposed to be Vice?" I asked.

"Have you tried to hold a conversation with him?" Durin asked. He sat straight and put on a lower voice. "I need to go study. No, I can't come out tonight, the moons aren't in the right place. Blah, blah, blah." Durin slouched again, eyeing the eggs.

I sat on to the cold, hard ground, my calves aching from squatting next to the skillet. "I thought I would have been trained by one of Nerice's people. They seem more like what Colonel Theone wanted me trained for. I have not seen any of Commander Lachlan's troops with a bow, let alone duel-wielding swords, except for Gwen. He said Gwen used to be one of Nerice's though. Is that true?"

"Aye, Gwen *was* one of Nerice's. I should call her a *scout* as to not scare others." Durin looked around to the townsfolk and smirked again, his attention returned to me.

I pulled the eggs from the fire and held my hand out for the loaf of bread. Durin tossed it to me.

"I'm not completely squeamish, Durin. I puke because I have bad anxiety and my pain tolerance can only get me so far, not because

I'm scared of what people do for a living."

Durin's voice hushed to a whisper, and he leaned closer to me. "Gwen was an assassin," he said, his eyes sparkling with the information.

I tore the loaf of bread in two then split the pieces in the middle to stuff each half with fried, yolk-dripping eggs.

"No one back home would ever believe I knew an assassin." I handed Durin one of the sandwiches.

Durin seemed entertained by my statement and took a bite of the sandwich, nodding approvingly at the taste. He swallowed and watched me dip my sandwich into the stew still hanging over the fire and copied me. "You're a damn good cook and baker," he said dipping his sandwich again.

I lit up at his compliment. "Thank you. I believe I would be of better use in the kitchens than out at war, but the Council believes otherwise. I don't think I have never been so tired in my life with all this training."

"To be a tavern cook and not have to train for battle from childhood…You seem to have lived a very good life before you dropped in, if this is the most tired you have ever been," Durin observed. He was correct. All the things in my life that had caused me any sort of inconvenience did not compare to the things I experienced here, and I had only been here less than two months. "Tell me more about your old job, Shorty, I'm curious."

I smiled fondly thinking about my jobs back home. What a different life. Despite the feeling lifting, I still felt displaced. "Well, I had two jobs. I worked in a kitchen. I started working as a night baker, and I was alone during the shift. It was quieter. I liked doing my own thing. Then after my time there I went to my other job where I selected music for people to listen to and told stories about my travels."

"You were also a bard?' Durin asked, almost in disbelief.

"I suppose I kind of was," I laughed.

"You have to share a song with me," Durin said finishing off his sandwich.

"I didn't sing the songs! I picked them out. Other bards and bands would do the singing," I explained.

"Everybody knows how to sing!" Durin quickly noticed my nervousness at his request. "How about I sing you one of my favourite songs and you can sing me one in exchange?"

We stared at each other. Durin took another bite from the sandwich and chewed slowly, waiting for my reply. Townsfolk bustled around us, many already fed and their daily chores in full swing.

"I'll sing to you while we are on our way to the Stills. But you have to sing first," I agreed.

"Deal!"

It was noon when I went to find Vice.

Durin and I talked nonstop in the hours prior. He told me wild, elaborate tales of valor and hilarious ventures he had with a good friend who he revealed, after a little prying, to be Commander Lachlan. I was stunned. With all the antics leading up to the Commander joining the army then leading it, he was a changed man, at least publicly. The two were long-time friends.

When I reached Vice he was reserved.

"Are you feeling unwell?" he asked as I greeted him, after knocking on his chamber doors.

"Um…no," I said. I stood in his doorway.

Vice stood, blocking me from entering. He was taller than I remembered, and his dark hair was down, his brows furrowed, worried. He appeared frazzled that someone had called on him.

"I just wanted to come say hello and get to know you, since we'll be hiking out together," I explained.

"I see," he said eyeing me.

Vice shared a large bunkhouse with several army lieutenants. Vice's private room was down a dark, cold hallway away from the large fireplace at the front of the cabin. I had been lucky that one of the other lieutenants had been in the common area of the cabin and directed me to Vice's room, or else I probably would have given up on finding him. I only knew Vice lived in this building because Durin walked me to it when I asked.

We were both quiet and I felt awkward. Vice continued to eye me, as if analyzing my every action and breath.

"So," I said peaking over his shoulder. His room was a space overflowing with books, scrolls and herbs hanging from the ceiling. Dozens of bottles filled with various liquids were stacked on shelves.

I found it easy to talk to Durin. Bellamy, Nerice and Gwen were wonderful conversationalists too. Colonel Theone started conversations on their own. I did not know how to start a conversation with someone I had only briefly spoken to weeks ago.

"Did you join the army on your own?" I asked. I had gathered a lot of people either joined through the church or were inspired to join seeing people they love do so.

"I did," Vice said curtly.

"Care to elaborate?"

"No."

I sighed. Maybe a different direction. "You kept me alive?" I asked.

"As did the Commander." Vice moved to sit at his desk and tucked some of his hair behind his ear. "Your tattoos are fascinating. I'm curious to their meanings." There we go.

"My tattoos aren't very visible most of the time," I said accusingly.

Vice grabbed a book from one of the piles on his desk and pulled it to him. "Yes, but you were without trousers or boots when brought to me. After the Commander and I stabilized you, I couldn't help but make speculations behind them."

"What do you think the meanings are?" I asked curiously.

Vice looked around, as if people were watching, then looked back to me as he opened the book. "Perhaps we can discuss this more in the evening? I have some previous engagements, if you don't mind."

I pouted. I had hoped to become better aquatinted with him now, but I suppose getting a raincheck for later in the day was not bad a bad start. After all, there was still time before we left and I had surprised him.

"Sure, you can come by my chambers after dinner," I said.

Vice was looking through his book. The conversation was over.

By late afternoon I decided to go somewhere familiar. In the weeks I had spent in Blackwick, the sparring field had become one of those places for me, strangely.

The soldiers were as they usually were, and Commander Lachlan stood watching over them. He barked some orders at a group who were practicing a shield wall then spoke to another a man standing next to him. "Captain Mosland, if there's a breach, we must be ready. Make sure they are."

"Aye sir," the captain said before leaving his side to adjust one of the soldiers in the lineup.

The Commander must have sensed my presence because he began to speak to me before he looked at me. "I didn't think a trip to the recruit camp would be relaxing but call me surprised."

I stepped beside him, and he glanced down at me, a playful smirk on his lips. "Hello Surprised," I said.

Commander Lachlan's smirk widened into a toothy grin, and he looked back at his troops. "Locals from Blackwick and some refugees have enlisted since you arrived. I was recruited to the army here myself, but I was not inspired to for the reasons they are." He began to walk, waving for me to follow him as he made his rounds and I happily did, excited he wanted to speak to me.

"I had however transferred out and was in the South Province during their official denouncement of the gods –I saw the destruction firsthand.

"High Priestess Katerina had sought resolution during her career and Colonel Theone upholds their mother's beliefs. The Colonel had sought me out after Durin highly recommended me for this position. If they chose to take position in place of their mother, I believe they will do a good job." The Commander looked at me with half a smirk as if he was spilling a secret to me. "The Colonel had

Durin convinced overnight to join the cause. I left the Keepers to join five years later; it seemed like the right thing to do, especially since Theone decided to use Blackwick as a base." We stopped at the opposite side of the sparring grounds, and he gave me his full attention. He faced me, stepping close like he had been last night, our breaths puffing out and mixing together in the cold.

"The Temples lost control when South Province fell from grace; despite what the Temples will tell you. Keepers are pulling away from the Temples, mages are becoming apostates. All they can focus on is replacing two Divines. Everyone has had barely any time to mourn. We can-" the Commander cut himself off. It was nice to hear him talk. He had said more to me in the last two days than he had in the last two months. "I apologize, my words can get away from me sometimes."

"Actually, I like your fervor, so I'd love to hear more," I said.

The Commander fought another grin and looked around the recruits again. My heart fluttered.

When he looked back to me, his eyes went over my face before settling on my lips. "I, umm…" He cleared his throat and resettled his gaze to my own. "I could arrange that."

One of Nerice's scouts approached, a parchment rolled in her hand. Captain Florence.

"Commander, an owl came in from Major Vale!" she said holding out the report.

Commanders Lachlan took it and Florence bolted back in the direction of the village as the Commander unrolled the parchment to read it.

We started to walk again, making another round and I followed him through the troops. He genuinely seemed to enjoy the company.

Major Vale was still alive, though his resources were all but gone. He was apparently one to crack a couple jokes in his reports because the Commander caught himself from laughing a few times while reading it. He was relieved his Third was surviving.

When the Commander rolled the report back up, I spoke.

"I have a question for you," I said, my voice hitching a little as I realized how much I wanted to talk to him.

"Of course, Seer."

"You and Vice helped heal me after the Temple exploded."

"That is not a question."

"I'm wondering, why did you help? Durin said you don't exactly flaunt your healing abilities since you have an army to lead. I mean I understand, but I'm just curious." I was rambling.

"Why would I not help? We saw you fall from the sky, one among hundreds of other falling stars. We had never witnessed something so frightening. We thought the gods were angry. Angry at those who had forsaken them, angry at all the bloodshed. I took half my troops to investigate and made it up the mountain fast. Many were fearful of what was awaiting us, but I was determined to make it there for our Divine, for *Theone*." He paused, looking towards the village, to where I suspected he believed Colonel Theone was working. "Hundreds of people had been there with High Priestess Katerina; their lives mattered. I made it to the site first with a couple others. There you were, amongst the flames and rubble without any broken bones, just your hand and eye bloodied as the stars finally slowed in their descent from the heavens. I carried you back to a summit camp to look you over as my troops stayed behind to survey the ruins. We did not think there would be any survivors."

"You carried me back?" I looked at the handprint burned into my palm, the print of fingers and a thumb wrapped around the base by my wrist. I rarely looked at my palm, fearful of the scar. My long sleeves usually covered the fingers.

"I did. I was amazed you didn't suffer any frostbite, considering you must have been there for several hours before our arrival. You are a miracle."

We had stopped walking along the outer edge of the training grounds, close to the trail that led to where Gwen and I would practice. The incoming clouds suggested another snow was coming. The Commander and I stared at each other, and everything seemed quiet for a moment as if we were the only two people around.

"How do you know I fell out of the sky too?" I asked.

I watched as the Commander thought over his words and pushed his hair back. "I…" He paused, his eyes looking beyond me.

I felt a familiar presence. The moment I did, I kicked my leg back like a mule. I heard a thud on the ground, and I whirled around.

Gwen.

I smiled.

She swung her legs towards me, a trick I now knew well, in an effort knock my feet from under me. As her legs closed in on my mine, I hopped over them and jumped back, narrowly missing a collision with the Commander. "Nice try!" I said victoriously.

Gwen sat up. "Okay, I'll give you this one. I'm very proud of you, Seer."

"Gwen, *please* call Delilah. I think you and I are past formal titles; you're my friend. We should be on a first name basis." Joy filled my heart when the word 'friend' left my lips. An official declaration of any sort of relationship here. It felt good to say it. Now only if I could stop asking people to call me by name.

Gwen smiled wide. "I'm glad to have you consider me a friend, Seer-" Gwen pressed her lips together trying to force back a smirk. "Delilah." Her eyes darted to Commander Lachlan, and I could see a silent conversation between them. Gwen's expression was almost challenging towards him. A suggestion that he should try something and see what her reaction would be.

I held my hand out to Gwen and pulled her up with ease to my surprise. I felt oddly triumphant how we had switched places, even if it was just this once, and I was glad it was in front of the Commander. I knew I had not yet surpassed Gwen in skill, but the fact that I had not fallen on my ass for once was a win. Commander Lachlan nodded approvingly, and just for a second, I thought I saw him smile at me before returning to the troops.

"You two have a nice afternoon, I should be getting back," he said.

Gwen and I exchanged pleasantries for a while before I returned to my room. She caught me up on her day and told me how she expected me again the next day. I expressed gratitude to her for being able to have a day to not do anything. Gwen told me, despite what I believed, I was their Seer, which meant I was everyone's boss.

Nerice had tricked me. A Mother of a religious order had known that I, their apparent Most Holy, needed to be in a better mindset and train for the war. She got me into a routine. When I was finally in it and told her I was not working, she had agreed to it because she had to.

I felt both jolted and impressed by her. No wonder she was the spymaster.

When I arrived at my chambers, Vice was waiting for me by the door, staff in hand, eyes coming back into focus like he had been somewhere far away in his mind before noticing my approach. He greeted me with a simple "Hello."

"Hey Vice," I said, yawning as soon as the words left my mouth.

"*Hey.*" Vice repeated.

I opened my door, waving Vice to follow behind me.

I pulled off each of my boots, one at a time, hopping around on one foot to yank them from my body. I felt Vice's eyes on me as I bounced.

"Sit down," I instructed, indicating the chair or the bed to sit on. Vice chose the chair by my desk. He sat very straight and formal. I was starting to understand Durin's impression.

After I got my boots off, I yanked off my socks, something I sewed together with some old clothes one of the laity was going to throw away a few days before, then started running my hands through my hair, trying to get the knots out. No one had a brush to bargain for and combs were a luxury item.

"You watch me very *curiously*, Vice," I observed after I was satisfied with my hair and Vice had not said anything to begin a conversation.

Vice did not skip a beat, "You're a very curious individual, Delilah." I could not be sure how Vice did it, but he made my name sound almost like a song, something that easily rolled off his tongue.

"Thanks?" I crossed my legs on the bed so I could face him and poured myself a glass of water.

"Do your tattoos have meaning to *you*?" Vice asked.

"You know, I have friends I've known my entire life, and they forget that I have them sometimes. I even do." Both my legs and one of my arms were covered in different designs. None really held a lot of significance to me, I just enjoyed the art. Some related to movies, shows and video games I enjoyed, others were just flash art I thought looked pretty. They had become a part of me, and I barely noticed them anymore.

"I have not seen many people with their bodies quite so covered like yours. I had time to study you. What about the one on your back? The dragon takes up a good portion of your skin."

"Oh, I just thought it would look nice," I admitted. I always forgot about that one. The body of the dragon was drawn over my spine and the wings spread over my scapula. It looked like it was chasing an owl, an older tattoo on the back of my neck. All my work was black ink.

"Interesting that you chose animals associated with some of the gods," Vice said.

Vice stayed for a couple hours, picking my brain and asking me questions about my life before arriving in Blackwick. I tried to sensor the best I could, to not give much away or suggest where I was from was different from this planet, but he asked so much that at some points I got excited. I would be talking about something I love, reminding me of home, like when I spoke with Durin, and I could not remember if I had said anything *unusual*. It just felt so good to talk about home, to remember it, to share things about it.

I had to *tell* them.

The time was not right yet. I did not know ow to even begin to explain the truth to these people.

Vice asked about my lineage. He asked what I remember before my memory loss at the Temple, looking at his staff, picking lint off his cloak. His voice was lax in the privacy of my room.

"It was just a regular day. I was going on a vacation and then," I paused. How could I even begin to tell him that I used to have a time travelling machine? "And then I was here."

"You did nothing beforehand? Nothing was out of the ordinary? No spells? You did not go somewhere where you could have angered a spirit or-"

"As odd as it may sound, Vice, where I am from there is no magic. No mages. No dragons and demons. Swords are usually used for decoration, if not on display in giant buildings for people to look at art and ancient workings of our ancestors."

Vice stood up, and I made a face, expressing an apology, thinking my voice had become heated and I said something wrong.

"I'm glad to see you are open to a place in a world where people are not, Delilah." My name again sounded so smooth coming from his lips, and it stirred something inside me; not the way that the Commander stirred something, but enough moved to make me wonder how he was doing it.

"You're leaving?" I asked.

He nodded. "It is late; you should rest before you return to your training tomorrow. The mind must rest just as much as the body."

I stood up and walked him to the door. Once again, I knew nothing about him. I felt like I had been thwarted for sharing so much about myself and not knowing anything about him in return. I had completely forgot to ask him about himself.

"I don't mind staying up late if you wanted to stay longer? Maybe tell me about yourself? I'd enjoy to getting to know you more," I said, trying not to sound like I was pleading.

"I need some time to myself. Have a good night." He left, disappearing quickly and quietly into the darkness of the quiet Tabernacle halls.

Chapter Seven
Day Sixty-One

I had time to get to know my companions. I had been given a nice routine. The time in the kitchens helped me feel I could contribute something to these people other than what they believed, and I did not.

As much as it was strange to admit, the meditation and prayer practices I shared with Nerice and Bellamy eased the shaking, unrelenting anxieties within me more every day. I felt more at ease within these walls and a great sense of connection to everyone each passing day. I enjoyed my weekly slow mornings with Gwen. We exchanged stories with one another, and I learnt, albeit vaguely, how Gwen had lost her eye.

"Life demands sacrifices," she had said, her tone darker than usual. "It led me here, and there is nowhere I would rather be." Her dazzling smile relit the mood and the subject was changed.

The evening prayers and stretches became something I looked forward to. My reflexes were getting better, and I became astonished by my body's ability. I felt stronger, exhilarated, and could not help but wonder if the routines Nerice had curated for me had been made to do exactly that for me.

Gwen had made me feel her wrath for knocking her over that day in front of the Commander, but only for the first few rounds. Our training had turned into a fun game. Gwen showed me stunts that I only ever saw in movies. She taught me efficient techniques to dodge and ways to lock weapons into mine, by my favour.

"You are small. You can slip underneath your opposition," she smirked darkly and in a hushed voice she said, "Then slice them in half from below!"

I often laughed as we sparred and twisted around one another. I knew she was only matching the skill I had to allow me to grow more confident; but every time I got comfortable, she would become a harder opponent.

After receiving my own canteen to drink from there was no longer a break for Gwen to retrieve water. Rather an opportunity was given each day to sneak a peak at the Commander when Gwen and I went to refill our bottles.

We continued to stay in the area by the trees, down away from where other recruits and soldiers practised. Occasionally I still felt something watching us from the woods, but one day, I felt a different set of eyes on me. I glanced to the top of the hill, identifying Commander Lachlan's figure overlooking my training. Later in the day he had returned, but this time with Nerice and Colonel Theone by his side.

I smiled as metal connected between Gwen and I, and I returned my attention to her.

It had suddenly become easier to bear this world.

No longer did I exchange my evening between nightly cries or dinner with Durin. Come nightfall, if I did not share a plate with my friend, I would walk through Blackwick, dinner in hand, talking to new faces and one's I had come to know. Occasionally Bellamy joined me as she was often among the scouts who did night patrol. She expressed love her job and boasted about being the best Rider in the province. Nerice had seen her on the field, practically flying through battle with her uncle Major Vale close behind her. Nerice wanted her enlisted immediately. Her coin had been a bonus addition to Nerice's team.

Bellamy's delicate features and long silky hair seemed out of place in a rural mountain village. Her extravagant fur cloaks and gold hair chains and jewelry even more so. I learned of her life in the Northeastern Province, a rather tropical area of the world. Her mother had moved there to marry her father. Bellamy came back to learn medicine from her mother's village and instead found herself in the heat of many battles with her uncle by her side. Once enlisted, she was stationed in Blackwick, leaving her husband behind in the other province. They wrote letters regularly. It had been three years, and she was still not used to the cold or sleeping alone.

Some nights when I returned to the Tabernacle Vice would be waiting for me outside my room. He was ready to bombard me with more questions then always left abruptly. He always strategically steered the conversation in a way that I would get excited about myself and forget I wanted to get to know him.

Other nights Vice would not be there. These nights became my favourite because Commander Lachlan would find me strolling the streets and walk me back to my room. Usually, he did so in silence or with small talk about the weather or how he was impressed with my improvements. Whatever possessed him to do so, I was glad he only did so in the evenings because he was less likely to see me blush any time he smiled at me.

The following day, if Durin and I were shooting the shit at dinnertime, Durin would tease me knowing I had been alone with the Commander the evening before.

"Believe me, Shorty, you're not the only clue I have to know when he's been with you."

"Oh?" I pressed.

Durin waved it off. "Aye, but I'm not going to elaborate." He smirked.

One afternoon, halfway through my regular training with Gwen, I was asked to join the Council in the Tabernacle. According to Colonel Theone, the Council had been waiting for me to be healed and my training well underway before I began to take on regular responsibility. The plan to work with them directly had always been on the table and I only figured that out as I sat in on their discussion.

It was time for me to leave for the Stills.

Captain Florence Pirc, who turned out to be Nerice's Third, had gone ahead to await my arrival. She was securing us a place to sleep at one of the Tabernacle's close to the Stills and was speaking with a Priestess there named Mirna. The Priestess was involved directly with Temple Krix and close friends with High Priestess Caoimhe of Temple Ilona. Priestess Mirna and High Priestess

Caoimhe were to be two of my three judges for my upcoming trial. There was hope that while I was there, I could make a good impression on Mirna and she would express her thoughts to the High Priestess.

I had been briefed on the missions the army was doing outside of Blackwick, including mine.

Priestess Mirna had travelled from Zaanthru two decades prior, when war spread to these lands, to help take care of one of the Tabernacles. She pushed for more supplies in this part of the province when others had given up on aid from the Temple's. At the time there were a lot of displaced refugees hoping to find a new home away from the main war in the South and Northeast Provinces. Now, people were travelling further north and west, into the mountains, to places like Blackwick, because it was harder to fight in steep, cold hills. It was Colonel Bellamy's hope that the Priestess would be convinced to travel again, this time to the Tabernacle in Blackwick. If she did, perhaps then the Temples would be persuaded I was not a blasphemy against their religion, as Grand Deacon Adder was suggesting. Of course, my trial still had to happen, and Captain Florence would be doing her best at persuading the Priestess to my innocence before our arrival.

However, Major Vale needed to be extracted. He had connections to people in the north that were invaluable and if he died, the army would lose that connection. I needed to be the on the extraction team because I could cleanse the areas of demons.

I was given a pack and some scout armour, which was thicker and more protective than the leathers I had been wearing on and off for weeks. I would be carrying my share of dried goods that we could rehydrate with water for meals. I sharpened my blades to make sure they were ready for whatever we faced, though I did not want to think of what that may be. I desperately wanted to bring my jewelry and night shirt, but I only had enough room for my wool sweater, which I knew I would need on the cold nights in a tent without a fire. I set my rings back into their pouch on the mantle above the hearth. I took my rings off for daily training anyway, but it always felt good to put them back on at night and I would miss them until my return to Blackwick.

Every part of me was dreading not being able to be return to my room at the end of the day. I liked my routine. I was going to miss hoping for an evening walk with the Commander. I would miss having breakfast with Gwen.

"If everything goes to plan, we should be back within the month, Seer," Colonel Theone said as they watched Durin tuck the sleeve of my sweater into the pack on my back. I was apparently bad at packing, and it had begun to come loose while we walked down the mountain. The Colonel could definitely sense my unease with leaving the village.

"Theone, no one is around!" Durin exclaimed. He extended his arms out to the landscape before us as we made our descent. "The poor lady wants to hear her name!"

After several hours I recognized the trail we used. We passed the old mill camp and the big gate where demons had been attacking. Each spot had a couple soldiers or a scout stationed there to help with refugees coming up the mountain. The crater from the crash site was almost filled in from two months of snowfall and all the debris from dead Machine's seemed to be buried with it.

As we continued our descent the snow became less thick and easier to travel through. Only sounds of birds carried with our voices, the trail less menacing in the late morning and early afternoon light.

Colonel Theone huffed and looked at me as they spoke. "If we are to truly drop formalities, you may simply call me Theone. If you insist, of course. I want to show you respect. That is why I call you *Seer*," Theone explained.

I felt hopeful, perhaps with dropping titles, it would mean I was making another friend. Theone was already popping over to my room occasionally. This was another opportunity for me.

"I *insist* you call me Delilah. Please," I said.

I could see a little smile on Theone's black-painted lips, and I wondered if they were happy to make a friend as well. I could hope, at least.

"Alright, it is done," Theone agreed.

It would take a week to get to the Stills and that was only if we kept on schedule, which meant a hell of a lot of hiking. It also meant more time to get to know my companions.

Durin and I practically never stopped talking as we walked, and I quickly decided he was someone I could never tire of. Vice remained quiet while Theone would occasionally throw in their own opinions on the conversation.

When we made camp the first night at one of the flatter hills that made up the mountains, I was blown away by natures extravagance. I tried to imagine springtime, and summer and autumn; how beautiful this place must be. Many trees were bare of leaves, but many were also covered with snow, frozen and waiting for spring. The snow glittered, untouched save the trail many used to move up the mountain to the refugee camps then to Blackwick. We had left early to make it past the camps, to leave room for anyone coming up and would make our own camp further down. The snow brightened the darkening evening, but it was still a hurry to set up our camp.

After the tents were up and the fire started, Theone sparred with me, to keep me in practise, while Vice and Durin established a string perimeter like the one I had seen at the soldier's camp outside of Blackwick. Bells jingled attached to butcher's twine and I kept my eyes from the trees, though the temptation was strong.

It was a challenging practise to fight someone other than Gwen. Theone unleashed fury on me, and it was simply thrilling to be faced by them. They refused to go easy on me. I had been put on my ass a hundred times before with Gwen, but at least now I could *almost* fight evenly with her. With Theone, I stood no chance.

When the four of us were settling down for the night, Vice broke his long silence and asked to take a short walk with me, assuring Theone we would not be out of the light of the fire. Vice said he would merely test me against battling a mage, since I had no experience with them. "She needs the training," he said. Theone approved.

I brought my daggers, but to my surprise, Vice revealed that what he said to Theone was not his true intention. We were out of earshot of the camp, and I saw Theone slip into a tent with Durin.

"I admit that since you fell out of the sky, I have been vexed by you, Delilah," he began.

"Everyone has been," I shrugged. It was a common comment in any discussion.

"Studying you, running tests on you, analyzing your answers to all my questions…" He took a deep breath and walked in front of me to face me, stopping me from walking any farther beyond the bell perimeter. I was taken aback by it. He normally kept his distance. His red eyes scanned over me, analyzing every possible move I could make. I watched falling snow melt against his cheeks and thick braided hair. His eyes glowed in the fire light behind me, and he scanned the area around us in a way to suggest he wanted to make sure nothing was going to surprise us from the trees.

"I will tell you that I am the one who placed books about Alhan in your chambers. I had made so many guesses to where you had come from. The Other, lost kingdoms that have been hidden away far longer than history allows those to remember, but to have come from a completely different world…That is truly something to behold," Vice said.

I took a step back from him, my lip quivering as a panic attack threatened to unleash at his words. It had been weeks since my anxiety had made a true appearance. I had been busy preoccupying myself with anything I could get my hands and thoughts on; books, meals, thinking about the Commander…The routine had been perfect.

To be confronted with something that was such a fear was different.

I had been right.

Someone *knew*.

"You do not need to worry; I will not tell anyone. It is your decision to do so. I am only telling you this because I would enjoy

learning more about your world without you controlling your words."
Something had changed in the way Vice stood before me, as if he
almost regretted his forwardness and confession. He saw my eyes
grow shiny, trying to hold back tears, hold back fear.

I nodded to show him I heard what he said, that I
understood. I knew he could sense how uneasy I was, that I was on
the brink of crying.

"I —" Vice began. "I apologize. I did not mean to upset you.
You can tell me more, only if you want to. Let's return to camp." He
motioned back in the direction of the fire and tents, his hand
hovering near my arm as if to reach out and comfort me with a touch.
I walked away before he could. I walked back to camp fast and
hurriedly crawled into the tent that Theone and I were supposed to
share.

Sleep did not find me that night. I cried, though I did try to
do so quietly.

The balance between thinking of home and dwelling on it
had been carefully curated in my mind. I knew that thinking of it too
much would make me emotional, and I had chosen to try to be
professional. I could not dwell on things I could not control.
Describing what I missed to Vice and Durin, even Gwen, was a
happy medium for me. I was able separate myself from missing
Earth. Distractions helped; Blackwick's kitchen; picking a star to
pretend was Earth; wondering what the Commanders lips would taste
like one mine.

Some nights were still sad, but they had started to numb, I
had begun to settle, until tonight. The truth that someone knew I was
an alien made everything real again. I could not pretend I was from
this world because I did not belong. I never had.

At some point in the night, I heard Theone yelling, an
argument that was very one-sided. Theone's voice scrutinized, who I
suspected was, Vice. Though they spoke in a Bygone Speech, the tone
clear: they knew Vice had upset me and he was in trouble. Eventually
Theone crawled into the tent next to me and pulled the furs up over

me in an almost parental fashion. They kissed the back of my head and rubbed my back for several minutes until I stopped whimpering. Theone turned over, their back against mine.

"*Lahko noč*, Delilah."

Our journey took us through an area that was called the Groves. The mountains flattened out, but the forest thickened with sleeping fruit trees. Nights became darker and trails became quieter. Occasionally we would pass a family or small group trying to flee the war. Theone patiently gave them directions to Blackwick.

There was one night when we heard a scream. A blood-freezing sound echoed out around us, and I sat up in my blankets, frightened. Theone hushed me and told me to go back to sleep. I almost asked why, until I realized Theone was pretending that they did not hear the sound.

We passed through more crash sites, blacked and scorched earth scratching at the fresh wound of someone *knowing*.

I was conflicted.

Both worlds collided and I could not process the existence of them together. I spoke the words of the cleansing spell, opening a portal to drink up the demons that congregated near each destroyed Machine. I saw the singed metal, the dead wire. I cast magic effortlessly. My eye stung and throbbed with every spell. The pieces of metal mocked me, crying out for recognition. I was exhausted all over again, the magic taking more energy from me than a whole day of training.

I did not know how much longer I could go without saying anything. I wished I had someone to talk to about it. Find council with someone who would understand.

Vice.

We had not spoken since he told me he knew. I could feel his eyes on me, waiting patiently for me to come to him, fearful of pushing me on his own accord. If I ever looked at him, he would look away or fall back behind Durin and I, Theone always leading us forward.

I wondered if the others would be as understanding as Vice appeared to be.

What I had not grasped about our missions was the sheer amount of death that I would witness.

Any time the trees thinned, and a space opened up, I could hear the bloodshed echoing for miles. Cities that once thrived were now only blighted by blood, disease, and death. Old homes lay in ruin, trees burned to hollow shells. A fresh snowfall was already stained by the slaughter. Bodies lay scattered with weapons still sticking out of them. Who won which battles was based on the amount of fire; those who followed the old gods burned their dead, those who did not left bodies behind to rot. Theone pulled out a large parchment with a map on it and marked areas as we walked further into the Groves.

"The four of us aren't enough to clear these bodies. Theone will order the scouts who went ahead to burn them on their way back. We don't need or want any more dark spirits and demons haunting this place than there already are," Durin explained to me seeing me watch Theone closely. If it was this bad here, I could not imagine how bad the bloodshed was in other provinces where heavier battles were fought.

Once deep into the Groves it did not take long before we found our own fight. There was a mass of battling soldiers we had to go through. Until now we had been able to avoid those at war, but going around this mass would add days to the mission. We could not make Major Vale wait longer. At the edge of the battlefield, Theone stood in front of me as they checked my armour, making sure it was fastened securely. We were going to go straight through them, moving from the treeline into the thick of battle and back out passing *hundreds* of people.

"We are going to run. You run as fast as you can, as far as you can until you are out of the carnage," Theone instructed.

I could feel my heart speeding up with anxiety.

"I will stay beside you for as long as I can, Vice and Durin will flank us. Only engage when it is absolutely necessary. We wear no banner, so it is possible we will not be attacked, but sometimes that doesn't matter," Theone stated. Their golden eyes locked with mine and they drew their sword and unfastened their shield. "Keep your weapons at hand. Do you understand?"

I nodded.

We ran.

I was terrified.

It was hard convincing myself to go towards the battle. It was even harder doing so while running with supplies on my back and a dagger in each hand. I put in great effort to stay alert to every movement before me. Dodging fighting soldiers tired me quickly, but I knew stopping was not an option. I would jump over falling soldiers and stumble here and there. I would be thrown to one side by men who grappled with one another, and Theone would catch me before I could fall, hauling me forward. Lightning shot out before us from Vice's staff if someone was blocking the path too tightly. Arrows whistled by from Durin's bow if someone saw us coming, and decided we were next.

Soon, we were in the heat of the battle and there were too many people surrounding us to continue to sprint past them.

Theone threw themself before me and pushed an onlooker off the path as he glared at us, beating their shield, ready to take us on. "Go!" Theone commanded as their sword colliding with his and igniting in flame.

The look in the soldier's eyes, it almost seemed sick, unreal, *empty*. I could hear more arrows whistle through the air and knew Vice and Durin also had their hands full. I kept running but did not make it far. As I ran another soldier with a crazed expression slid his sword deep into the chest of another. He spun around as I approached and locked on to me. I tried to run past him, but he grabbed my pack and threw me to the ground. He charged, ready to stab his bloodied sword into my body. I rolled out of the way, narrowly being stepped on by another soldier. I threw my body up, holding my daggers out, ready in an offensive position that Theone had made me practice only the night before. My balance was off because of my pack, but I caught myself before stumbling again. He growled in response and charged me.

I narrowly parried his first strike and then caught the second with my two daggers before my face, our blades inches from my nose. My arms burned trying to hold him off me.

"Somebody!" I screamed.

The man's eyes widened, and he fell to my feet, an arrow clean though his temples and black blood dripping from the entry point. I looked around and spotted Durin. He saluted me before turning towards an oncoming soldier . He ran at them then dropped, sliding underneath the soldier's legs at the last moment, his bow clung tightly against his chest. Durin moved swiftly, jumping up behind him and shot another arrow into the soldier's neck.

I focused on what was before me. I could feel my heartbeat pound heavily against my chest and my breath on the edge of panic. I heard someone yelling, their voice full of rage. When my attention fell on them, I braced for impact from their sword. The man stood too close. Instead, his shield bashed against me and the wind left my lungs. I barely caught myself from falling, stumbling back a few steps, trying to hold my body up. I moved my daggers back up and only *just* caught a blow from his sword. I could barely hold against his strength.

This almost felt worse than my battle with demons. His sword was so close to my face, and I could feel the sweat bead on my forehead.

All my training could not have prepared me for this.

"Help me!" I screamed. "Please!"

Nobody came to my aid.

I took a step back, releasing the sword and he advanced. I bumped into another soldier , but they seemed indifferent to me, only throwing me forward, back towards the other. I groaned and moved around my pursuer, barely missing his swing again. This was so much harder with the pack on, but I did not have the time to drop it. I blocked him again, and as I struggled to hold him off, I took the chance to push-kick him straight in the balls. He was only wearing leather armour.

He grunted loudly and doubled over, but not long enough for me to escape. I danced around him, continuing to block his advancement.

It occurred to me then, as I continued to evade him, catching his strikes, moving back and fumbling against other soldiers. These battles, the one I was in now, were fights to the death.

I swallowed and caught another attack with one dagger, my arm ready to give out, but the soldier stilled and dropped. I swallowed, staring down at the body before me, the dagger from my free hand still deep within his skull, the hilt of it at the base of his jaw and the tip bloodied, sticking up through the top of his head. I released a long breath, my ears beginning to ring and the battlefield quieting around me.

I killed someone.

"Seer!"

I was still, the world silencing.

I *killed* someone.

"Delilah!"

I stared down at his lifeless form and swallowed again. I slowly knelt down.

"Delilah, move!"

I gripped the hilt of my dagger, trying to tug it free from the corpse though it resisted release. Gwen was right about it being difficult to pull out. I let out another slow breath and finally got it out. His blood covered my hands from dripping over the handle and beautiful owl head pommel.

A body slammed into me, an arm wrapped around my side, pulling me with them as they ran.

"Breath of the gods, woman, put your head in the present and move!" It was Theone. They pulled me with them until I refocused and held my daggers back at the ready, running on my own accord. I shook my head in disbelief, and I could hear everything around me again.

"I'm sorry!" I cried.

"Keep moving, we're almost out!" Theone shouted.

I stole a look behind me and I watched as Durin practically tumbled out of a big group of grappling soldiers beside Vice, who trailed a few feet behind us.

"Go!" Durin shouted, his face splattered with blood.

We ran, and we kept on running for a while.

Theone had their shield hooked on their hip, their sword in their nondominant hand returning my arm as we ran. It felt like forever before we were out of the main horde. Even longer before we were through the scattered fighting clusters of enraged soldiers on the outskirts. When the screams of battle finally fell into the distance, we slowed to a brisk walk.

Everyone's breath heaved.

Finally, Theone stopped us when we reached the trees.

"Let me look at you!" Theone demanded, their hands going onto my shoulders, their eyes wide with fear. "Are you hurt?" They were covered in blood themselves, some of their liner was smudged by their eyes.

I shook my head, and I looked down at my armour. More blood. Not mine. I glanced at my dagger, red and wet.

Theone thoroughly looked me over and I glanced over at the boys. Vice handed a vial to Durin, who was hunched over his knees, his bow discarded on the ground by his feet.

"Seer."

I watched Durin slowly straighten and put his hands on his back, stretching backwards before snatching the vial from Vice and downing it. He winced at the taste before pulling a cloth from his belt and wiped his face, cleaning it from the blood and sweat. His hair had come loose from his bun, and he began to retie it as Vice held his hands to his eyes, trying to collect himself.

"*Delilah.*"

I looked back at Theone.

"Are you alright?" Theone asked.

I shook my head. "No."

Theone looked me over again and then watched me for a long, intense minute. "This is the first time you took a life," they stated.

I nodded and felt as my eyes began to well. "Yeah," my voice hitched.

"It is alright, Delilah, either you kill or be killed. It is the way. You did what you had to do."

I shook my head and felt my lip quiver.

"Look at me."

I let Theone catch my gaze. I looked into their sharp yellow eyes and saw years of trials and tribulations behind them. Years of doing what they had to do to stay alive. The empathy for me.

"This is why we are training you, Delilah. We are training you to survive. To live. We *need* you."

I let out another slow breath and felt as tears slid over my cheeks. I looked up to the sky. Above us a sunny day was unbothered by the massacre below. I tried to find music somewhere within me to distract my growing panic, the pinching, the nausea. I looked back to Theone who had a concerned look on their face as they let go of my shoulders.

"We must keep moving. We will reach the Tabernacle by nightfall and when we are there, we can breathe, okay? Wash this whole ordeal away and forget about it. They have a beautiful bathhouse. It will cleanse us." I could tell Theone was trying to distract me.

I nodded.

Durin came beside me and patted my back, his bow back in his hands. "How about I sing you that song I promised, Shorty?" he said. I nodded, my arms limp at my sides as I followed my companions forward. He sung about love, and Theone's gaze softened.

The Tabernacle had a similar design to the one in Blackwick. A stone base with wooden additions, towering high into the sky. This one was not built into a mountain and appeared better maintained.

Two people dressed in religious garb stood guard at the doors with swords on a belt around their hips. Several hours had passed since there was last any sign of battle, but I felt safer knowing there were guards here.

"Keeper!" one person said to Theone as they approached ahead of us. "We've been expecting you. And the Seer? She is-" Their eyes landed on me, and the two gasped almost in disbelief.

I waved; my thoughts still not caught up from battle.

"*Dobrodošli*! Please come in!" the two guards said together.

It was refreshing to be greeted with kindness, as I half expected for the people here to treat me as Deacon Adder had. Inside the Tabernacle was considerably brighter and cleaner than the one in Blackwick. The space was warm even in the halls and the smell of incense made of jasmine and cedar lingered heavily. Musical chanting by the monks and nuns who lived there swam through the air and could be heard clearly in every room we walked through.

I closed my eyes, still walking forward with the others, and let the chanting wrap around me, tuning out everything else. Slowly the shock of the battle drifted away and all that was left in its place was what Theone had told me. *We* need *you.* I was not the first person to kill someone here. I had been right, knowing it was a kill or be killed situation.

Was my life really worth more than the person I had slain?

The music washed it all away. I needed this.

In a world at war, the Tabernacle did its best to be a haven away from it. We were brought to a large dining area, where we sat on the floor with low tables and presented with a warm meal of fresh bread, grilled vegetables, humus, infused oils, smoked fish and ginger tea. The dining hall was decorated with soft violet and peach walls, more painted embellishments depicting people at work and worship. Tapestries of individuals healing the sick and forging weapons, themes representing different gods. Candles hung from the ceiling in chandeliers made of antlers. The soft light mixed well the echoes of singing voices from other rooms. My belly grumbled at the sight of the food, and I was enthralled by the flavours that were not in the mountains.

Afterwards, Theone and I were led to separate quarters from Vice and Durin. Captain Florence caught up with us, glad that we had made it. She told us Priestess Mirna wanted to meet me the following day when morning worship was finished. Everyone within the Tabernacle wanted us to rest and feel refreshed before continuing to the Stills to get Major Vale.

From our quarters we were shown where the bathhouse was, and I was grateful for my first actual bath in months. Prior to this, I dumped warm water on my head in my room and combed through it with my fingers and lye soap when it got too gamey. I used leftover tea water and cloths to wipe the rest of my body, longing for a shower.

This was different and so much better.

I sunk into the hot water of the bathhouse naked, and a nun brought me scented oils and soap to clean myself. She even gave me a comb.

"You may keep it," she said with a smile as she saw my expression change into excitement when I saw the comb.

"Are you sure?" I asked, trying to hide my breasts beneath the water.

"Of course, Seer. You are welcome to anything here."

She then lay it on top of soft blankets that were folded neatly by the edge of the baths. A black clergy robe, resembling the one she wore, lay draped next to them, awaiting me. With the chanting echoing through the halls and the warm peppermint scented water steaming into my pores, when I closed my eyes no longer was I in the middle of an ancient war. Instead, I was in a spa.

The bathhouse was made of cream and blue tile, floor to ceiling. Mosaics of sea creatures were designed into the tiles. Beneath the water I relaxed in was a scene of a giant squid wrapping its tentacles around a ship. The ceiling mosaic depicted a large man coming from the sea, holding a trident in one hand and a large fish in the other. I wondered if he was supposed to be Dagr, the god of night and day, rivers, storms and seas.

Theone joined me briefly, using another pool in the room to clean themselves. Shockingly modest, they kept a robe over their body, between them and I, until they were submerged in the water. A completely satisfied sigh echoed around the chamber and they ducked under the surface and came back up, their short black hair sticking to their skull and their make up running down their face. They cleaned their face, rubbed oil in their hair and sat happily in the large bath for a half hour before leaving me alone again.

When I felt the water begin to prune my skin and I finally felt clean, I dried myself and dawned the silken robe. It was soft and welcoming on my skin and combing through my hair with something other than my fingers was a simple pleasure I missed terribly.

Back in the sleeping quarters, where Theone was already fast asleep, I looked around the clean room. I had not really looked at it when we first arrived, having been too excited by the thought of a bath. Theone had thoughtfully laid out my sweater for me on my bed and a pitcher of water with citrus fruits sat on a small table with two crystal glasses. I went to pour myself some water, when I noticed a small hand mirror on the table next to the pitcher.

I was thrilled.

Then I horrified.

I held up the mirror to look at myself, but what looked back to me was not who I remembered. I saw the remnants of the scar I had been given by the demons, the Commanders handywork working almost flawlessly except for one eyebrow that had not completely grown back through the scarring. My left eye, the one that kept bleeding and causing me so much pain, was not *my* eye. The pupil was long and thin, like a cat's eye or a snake. The colour had changed to a deep red, more supernatural than the colour Nerice and Vice had. I dropped the mirror, alarmed by the reflection. It clanked against the glasses on the table. Shakily my hand went to my eye.

Had my eye looked like this the whole time?

I lay in bed, the blankets soft and cool against my skin in the warm room. Tears escaped. Though I saw traces of my face in the reflection, to me it was not recognizable with the thin shiny scar and supernatural eye. My cheeks had thinned out. My roots had grey hairs. This was not the reflection I had been used to my whole life. I tried to breathe steadily and wiped my eyes.

Theone snoozed lightly.

I was eventually lulled to sleep by the chanting from deep within the halls of the Tabernacle.

It seemed they never stopped singing here, and I was grateful for their soothing song.

The following morning, we met with Captain Florence, who was lovely to be around, and much more animated than she had been back in Blackwick. Theone handed her the map where all the bodies we passed lay and ordered Florence to release the spirits on her way back through to Blackwick. The Captain salute her in farewell and left after breakfast, bringing word back to Blackwick that we had arrived safely and would be returning with Major Vale and his team at our side, hopefully.

An owl from Major Vale, had arrived in the early hours before I woke with his status and Theone, who was awoken with the news, sent several back indicating we would be on our way within the day.

Upon meeting Priestess Mirna, I was met with an overwhelming sense of peace, just as I had been greeted when I entered the Tabernacle. She was a woman in her sixties and held wisdom and hope within her. She had bright blue eyes and blonde hair wrapped in a head scarf. Her skin was almost as dark as the night and she had an enchanting smile. I understood why meeting her had been important. She had good influence just by existing.

Priestess Mirna wore long black and grey robes that were more elegant than the ones the nuns and monks wore. She had a nose ring and when she saw mine, she tapped her nose, smiling at our matching piercings.

Our conversation was brief. She asked about my life before I became chosen. I told her I worked in a tavern as a cook and a bard elsewhere. She asked what I had been doing since arriving in

Blackwick, and I told her my daily schedule of meditation, prayer, combat training, and stretching between meals. She asked me how I felt about having the title of Seer, and I was honest. I told her I had not fully grasped it, that it was hard for me to believe I was the chosen, and up until I was found by the Commander and others, I had never wielded magic in my life. I was still uncomfortable with the title, not believing I was worthy of it when I was amongst other much more capable people.

Priestess Mirna was content with my answers and told me she looked forward to seeing me again at my trial. Her and Theone spoke briefly before we set out again. They spoke words I did not understand, but I heard them mention *Ilona* and could only assume the Priestess was going to be speaking to the High Priestess of Ilona about her observations of me.

More battles awaited us as travelling to the Stills. These encounters were nothing compared to the one we had experienced when we first arrived, but I still found myself uneasy and lost within them. A part of me screamed to run every time a group fell upon us, but I stood there as my friends fought around me. Something in my brain switched on, or maybe off.

A raging soldier came running towards me. At the last second, I pushed my blade through him like a hot knife in butter. He held my gaze, his eyes stunned as he settled on my one eye. He had different coloured eyes, one brown and one blue, and I watched as the life left them. When he dropped, it took me several tries to pull the dagger from his stomach. The blade pulled out pieces of his innards and skin. His blood melted the snow his body fell in. I swallowed, overcome with nausea, and puked beside his corpse once the blade was free.

I never hesitated to defend myself after that. I did not run or freeze. I did not call for help. I just acted.

It was another long day and at first it was a lot to take in, all the death, but I continued forth. Hundreds of people died in the Groves from the warring daily, even more elsewhere in the province and world. I could not pretend it was not happening. The smell of rotting corpses was sickly, but nothing compared to the stench the demons left in their wake. Theone set bandits and soldiers on fire when we were through with them, to release their spirit, but eventually the numbers were too many and Theone started marking a new map of where the bodies were. I did not know who would be taking care of these once with Captain Florence already on her way back to Blackwick.

Major Vale had not exaggerated when he said the Stills were in dire straits. A town barely larger than Blackwick had been run empty on supplies and the townsfolk could barely keep the demons away. Many were through the forest along the coast, however there had been several star collisions directly into their Tabernacle. All the monks within it perished months before, having tried to contain them. People were dying quickly, and Deacon Adder, who lived there, preached sermons about how the sacrifices those folks made were worth it.

At the gates to the town a person named Asa met us, smiling warmly at Vice as they greeted each other. Asa explained the situation further and guided us to the Tabernacle. Asa, who was apparently Deacon Adder's only child, had known about our arrival thanks to an owl Vice sent and explained they had grown suspicious of their father's behaviour. They wanted to help us in any way they could.

Looking at them, I did see similarities between them and the deacon. Asa had more approachable features than their father, but I could see the deacon in the sharpness of their jaw and colour of their eyes. Asa's smile was welcoming, and I could not imagine Deacon Adder with a smile on his face. Asa led us to the part of the town that was barred off from the rest of the population, telling us how they disapproved of how the deacon had been running things within the town and how he treated his own refugees.

Vice turned out to be an old colleague to Asa and Deacon Adder before Adder had been appointed *Grand* Deacon. He had left behind the two of them to join the cause in Blackwick, claiming

Adder grew selfish. Asa backed up what Vice said.

"I must warn you to be careful, few return from the Tabernacle who go in," Asa told us as we approached its barred doors. Several city guards stood at arms facing it, waiting for creatures to come out as the door shook and inhuman screams echoed from within. I knew the sound well, the images and sounds burned into my mind forever.

"I can open a portal to the Other," I assured them. I tried to sound confident.

Asa gave me a fond expression. "I've heard. A true gift, you are to this world. I can't wait to see you in action."

The guards tentatively approached the doors when Asa waved to them, their eyes darting to the doors and to us as we moved forward. Asa explained the deacon had sent mage refugees inside hours before our arrival. He had omitted his plans to use them to the Temple's and they had not come back out. When Theone indicated to the guards to open the doors, the guards unlatched and pulled them open before running as far as they could from the entrance. A dark spirit came flying forth from within the Tabernacle. Spiked wings, primate face, long claws of a monster, black sludge clumping out of its mouth. I did not think I would get used to these things.

Theone's sword alit in flame and decapitated it without hesitation before anyone else reacted. The creature turned to dust.

"Forward!" Theone roared.

We charged in. The guards closed the doors behind us.

Vice stood beside me, covering for me as Theone stormed the demons. Durin was at the doors with Asa, who surprisingly came in with us. Asa's hands held bottles ready to throw, their coat was unbuttoned revealing more mysterious potions on their belt. Together they were the last line of defence in case the demons overwhelmed us.

I glanced to Vice, who nodded to me to concentrate on opening a rupture. I looked around the Tabernacle, now covered in blood, rotting corpses and debris from the ceiling falling in. Amongst the stone rubble, I saw the remnants of another Machine. My heart ached for its pilot and whoever had Travelled with them. I refocused on the spell I had to cast.

Vice kept the demons off me, and I braced myself for the coming pain that would accompany the magic. I spoke the words forcefully, a rupture ripping open before us as wind shook the doors and stirred fear within the creatures. Loose debris shook and the creatures clawed and screamed for escape. I concentrated harder, willing them to relieve this town of their torment. They were sucked up one by one, red light shining out again and again, brighter and brighter. With the last one the portal closed and red light shined out so bright we all winced away as the final vibration of the rupture shot out.

It was over much faster than anticipated.

"By the gods, you did it!" Asa exclaimed, clapping. "What a miracle to have you here."

I turned around, wincing at my headache, yearning for rest though I knew more demons lay ahead to rescue Major Vale.

"You poor soul!" Asa said as they looked at me. They rushed forward, snatching the cloth from a pocket of their coat and dabbed my cheek to clean the blood. "It appears you have not yet accepted your gift." When they were satisfied with the state of my face, they plucked a vial from their belt and set it into my palm, closing my fingers over it. "For the headache."

"What?" I squeaked as I clutched the small bottle.

"The potion. You must have a headache with so much blood leaving you. This will help quickly," Asa smiled.

"No, not that," I said. "What do you mean I have not accepted my gift?" I looked down at the glass vial in my hands. The liquid within was bright yellow, a glimmer sparkled back at me like Vice's potions did.

"Oh! You speak a cleansing spell in Bygone Speech, but it appears the power to completely close the rupture is because of," they tapped their own eye, which mirrored the one that frightened me when I looked in the mirror. "Your gods eye. Andreja's, right? My father was trying to dismiss the rumors but…"

No one had explained it to me.

Had my eye changed because I held the relic?

Would things had been different if I had not taken it when Katerina gave it to me?

"I have to *accept* my eye?" I asked quietly.

Everyone was looking at me.

Asa met Vice with a confused expression. "Does she not know? How?" they asked.

Vice did not reply, though Asa did not leave much time to as they turned their attention back to me quickly.

"Of course you have to accept your gift, sweetheart. It would be like being given a bottle of fine wine and you leave it on your doorstep to sour in the sunlight. You must take it inside to enjoy it. Your eye would most definitely stop bothering you!" Their voice was gentle in their explanation.

How had no one else said anything?

"We should get moving if we want to reach the Major before nightfall. Asa can let Grand Deacon Adder know of our success," Vice suggested when no one said anything further. He turned to face Asa and gave them a friendly smile; something I did not know Vice could do. "It was good to see you again old friend, hopefully we will meet again under more pleasant circumstances."

Asa's concerned expression shifted to one of expectancy and they smiled at Vice. "Of course," they said.

As we left, Asa gave me a tender look. They seemed like a nice person, and I wondered how they could have a father who could just throw people at demons without empathy for them. How someone so kind-natured could be related to someone so hot-tempered and rude.

Storm clouds were thick, marking the cross into the Stills. The area was untamed, and the storms wicked. The sky cast a dark grey over the land, lightning cracked in the clouds, and the snow was gone, replaced with rain if it was not turned to ice while it fell. I was told how much worse this area was during storm season. The Stills had to be an ironic name since rain pelted us so hard I thought my skin would bruise.

An ungodly sound echoed around us.

Looking up, an actual dragon sored by. Its shadow darkened every inch of the land. I almost followed it, out of awe, but Theone pulled me back.

"No!" they said sternly, and the dragon disappeared into the dark clouds. Theone gripped my shoulder firmly to stop me from following further. I was both terrified and enthralled to see such a creature. I wanted to think it was beautiful and that this worlds magic wrapped itself around me by the sight of the beast, but something about it did not feel right.

When my attention returned to my companions, I saw them looking at Vice who appeared extremely disturbed by watching the dragon fly off.

"What's the matter?" Durin asked him.

"Something is wrong with that dragon," Vice replied. "Something is deeply wrong."

We pushed forward, the wind whipping around from every direction. Not a single part of any of us was dry.

Dead, hollowed out, ancient trees lined the area before a cliff. Sea water carried in the air. At the cliffs edge we looked down into a heavy fog, hearing the shrieks of the demons below on the beach.

Major Vale had not exaggerated when he wrote about all the demons guarding the sands. The creatures slithered and clawed their way around the shore, their cries more unnerving by the second as we planned our approach. An unnatural howl echoed over the wide ocean making the demons more intimidating.

"What is that?" I whispered as we crept down to the seaside. Small waterfalls of freshwater poured over the cliff rocks and tiny streams led to the salted ocean as high tide pulled away from the shoreline. We had to step carefully, or risk being caught in the rivers and swept out to sea.

"An old foghorn, probably," Durin said. "Enchanted stones

to warn sailors of the rocks offshore, so they would not crash in poor weather."

The fog over the water was so thick and sea so angry we could barely see the ugly shapes of demons creeping along the sands, blurring together en masse. The ocean was hidden, though the sound of its waves crashed to the beach every few seconds.

Commander Lachlan said his Third had been trapped in the rocky waves offshore, unable to make it past the demons commanding the sands. He was confident his Major and his men were still alive when we left, and Major Vale's owls confirmed they were just unable to make it past the shore for every demon they killed, two more would appear to replace it. He said that their supplies were running thin weeks ago, and he had already lost several good men to both the demons and exposure. His letter that morning said he was sick of eating fish from the nets and the other sea creatures had gotten wise to their huntsman.

I had to open a rupture, I had to cleanse the shore of the demons. That way the Major could have a chance to leave his ship.

Demons surged with anger as I took a deep breath, steeling myself for what was to come. They were determined to not be contained and knew what I was there to do. Our weapons were drawn, I began to chant the spell.

Theone's sword burst aflame, and the top of Vice's staff sparked with electricity as he moved to hold it in both hands like a polearm. Durin scraped the tip of several arrows to his heel, and they were set on fire as he drew his bow. We were about to attack blind.

"We will cover you long enough to open it," Theone said confidently. "Hold it as long as you can."

Durin's arrows flew through the air. The silhouette of one of the skeletal demons arched back in pain when one connected into its shoulder. Meat slopped off it, tainting the sand below. It faced us and the arrows exploded. The demons scream echoed into the storm, falling. More shadows moved around the fog. Theone charged.

Before this moment, I would find a piece of Machine, focus on it as the spot to open a portal above.

The fog was too dense, and I could barely see a few feet before me. Vice stayed close, a wave of his staff pushing some of the moisture away, but it was not enough. I pretended I had a focus somewhere within the fog, my eye began to leak.

I could feel the wills of demons around us, their determination fighting against my own. Sharp fingers tried to claw their way to us. I finished the spell, and the fog was suddenly blown away by the rupture, revealing dozens and dozens of demons wreaking of sickly-sweet rot. A ripple in reality now floated over the beach, drawing the demonic forms towards it.

I wished I had not wanted to see debris from a Machine to focus on. I wished I could be back in Blackwick, away from everything.

Hundreds of thousands of pieces of metal lay ashore, going on for miles along the sea. Waves crashed against the metal, now rusting from saltwater. The sea sounded angrier, large splashes echoed against the cliffs. We warred against the horde.

I wiped at my face and drew my daggers as I stood at the ready, all the demons coming for us. I had to prepare to hold the portal open and fight at the same time. That was only two things. I could do two things.

Demons screamed as they were dragged over the sands towards the portal. Theone and Durin focused their efforts on the creature's legs and arms, making sure they lost their footing and could not cling to the debris on shore.

Swords crashed against claws that hung onto pieces of Machine. Vice's staff lit up, electrifying anything that came close.

One creature got past him. I felt something beyond the portal, within the Other, angry and clawing to get out. The rupture surged as something tried to get out and I dropped. The portal closed.

"Shit!" I cursed on my hands and knees, my daggers still in my fists. I saw a couple drops of blood drip into the sand. Lightning shot out before me and the demon that was close, shrieked before it fell mere inches in front of me. Its body charred and smoking, its horrible teeth still bared, ready to attack in death, the black sticky ooze poured from its mouth and eyes.

Something frightening emerged from the waters as I scrambled back up. I wiped at my eye with the back of my hand and watched it slowly lurch through the waves, the storm unable to sway the form. A horned beast with black seeping down over its face, teeth sharp as a shark's, arose from the waves.

I screamed.

Theone spun around at the sound of my fear, but as their eyes landed on the form in the water their voice was relieved as they called out to it. I watched as other horned creatures rose beside it.

"Cathal! You're still alive!" Theone shouted. Theone pierced the chest of a demon next to them, skewering it long enough to slice its head off with the sharp edge of their shield.

I looked closer at the form coming from the water, seeing large axes in each hand. It smiled wickedly at us.

"Of course, I've been waiting for you," it purred.

I focused more on the face, my fists gripping my daggers tighter.

A man.

He kissed the air before pulling the hood over his head down, the antlers falling with it.

A handsome man.

The black that had been seeping down his face had been thick liner around his eyes, washed away from begin submerged in the water.

Demons turned in his direction, and the man spun the axes with a flair I had not seen from other warriors, before beheading two demons at once. He laughed, entertained, and the other horned creatures charged from the water with a mortal battle cry, their weapons drawn as they fell upon the demons with excitement.

"It took you long enough!" he teased as he threw one of his axes at another demon, beheading it. The axe landed in the sand by Vice's feet and the demons form turned to dust, fading into nothing.

Vice looked at me, his eyes still pained from our

conversation several nights before, apologetic for not telling me I had to accept my *gift* sooner, pleading. "Open another rupture," he said.

I nodded, sheathing my daggers.

With the additional warriors help I could focus on the spell. I opened it quickly and the demons were slain or sucked up in an instant. The last of the creatures were pulled in and a rush of air shot out, sand covering our toes.

The man walked over to me after retrieving the axe near Vice and tossed it to his other hand after he slid the first one into a loop on his belt. He held his now free hand out for me to shake.

"Aren't we lucky a little tart like you fell from the sky with all the answers," he said, his tone low, enticing. "Major Cathal Henry Vale, at your service, my lady."

I shook his massive hand, and he gripped my wrist. He smiled with an inhumanly sharp grin back at me.

"Pleasure," I squeaked.

The Major brought my hand up to his lips and kissed my knuckles. "Pleasure is all mine," he said.

I blushed.

He was entertained by my red cheeks and a hearty laugh echoed around the beach. "What do I call you, darlin'?" he grinned.

"Delilah," I said.

"Mmm, a first name," he purred. The Major let go of my hand. "You may call me Cathal."

Cathal was huge; tall like the Amaranthine's, but thick with muscle and fat, like a bear, just like his team was. I had to angle my head all the way up to look him in the eyes. He had black hair, which was braided tightly to his scalp, though the sides of his head were clean shaven, and a mighty beard, for the most part, covered his demon-like fangs for teeth. His smile was friendly when you ignored the creepy teeth behind it. I could his resemblance to Bellamy. The colour of his hair, the friendly smile. The difference was his skin was paler, his build rougher. Bellamy was petite and had nice, normal teeth, her eyes like sun-lit sand. Cathal's were grey, like a raging sea.

Cathal and his men were called *Fury*. Fury were good with

medicine and exceptionally violent in battle, sharpening their teeth in order to tare into the flesh of their foes if they lost their weapons. I had read about them in one the books Vice had placed on my shelves. It was why Cathal was invaluable to the Commander's army. He was in the middle of convincing people from his village, a rather large one, to come help with the war.

The team practically rolled around in the sand, thrilled to be off their ship and unphased by the raging storm still pouring over them. They cheered and talked about how excited they were to return to the mountains. The ship they had come from was immense, looming over the waters like a giant sea creature through the fog. Cathal only had about six men with him. He had only lost a few men during his wait. How less than twelve people were enough to man such a huge ship was beyond my knowledge. Its sails were rolled up, several chains hung down to hold it off the shore. Cathal, Theone and Durin all seemed to be happy to be together again, a friendship forged long ago.

I nursed some water from my canteen, distracted by the rubble.

I thought about all the portals I had opened. Pieces of Machine's always accompanied a collection of demons. My chest felt tight, and I swallowed back the anxiety swirling in my stomach. A few yards from where I stood, a shiny dark box clinked as rain assaulted it. I walked over, brushing the sand from it with my boot. A serial number was embedded into the metal.

A Machine's black box.

Vice came beside me, and I jumped at his voice. "Do you know what this is?" he asked, his tone carrying the second question of *can we talk again?*

"I'm afraid I do," I said quietly. I glanced up at Vice, who's eyes remained on the black box. "Can you keep another secret Vice?"

He nodded once.

"My people can travel through time." I felt like I would throw up. "This box and all the metal littering the beaches and forests that we saw coming here are remnants of the vessels we use to do so."

"I see."

I struggled to form the words in my head. I felt sick by their thought. "Your people burn your dead to release the spirit, right?" I asked.

"Correct. We must release the spirit. The fires signal Manoach, he will send Samu to guide them to the After. If someone is trapped within their body, they watch it decompose. They can go insane doing so, trapped to their bones and rotting flesh. Demons are made that way, with tortured spirits."

Vice knew where I was going with my questioning as the last words left his mouth. I could feel his energy change. I felt hot, my chest tight as I tried to control my breathing.

"I think all these demons were people from Earth."

Chapter Eight
Day Seventy-Eight
I'm starting to lose count…

I had been having trouble sleeping for days, conflicted with how to bring up my true origins to the others, how to tell Vice I was not mad at him, just scared. I had not been a very good friend to him, even though I had desired to be one. Our mission would be finished tomorrow, when we arrived to Blackwick. Cathal travelled with us while his crew members slowly followed behind to burn the bodies Theone had discovered in the Stills. They were instructed to also burn any more that they came across.

Tonight, I had fallen asleep hearing Durin and Cathal chatting, their shadows animated and enthusiastic through the canvas of the tent. Theone had quietly listened to them, their laughter a welcome sound in the night.

The feeling of something watching me stirred my body. When I sleepily looked at the entrance of the tent, my eyes widened, panic shot adrenaline through my body. The camp had grown quiet despite the fire still crackling bright between tents and a wolf stood mere feet away, staring me down like I was its next meal.

My eyes widened and I sat up my hand searching for a dagger. What stood before me was bigger than I imagined a wolf to be, ganglier. Though the head and claws were distinctly an animal, the body, covered in black fur, was thin and long, almost humanlike. Its eyes glowed in the shadows of my tent, a hint of red in them. I inhaled deeply, ready to scream for help as I found my daggers hilt, but then its hands were on me. A warm palm settled over my mouth and long finger pressed its lips as the wolf form seamlessly transformed into Vice.

His red eyes so close to mine and his hair loose around his face, unbraided and unkept. His piercings were gone. Not once had I imagined Vice could look so feral.

"My apologies," he said quietly. His free hand moved from

my face and grabbed the fur that was over my legs, pulling it towards his naked body. "Speak softly." His brow cocked, waiting for me to agree to his request.

I nodded, taking in what I had just witnessed. Vice relaxed, lounging back onto a lump of our packs piled in the tent.

"You're a werewolf?" I whispered in utter disbelief, discarding my dagger.

Vice stretched his arms over the pile, relaxing further. "Aye." His voice seemed indifferent. He expected my surprise.

"Do the others know?" I asked.

"No." He watched me, beginning to braid his hair, the wild aura surrounding him slowly disappearing as his fingers worked his hair into submission. His eyes still had a slight glow, reflecting any light that hit them. I connected the dots, realizing no one else's eyes did that in the dark here. Just his. He was a *werewolf.* "What I am does not concern the others if I do not pose a danger to them. I know when the change will occur, and I take myself away from the village long before any transformation can happen. I tried to get out of this mission, but Theone and Nerice were suspicious when I couldn't give them a reason not to come."

It was late in the night. The feeling of it carried in the cool air with the drowsiness that escaped me when I had been spooked awake by a wolf. I was surprised Theone had not made it back to the tent yet and that Vice had made it here undetected by them and the other two party members.

"How long have you been one?" I asked, still shocked. I did not know what else to say or where the conversation was supposed to go.

"Not for as long as I have walked this life, but long enough to have control over it. Many others do not get that luxury."

"How…?"

"Do you not have werewolves where you are from?" His ruby eyes caught mine again, and I felt slightly enchanted. There was an actual magical creature sitting in the tent with me.

I looked him over, still taking in everything. His body was

remarkably athletic, something that was not apparent through the layers of cloaks he typically donned. I blushed taking him in, trying to keep my eyes on his and not his chest. For a thin man, he was clearly a lot stronger than he appeared. I shook my head then pulled my jacket over my shoulders as the night air settled into my skin.

"They are fictional on Earth!" I hissed quietly, trying to keep my voice low in fear of raising suspicion outside.

Vice laughed, an amused, wolfish grin coming to his lips. "Truly interesting, your world. Perhaps they are real and, like this one, are simply hidden. Is Earth the name of your home? Earth is beneath us, how simple to call it that."

"Did you want to be one? How did you become one?" I asked.

"Why would you like to know?" His smile grew wider. This was a completely different side of Vice. He pulled the fur up his body more, making sure they did not fall below his hipbones. "Do you want to be one?"

A shiver ran down my spine. "No!"

He laughed again; apparently not worried about the others noticing him in here with me. Once Vice finished his braid he rolled his neck, cracking his bones with the movement, and obliged me. "Well, some people are born with the wolf inside them, if one of their parents hold a wolf inside or both. Others retrieve it from those who have it and bite them."

"That's how it worked in the stories back home," I commented.

"It seems our worlds are not that different," Vice said. He looked around my tent, seemingly thankful that Theone had not yet returned and motioned to the tunic I wore today folded near me. "May I?"

I passed it to him.

Vice slipped it over his pale body and stood, blanket in front of him , the tunic covering his torso. He then tucked the fur around his legs like a skirt. I looked away, my eyes wide, as I saw a trail of dark hair that led dangerously close to-

"I didn't plan on getting it, if that is what you think," Vice said. I looked back to him, and he had grabbed the small mirror Theone took from the Tabernacle in the Groves to check his face. Theone liked using it to check their makeup. Vice licked his finger and wiped some dirt from his nose. "Long ago, I had loved someone very much. Unfortunately, he had been cursed with the wolf and had not told me. One night I came to his cottage as a surprise and he, well…I know you are smart enough to figure out the rest. He passed on a few centuries ago."

Centuries.

"I'm sorry," I said.

"Oh it's quite alright, Delilah. He lived a long life, and we were happy together." Vice smiled thoughtfully at his memories before his expression returned to what I was used to from him: stoic and almost unemotional. "But my people live a lot longer than others here so you must be prepared when you choose to love someone who is not Amaranthine. I believe I will see him again, weather it is in this life or in the next. Perhaps even in the Other when I finally decide to go."

"Wait. You can *decide* to go?" I asked.

"Of course. If I stop taking the life energy of others, I will age as the rest of the world does and eventually pass."

Wow.

"Can't others become Amaranthine? I know there's a process but-".

Vice looked at me, something about the night and his eyes were just… "He did not want to live forever. Not when there were so many other lives to live." I almost thought I heard a hint of sorrow in his voice. I wondered if Vice had asked this man to walk with him for centuries and he declined.

Vice leaned down towards me, catching my gaze. His form took up most of the free space in the tent while standing. His ears twitched at the sound of movement outside.

"In Blackwick you said you wanted to know me. I wanted to show you this part of myself. I felt it only fair to give you my secret since I know yours. It is what binds us as friends," Vice said.

Vice considered me a friend. I never would have guessed that.

A quiet moment passed between us before Vice kissed my cheek and straightened, still slightly hunching over since he was too tall to stand fully in the tent. The blush on my cheeks warmed; his lips were soft, and I had smelled his sweat and the forest on him. "I will return your blanket and tunic. I just need to go back into the trees to retrieve my clothes."

I risked a question I had been dying to ask for months. "Aren't the trees dangerous?"

Vice shrugged, looking over his shoulders at me before leaving. "Not for me, usually," he replied.

I lay back down. Whatever fluttered inside me was strange. Pinpointing whether the flutter was because I found yet another one of my companions beautiful or because something within me knew something within Vice was a predator and I prey was an effort. I almost wished I had not seen him without clothes. I could have blissfully gone on with my life just seeing him as a serious scholar.

Sitting in my tent for several minutes, I let it fully sink in that Vice had shared a part of himself with me to ease my concern about my secret being known. He trusted me with a secret of his own so I would trust him. I let out a long breath, my heart finally slowing and tiredness returning.

I was barely awake when I felt my fur blanket cover me. I yawned and pulled it tighter around my body. "Thank you," I said softly. A few moments later I heard Theone come in the tent; how Vice had dodged them, I will never know.

The return to Blackwick was quiet. Arriving in the evening, long past when the sun went down, only a few scouts roamed the streets. Durin sleepily set up his tent in a free area by a street fire while Cathal wandered into a building that I discovered was the inn and tavern. Vice returned to his suite at the bunkhouse and Theone walked with me up to the Tabernacle.

It was good to be back. The familiar smells and the safety of the walls around the village had been something I actually missed. A fire had been lit before my arrival and the room assigned to me was welcoming after all the rain and snow. The cold outside had a hold to it unlike any other and I felt a stuffed nose and scratching throat threatening to become a flu. Where I used to live had winters where wind hurt my face, but this cold was a whole different level, chilling the bones to a point it felt as if the cold would never leave my body again.

Gwen sat on my bed waiting for me and leapt off when I realized she was there. She threw her arms around me, giving me a big hug.

"How did you know I was coming back tonight?" I asked, hugging her back. I was thrilled to see her.

"Honestly, I've been staying in here the last few days. An owl came saying your party was on the way and I guessed when you would be arriving," Gwen laughed. I doffed my armour and changed into my nightshirt while Gwen picked through my pack to see if I had brought anything back with me from the mission.

We sat on my bed together. She combed through my hair with the pretty comb I had got from the Tabernacle in the Groves then braided my hair tightly to my scalp. We were silent for a while. Gwen hummed a song before softly singing it. Her voice was angelic and lulled me to sleep sitting up against the wall my bed was pressed against.

I had heard many songs since living here, mostly thanks to Durin. All the songs were soft and whimsical, telling tales of great adventures or history. They were all lovely to listen to, though many of them had sad endings.

I stirred when Gwen was brewing a tea in the hearth.

"I have to tell you something," I said as I watched her.

Gwen smiled excitedly. "Is it that you fancy someone?" she joked. Gwen glanced at me as she set up some cups for the tea. The tea smelt like orange, ginger and oregano. While I had been resting it appeared she had gone to the kitchens and helped herself to some bread and cheese as well. Her smile widened seeing me blush.

"You fancy Commander Lachlan, right?" she asked.

Once drowsy, I woke right up to try to summon words. Gwen's expression was triumphant.

"I knew it!" she said. She poured the tea then picked up the tray with the cups and snacks on it, hustling over to my bed with a dance in her step.

I was stunned silent. I had not expected the conversation to turn in this direction. Gwen set the tray on the bed and climbed beside me. She gave me a playful shove then plucked her cup of tea up.

"He asked about you a lot while you were away," Gwen said. "You should talk to him more," she said.

I put a piece of hard cheese in my mouth, chewing slowly while Gwen repeated all the questions the Commander had asked her.

Did I ever talk about other people?

Was I benefiting from the morning and evening practices?

Did Gwen know if I enjoyed any hobbies? Had a favourite flower?

I had to spit it out before I was completely absorbed by the thoughts of the Commander thinking about me in my absence.

"Gwen," I blurted out her name loudly. She quieted, her expression now that of concern. "I'm a time-travelling alien."

Gwen stared at me. She remained silent, waiting for me to say more.

"I was supposed to be going on vacation the day I arrived here. Something went wrong, I still don't know what. I've been seeing the wreckage of hundreds of other people's Machines here. I have no fucking idea how I'm alive right now. I've been freaking out over my eyeball changing colours and shape and the constant bleeding and apparently I have to accept that my eye is like that or something and *fuck!*"

I covered my lips with my fingertips. I tried to find my breath because I could feel another anxiety attack approach. I had only touched the tip of everything I wanted to say to my friends, and I could feel my eyes water with the fear of every bad scenario going through my mind.

Gwen slurped at her tea loudly and I looked over at her again. She no longer looked concerned. When she noticed me looking at her, she smiled reassuringly.

"I don't think it matters to the Commander where you're from," she said simply.

"How could you know that?" I whimpered.

Gwen set her teacup down and wrapped one arm around my shoulders, pulling me tight to her for another hug.

"Because it doesn't matter to me. You're still my friend and lifetimes, and planets, apart will never change that. A man descent from a god is hardly someone who would judge a person descent from beyond the stars themselves."

*

I knew I would be given the chance to speak to the rest of the council at the debrief. Gwen had stayed the night, listening to everything that I had been carrying with me for months. I poured my heart out to her and when prompted about the courage to speak up, I told her Vice had inspired me to come forward. Gwen was impressed he had figured it out before Nerice.

Skipping my return to the kitchens, I sat in with some laity and villagers singing in the main chapel of the Tabernacle after I woke up. Nerice clocked me from the front, having been leading the choir of people, choosing which prayers and hymns to follow. She smiled when she saw me and did not follow me when I felt content with my practice.

I found myself wandering down to the troop encampment in the late morning. Many were already sparring or at target practice. The day was turning out to be a sunny one. The moons were wanning. The breeze did not cut into me as it usually did.

I found the Commander quickly, his form sticking out amongst his troops. Gwen acknowledged me from across the field and continued sparring with another soldier as I approached him. I saw Cathal tackle a whole group of soldiers to the ground and the groups laughter echoed around the field.

"Commander Lachlan," I said from behind him.

I watched his posture ease, and the Commander practically flew around in excitement to face me. "Seer! I mean…" his voice lowered to say my name, "*Delilah*." The excitement in his voice sent a pleasurable tingle through me. He cleared his throat. "I'm glad to see you returned safely. How were your travels?"

"The mission was tiring," I said. I bit my lip then let out a long breath, "I have a proposition for you."

Commander Lachlan seemed intrigued, and his voice had a hopeful note to it when he responded, "Oh? What kind of proposition?"

"More time, together." I hoped with all my heart that Gwen was right when she said he would not care when I told him, and the rest of the Council, my secret.

"That's a fantastic idea!" the Commander looked surprised by his own voice, the loudness and enthusiasm to it. He lowered it again. "That would be nice." He gave me a charming smile, looked back over his troops, and then motioned for me to follow him. "We could start right now. With my Major back, he and Colonel Theone can watch my troops. What do you say?" His brows rose with his offer, the corners of his lips remained perked.

I felt heat build inside me and nodded. "That's a fantastic idea," I said.

The Commander grinned wider and I followed him as he strolled towards the village.

We went along the outer path of Blackwick, the one against the fence and mountain rather than walking the many streets that weaved between the tight-knit homes and shops. I often saw scouts on this path, not villagers.

"What would you like to do?" the Commander asked. "I pray you don't wish to talk work," he laughed and then cut himself off abruptly to look down at me, suddenly afraid he had been right.

"Where are you from?" An odd question since I avoided answering it at all costs. He would know soon enough.

"Oh, umm, well my great grandparents founded Blackwick, and I grew up here."

"I didn't realize you were born here," I said.

The Commander chuckled. "Was my family name not enough of a clue?"

I was embarrassed. I supposed that should have been obvious. "I was told you were descent from a god?"

He had an almost sly grin on his face, an expression I had not yet known from him, but I could feel my insides swirl at it. "It's not something I publicise. Who told you? Nerice? Probably Nerice, nothing escapes that woman." He looked forward continuing to walk.

"Did you know them?" I asked.

Commander Lachlan nodded. "She was around when I was very young, before I went to her Temple to train as a Keeper. I only have one memory of her before she died."

"Gods can die?"

"In their mortal forms, of course. What did they teach you where you're from?" The Commander made a face, as if to tease, and I bit my lip, nervous; I had almost exposed myself ahead of schedule.

"I didn't pay a lot of attention during religious and history studies…" I lied.

He laughed. "Clearly." He moved closer to me, his fingers brushed against my own while we walked. I slipped my scarred hand into his and he gave me a satisfied squeeze, holding my hand. The Commander continued talking.

"From our understanding, when a god comes to our plane they can come in one of two forms. There's their mortal form, which keeps them here longer. Their powers are limited, if contained within them at all, and they grow old very slowly; unless they make the decision to age as we do. You can kill a god, but only in body. Their essence returns to Other, and their powers are returned. They can also come to our plane in their true form, with all their powers, but they can only stay for maybe a few hours, a day at most. I *believe* that's how my great grandparents met. My *pradedek* was a Commander too and he prayed to Andreja every day for victory and spoils of battle, to keep his people safe. One day she came to him. Tales of this happened a lot in the early years of our history. Our people would pray, and the gods would physically answer. It's how so many became blessed with magic. The gods were…well you know how they are." The Commander smirked again, and he squeezed my hand.

"She liked my *pradedek* so much she took mortal form and formed Blackwick with him as a haven for my *pradedek's* people. Many who desire war do not travel this far into the mountains. My grandfather had said his mother loved this village so much that she promised to always watch over it. He had thought she would just elongate her life, but she passed soon after my *pradedek*. I suppose she watches from the heavens." Lachlan smiled thoughtfully. "And then she sent you to us." He looked directly to the eye that had been *gifted* to me. "With her eye."

I understood it now. Why Lachlan was such a religious man. To hear his story, his family's story. A village built so close to a Temple belonging to a goddess that protected his people. A goddess loved by the world. A goddess whose blood ran in his veins.

It was real.

No matter how much I resisted it, it was real. I had seen and cast magic. I had witnessed a dragon flying and demons attacks. This whole world was run by the belief in their pantheon.

Was this how she would watch over the village now that she was gone? Through me?

It was hard to grasp, but there was a part of me that wanted to believe as they did. A piece of me that wanted to be part of something bigger, to give all that had happened to me meaning.

The village was loud off the path we walked. We had passed a couple scouts who saluted us each time they walked by, and villagers were busy with their workday and chores. I knew we passed by the inn when music was loud around us, muffled by just one wooden wall. The Commander ducked under a low hanging branch of needles while I let the tips wet my hair with frost.

"You were at God's Wall with Durin. What was that like?" I asked.

"While we were there, relations between different regions of the province fell apart and the Grand Deacon went insane."

"Theone introduced you as Champion there," I noted.

"You remembered!" the Commander said warmly. "I am. There were not enough Keepers in the Southern Province to keep order. Dark magic made Grand Deacon Persephone believe the gods were dead and joined those south of the wall we were trying to build. The battle at God's Wall was a turning point in this war. The Southerners forced a wider invasion to other provinces. Persephone threatened to kill me and turned on her troops. I stood as Champion against her, and I sent her to the gods for judgement. I wish I had seen through Persephone sooner. It usually isn't the women who go mad, but it was my duty as her Second to challenge her. My duty as a Keeper." The Commander was momentarily lost in thought before he returned his attention to me, giving my hand another squeeze. We were on our second lap of the village.

"Durin and you are friends, right?" I asked.

"We are best friends," Commander Lachlan said. "We've spoken more again since I joined the legion here. Largely at Durin's insistence. According to him, I don't spend enough time in the tavern and it's bad for my health."

I giggled. Durin had a lot of opinions, and they always entertained me. "What do you do if you have free time?" I asked. I felt like I was on a date. I wanted to live in this moment for as long as I could, fearing the worst when I addressed the Council later.

"I love coffee," he confessed. "I have tried many different roasts thanks to Bellamy's connections. I also enjoy gardening in the springtime and summer. I dry my favourite flowers for special occasions if one were to arrive in autumn or winter, but until now I never had a reason to really give them out."

The primroses in my room…

"I used to garden," I said. "I lived on a farm. The old couple who owned it gave me a low rent if I helped them."

"Ah, well I insist you help me with my flowers come spring!"

We slowed, another scout passed us.

"Well I suppose if it's the Commander's orders, how could I refuse?" I teased.

He seemed undaunted, simply content with our conversation. The stroll had brought us back to the gate. The clash of weapons echoed over to the village, the quartermaster was at work. I thought I heard Cathal laughing again. Here, out in the open, the Commanders gaze lingered on my lips. He still held my hand. I longed to pull him in closer.

"Does your mind ever wander?" I asked.

He caught my implication. "What if it was at present?"

I blushed. I could not let this man kiss me without knowing the truth. Despite what Gwen said, I was still afraid everything would blow up in my face. "I should let you get back to your work, Commander," I said reluctantly. I had not expected him to excuse himself from his duties so freely.

Commander Lachlan nodded. "If you must. I'm sure you have other things to do as well." He took a step close to me, and leaned down to make sure only I could hear him as villagers and soldiers moved around us. His voice was low and husky in my ear. I could smell coffee on his breath, and my heart sped up. "Oh, and my name is Lachlan. To hear my name on your lips, would be to witness a beautiful summers day, *Delilah*."

He winked at me as he stood straight again then turned to return to his troops, his hand slowly, longingly, leaving mine.

Until the meeting, I spent more time in the Tabernacle. I sat in a prayer room, trying to find a calm to soothe my restless spirit. Sandalwood incense wrapped itself around the room and I had the space to myself. I meditated, letting my mind ebb and flow through every outcome. Not only the possibilities of tonight, but for every night, month, and moment afterwards. I let the worry fill my mind and then with all my might I tried to let it go.

I let myself exist. Something I craved for a long time.

The Tabernacle bells only rang twice a day. Once in the morning, when the sun was cresting the mountains and, in the evening, when the sun was about to tuck behind the horizon. They chimed out now, rousing me from my meditation. I could smell dinner in the halls stronger than the long burnt-out incense. I moved towards the Council Room.

I tensed with each step, the blissfulness of not having any worries fading as I continued closer to the council. In the main hallway nuns moved around with dinner trays, curtsying if we made eye contact. At the Council Room door, I heard Nerice and Bellamy talking beyond it. My heart sped up, hoping beyond hope that everything would turn out.

If these peoples' gods could hear me, please let them understand.

I opened the door.

Lachlan's face lit up when I entered. Theone nodded to me and Nerice and Bellamy waved as they finished their conversation. I heard loud thundering footsteps speeding down the main hall behind me. Stepping aside, Cathal leaned against the doorframe to brace himself after running.

"Am I late?" he asked.

"Not at all, Major, we haven't started," Lachlan said.

My chest felt tight, my breath catching before I recentered myself. I had not anticipated Cathal joining us, but I understood.

"Is Captain Florence coming as well?" I asked.

"She's back out on the field," Nerice said.

I looked around the people before me. The people I wanted to call my friends.

"Could someone retrieve Durin?" I asked. Everyone looked at me. "It's important."

Nerice whistled, and a scout ducked under Cathal's arm from the hallway and stood at attention.

"Get Lieutenant Hawke," Nerice said.

The scout ducked back under Cathal, who then stood straight and walked in. I watched the scout sprint down the Tabernacle hallway, dodging around laity members before I heard the creaking of the big doors at the front. I looked up at Cathal. He smiled his sharp, toothy grin at me before he walked beside Lachlan.

A large provincial map lay open on the table and Theone began to point out all the areas we had passed containing bodies. They then emphasized where we had delt with demons, placing small markers on the spots I knew were dead Machine's. Nerice commented on regions further out in the province that had been reporting demon activity, though none of it was as active as all the sites near the mountains and Stills. Owls had brought news of the sky falling everywhere in the province the same night I had arrived. The demon accounts aligned with a lot of fallen star reports.

I felt unwell.

Durin knocked once before opening the door tentatively. He looked actively uncomfortable being in this room. Almost as uncomfortable as I was. "I was called on?" he said when there was a pause in conversation.

Nerice motioned to me, standing straight from leaning over the table. "I get the inclination you have something important to add to this meeting?" She had her professional voice on. It was so different from the one she had when it was just the two of us, or the one she put on when she led the laity in prayer. She had asked a few times if I wanted to go for drinks at the tavern with her, her tone sultry and lovely. I had struggled to decline.

I had to just spit it out, like I had with Gwen.

"I'm not from here. I cannot be your Seer," I started.

"I am not from this province either, but that does not make me any less of a Colonel," Bellamy said before I could elaborate.

"No, I mean," I took a deep breath. "All that metal at demon sites. The strange copper cord and pieces there, I know what they're from. I do not belong here. I am a time-traveller from another planet. My people invented a way to move through time and space. I owned a vessel that could do that, I-" My eyes darted between everyone. They all watched me intently, waiting patiently for me to finish talking. "The night the stars fell from the sky, I had been Travelling on my planet. I had been planning on going to another country there. Something went wrong. I ended up here instead. That metal, it's what our vessels are made of. *My* people fell from your skies." My eyes welled with tears. "I think it is *my* people who are now plaguing your lands as demons." My breath caught. "I cannot be your Seer. Not when I am not from here. Not with my people tormenting yours!"

I was shaking. My chest tightened. I could not find my breath and nausea bubbled in my belly, threatening to come out as my head swam with dizziness.

A hand touched my shoulder.

Everything stilled.

I looked over seeing Durin, his expression empathetic. He squeezed my shoulder.

Nerice laughed. "Oh, that explains so much!" She leaned over the table again, bracing herself against her laughter as she continued to cackle. Bellamy seemed thrown by Nerice's outburst.

Theone gave me a puzzled look, their black painted lips slightly ajar. "I don't understand. You are saying you cannot be a Seer only because you were not born here? The gods are not born here, they are still our gods. Just because you believe it is your people who are the demons in the province, they still are not the ones causing this war."

"Well said, Colonel," Lachlan said.

It was the first time I looked at him since entering. I had been so ashamed of holding this secret. Yet Gwen was right. How could I have been so scared of telling them when they had been so understanding from the very start. Lachlan smiled at me with an unexpected warmth.

"Can I have a hug?" I asked quietly.

Durin pulled me into him. He was a good hugger, his arms tight around me and one hand rubbing my back. Soon others enveloped us, a lump of friends all embracing. Someone kissed the side of my head.

No one let go of me until I began to pull away. When I did, I was relieved. Cathal rubbed the top of my head messing up my hair, Nerice held my arm and gave me with an approving smile. Theone gave my hand a firm squeeze. Bellamy cupped my cheek and giving it a soft pat before clapping her hands together, gathering everyone's attention to her.

"We have a lot more to discuss! But how about we have an early evening," Bellamy proposed. She gathered the papers spread on the wide table. Once in a neat pile, she set a bottle of ink on top to keep it in place. Her expression was sympathetic when she looked at me again. "Tomorrow is a new day. There will be time then to discuss your theories and also answer any questions we may have for you."

I could tell Bellamy wanted to give me some space. I knew that she understood how hard it had been for me to confess what I did. She knew how much it meant to me that no one turned against me and instead embraced me as one of them all over again.

"Back home, I used to have my friends over to chat and drink and eat all night. I've really missed those nights and could use another night like that. May I extend an invitation to any of you to stay the night with me? Just a night where we can just be companions," I replied.

Bellamy's face lit up at my suggestion. "That sounds lovely!" She looked at Nerice, then Theone. "We would love to come, wouldn't we?" she said.

Nerice flung her arms over Theone's shoulder, pulling them closer so she could put her arms around Bellamy's as well. "We would!" Nerice said enthusiastically.

Only an hour passed between the meeting and friends arriving to my chambers. I had requested someone send for Gwen, who arrived with a bedroll and a bright smile sooner than everyone else did.

I thought about my friends and family back home. I thought about how, if I had lost any of them to a missing Machine, that I would be inconsolable for weeks, months, *years*. I had come to terms with the inevitability that I would never return to Earth, but I knew I found solace with having found the companions here.

Every day they surprised me.

I looked over the gaggle of companions who sat before my hearth and thought of the others who had gone to their own beds for the night. They had left with the promise of dragging me out to the tavern another night or a hearty chat during my next mission. I could easily say I loved my new friends just as I loved the ones on Earth.

Gwen always let her hair flow freely after training with me. She let her red curls escape restraint now, her laughter loud with the others as we chat. Gwen had truly become my best friend and helped my heart heal when I no longer thought it was possible. We spent so many afternoons getting to know each other on the sparring field and I was grateful for her. Some days, when I was with her, I almost forgot this place was not mine. Sitting with her, I could *almost* be convinced to call this place home.

Though Durin had not joined the others for my little party, he had dropped off a deck of tarot cards for me. He arrived with Theone, walking them to my door and giving them a kiss on the cheek before wishing me goodnight. Durin almost felt like a big brother to me. It was fun trying to outdo one another with our stories at evening fires or during our mission to the Stills. He wanted to keep me safe. He too had a way of making me forget I had a life before the one I lived now.

Theone felt like another older sibling, and I cherished them, not having any siblings on Earth. They would get upset every time I was hurt and would be proud that with each battle I grew stronger. When we found a place to rest and bandage ourselves during our mission, occasionally I would find myself tearing up from what I had just been a part of; at the death, at the savagery of it all. Soldiers who fought against each other, not knowing which side we were on when we went through the carnage, would look at me as if I was part of a sport. Theone would be there and hold me until I gathered myself when we made camp. With my eyes closed and their strong arms wrapped around me, their voice quietly humming bardic tunes, I felt safe from the rest of the world.

Since our return Nerice had figured out I had eyes for another member of the Council, and we talked about my life on Earth and here. I told them about my afternoon, what pushed me to come out to them. She supported me fully. It was nice to see a part of her that was different from the shadows and razor-sharp fingernails and prayers.

"I should have made a move sooner!" Nerice joked. "I'm so jealous of the Commander. He's going to get that delicate face and that luscious ass!" she said with a teasing tone, her hand making a grabbing motion.

Theone swiped at Nerice's hands, though I could see them trying to hold back a smile at Nerice's taunting.

Gwen and Bellamy cackled in delight. I blushed intensely. No one had spoken to me with a hint of vulgarity yet, but seeing my friends' walls come down just as mine had to them was a true gift. It turned out people were the same on every planet. I loved it.

My mind drifted to thoughts of truly building a life here. Weekly evenings or dinners with my friends. A small cabin by a lake with Lachlan maybe...

"We have only talked to each other! Nothing else!" I said in defence.

"Yes, but I bet if you offered, the Commander would let you climb him like a tree!" Nerice said with a wicked grin. "You looked good when we found you, but since you started training, *look* at you!"

Gwen smacked my ass as Nerice stopped talking. I swatted at her before sitting down next to her in the little circle we made in front of the hearth. I looked at the tarot deck Durin had given me, so similar to the ones I had on Earth. I shuffled the cards, preparing to draw them for my friends.

"Oh, I feel as if I shouldn't know of these conversations. They are so-"

Gwen cut Bellamy off and ruffled her silken hair which, without it's pins to keep it neatly to her scalp, fell beautifully around her cheeks, framing her face with gentle dark curls. "Duchess, we're all friends here. Is it not nice to take a break from the real world and all the stinky boys and just gossip?"

Bellamy sighed, a small smile on her lips, and nodded in agreement. I had been fond of her since we met. When Bellamy walked into the room, it felt like the sun was coming out after days of raging storms. She was a ray of sunshine, and I was so glad she wanted to join me and the others at my sleepover.

I smiled, knowing these were memories I was creating. These people were becoming not just my friends, but my family here. They would never take the place of the those I had lost, but they could fill the dark space in my heart from missing Earth. If not for them, I did not know where I would be mentally. If I had continued to be alone, isolating myself, lying to them, I would be a very different person indeed.

I sat in my breeches and my sweater, the others in either their breeches or nice linen night dresses. We were laughing, telling each others' futures and drank hot chocolate Bellamy had brought over. The chocolate was a secret stash she kept in her own chambers from her home in the Northeastern Province. How delicious it was to taste chocolate again. It was creamy with hints of caramel and spice, an absolute delight.

We ate pastries, fruit and cheese, and sipped mulled wine when the chocolate ran dry. Bellamy's face was red, and she was extra giggly as Nerice and Gwen flirted with her. Nerice had her mouth full of an apple and was more charming than she should be talking through food. Gwen had a similar flirting style, her fingertips walking over Bellamy's shoulder before poking her nose and complimenting Bellamy's tastes in fashion and food. Gwen and Nerice caught eyes several times, smirking at each other like they were playing a game to see who would win Bellamy's favor. Theone simply rolled their eyes, picking at a board of meat and cheese as they watched on.

When we were all a little more than inebriated, especially Bellamy, the door knocked. I expected it to be Vice, perhaps coming to educate and elaborate on my eye, my *gift,* that I was supposed to accept. My chambers were, after all, much more private than camp. I suppose he obviously did not know that I had confessed everything to the Council the day after our return and invited the others over as an act of friendship.

"Come in!" I called, ready to send him away with a pastry.

The door muffled the voice that spoke beyond it, making me

unsure of whom was actually there, but I managed to pick out, "I'll just be a moment."

I got up, crawling away from the snacks and wine. I stood when I reached the door. "Breath of the gods, just come in!" I opened the door. Lachlan stood there, his mouth agape, ready to respond, but his words had escaped him as he looked down to see I was barely dressed. I watched his eyes look me up and down and I felt heat raise within me by the excitement of it. The others behind me squealed with joy and Bellamy spit out her wine sending Gwen into an even wickeder cackle. I knew Theone was fumbling to clean up the mess hearing them mumble, as if Lachlan would judge them on the mess.

"Oh, I, umm-" He turned his head, pretending he had not just checked me out and obscured his view to give us time to dress if we chose. I could see him fighting a smile.

"Lachlan!" I practically screeched. "I wasn't expecting you tonight!" I tried to pull my sweater down but doing so only revealed more of my chest.

I heard everyone giggle again and Bellamy try to shush them. "Quiet down and let them speak!" she hissed quietly. "I can't hear them!"

Still facing away from me, Lachan's hand rubbing nervously behind his head, he said "I didn't expect you to expect me, I just, umm," he cleared his throat. "I just wanted to-" His voice kept catching.

"Care to come in, Commander?" I asked my voice high as I stepped aside for him to enter, still pulling at my sweater with the hope of it suddenly becoming longer.

"Are you certain, *Seer*? If this is not a good time…"

"Come in!" I demanded, a panicked and embarrassed tone to my voice. I looked behind me with a wide-eyed expression and my friends whispered to each other in an entertained fashion. Bellamy and Theone wrapped themselves in long furs for more modesty around their leader. Gwen and Nerice did not seem to give two shits if Lachlan saw them without their uniforms. Nerice just sat in her knickers, her breasts barely contained by the bralette over her chest. Gwen had a loose pair of wrap pants and a tunic scarcely held together by the strings tying the front. Her blind eye seemed more alive tonight and she took a big sip of mulled wine before turning her attention back to the others, speaking to them in Bygone Speech in an effort to distract them from Lachlan and I.

Lachlan carefully stepped inside the room, closing the door behind him as I scurried over to the chest where I kept my clothes to find a pair of bottoms.

I fumbled getting pants on, and when I did, I told Lachlan I was decent.

He finally looked at me, from the door, which he now leaned against, trying to take a more relaxed attitude amongst friends. "I'm sorry, I know you were having a little night gathering," he glanced at the others again then back at me with the smallest smile on his lips. His eyes scanned over me again, drinking me in and I swallowed. For a moment I forgot the others were there as he watched me.

I beckoned Lachlan to come closer, though he remained by the door. Instead, I approached him. He had so much presence. It was admirable and intimidating and... "What can I do for you, Commander?" I asked, pulling my hair over to one of my shoulders, moving it specifically to cover the skin that was exposed over my chest. It was so hard to pretend to be professional with a head full of wine.

Lachlan watched my movement, and his expression seemed conflicted with what he wanted to say. It was almost like he had hoped I was alone, regardless of knowing how I was going to spend my evening. He stepped close to me, like he had earlier in the day when we had finished our stroll around the village.

"Well, if you would be so kind, as per our previous conversation, you may address me simply as *Lachlan*, since we are in such an informal setting." I could feel his hot breath on my skin, and it was more enticing than I wanted to admit.

My friends giggled again, having clearly tuned back in to the conversation he and I were having. Nerice went "oooOOOooo!" and someone shushed her so they could continue listening.

I smiled, and Lachlan smiled back. He smelt so good, like coffee and cedar, evidence of his love for the hot beverage and his constant life outside. I wanted to eat him up. I felt the rose in my cheeks deepen. "*Lachlan.*" Saying his name, to him, brought life to me. "What *else* might I do for you?"

Something crossed his expression before he replied. "I came to tell you I'm proud of you for telling us the truth. I know how hard it can be to share very personal things about yourself. I'm sure Nerice, Theone and Bellamy are proud of you too." He broke eye contact with me only to look behind me to the others, his brows raised, waiting for them to confirm what he said.

"We are!" Nerice exclaimed.

"You're proud of me?" I asked. My gaze had not left him.

His expression shifted, his eyes drifting to my lips before clearing his throat. He forced his mind back to the conversation and met my gaze. I loved his eyes, the pale green a respite from the exotic, vibrant colours of the rest of my friends.

"Aye, I am," he stated.

I hugged him. He was all armour and furs, but I knew somewhere amongst the layers he could feel my embrace. After Gwen's hug last night, I had desperately wanted more and the group hug earlier this evening was not enough to quench my need. It took him a moment before he wrapped his arms around me, but he did nonetheless, and I felt shivers run through my body as the excitement within me grew by his gentle touch.

If this was back on Earth, and not in front of other people, I would have kissed him. I wanted to feel his lips on mine, to taste his breath and feel his skin against me. I tried to squeeze him, telling myself that I did not want our first kiss to be in front of everyone else. Lachlan squeezed back.

"Thank you, Lachlan. It means a lot to me that you said that." My head rested against his chest, my face buried into the big fur on his shoulders, feeling the rise and fall of his chest beneath me. He was surprisingly warm. I felt his head rest on the top of mine. He let out a relaxed breath, a worry he had seemingly been carrying had left him alone.

"You're very welcome, Delilah," he said softly.

My friends *awed* at us, and I raised my middle finger to them while I was still in Lachlan's arms.

Slowly, hesitantly, almost regretfully, Lachlan pulled away from our hug. "I..." One hand still rested on my hip, and he moved his lips to my ear, his voice lowered so only I could hear. "I also wanted to ask for some more time alone between you and I before the trial. I was delighted with our walk today and thought we could enjoy one another's company. May I be so bold to suggest in my chambers." I felt his lips gently press in the space on my neck between my ear and shoulder and linger there before his voice returned to my ear. "Know that hearing your voice is like cranberry wine and I draw life from hearing it."

A pleasurable shiver ran down my body from where he had kissed me. I blushed fully and nodded before I could process words to reply to him. "Your suggestion sounds delicious," I squeaked. "I mean— wow. Umm. I. Holy shit."

Lachlan grinned, pleased by my response, and removed his hand from my side. "I'll be on my way." He nodded to my companions behind me. "Folks." I could not help but imagine there was supposed to be more to Lachlan's visit, to his words, to his touch. I almost followed him out to find out what awaited me in his chambers.

Instead the second the door closed behind him, Nerice and Gwen clapped and teased, reminding me I had guests. Gwen gestured for me to return to the cozy circle we had made on the floor.

"I *told* you!" Gwen declared.

Bellamy giggled as she sipped at more mulled wine. "I have *never* seen the Commander like this!" she exclaimed.

"Neither have I," Theone agreed. Theone almost seemed shocked by how bold the Commander had been in front of us all. They blinked a couple times before taking a deep drink of wine.

Gwen and Nerice screeched with excitement. Nerice made

kissing sounds, and Gwen poured herself another cup of wine before topping up dwindling glasses.

"The scout's gossip about what they see around Blackwick. Not *everything* is behind closed doors," Nerice smirked at me.

Gwen pointed an accusatory finger at Nerice. "You know everything that goes on around Blackwick. Guaranteed, if *they* decide to worship, you will know before they do!"

Nerice and Gwen cackled together. "You're right!" Nerice agreed.

Theone made a face, as if not wanting to know the goings on of their equals and chugged their cup.

Chapter Nine
Day Eighty?

The following morning, I was summoned to the Council Room. Gwen and Theone had woken up earlier than the rest of us, leaving in the early hours before the sun or first bell. When Theone returned to my chambers, their voice loud enough to stir us from our slumber, Nerice and Bellamy shot up disoriented from the cuddle pile on my bed. Nerice groaned, mumbling in Bygone Speech to Theone as she rolled out of the bed. Her cheeks were flushed, and eyes hooded with the tiredness that accompanied a hangover. Bellamy yawned and stretched before delicately stepping to the floor with a grace Nerice lacked. My head hurt with wine.

Nerice and Theone exchanged a few words before Theone left. As I poured the two ladies some water I asked, "What's going on?"

"We received an owl saying it's time for your trial," Nerice said tiredly. She looked around searching for her robe. When she found it, she slipped it on. Nerice did not tie it in the usual method that the other nuns did, leaving it open to see her knickers. "We must prepare to send you back out. Dress and meet us in the Council Chambers." Nerice yawned then chugged her glass of water before excusing herself from us.

Bellamy pulled her own robe over her nightdress, tying it more mindfully. She sipped her water with less urgency then gave me a hug. "You must have made an impression on Priestess Mirna. This is good news," she assured me before leaving.

I stood quietly in the Council Room listening to the others as they planned the strategy for the trial. They hoped showing Temple members my memories would make it an easy decision to officially name me Seer. Theone still had their mothers ring, a significant piece of evidence they planned on bringing to the trial's attention while there. They knew High Priestess Caoimhe would be particularly swayed by them having it, and I had yet to completely understand why.

An owl was also received from Asa, letting us know they would stand witness against their father's accusations. If the Temple's accepted me, the army would be allowed more resources. The Council would leverage anything they could afterwards to make sure we found a solution to this war.

I agreed with their decision, believing our best chance would be with the help from more mages. Mages were powerful, magic was valuable. Aside from Vice and the Commander, there were no other mages within Blackwick. The mages would be an asset in the war. It was always going to be a hard feat to find mages, especially since a large population of them had disappeared into the thick forests of the province to hide. Temple resources meant mages at their disposal. The mages Grand Deacon Adder had been using for himself to be exact.

Finding out that the deacon had been using mages without Temple consent drove Theone to great anger. They called it slavery. Mages were to be revered, not used. Their mother had been a mage; the only mage amongst the other High Priestesses. All we could hope was that the Temple's would side with us. Our third feat would be proving to the refugees that we would not restrict or use them as Adder had.

"You must be on your best behaviour," Bellamy chimed, shockingly cheerful and awake considering the amount she had drunk the night before. I had really thought, of all of us, she would have had the worst hangover. "The Temple's are already on high alert because of the war, but the rumors of heretics harboring a Seer has caused much imbalance within. We have a letter from Deacon Adder inviting Delilah to stay at *his* castle during the trial rather than the local inn. We should accept his offer but remain cautious."

Suspicions had grown too high in the last few months. Fears of another attack on a Divine caused unrest. Keepers were on their way to the Stills from the Temple in the Southwestern Province to sit in on the trial. They were under command by a High Priestess who, so I heard, had a bite worse than her bark; Caoimhe.

"Deacon Adder's *castle* is one of the most defensible fortresses in the province. He was given it by the Temple's to help oversee Temple work and aid refugees, which obviously he has been abusing. This castle rivals even some Temples," Lachlan said looking at me, his posture fierce, straight. Memories of his lips on my throat flickered through my mind. I refocused, sensing the worry behind his words. "But we should assume the same people who attacked at Samu's and Andreja's Temple know about your trial and that another Priestess will be attending. We cannot leave it completely unarmed."

"The Temples know Delilah will be accompanied by handlers from our forces. High Priestess Caoimhe will surely see us as raiders if we bring a large party and will either attack us or report our sins to the other High Priestess's across the globe. We cannot lose the only means we have of stopping this war, but we also must show good faith to the Temples," Bellamy stated. "We must attend this trial with as little people as possible and trust her Keepers will protect her and everyone else."

Everyone appeared frustrated.

"We will work on a solution to the demon surge while you're gone," Nerice said. "But getting those mages and maybe some Keepers will definitely help."

"There must be a solution," Theone sighed. "We can't go in with only five people. I would be more comfortable with ten. I don't trust this, even with Keepers there."

"Most buildings like this have secret passages below," Nerice said thoughtfully. "We can send a half a dozen of my scouts through it, and they can watch from the rafters of the trial. No one will know they are there unless things turn."

"Too risky," Lachlan protested. "Keepers are smarter than that."

"Adder isn't. This is all under the assumption Southern sympathizers will be hidden within the Holy Order and audience," Nerice said. "Theone is right. We must have a backup plan. Sitting and hoping for the best isn't ideal."

The Council Room door burst open, and I jumped at the sound. Bellamy withheld a giggle at my surprise and Theone gave me a look to suggest *you're supposed to be a symbol of the gods, do not be so skittish.*

"I have proof of Adder's betrayal!" Vice's voice said from the door.

One of Nerice's agents ran in after him. "Commander, Mother Nerice I tried to tell him you were in a meeting!" The scout seemed out of breath as if he had been chasing him. Vice was animated.

"I used to work with him, I know his magic. If you're going to the trial, let me be one of the Seer's handlers. I can assist in casting the memory spell and Asa sent me *evidence* for his treason," Vice said.

"Adder is a *mage?!*" Theone practically boomed. "What proof do you have?"

"Asa, Adder's successor, has sent me an owl from a Southern captain addressed to Adder. You can arrest him when Keepers arrive, and the mage refugees will follow Asa out. Pretend to play Adder's game." Vice turned to Nerice. "I will give you all the anti-charms for your scouts move through the castle unnoticed."

"Asa controls the people there?" Nerice asked.

"Asa, like Adder, is a mage, but far kinder. They rarely use their mage, save enhancing their tonics. Adder only accepted the refugees after Asa's pleading. Adder promised to protect them and, as we know, lied."

Theone slammed their fists down on the table. "I knew it! The gods granted me a gift and it is to smell out traitors!" they hissed. Bellamy moved closer to Theone and quietly shushed them. "Why would Asa send separate owls about the trial? We received promise from them to speak against Adder. Why give-" Theone stopped their own questioning, their voice lowering as they realized the answer to their own questions. "Adder would be less suspicious of owls if they are carrying smaller letters. It's safer to send crucial information to you than it is to us. Clever."

I took a deep breath. I had been dreading the trial. I was

terrified of a negative outcome, but the Council seemed confident the Keepers would see reason, that Caoimhe would see reason. I had not been steered in the wrong direction yet with them. This would be a large quest to face. A part of me feared that leaving Blackwick meant I would never return to it, never sleep in my bed again. I worried I was not strong enough, my tongue not quick enough to stand up for myself or my companions.

I hated politics.

I remembered last night and how proud all my friends said they were of me. Certainly, if these amazing people believed in me, I had the strength to do this.

"Let's do it," I said.

Vice turned to the Council with confidence. "I promise on my life, that I will keep her safe." I almost thought his words were directed at Lachlan.

Nerice's brows rose, impressed as she turned to look at the others. "It looks like we have direction," she said.

Bellamy nodded and began to write things down on a piece of parchment on the table.

Theone looked at me, then Vice. "You have helped keep her safe this long, there stands no reason you wouldn't now," they said.

Vice nodded to her before stepping back out of the room.

"Collect your pack, Delilah, we need to move as soon as possible," Theone told me.

*

Cathal, Theone and Vice accompanied me to the Grand Deacons castle in the Stills. I was disappointed Durin could not come, but I knew it was strategic planning that Cathal came in his place. Theone would watch over me and act as both a representative of the Temple and our cause. Vice's magic was vital for the trial, plus he knew the castle. Cathal was extra muscle in case things went sideways. Durin assured me I could fill him, Bellamy, Nerice and Gwen in upon my return.

When we arrived at Adder's Castle a half a dozen guards

greeted us. They were not Keepers. These guards wore exquisitely detailed tunics over golden chainmail. It fitted tightly to their athletic forms. The silver and gold beadwork were expensive for wartime. Adder was showing off with his guard. A sigil on their chests provoked recognition in me and I tried to place it as we approached them. People who I could only assume were refugees scrubbed the castles walls and tidied the courtyard where we entered. For once it was not raining here. We stopped at the door, where a single guard stepped out from the line watching us.

Theone gave our names and positions and there was a long silence for more time than I would have liked after they finished. I could see their irritability begin to bubble at the guard's silence.

"Are you not going to let us in?" I asked, sternly, looking at the guard with my best unimpressed expression; something Nerice encouraged me to practice on my way here so others would be unable to tell how uncomfortable I was. It had been a long trip, and I was very tired.

The guard had an arrogant expression on his face, his brows peeked at the sound of my agitated inquiry. "We were not expecting anyone other than Miss Golding," he said. "Your party can stay at the inn."

"Then you must not have been informed that the Temples require I have handlers for the trial," I said simply. "If they leave, I will too."

The man looked at me then looked at my friends then back at me again. He sneered at my defiance, an expression he learned from Adder no doubt. He was annoyed, but compliant. The guard waved us to follow him inside.

The other guards watched us as we passed them, only their heads turning in observation. Again, I tried to figure out where I had seen the sigils on their chests. I could almost pinpoint it, the source on the tip of my tongue.

We passed through a long corridor of the castle. It was kept clean and warm, probably thanks to all the poor refugees Adder had been putting to work. I could not understand why they had not gone against him. He was only one man, though his guards appeared to be several dozen. The number was surprising for a Grand Deacon, almost suspicious. We went deep into the castle, descending a wide staircase that led to a large entertaining hall. At the far end of the grand hall, positioned lavishly on a platform, Deacon Adder sat in an extravagant throne.

Of course he had a throne.

I let out slow breaths, trying to keep my wits and not show how anxious I was to be here. How irritated I was at this man's audacity.

"Grand Deacon, your guest and her *ensemble* has arrived," said the guard, a note of superiority in his voice when he referred to my companions.

Deacon Adder stood from his throne. "I see you brought associates with you, despite my invitation for you alone." His eyes focused on Vice briefly and I watched as his face scoffed upon recognizing it. He avoided looking at Theone and returned his attention to me.

"And go against the Temple's instruction that I come with handlers? Do you think me foolish?" I asked.

The deacon huffed, his jaw working and holding back what he really wanted to say. After a long pause he said "No."

Standing in this castle, looking at all the embellishments, the luxury it exuded, left a sour taste in my mouth. Adder was a man living beyond his means. We had thwarted whatever he had been planning by coming in together and he was doing his best to not throw a tantrum like he had at the camps near Blackwick, but I was still on edge.

"I know you want the mages," the deacon said after another long pause. "Maybe we can work out some arrangement that is equitable to all parties before your trial." He looked between us again, something about him provoking more suspicion in me. "How about I give a dozen or so to you, on lend immediately, if I'm paid a just sum each week until their return and you confess your heresy?" Adder said. A smug grin crept onto his lips.

He had to be joking.

"No fucking way," I hissed.

The deacon's expression hitched at my vulgarity and Vice tapped my ankles with his staff as if suggested I hold my tongue.

"Are you really bartering peoples *lives*, father?" Asa cried, stepping from a dark corner of the room. I had not even noticed them there. A guard came forward and grabbed Asa's forearm, trying to pull them to a nearby door. Asa resisted.

"You are supposed to be resting," the guard murmured when Asa tore their arm from his grasp.

"Asa, my pet, you would not have convinced the mages to stay in our care if you did not trust me with their lives, correct?" Deacon Adder asked.

Asa moved closer from across the room. "I thought you would be good to them, like you are to me. Instead, you threw innocents to their deaths! You've barely protected them! I trusted you and you used me!" Asa hissed.

Deacon Adder sat back in his over-sized chair, relaxing, his posture still arrogantly confident that the situation would go in his favour. "These *people* need mages to help them," he looked at me, his expression hardening, "do you not?" He snapped his fingers out to the left and a young woman rushed over with a platter of preserves and crackers. She placed a piece of bread with orange jam on it into Adder's hand and he popped it in his mouth. "Who says they won't do the same thing I did? The majority of the province's mages have fled into the trees and are probably dead. *I* have what *you* need. So, we have a deal?"

"No," I said in disbelief. "You're the fool if you think I would ever yield to you."

The stillness in the air was sharp, the audience of guards and my companions stunned or delighted by my response to the grand deacon. Theone struggled to keep their lips sealed. They wanted to comment on his simple impudence, to support my boldness. I could see it in the glimmer of their yellow eyes as they stared down the man and awaited his next move but remained silent. This was the part of the plan, letting me speak for myself, for our cause.

I glanced over to Vice, always statuesque, and his gaze caught mine. He nodded approvingly. Cathal's booming laughter cut the silence, but he quieted quickly when Theone gave him a sharp, disapproving look.

"Then why would I ever help you?!" Deacon Adder hissed, standing again from his throne in a rushed, angry movement. His cheeks had grown red by my defiance.

All I saw before me was a little boy not allowed an extra portion of dessert. I rolled my eyes and took a deep breath. I was not a politician or a negotiator. I could not for the life of me understand how I was in this position. Why Theone or Cathal could not speak for me, for Blackwick and the army. The Council wanted to make me the voice, the face, and have the confidence and the finesse to play whatever game Grand Deacon Adder was playing. I just wanted this over. I wanted to knead some bread. I wanted to feel Lachlan's hands on my body.

I bit my tongue from snapping at the deacon. Again, I was reminded why he tested Theone's temper. It made me wonder how long Theone had delt with him before they began snapping at even a mention of his name.

Asa glared at their father, charging towards him. I had not noticed from the distance between us, but as Asa got closer the torches and candles alit their face. Their complexion had drastically changed from mere weeks ago. They looked so *tired*. The deacon seemed surprised by Asa's movement.

On our journey here, Vice had mentioned that Asa's body was failing them. Asa was a skilled healer, so skilled in fact that it was them who taught Vice many of the recipes he used after battles. Sadly, no medicine, potion or magic could cure them from what they suffered. They were bound for the After with the gods and their mother. I had asked if any surgeons or other healers knew what was happening and Vice simply said what was in the woods had infected them. This was something Asa had accepted. Adder had not.

. "They know everything, father," Asa said gently, trying to not provoke the deacon further. Their struggle to yell at him was mighty.

I let my breath out gradually, feeling my heartbeat slow from the aggravation of trying to speak civilly with an asshole.

"What do you mean? Asa, what have you told them?" the grand deacon asked, his voice betrayed. His expression twisted as he came to realize what his progeny had revealed. The hundreds in the area who had died by his order in attempt to vanquish the demons, his wild disregard with living people, his alliance with the southern armies. According to Vice, in Asa's letter, Asa revealed that the mages did not even have proper sleeping quarters at the castle, despite having the space to do so.

Deacon Adder stood and stomped down from the platform his throne sat on. The girl that had brought him a platter of food scurried off, frightened by his sudden movement. "Fine!" he growled. His eyes darted between us and his child. "Take those apostates, you'll be doing me a favour!" Deacon Adder's fists clenched and unclenched at his sides before he held out his hand to me. "I will concede and tell the Temples the truth."

It could not be that easy, I thought.

I raised my hand to take his, hesitant, debating if this was the exact trap the Council was concerned that he would make for me. The Deacon grabbed my hand a little too hard and I tried to jerk my hand back, realizing my mistake.

"How dare you turn my own child against me! You're nothing but a *mistake*," Deacon Adder snarled. I continued to try to pull from his grip, trying to pry at his fingers with my free hand, digging my nails into his skin. I heard as Theone drew their sword, the swift *shwing* of the metal in the air as it left the scabbard.

My heart sped up, I could feel my stomach in my throat, the panic setting in. "Let go of me!" I hissed, my voice raising, my stomach churning. I continued to try to yank my hand away, his grip hurting my wrist. I heard running behind me, unsure of who was coming to my rescue.

I heard the unravelling whirl of ropes above my head and my attention shot up seeing Captain Florence descend from the old wooden beams of the main halls ceiling. Four of Nerice's scouts repelled down, following behind her. They landed around the room. Florence and another scout flanked Deacon Adder faster than I could process the scene. Three other scouts pursued the grand deacon's guards, their weapons drawn faster than the guards could react. Florence pinched an area on Adder's neck, and he collapsed, releasing my wrist. I jumped back, rubbing my arm where he had gripped it. Theone and Vice were beside me, Cathal's axes were drawn. Back up in the rafters a fifth scout stood with a bow at the ready.

"You are under citizens arrest until High Priestess Caoimhe's Keepers arrive. A second trial will be taking place!" Theone growled.

Captain Florence knelt next to Adder as he groaned on the floor. She bound his wrists behind his back quickly and tight. I could feel my heart pumping in my head, and I took a deep breath to calm down.

How would this have gone if the scouts weren't here?

My three companions were talented, but I was unsure if they could have defended against whatever the grand deacon had planned. I let out another breath, fighting my eyes from watering. My wrist was sore. I examined it, only a red mark remained from the deacon's forceful grip.

"It's alright, you're safe," Vice said quietly. He put his arm around my shoulders and steered me away from where the grand deacon lay on the ground.

Theone and Florence spoke to one another in Bygone Speech, and I could see as Adder's guards stood on edge, their hands by the daggers on their hips, but fear evident in their eyes. They knew if they tried to draw their weapons, Nerice's scouts would get to their very exposed throats first.

"The scouts have spotted Keepers on the other side of the valley. They should arrive by nightfall, and we will push for your trial to begin immediately," Theone told us, jogging over and putting their sword back in its scabbard. "How are you feeling?"

"Nervous," I admitted.

"You're allowed to be," Theone cooed. They turned to one of the guards who put his hands up quickly when Theone glared. He was the same one to lead us to this chamber. "Where can we wait until the Keeper's arrival?"

The guard kept his hands up. "This way, Colonel," he said. His voice no longer carried the arrogance it had before.

We waited in a spacious parlour, decorated with elegant silken couches and lush gold curtains, another example of what Adder was using Temple funds for rather than helping the refugees. A couple soft blankets were lumped on a lounger and next to it was a table with empty potion bottles and an herbal smelling pitcher.

Asa eventually joined us, looking drained and sat on the lounger, pulling the blankets on top of them. "I'm sorry about my father," they said. "He's so stuck in his ways, especially after auntie passed."

When the Keepers arrived, Theone left the parlour leaving me alone with Vice and Asa to speak with them, Cathal having stayed in the main chamber with Florence and the scouts. There was a lot of noise beyond the parlour door. The sound of furniture moving, metal boots clanking against the stone floor, dozens upon dozens of voices; Grand Deacon Adder's furious voice amongst them.

Vice patted my knee, seeing my growing anxiety. "We will perform the same magic we did when you first reached Blackwick, Delilah. Just tell the truth. The Keepers will see reason," Vice assured me.

"Lachlan was there before," I squeaked.

"Delilah, you are different from who you were then. Your mind more open, your magic stronger. I don't need the Commander. I just need you," Vice said.

I let out another nervous breath.

"If they even just see you, they will believe," Asa said encouragingly. I looked at them. Through their exhaustion they still had a sweet smile, their words soft and warm. I wanted to believe them. I wanted to believe all my friends when they said it would be alright.

"Then the magic will seal the deal," Vice stated.

I touched my eye again. We had crossed several other Machine crash sites on our way here, crossed more demons. My eye had bled with every spell cast. I was still so scared to look in a mirror and now that Theone had one, they offered it often though I just as often declined.

"You enjoy music, right?" Vice asked. "I could sing you something, if it would help calm your thoughts."

The hours dragged slowly. We were brought tea and the potion bottles on the table near Asa were refilled. Asa drank one potion every hour. The night was late when Theone crashed through the parlour doors, startling me awake from Vice's lap. I had not even realized I had fallen asleep, but his voice had been so relaxing. I sat up quickly and Vice pulled his hands away from my hair where he had been petting me.

"Priestess Mirna and High Priestess Caoimhe is here!" Theone exclaimed "The trial is beginning, and Adder is feeding them lie after lie on the podium without us!"

Florence jogged in after Theone. "Colonel, please find your calm. This will be an easy decision as soon as they see her!"

"Gods grant me serenity," Theone growled.

I stood. "So, they're ready for me?" My voice seemed to defuse Theone.

They looked at me, with care in their expression. "Yes, please come with me," Theone said.

Vice followed close behind us, his voice low as he leaned to speak with Theone as we walked. "Were the Keepers upset by Nerice's scouts?" he asked.

"There was some debate, but we still have less than a dozen people with us, so they aren't too concerned, thankfully," Theone clarified.

"Good."

When we entered the main hall again, it was a changed space. A large podium stood on the platform in front of Adder's throne, which had been pushed back against the wall. Mismatched chairs that seemed to have been collected from different rooms around the castle were set up on two sides of the hall in long rows. Four chairs were facing the podium, and I recognised Priestess Mirna and Grand Deacon Adder, still bound, among them. As I walked forward, Theone held one of my arms and the once quiet room began to fill with whispers. When the deacon looked over his shoulder to watch us, I could hear Theone cuss under their breath. I took a deep breath, trying to keep my shoulders straight and my gaze forward to appear unphased by the crowd.

When I glanced to the people in the rows of chairs framing the walk to the podium, I saw who I guessed were Keepers. Their violet robes resembled the ones Nerice wore, but they dawned more armour. Their expressions were stern, but if I caught their gaze I watched as wonder replaced disbelief. More and more eyes fell on me and whispers became louder.

I was led around the group of four sitting near the podium. In front of them was a table with parchment and quills. I accidently made eye contact with the deacon, and he sneered at me. I held his gaze, and Theone brought me behind the podium. They stood on my left and we waited in silence as Theone motioned to someone in the audience. A Keeper from one of the closer rows of chairs walked forward and stood on my right. My heart pumped heavily, and I looked over at the others sitting with the grand deacon and Priestess. The other two appeared to be members of the Temples. Both appeared surprised by me standing before them.

"Esteemed clergy," Theone bellowed. The crowd hummed to a silence. "Ladies, gentleman and variances thereupon, I present to you, for your evaluation, Miss Delilah Golding. Our Seer."

The chambers were silent, save Grand Deacon Adder who huffed loudly.

"Supposedly," he called.

"Grand Deacon," a woman beside him said. She was adorned more extravagantly than other people in the audience. "I would suggest your tongue be held until we see and hear everything."

The deacons mouth snapped shut abruptly, his eyes big like a scolded dog.

Theone continued to speak. "We have brought Sir Vice, an Amaranthine academic and mage with us from Blackwick." Voices stirred at the word *Amaranthine*, though Theone continued. "Vice and Commander Blackwick preformed a memory projection spell on Golding after the incident at Andreja's Temple. She had suffered memory loss prior to it. The spell was enlightening, and I pray you see reason as we did. If we may perform it again, this trial can be wrapped up quickly and we can all go to sleep, as I'm sure we all want."

"Proceed," the woman next to the grand deacon said, leaning forward on her elbows, anticipation brimming from her eyes.

Vice moved behind me and Theone took his staff. His voice was quiet, only I could hear him as he spoke. "Concentrate on the words I say, let your mind relax. Remember when the Commander and I preformed it. If you are able, repeat my words and open your memories for me." I nodded and felt Vice's fingers place themselves softly on my temples. "Breathe," Vice whispered.

Vice was right. My power had grown since the last time we did this, and he had gone over the steps with me on our journey here for this spell. I focused on Vice's voice, despite my nervousness, and began repeating what he said. Reality shifted around us, my memories shot forth from my mind and the room gasped loudly. Voices picked up in a clammer, seeing their late High Priestess run into me. I concentrated on clarity for the vision, just as I concentrated on forcing the demons into the Other. The flicker of my memory became clearer, the voices in it louder.

The audience watched as their late High Priestess gave me the sacred Eye. They heard her words to me and witnessed as I was bestowed the power of a god. They saw Katerina drag me to safety, be given instruction with her ring. Many audibly gasped. They watched High Priestess Katerina be held hostage by something deeply sick and monstrous. They watched men turn into demons and their Divine sacrifice herself, trying to destroy them and save *me*.

The memory finished.

Slowly Vice released my skull, and I could hear him collect himself behind me. Theone passed his staff back to him. I looked over the audience, seeing tears in the eyes of the Keepers, of Adder's guard, of Captain Florence and the scouts. I felt the familiar sensation of blood trickle from my eye, and I wiped at it. My head ached.

"I see," the woman other than Priestess Mirna at the table said. "Do you have her ring with you Theone?"

Theone removed their glove and stepped down from the platform to approach the woman. They wore the flower-shaped ring on their hand and held their fingers out for the four to see.

"I did not want to bring it up until the trial," Theone said.

The woman took Theone's hand in hers. "I always knew it would be you."

Deacon Adder was fuming.

The woman let go of Theone's hand and leaned to a man on the other side of her, her voice quiet and the man nodded. Voices got louder in the chambers.

Theone returned to my side and spoke to Vice.

I saw movement from the corner of my eye.

Something did not feel right.

I saw the deacon tap his fingers angrily on the table. Priestess Mirna was writing something down on parchment and seemed to have written a lot during the vision, several parchments already filled with ink. The grand deacon's eyes shot over to where I had noticed movement before and a wicked smile settled on his lips. I followed his gaze. One of Adder's guards was sneaking around some pillars, away from where the audience was. He was coming towards me.

"Guys…" I said softly.

The guard moved closer.

Theone and Vice turned their attention to me, but their eyes quickly landed to where I looked.

The guard was *fast*. He was on me faster than anyone could react. The audience voices moved into an uproar. I could hear the one woman in the front who had shushed Adder calling for Keepers. As the guard grabbed me, the illusion was broken. His form shimmered into Adder. He gripped my arm, hard, with one hand.

The Keeper on the platform near to me moved, attempting a peaceful solution. Her voice said, "We can talk about this, Deacon, unhand the Seer and step away slowly." Her hands were in a calming position, her eyes on him far kinder than the look on Theone.

How had he gotten out of his ties? How was he in two places at once?

"That's *Grand* Deacon, you imbecile!"

The man who was originally thought to be the deacon shimmered into the guard who I had thought was coming for me.

Had this been the plan all along? Fake an unsuccessful attack so our defenses would be down? Or had they switched places when someone was not looking?

Theone drew their sword quickly, people ran around the chamber, but I could only concentrate on Adder. I tried to yank my arm away from his grasp. Adder's free hand pulled something from his pocket, and he slammed it against the back of my hand, the same one with the handprint scar. The object burned.

"This power belongs to my master!" Adder snarled. "You wouldn't even begin to understand true purpose, would you?!" My eye ached as Adder started chanting something in Bygone Speech.

A spell.

Asa's voice called from across the hall, their tone terrified. "Father, you sound insane!"

Vice discarded his staff to the platform, its wood clanking roughly to the ground, and grabbed onto Adder. He too began to try to pry Adder off of me. I could not understand how Adder was so strong, so immoveable. I looked over my shoulder and saw Theone's back to us, her sword and shield drawn as the two of Adder's guards approached from behind the throne. Keepers encircled the podium, yelling orders in Bygone Speech, but their commands went unheeded. Adder and his guard did not budge.

"Listen to your child, Adder!" Vice hissed.

Adder spat on Vice's chest as he continued to grip my wrist. "I gave you a chance to be part of this, Vice, and you turned me down. My master has power you would not believe. He will raise this world from the ashes it spoils in! He will create a world better than the old gods ever could! Divines be damned!"

"Who the fuck is your master?!" I asked bitterly, shakily. I wanted to puke. My hand hurt, I could feel my eye leaking, and it took a lot in me not to cry out from pain.

"He will be our new god! He will make the world bow to us! Together we will rule from the Sea of Mia to the Kane and Trickson Oceans! We will not feel like the gods have forgotten us ever again, because we will have Him to watch over us!"

Asa's enraged voice echoed from behind us, closer now. "The gods have not forsaken us!" they exclaimed, their voice out of breath.

"Release the Seer!" a Keeper demanded.

"Adder, this is exactly what you and I talked about never wanting to happen! Why would you support this? People have been trying to forsake the gods for centuries and you saw what happened to the South Province, to your sister. Is that what you want for the rest of the world?" Vice asked.

How was Adder's grip so strong?

"Stop it father!! Let them stop this war and let's go back to the farms," Asa begged.

"No, it's the only way for you, Asa. My master can save you. He promised," Adder hissed.

"Save me?" Asa asked.

"There is a way. Master promised if I undo the mistake at Andreja's Temple…" He glared at me as he trailed off. As if I was the cause of all his problems, a pebble in his shoe.

"I'm going to die. You need to accept that," Asa said. "I will be with mother, I will wait for you before I come back, you will see me again." Asa's pleading words landed on deaf ears.

I swallowed back my nausea and glared at Adder. I tugged

again and again. Vice's fingers prodded at him. Nothing seemed to make Adder's hand budge. "Give this up!" I hissed. I could barely steady my voice, but it sounded convincing enough, I think.

"You should be *dead*. You should never have existed!" I could feel as my skin tore beneath whatever was between Adder's grip and my hand. It was sharp. Adder looked at Vice, a knowing look exchanged between them and Vice shook his head at him.

"Don't you dare," Vice hissed.

"*Potovanja*," Adder hissed back.

"No!" Vice shouted, his own hand slamming down over my hand where I could see my blood pour from between Adder's fingers. Red light burst out from our connection, people screamed, and I realized that Adder had completed his spell.

The red light blinded me, unlike the one that shine from the Other. I had seen this light before. I felt the *pull* of something.

My body thrust forward then dropped into cold, stinking water.

Adder's hands were no longer gripping mine and I was shrouded in darkness.

I could hear Vice cursing.

The water sloshed around him as he stood up and coughed out water.

"Delilah!" I had never heard his voice sound so worried. "Are you alright?" he asked.

Fire appeared hovering above his hand, he looked down to me, water dripping off every part of his body, his cloak clinging to his shape, and his hair dishevelled and flat from being wet. He must have landed completely in the water. I landed on my ass.

Nodding, I looked around, the water coming almost to my shoulders where I sat in it.

Where was Adder? Where was Theone and the tribunal?

I stood up in the water and got a head rush. I looked at the back of my hand where Adder had been pressing the sharp, burning object and a deep gash lay across the middle of seared flesh.

"Where are we?" I asked. My body hurt. I felt displaced.

Two guards wearing Adder's colours appeared at the far side of the room we stood in. Their torches illuminated what I recognized was once the entertainment hall where the trial was being held, now flooded, chairs from the trial either broken or floating in the murky water. It smelt like salt.

This was very wrong…

"Blood of God!" one guard gasped.

"Where'd they'd come from?!" The other asked.

We killed them.

To say I was overwhelmed and scared was to put it lightly. It had been a mentally taxing trip to the Stills. I barely got to rest from the first mission before turning around and coming back. I had sleepless nights coming here, nervous for the trial. Now this.

When the two guards drew their swords, it was clear they intended to kill us. Something I had learned over the last few weeks was I would always choose myself over them. A switch had flipped inside me weeks ago, and I was upon the closest guard before he could raise his weapon to attack. Before he even made it to our side of the hall. I had no idea how I had crossed it so quickly nor did I even remember drawing the blade in my hand, but my dagger was deep within his belly. He spat up thick black blood and collapsed moments after I withdrew my dagger. I turned just in time to see a ball of fire collide with the second guard. I glared down at their corpses floating in the water, black blood seeping from one corpse and the other crispy.

I swallowed and my body shivered with unease, remembering how many people I had killed in under three months. I tried to convince myself it was something I had to deal with another time, though I recognized it was chipping away at my ability to hold it together. I pressed my hand to my belly as it churred.

I would always choose me over them.

"Delilah?" Vice's voice was far away. I could hear him move through the water from the other side of the room towards me.

I hinged forward and hurled into the dark water. I hated

killing people, but it was always me or them.

Me.

Them.

I would die.

Or they would die.

I had to choose me. I could not have travelled through time and space just to die here. Not with whatever gift I had been given…

I wiped at my mouth and stayed bent over, catching my breath, trying to breathe in the resistance to puking out more dried meat and cheese. Vice reached me after a few minutes and rubbed my back.

"Interesting," he said thoughtfully as I slowly straightened. The torches were extinguished when the guards dropped but Vice created another light in his hand, his fingers bright like an iridescent mushroom in the darkness. He knelt and patted the guards' floating corpses until he found a ring of keys on one and unhooked it.

I groaned then burped as my body threatened to vomit again. I could feel my eyes well, and I bit back the tears. I looked at my hand again and watched as blood dripped from it and into the water below, stinging my newly burnt flesh. If I looked closely, I thought I saw a familiar pattern burnt onto the roof of my hand, but then I noticed bone, got distracted by it, and gagged.

"The last thing I remember is standing in by the podium…" I said as Vice stood back up, hooking the key ring to his belt.

"We're still here," Vice said, his voice calculating.

"The red light from the spell," I said. "Right before I was pulled here, a red light came in my windows just like that." *I was starting to remember…*

"Red is a colour associated with Andreja." An idea crossed Vice's mind. "We had been studying time magic before I left. Perhaps Adder…how could he…"

"What is it?"

"Adder must have sent us through time. I can think of no other explanation," Vice said.

Vice looked at me, his eyes darting down to the welt on my

hand. He pulled one of his potions out for me to take. I downed it, gagged again and then looked at the wound as it healed into a large, ugly scab over the handprint. I watched Vice mentally run through different situations, different outcomes, different endings.

"Excuse me?" I felt my face pale.

I had already done this once. I was still learning to cope with that, or at least attempting to. Telling my companions the truth had helped. I knew the magic here was powerful, but I did not think I could adjust to this again. I thought I had arrived here because of a malfunction with my Machine, despite everyone telling me the gods had brought me here. I could not use my Machine as an excuse this time. This time my Machine was not involved. There was only a second to think about it.

Was it possible that magic, and not the science within my Machine, did this the first time?

Was everyone else right?

Was I chosen by the gods?

"Did we go forward in time? Or backwards? And how far?" I stuttered out. Travelling to a whole new world was bad enough. I could not restart my life again. Not when I was just starting to get comfortable.

"Good questions. We'll have to find out. Let's see where exactly the grand deacon sent us. Then we can figure out how to get back and if we can," Vice said. He was putting on an act, his tone far brighter than the situation let on. I thought maybe he was putting on a face for me. "Adder was not a follower of Andreja, but a fan of her time magic. No one in many lifetimes have been able to uncover her secrets and yet…"

"I'm barely holding it together, Vice" I confessed. "Please. Just tell me if this can be fixed."

Vice paused. I felt tears run down my cheeks and I was sure there was blood still on my face from the trial. Vice took a step close to me and pulled out a wet handkerchief, frowning at it as if he forgot we had just been almost submerged in the water. My feet and legs were soaking in the flooded room. "I'm here to protect you. We will figure something out!" Vice said hopefully. He gently wiped at my face. Actual concern for me planted roots in his features, but I realized he was definitely hiding his own fear to keep me calm. As I let him wipe my face, I saw the residue of my blood on his palm from when he had fully grabbed on to me right before the spell finished.

Was it my blood that sent him through time with me? Had I been moments from coming here alone? I burst into tears.

I crumbled, Vice catching me and holding me against him for support. He did not let me slip into the water. I wept, crying into his wet leathers and he was silent as he hugged me. I clutched at the furry part of Vice's cloak. The headache I had received from Adder's spell still pounded behind my eye and only intensified by my crying.

Vice continued to hold me, one hand supporting me, rubbing my back while the other worked its way through my hair to cradle my head against him and comfort me.

"I can't do this again, Vice," I cried.

"We'll figure it out, Delilah," Vice assured me in a soft tone.

"I was finally beginning to settle!"

"I know," Vice whispered. He hugged me tighter. Vice gently pulled away from me, but enough to hunch and press his forehead to mine. He spoke gently. "Delilah, breathe with me. The sooner you are calm, the sooner we can figure out our way home. Breathe with me." Vice took a slow breath in, and pet down the back of my hair. "Come on," he encouraged. He breathed out. His breath was sweet.

I followed his instruction, my breath hitching as I tried to stop sobbing.

Vice breathed in again and I did so with him. "Good," Vice coed, and he breathed out.

A few minutes passed as we breathed together. When I finally stopped crying, Vice let go of me, his hand coming out of my hair while the other slid to my hip, waiting for me to confirm I had calmed down enough to continue forward. Vice stood straight and I stepped away from him, his hand leaving my side.

Vice motioned to the open doors the guards came though before we killed them. I was very aware of their corpses still floating next to us in the water. "Let's go," Vice said.

We wandered the castle for hours, stepping quietly to not draw attention. There were seemingly endless passageways existing within this castle, almost like all of the Stills sat atop the catacombs beneath. Thankfully Vice was familiar with it. The goal was to go up, since the entertainment hall was deep underground and flooded from the sea encroaching nearby. A few times we encountered very angry, surprised guards, but eventually we found our way to what appeared to be the dungeon. It was in the dungeon, where sharp angry vines crept from the walls that we heard a someone praying.

"May light lead her safely through the paths of this world and into the next. Trust in Krix, may her soul not be lost."

"Theone?!" I shouted. The voice quieted just as we turned a corner and saw two of our friends, Theone and Cathal, within a rusted cell. Theone sat with their knees on the ground and hands clasped as they prayed, black vines wrapped around them like snakes waiting to squeeze life from a mouse. Cathal stood with his back to us. I could hear him mumbling curse words under his breath. Perhaps he thought we were guards coming to taunt them.

I watched as Cathal pulled a piece of black, cracked vine from his arm, blood splattering down over the cell floor. He cursed louder then turned around slowly, readying himself for whatever torture he expected to receive and looked down at Theone. "Colonel, don't let those things crawl on you," he growled, yanking the vines from Theone's body. Black blood seeped from small entry points the vines had made on their flesh, but Theone seemed unphased by them being pulled out.

Cathal appeared in better shape than Theone. His skin still had some colour to it. His eyes…

His eyes were blood red.

I did not remember his eyes being that colour.

He looked up from Theone, his expression changing to that of surprise when he saw us. A big toothy grin spread over his lips. Black stained his teeth. "You're alive? We saw you disappear from existence," Cathal said.

Theone's eyes remained closed. They continued to pray.

I ran to the cell and grabbed hold of the bars nearly weeping from excitement to see them. "You're here!"

Theone finally looked up from their clasped hands, eyes filling with disbelief. A single black tear escaped from their eye as they gawked at me. I could see black ooze that had leaked from their ears, now dried to their skin. They looked aged, tired. Much worse for ware than Cathal seemed. Starved even.

"Breath of the gods, have we been given another chance? Gods forgive me, I failed you, I failed everyone. My mind and its tricks…"

"No, we're here Theone!" I unhinged the lock on the bars with the head of one of my daggers and swung the cell door open to drop in front of them, clasping Theone's hands in mine. "It's me, Theone," I said softly. "Look at me." Theone's hands were frozen.

"I was there…you and Vice were *gone*," Theone said, still looking at me in disbelief. They searched my face for answers I did not have, the yellow that was once vibrant in Theone's eyes, dulled like wet autumn leaves. A cold hand cupped my cheek, and they looked past me, their attention finding Vice. "Vice!" they gasped.

Vice stayed beyond the bars, his concentration hard on Cathal, his expression now the one of disbelief. Something else on his face expressed disappointment, not in me or our two friends, but in himself. "You're-"

"I know what I am. Why do you think they have me with the Colonel? I keep eating everyone else," Cathal cut off Vice.

Vice whispered, "I should have known."

Theone's face was not aged in a way that suggested we had been gone for many years, but when as I looked over them, I knew time had taken its toll. Their sun-kissed skin was now pale, their eyes void of life. No makeup was on their face and their hair hung long and tangled over their shoulders. Theone did not wear armour and their once honed, muscular form was thin and wasting away. They looked exhausted beyond reason and uncomfortable in their body.

"Are you alright?" I asked my friends.

Another black tear trickled down Theone's cheek, their eyes focused back on me. Their face had grey stains around their eyes and nose, reminders of many tears shed before our arrival. I wiped at their face, as they had to me many times before.

"We've certainly been better," Theone stated. "Dark magic lives in these walls and it eats at me. Being around all this evil taints the spirit and our bodies contain the stain. I believe we are the last," Theone winced trying to stand.

"Is that the black liquid? Dark magic?" I asked.

Theone nodded. "It is hatred, sadness, pain." It had to be agonizing, to have your insides slowly melt into dark magic. I frowned and helped Theone to their feet. This was horrible, seeing them like this. Seeing Cathal leaking from his arm where a tainted vine had been growing inside and his eyes crimson with the lives of many.

"Can you tell us what year it is?" Vice asked.

"Two and one thousand," Theone said weakly, coughing up black ooze and then wiping their mouth on their battered tunic. "Probably." I struggled to keep myself from crying again. I could never have imagined Theone in such a feeble state.

"Two and one thousand?" Vice repeated. "It's been three years."

"What does it matter?" Theone asked, confused.

"Adder's spell displaced us in time. We only arrived here a few hours ago," Vice explained. "If we find Adder, we may be able to return to *our* present."

"You can go back?" Theone asked, a hint of hope in their voice. "Can you stop this?"

"We will do our damn best," I said, glancing over to Vice. I felt a little less lost now, having found our friends.

Theone gripped my hand, drawing my attention back to them. "Delilah, listen," Theone croaked. "Within weeks of your disappearance a dragon attacked Blackwick. I could not ascend to the High Priesthood. The Divines of other Temples were all murdered within the year. A dark army swept through Alhan, a horde of demons unlike anything we have ever seen. They looked like a storm in the sky. Nothing was left in their wake. This world is sick and dying, and the gods have sent you to us once more. When you get back, you must warn everyone! Change the outcome!" The fear on their face choked my heart. *How could all of this happened?*

I could feel a panic attack threatening to build, my heartbeat thumping in my ears. I could not let this happen. There was no time for a panic attack. It could wait when we got back –if we got back…NO! *When*. I had to stay positive, or I would puke, not that I thought there was much left to purge.

"Our only chance to return might be figuring out the spell that Adder used. To start, we need whatever he used as a focus," Vice said.

I looked back to my now wounded hand. In the torch light of the dungeon, I could see the pattern on my hand through the scab.
Fuck.

"I know what he used," I said to Vice. I looked up from my hand. "He has a piece of a Machine."

Vice nodded. "Adder was never a talented mage, he always needed something boost it. Your people's time vessel would make a good anchor for time magic."

"Let's find this bastard!" Theone said. I saw a flicker of their old self crossing Theone's eyes. "There's a torture chamber further up the Keep. Maybe Nerice and Commander Lachlan-"

"Lachlan?!" My voice cracked.

My anxiety choked up my throat again. Existential dread washed over me at in uncomfortable waves. I was lightheaded. Vice put a hand on my back, his touch helped, but I could still feel the pit of my stomach turn. All these emotions were too much. I breathed more deeply, concentrating on one of the cell bars.

"I will keep you safe, Delilah, I promised the Council I would, and I promised you," Vice reassured me. "We will find Mother Nerice and your…" Vice searched my face for answers, and I watched as the realization hit him. "We will find them."

"Krix guide us to this asshole and get you two back!" Cathal
boomed. He cracked his knuckles and neck, the act rejuvenating the
man slightly. When he saw me looking at him, he winked. "We can
get weapons in the torture chamber then pay a visit to the grand
deacon. I heard a guard say Adder barricaded himself inside his
bedroom. I bet he's still there."

"I know where that is!" Vice said. "Up we go!"

Ascending the castle was tiring. Copious amounts of stairs,
guards, and frustration followed us as Vice carefully led us through
corridors. Near the top of one tower, we heard muffled yelling from
behind thick stone walls. Demands mixed with the threats of
suffering.

"Make me!" *Nerice's voice...*

A loud slap sounded beyond the door and Nerice cried out.

Vice leaned close to me and whispered, "One more set of
stairs and we should reach the bridge that leads to Adder's
chambers."

I nodded and continued to listen, inching closer to the door
as Vice handed me the ring of keys he liberated from the guards
earlier in the day. There were dozens of keys on the ring, and I kept
trying one after the other. I glanced at Vice, hoping he'd know which
one was for this door, but he shrugged then shook his head, his
expression apologetic.

"Did your parents never teach you that hitting a defenseless
person is wrong?" *Lachlan.*

"Would you rather I return to you, Commander? There's no
use to this defiance. You have nothing left to protect."

I needed to get to them, free them. I almost dropped the key
ring but caught it and finally found a key that fit the lock.

"You're wasting your breath," Nerice hissed. There was
another slap.

"Hitting someone who's restrained? You'd stand *no* chance if
we were free of these chains."

I opened the door. I suppose the guard inside did not expect anyone to come in who was not under Adder's command, especially if they had a key to the door. I watched as the guard grabbed a jagged-edged dagger from a table full of torture devices. Rusted with blood, he brought the dagger to Nerice's throat. I was scared for my friends. Tears streamed down my face from my anger, my fear. I was unsure of how much more I could take.

"Yield!" The guard hissed as he pressed the blade harder against Nerice, two tiny drops of black blood finding their way out by the edge of the dagger.

"I would die a hundred lifetimes first," Nerice hissed back.

"Let's see if we can have that arranged," the guard purred.

"Hey asshole!" I called. The guard turned in surprise to face me, the grip on the dagger relaxing against Nerice, his hand lowering.

Nerice took her chance. She hauled her unbound her legs up around the guard's neck. The guard cried out, jamming the jagged knife into her shin. Nerice hissed, but twisted her legs more, her sharp toenails scratching against the mans face, drawing blood. I could feel both Cathal and Vice tense and Nerice breathed in sharply, the blood from the guard turning to mist before us. She took in another breath and the guard aged rapidly, his flesh hollowed out, and the blood spilled up and into Nerice's nose like magic. Some colour came back into Nerice's face, but she did not release the body of the man before crushing his skull between her thighs, the bone making a sickly crack. She had done it so quickly I was taken aback by the whole movement.

"Krix's dick, woman," Cathal breathed, both shocked and impressed by her action.

"Delilah?!" Lachlan gasped. His voice was raspy and aching, run sore from screaming. Hope had not dulled within it.

I ran to the guard's empty corpse, snatching keys on his person. I knew they would unlock the chains that suspended Nerice and Lachlan from the ground.

"Hurry up!" Nerice snapped. "He tasted like unwashed ass."

The others filed in after me. Cathal went directly to a chest that, when he opened it, revealed a bunch of weapons. He had been right.

I unlocked the chains around Nerice's wrists. "Are you alright?!" I asked trying to make my voice even, trying not to sob. My heart pounded against my chest, my hands shook with the keys in them, and I fumbled a few times before getting the right key. Thank the gods there were only three keys on this ring. Nerice landed gracefully to the floor from being suspended in the chains.

"Spite fuels me," Nerice said simply as she rubbed her battered wrists, torn and scarred from being in chains. She spit to the ground then moved towards the others.

I rushed to Lachlan, unlocking him from the shackles. I held one of his wrists between my fingers, frowning at the bloodied scars he also had after I freed him.

Lachlan wrapped his arms around me. I had never been squeezed so hard in my life. His head rested upon the top of mine, and I heard him take a deep breath of my hair. "I'm so grateful you're here," he said.

"I can tell," I laughed through my tears.

Lachlan moved so he could look down at me still in his arms, one hand cradling my face. "I thought I would never see you again." His fingers were rough against my skin, but welcomed. I remembered the feel of his lips on my throat, the way he smelled. The things he said…

For me it had only been a couple weeks, for him it had been years.

"It's okay, I'm here," I said smiling up at him.

Lachlan looked beaten and much older than his years, just as Theone did. His thumb wiped at one of my tears that left a long trail behind it. He seemed comforted that I was not leaking black magic like everyone was. Lachlan took another deep breath watching me. "I thought I…" He dipped his head down and his lips were on mine.

I had not realized that I had been walking around asleep until this moment.

His kiss awoke me.

My heart was set aflame, a shockwave running through me

like electricity bringing my body to life. His lips were soft and tasted delicious against mine. I returned his kiss, wrapping my arms around him as his tongue tasted me. He pulled me tighter and briefly all the bad that was happening in the world was gone. His arms were full of me, his hands wandering into my hair, around my waist, holding me like he never wanted to let go. I'm not sure how long we stood there, loosing ourselves in each other, but when he pulled away, his eyes still shut and his forehead to mine, I saw black tears run down his face.

Oh no.

"I thought I would never be able to do that," Lachlan whispered.

All the nausea in my belly had disappeared and my headache was gone.

I suppose everyone understood, for they had all remained silent during our embrace. Nerice had plucked a torture device from the wall and somewhere she had found a bow. I could hear her talking to Cathal in Bygone Speech and Cathal's tone was defensive. Lachlan kept his forehead on mine for a moment more, his hand holding mine, watching me still in disbelief that I stood before him. Nerice put a quiver on her hip and elbowed Cathal who tossed Lachlan a war hammer. He caught it with one hand, the other remaining on my waist. With reluctance Lachlan let go of me.

Everyone seemed now outfitted in some armour and weapons, having found items within the chest by the door. A chest plate over Cathal, a longsword tight in his grip. Theone donned silver bracers on their forearms with a sword in one hand and a large shield in the other. Like soldiers on the battlefield and Adder's guards, the shield was painted with a familiar insignia.

Where had I seen it before?

"Everything that has happened to you, we're going to try to stop it," Vice said, breaking the silence.

"I'm sorry," I said wiping the remaining tears form my face, "but if we can get back, we can warn everyone of what will happen without our intervention."

"This is not your fault," Lachlan said. He kissed my forehead then looked back at the hammer Cathal passed him. He whispered something at it and as soon as the words left his mouth, the hammer ignited in fire. Lachlan smiled triumphantly at it then held his hand out to the weapon in Theone's hand.

"We must get to Adder immediately. There is no telling what will happen the longer we stay," Vice stressed.

"The world has suffered enough," Nerice agreed. "Let's go." Nerice's eyes were dulled, like Lachlan's and Theone's were, but the red in them haunted me. I could see hunger. This was a Nerice I feared. The one who had watched me in the cell when I had first arrived. The cheerful know-it-all who I had come to know, was replaced with a cold, frigid spymaster craving the spill of blood.

Lachlan whispered the same incantation to Theone's sword and handed it back to them in flames. Theone gave it a shake, the flames disappearing, a hint of a smile on their lips with the memory of years past lacing it. Lachlan did the same thing to Cathal's weapon, and we moved on.

Adder 's chambers were one tower over. We travelled through a connecting covered stone bridge, dirty and unkept for years. Several large holes were blown through the stone, large boulders collected on the opposite sides of the wall that cracked threateningly up to the ceiling and into the floor. A large board was hooked over the doors to Adder's room indicating the intent of keeping whoever was in there inside rather than keeping those outside from getting in. The board was the length of a tree and almost as thick. It was impressive that it had been placed there. Cathal walked up to it and tried to lift it. The board barely moved and looked back at the rest of us. "We can do it if we all boost it," he said.

Everyone set down their weapons and wedged themselves under the board. Vice murmured a spell, casting it on the wood. When the board hit the ground, we heard yelling from within and weapons were back at hand.

Adder was inside a huge bedroom chamber, another unnecessary luxury from embezzling the Temple's funds. His presence expressed defeat, not defiance, seemingly waiting for us all this time. "*Seer*," he said sadly as we pushed the doors open.

The air inside smelled vile, and the room was dirty with waste and cobwebs over its once elegant furnishings. Clearly Adder had not left his chambers in a while. I breathed through my mouth, but the stench was strong enough to tasted it. Cathal audibly gagged. A desiccating body lay on a pile of soiled pillows and blankets, but it was not the only source of the stench.

"Was it worth it?" I hissed. My stomach turned from the smell. I concentrated on keeping a steady head. I felt tears welling in my eyes again and I wished I was not a crier when I was mad.

"It means nothing now…" Adder said solemnly. "I knew that I fucked up the spell. Even with trinkets I was never a master of magic…" He glanced at Vice and a hint of distain crossed his expression before misery overtook him again. "I had done everything for my child, for our province. Nothing matters anymore. All I can do is pray that the gods forgive me for what I have done." He looked down with a deep shame in his eyes and tear ran down his cheek, black as night, staining his placid skin.

"Things still matter. We can undo this," I said forcefully. I would not take no for an answer.

I could not let this happen to friends. Looking at them in this state made my heart hurt. They were so deteriorated, so starved. Their bodies were infected with whatever dark magic now plagued this world. I could not imagine the pain they had gone through during my absence and were still in now. From the moment we dropped into the flooded grand hall, I knew I could not live in a world like this. I could not let them suffer

"The past cannot be undone. Salvatore will know you're here…Krix have mercy on us."

Salvatore. Something picked at my mind again.

Vice moved suddenly, vaulting across the room when he realized something. His hand clutched at the pale hand of who I had originally thought was a corpse. Looking now, I saw that it was Asa barely clinging to life. Pale, paper-thin skin and black veins climbing through their body like the sick vines that had been digging into Cathal and Theone's flesh. Their eye sockets were hollowing, and their eyes were glazed over, far away from this place. Asa's hair was thinned, and their skin clung to bones. Vice lifted them to his lap from laying draped over the dirty pillows. Whatever cancer was within Asa had fully sunk its teeth into them.

A forest could do this to someone. I swallowed, the shock of the scene setting into my churning stomach.

Adder reached out wanting to stop Vice from touching his child. "Asa!"

"Breath of the gods, Adder, how could you do this to them?!" Vice cried.

"They were dying, Vice. I saved them. I *tried* to save them...Please, let Asa be. I'll do anything you ask!"

"Where did you get the object you used in your spell? Where is it now?" I demanded. Vice had said we had to move quickly. We needed to do this faster.

Adder's eyes darted between Asa and I but settled again on his child. All the anger that used to live inside him had long disappeared and an Adder I wanted to believe used to exist was now but a shell of who he used to be. "Salvatore," Adder said. "My master gifted it to me from his body. He- Please stop!" Adder begged taking a few steps closer to Asa and Vice.

Vice glared over his shoulder at Adder, tears in his eyes, and snarled through his teeth like...a wolf. "You cannot bend the gods will Adder! Asa made peace with the gods years ago!" Vice looked back at his friend, I could hear his voice catch. "I'm so sorry," he croaked to Asa.

Nerice appeared beside Vice, quiet as a shadow, her eyes moving between him and Asa's body. "Put them out of their misery," Nerice said.

"No!" Adder begged. "Please. They are all I have."

Vice raised a shaking hand and brushed some greasy hair from Asa's face. Asa did not seem to notice.

I looked back at Adder. "Give me the object you used for the spell," I said. I held out my hand to him, took a step closer.

Adder paid me no attention.

"I can't," Vice said softly, looking at Nerice.

A dark glint covered Nerice's eyes, and her jagged nails pressed into Asa's throat, blood seeping where her nails were. "You will no longer know this worlds pain," she ripped open Asa's throat. Blood pooled down their soiled tunic and trousers to the floor. I watched as Nerice licked the blood from her fingertips. She did not suck in whatever life remained in Asa like she did the guard. I gasped, watching as her ruby eyes shined a little more vibrantly. Vice kissed Asa's forehead.

"No…" Adder breathed. "ASA!" Adder collapsed to the floor, wailing. He crawled across the floor to the pool of black blood around Asa's body and Vice. Nerice stepped over the corpse and came to stand next to us as Adder pulled his child's body from Vice and into his arms. He sobbed into Asa's chest. Both men were covered in black blood. Asa had been unrecognizable. Whatever was keeping Asa alive was criminal.

"Nerice…" Theone said softly. "Was that necessary?"

"This world is not necessary!" Nerice said through her teeth.

Vice put his head in his hand, barely holding it together himself. All the effort he had been putting in for me, to pretend to be strong, unphased by being thrown through time, now ruined. Vice slowly rose and held his hand out to Adder. I watched as he attempted to harden his expression again.

"Please, give us the piece, Adder. We can try to fix all this," Vice said. "Asa still lives in my time."

Adder looked up, rage in his eyes, his chest heaving increasingly faster as he stared at us. Something shifted in the air. He gently placed Asa's body back to the sullied floor, standing as he stuck his hand deep within one of the pockets.

Everyone tensed. Lachlan took a stance, and the hammer ignited to a blue flame as Adder began to murmur a spell.

I looked to Vice the same time he glanced to me. "Adder…" he warned.

The grand deacon started to chant the spell more forcefully, his voice echoing throughout the chambers, the thing in his hands beginning to glow.

Fool me once...

I took a deep breath and fell into the shadows. I could hear Adder's voice hitch at my disappearance, but then he raised it higher, more forcefully. Vice held his hand out to the others, trying to keep them still while Adder continued the spell. I glided across to room to where Adder stood and as I let my physical form return, dagger in hand, I pierced his heart. Adder gasped, whatever spell he had been planning to cast stopped in its tracks. My blade was deep within his chest, and I slowly pushed it further until the hilt hit his breastbone. I kept my eyes locked to his, smelt the rot in his teeth and grime on his skin.

I would never claim to understand whatever magic I had cast, but I knew it was the same magic that brought me across the entertainment hall when the guards found us. It was an old magic, and it was *mine*.

I watched the life slowly leave Adder's eyes. The defeat and regret within Adder's expression faded, his voice quivered. His eyes searched for something in mine: *forgiveness?* I swallowed, another tear running down my cheek as I grabbed onto his body and guided it to the floor, next to his child. After I laid him down, I pulled my dagger out, the *sloosh* of the blade not haunting me the way it usually did as I wiped the bloodied metal on Adder's robe.

Vice came beside the corpse, gently prying at his old friend's fingers. When he found what he was looking for he showed it to me. I was gutted. I had been right; it was a piece of Machine. This particular part resembling a petrified keyboard key with a raised letter. Vice looked at me, giving me a full view of it. I nodded, confirming his silent question. Vice looked back to Adder's body. "Oh, Adder..." he sighed.

"He will see reason. We can fix this," I said firmly. I could not have left Earth only to see this one destroyed. We were the good guys. The good guys always won in the end, *right?*

"We can hope," Vice said. He stood back up, wiping his face and his expression returning to its usual one. "Give me some time to work out the spell."

Nerice abruptly finished cleaning the blood off from her hand and charged towards us. "You need *time*?!" she hissed. "Time isn't important! Life is! You must go immediately! Can you not sense it?"

As the words left her lips, we heard an awful, most terrifying noise. The whole castle rumbled with its power. Stone walls vibrated as though the castle itself was shaking with fear. Dust puffed down from the ceiling above us. My eye began to ache, a different kind of ache than what I was used to. Not one that hurt or hummed but *sung*.

"The dragon…" Theone breathed.

"You cannot stay here," Lachlan commanded, looking at me.

Theone composed themselves well, while Cathal looked concerned. They exchanged look with each other then with Nerice behind Lachlan.

"We will hold the outer door for as long as we can," Cathal said.

My chest hurt. "No!"

"Look at us," Nerice said. "Cast your spell and do it fast, Vice. Our world depends on it."

Theone went to one of the barred windows, tarring down the boards there. They leaned out into the darkness and a red glow beamed inside. They looked back at us, nodded, then climbed out. Cathal left the chambers to the bridge between towers.

Nerice raised her bow and drew a few arrows, clutching them in her sharp fingers. "Krix watch over us in this life…" she cooed following Theone's path out the window.

"And the next," Lachlan said as he trailed Cathal through the chamber doors. He gripped the hammer, the flames on it burning hotter. He turned to look at me with a weak smile as Cathal began to close the doors.

"Do not cry, my deepest love," Lachlan told me, his voice carrying across the room as clear as if he stood next to me. "I will find you again. I will always find you. Know I will burn the world for you."

The doors shut, the last glimpse of my friends gone. It hurt watching everyone leave, seeing them hold more suffering inside them than anyone should. My heart hurled itself harder against my chest and my stomach turned further. I found myself praying that this was going to work. I could not stand living in this world knowing my friends were about to die. That this could be the end for me as well. I vomited again, heaving until my body was happy with the spit and air I coughed up.

I stood wiping my lips and spitting the remaining acid from my mouth out next to Vice. He murmured to himself in Bygone Speech, glancing at me briefly, feeling as he focused on my *gifted* eye. I was called to repeat the words Vice said and felt as my eye began to sting. Vice promised he would make it up to me later, "If there was a later," he confirmed between the spell's words. I thought I heard Lachlan chanting the spell through the door. A large clank sounded, the board back in place on the other side.

My attention shot back to the chamber doors, voices in unison now. I wiped the blood leaking from my eye. "This is *mine*," I whispered into the air before picking back up with the spell. I heard Theone scream outside, Cathal's familiar cries of battle in the chamber bridge and the shrieks of demons. My heart ached further. Tears flowed down my face, and I could feel my stomach try to summon bile into existence.

Something was different.

The pain in my skull was not there.

My eye ceased to bleed.

The chamber doors flew open. Lachlan and Cathal were gone. Demons leaking with dark magic charged through the doorway, their stench more powerful than the room. A part of the castle exploded inwards, and a piercing screech echoed around us. I could hear nothing else.

Vice pressed the piece of Machine into my hand, holding it to my palm as he focused on the spell. Red started to glow around our hands. I knew I was distracted with watching the demons close in on us because I went to take a dagger from its scabbard and took a step towards them. Vice pulled me back as he chanted on.

I mourned for my friends, for the lives they had been living without us.

It was the end.

The…pull?

Whatever magic had moved us forward to the future surrounded us again. Time shifted, covering us, and I stumbled forward with the sensation of being shoved. Vice grabbed my hand, catching me from falling forward. We were still in Adder's chambers. The difference was that these chambers were pristine. The bed was turned down ready for the evening, expensive fabrics were stitched into beautiful blankets instead of furs. Torches and incense were lit. From the window the sun set, casting beautiful colours over the sky. I could breathe without the scent of rot entering my nose.

"Follow me!" Vice said, still holding my hand, the piece of Machine between our palms. He pulled me behind him as he bolted through the open door.

We sprinted across the bridge to the opposite tower, racing down the stairs. Vice did not let go of my bleeding hand, ensuring I would not loose him as we ran. He was fast. He knew exactly where to go and as we turned each corner in the castle my heart beat faster, scared we were too late.

"Listen to me, Delilah," he panted as we pushed forward. "Listen carefully."

As we got closer to the grand hall, I saw dozens of Adder's guards sitting defeated on the floor, their hands and feet bound. We passed by the door at the entrance, and it was wide open giving view to the refugees in the courtyard, all huddled together, talking, eating fruit around a large fire.

How long had we been gone? A whole day? A month? Did Vice's spell work?

We raced down the final fleet of stairs and were met by Temple associates standing guard in front of the halls closed doors.

"Words have power, Delilah." His eyes momentarily glanced at my gifted eye, and he slid to a stop several feet from the door, finally releasing my hand, my blood staining his palm. I had to grasp at the keyboard key to keep it from falling to the floor. The Temple monks stepped forward into a defensive stance, fists up. "With enough command, they can be magic. It's how the Bygone Speech became Divine. You want something bad enough, it will happen. The gods will hear you."

"Who are you!" one of the Temple associates hissed.

"*Z moje poti!*" Vice shouted, his hand swiping across the air and the monks flying into the wall following the motion of his hand.

"Holy shit!" I cried.

Vice looked at me and motioned to follow him. "Remember what I said!" he exclaimed.

"Are they okay?!" I screeched.

"Hurry!" Vice urged as he rushed to the door and pushed it open.

We were back in the entertainment hall, in the time it was supposed to be. Chairs were still set up for the trial, but no one sat in them. People were arguing, voices heated. Temple laity and Keepers were inside, mostly at other entrances to the hall, on guard. I spotted Nerice's scouts who surrounding Adder, his hands and feet bound like his guards and his mouth gagged. Theone and Captain Florence had corned some laity, demanding to speak to Caoimhe. Asa was trying to lend a calm voice to whatever argument they were having with the nun. Everyone looked *tired*.

My eyes settled on Adder again who had a satisfied grin on his face despite his mouth full of rope and cloth. Momentarily he glanced at me and then back to the argument then he sat forward in shock, eyes wide. He tried so scramble to his feet, unsuccessfully.

I was *enraged*.

My heart still pounded from running through the castle and my stomach still turned, but all my anxieties were gone. I did not want that awful future for my friends or my world. I never wanted any of my friends to die. Not before their time. Not because of some selfish dickhead. I stormed towards Adder.

The arguing stopped abruptly as my heavy footfalls echoed through the hall. Adder put his bound hands up in defence, shaking. Nerice's scouts parted at my approach, more had arrived since whenever we had left, no doubt a request sent out by Captain Florence.

"Is that the best you've got?!" I growled, grabbing onto Adder's tunic, lugging him up off the floor to bring him to my face. "You fucked around and now you're about to find out!"

Adder dipped his head, cowering behind his hands as I held him. He cried behind the gag, and I ripped it from his mouth. "I'm sorry, what was that?" I shouted.

"You've caught me, you win," he whimpered, defeat in his voice.

"Who's the heretic now?!" I demanded. My voice echoed around the hall, loud as thunder. I heard someone gasp at my tone.

"Mercy! I'm sorry!" Adder cried. He peaked around his hands to Asa, his expression ashamed. "Asa…"

Asa approached us, a thick woolen blanket draped over their shoulders like a shawl. I let go of Adder. He barely caught himself on his hands and knees. Asa knelt beside their father, their tired eyes still full of love for the man who raised them. Relief in their voice for their father's apology Asa said, "It's going to be alright, father."

Adder shook his head and clutched at Asa, leaning into Asa's chest as he began to cry. "I cannot live without you!"

"*Everyone* dies, father."

Adder struggled back up with Asa's help before Asa handed him back to one of Nerice's agents. Adder faced the scout, humiliated. Asa shook their head with a sigh. I could tell they loved their father, but they were also disappointed in the path he had chosen for himself.

"We made it," Vice said, a hand resting on my shoulder to reassuringly. I closed my eyes and took a deep breath, letting it out slowly to find my calm. I felt another tear escape. "We did it, it's okay." He squeezed my shoulder.

"I'm going to puke again," I said, finally feeling safe. When I opened my eyes, I saw blood slowly dripped from Vice's nose. Realizing what I was looking at, he wiped at it then handed me a small vial of what I assumed was concentrated ginger and whatever magic he incorporated with it to help my stomach. It was something he had been making me for my nausea in the Stills. He grabbed another potion from his belt and sipped it. Some colour came back into Vice's face.

"Are you alright, Vice?" I asked.

"It was hard," he replied. "Seeing them like that."

"I'm sorry you had to experience that."

Vice looked at me. "I'm sorry you had to experience all this too."

I looked beyond him to Theone and Captain Florence, who hurried over to us. I drank the potion and felt as my belly finally found stillness. I did not know where Cathal was.

Armoured footsteps echoed through corridor leading to the room. At least twenty Keepers marched into the chamber, two of them the ones Vice had magically thrown into the walls. Most of these monks and nuns wore heavy plate armour over their robes and the murmuring voices in the hall silenced again.

A middle-aged woman in fine violet robes walked into the room with distaste on her face. Her greying hair was full and loose around her face, she wore shoulder plates with chains hanging on them. Each nostril had a stud in it, and she wore a hoop in her septum. At first, I thought she had some sort of turtleneck on underneath her robes and armour, but then I realized her whole neck was tattooed black. I recognized her; she had been sitting next to the grand deacon Adder during the trial. I had not realized how special she was. When she entered the room, I felt a presence of great power.

A Divine.

"Colonel Ward," she stated stopping mere feet from where I stood. "It seems we have a lot of decisions to make."

Asa approached, scurrying across the podium to the woman and when they reached her, they bowed. "High Priestess Caoimhe, might I assist in the explanation-"

Asa was ignored. "I should also mention I am *not* impressed with the little party you seemed to have acquired while I rested. Especially since, correct me if I'm wrong, you are trying to show the Temple's good faith. How are two dozen scouts an act of such?"

Theone's eyes were wide with nervousness, and they slowly approached the Priestess. Theone seemed small beside her. "Your Holiness, if you would give me a listening ear-"

The Priestess clapped once in Theone's face, silencing their words and the murmurs in the hall.

"I had been hopeful," Priestess Caoimhe said. "I wanted to help you because of your mother, may we meet again, but you can see the predicament I'm in."

Asa raised from their bow, clasping their hands, pleading. "Mother Caoimhe, my father has been under control of a great evil. An evil that could be the reason for this entire war. The Colonel was just taking precaution."

"Yes, I've seen the letters, Asa, I was there while my Keepers interviewed you." The Priestess was getting agitated.

"Colonel Ward and their forces have been working hard to find a solution in the Temple's stead. We as a nation have never been closer to the end of this war than we are now, and we have a *Seer* on our side." Asa had a calming voice, and the High Priestess appeared little less rigid when she glanced to them.

Asa took a step back and held their hands out, presenting me as I stood gaping at Caoimhe. One of the nuns who had been in the room rushed up to the High Priestess, whispering loudly to Caoimhe as she nodded, eyes still on me.

"Delilah Golding," she boomed.

I swallowed. "Yes?"

"Do you believe yourself our Seer?" High Priestess Caoimhe presented the room full of silent people to me. "They have decided the truth, but have you?"

I let out another long breath. All eyes were on me, and the room was so quiet a pin could drop, and it would be heard. "Aye,

Most Holy. I am your Seer, and I have brought you news of the future if we do not stop it soon." Something in me recognized something in her and I watched as the High Priestesses expression looked ever so slightly impressed with my words. "Grand Deacon Adder cast a dark spell to try and kill me. All he did was show me a future full of black magic and wickedness allowed only because I was gone. I would love to fill you in, if you'll allow it."

The High Priestess scowled, her gaze going past me to Adder who now stood in the custody of Nerice's scouts. "Black magic? Are you dense?" she asked. She almost seemed entertained.

Adder hung his head again, still crying quietly to himself.

"He serves a master that wants to overthrow the gods. He has been tainted by the Southern Province and damned the Divine's!" Theone cried.

Caoimhe scowled further. "I see," she growled. Her attention returned to me. "Tell me of this future of dark magic and wickedness. Do you know his master's name?"

I nodded, approaching her.

"Salvatore," I stated. "His masters name is Salvatore." I glanced to Adder whose eyes were surprised by my words. I looked back to the Priestess and recalled Theone's haunting words from my memories. They were clear and loud in my mind. "A dragon will attack Blackwick soon. All Divines from the Temples will be assassinated in the months that follow. An army of demons will sweep through our lands like a storm. Nothing will be able to stop them. Nothing will be left. This world will become sick and die unless we intervene."

The High Priestess kept good composure. She waited a few moments to make sure I was finished talking then turned to Asa. "You and everyone else in this vicinity must vacate this castle immediately. It is no longer safe here."

Asa's eyes widened. "Please, Mother, give us three days to coordinate!" Asa cried. "This was my fathers doing not ours! I just need a little time."

"It doesn't matter. The sins of the father will be held by the children." Caoimhe glared at Adder. "You are to be stripped of your title immediately. I hope you are happy with all your decisions leading to this moment. They are your last."

Adder wept louder, his voice echoing throughout the hall. I could hear as his heart shattered. "I'm sorry!" he cried out.

High Priestess Caoimhe rolled her eyes at his continued plea's and waved him off before facing Asa. "I will pray for you. Do not retreat to the forest like the others, gods help them."

"They will come with us," I said, taking another breath; my eyes stung with all the tears I had been crying today. "We will give the mages our trust and they will help us in our cause. We had hoped to acquire them after the trial."

Asa looked at Caoimhe, hopeful. "As long as you approve, Most Holy."

"We would be honoured to have them fight as our allies," I told the High Priestess. Our whole goal was acquiring the mages. The trial had gone in my favour. Everything was turning out so far. "I would also request some of your Keepers. Maybe with them, my village will not burn," I said.

"We cannot afford to be divided any longer. You may take half my laity here today, but that is all I can offer you. We will send an owl if we can offer more later on." Caoimhe looked me up and down. "I will assume this offer goes both ways. If we are in need, your soldiers will come to us."

I put my hand out for her to shake. "Agreed," I said.

The High Priestess shook my hand then waved with her other hands to the monks and nuns who had accompanied her. She glared at Adder, who still whimpered to himself. "Thanks to this man's confession and numerous amounts of evidence we have more than enough information to attempt an infiltration to the Southern Provinces army. Ready to return to the Temple immediately and prep to bar these doors."

Caoimhe, the High Priestess of the Temple Ilona, had all the authority that High Priestess Katerina did, just with a different god. I looked at her she spoke with Theone, holding their hands in hers. She did not look like what I expected a High Priestess to look, dressed in plate armour with a longsword at her side and a nose full of piercings. In my memories, Katerina had dressed so differently, softer. Maybe it was a fashion choice for the war. After all, why else would the highest representative for a goddess of wine, sex, and celebration be donned in so much armour. Katerina had been safe within her Temple, Caoimhe was out in the open on the Stills.

When the conversation was satisfactory between them Caoimhe turned to leave the hall, her and the laity silent, though many of them looked back to watch me and stare directly at my gifted eye.

As the High Priestess reached the doors, Cathal ran through them, out of breath and a parchment in hand. Priestess Caoimhe stepped from his path. An owl followed him in and landed on a sconce on the wall, its flames extinguished by the wind of its wings.

"Excuse me, Mum!" Cathal said as he ran past Caoimhe and through the Keepers. "Theone!" His footsteps were loud in the chamber, and he sprinted up to us.

"What is it?" Theone asked.

Cathal handed the parchment to Theone and looked at Captain Florence. I had not yet seen worry in Cathal's eyes. His *grey* eyes were flooded with panic. "We need to haul ass, Colonel. An army was spotted east of the trail to Blackwick. There's a dragon with them."

Chapter Ten
Day Eighty-Eight.

"How will we get back before the army?" I asked pulling a cloak over my shoulders. The Stills were so wet and cold, I had a hard time deciding which was colder: the mountain or the sea. "They're ahead of us!"

Florence pulled several horses from around the corner of where we were collected with Nerice's scouts. "The horses will help," she said handing the reins to Cathal. Cathal nodded to her, and she ran back towards the castle where the refugees, Keepers, Asa and Adder still lingered, waiting for orders. The High Priestess had handed Adder to us for custody. She said if he survived whatever was about to happen, he could live out the rest of his days in a dungeon, under control of the very person he tried to condemn. Florence and the Keepers would take him to Blackwick. We were going ahead of them.

"We also aren't taking the main trail," Cathal commented. "It will be faster that way."

Theone mounted one of the horses and rubbed its neck. "I don't like this," they commented. Theone continued to coo at the horse until the animal whinnied at them. They tugged the reins from Cathal's grasp and steered it towards the entrance of the town.

Vice fastened his staff to the saddle of another horse, who seemed a little spooked by him. He kept trying to shush her, but she continued to fuss until he gave up on trying. He made a face.

"It's the fastest route," Cathal said.

"What's the fastest route?" I asked. "I don't understand."

Everything had been a rush. A rush to gather the mage refugees, a rush to pack up Asa. Captain Florence and Nerice's scouts had hurried from the castle to the inn where they had kept their horses. The castle was already boarded up and hundreds of people were waiting outside for direction. Captain Florence and the scouts would lead the mages, Priestess Mirna, and a handful of Keepers to Blackwick, if Blackwick would still be there upon arrival. In the future we had witnessed, we had a few weeks before the attack. This felt ahead of schedule. The four of us would push to get there before everyone else, taking a shortcut. I wondered why we had not taken it on our missions before.

My three companions looked at me with serious expressions.

Cathal handed the reins to Vice's horse to him even though Vice had not yet mounted the animal. Cathal then waved me over to him. In a swift movement, he lifted me up onto the third horse, the largest of the three beasts. He mounted behind me and then started to direct the animal to leave town, following behind Theone. "Through the trees," he said. "The fastest route is through the trees."

Vice finally got on his horse, but she fussed again, almost knocking him off. Theone trotted their horse next to his and their hand stroked through the horse's mane. The animal calmed, though it made a unsatisfied nickering sound as Vice tried to guide her.

The horses made their way out of town. Rain and hail pelted us from dark, angry storm clouds and froze quickly to the chilled ground. Buildings still lay in waste from crashed Machines. Snow had not fallen recently in the Stills, but the snow that covered the streets was hard as ice and unbothered from the storm. Notices were nailed on doors from Keepers, telling those inside that nearby Tabernacles would offer them shelter if they needed it. The townsfolk resources would be limited since their local Tabernacle had been destroyed, at least until the spring.

I often wondered about what was in the forests. I heard the screams at night. I remembered the glowing eyes my first day here in the mountains and they haunted my dreams some nights. I remember wanting to be one with the forest floor.

"Okay, but *what* is in the trees. Why are they unsafe?" I finally asked.

Vice pulled his horse next to the one Cathal and I were riding. "It's better to pretend they're not there," he said quietly, as if talking too loudly would mean the nearby forest would hear.

Icy wind blew around us, whistling sharply and carrying lost voices on it. We were more bundled up than normal, feeling a blizzard would be accompanying us on our journey. I stared into the trees, full of shadows, as Theone pulled their horse up to the other side of us. We passed through the front gate. It was late morning. I still had not slept since my nap before the trial.

"We must go," Theone said, staring into the woods with me.

The original road we had travelled on out way here twisted beside the forest. Mist hovered over the path and the trees looked dark despite it being daytime. I remembered how rigid Theone had been with me the first day, guiding me down the mountain. How carefully they picked the route. They had been scared then and were now.

Cathal smiled at Theone. "Race you," he said, snapping the reins. The horse took off and I clutched to the horse's mane, Cathal's huge arms around me. The moment we entered the forest the atmosphere changed, and Cathal's voice sounded husky in my ear. "Look ahead only. Do not look up."

Unlike the main roads and trails we had travelled prior, the forest consisted of narrow game trails and thick brush between trees so massive they seemed to touch the heavens. The snow was thick, but the horses were unperturbed as they sped through the woods, the snow crunching sharply beneath their hooves as thin layers of ice shattered. No one spoke as we raced against the sun. The horses did not fuss, not for a long time.

Hours passed.

The sun began to set.

I jerked awake when we slowed to a trot. We moved through a tight trail with large animal prints littering the snow ahead of us. I could not name what creatures they belonged to and everyone else paid them no mind. We were ascending a mountain, the trees and brush thinning out. The rain had turned into snow, but large pieces of hail still hammered down, clinking against the metal of our armour.

A scream in the distance echoed over the hills. One of the horses whinnied uncomfortably. Theone cooed at it. Cathal's voice was in my ear again, his chest pressing up against my back. "Go back to sleep, we're fine," he said. His tone was *almost* convincing. "I'll wake you when we get home."

"How long before we reach Blackwick?" I asked.

"Morning, if we're lucky."

*

The sun had not yet risen over the mountains when Blackwick was in our sights. Arrows still alight with fire stood jutting out of the snow beyond the protective barrier of the troops camp. A night guard came jogging out to meet us with a partner, each holding a torch and a weapon

"Colonel! Major Vale!" The night guard said. He walked with us towards the stables outside of Blackwick's massive fence. "*Seer*," he breathed, catching my eyes, focusing on my gift. "It is good to see your return."

"Notify the Council of our return," Theone instructed.

"Aye, Colonel," the night guard said, running towards the village. His partner stayed by our sides until we were within the belled perimeter of the troops camp. Cathal slid off then held his arms out for me. I turned on the horse and he plucked me from its back as easily as a grape from the vine. The snow crunched underneath me. The blizzard had calmed at some point in the journey, but it had been hard to tell in the darkness.

"Do you need me to walk you up?" Cathal asked.

"I'll walk her," Theone said. Cathal nodded to them then steered into the camp.

Vice walked with us into the village, veering off towards the bunkhouse. He had handed me a vial before leaving, its colour ugly. "To help you sleep," he said. The bags underneath everyone's eyes were heavy and dark. I feared how bad I looked surviving off naps alone.

When we entered the Tabernacle, Theone marched straight

234

towards the Council Chambers. I stood in the front hall, exhausted and relieved to be back. The Tabernacle was still quiet, but I knew the laity would wake soon. The cooks were probably already awake, readying breakfast.

I heard a door close behind me and when I glanced over my shoulder, I saw Lachlan locking the door to the small room I had woken up in weeks ago. He looked tired and was fully dressed in his usual furs, leathers, and plate armour. Excitement filled my belly.

He was here, he was healthy, he was *alive*.

"Lachlan," I said.

He turned, hearing either my voice or the sound of my footsteps hurrying back towards him. A big smile spread across his face, and he held his arms out just in time for me to launch into them. I hugged him, hard, and wrapped my arms around his shoulders to embrace him fully.

Everything is alright, it never happened, I told myself as I hung onto him, not wanting to ever let go.

"You're back!" Lachlan said happily. He lifted me up off the ground, giving me a squeezing hug. I clutched onto his leathers and buried my face in his neck, taking in the smell of him: coffee and cedar.

"I'm back," I said. I felt like I could cry. I had not given the others the details of what Vice and I had experienced. I barely had any time to process it. I could not imagine what Vice was going through and wondered if he was already asleep in his bed, surrounded by his books and tinctures, cuddled up to that cat.

Lachlan slowly leaned forward so I was not hanging off of him. He gave me another cuddle, all the pain I had felt before slowly being lifted by his touch. He rubbed and patted my back, pressing his lips against my neck again and again, kissing my throat with yearning. I remembered our kiss in the future. I remembered his words before I left for the trial. *Know that hearing your voice is like cranberry wine and I draw life from hearing it.* It was hard to ignore the future I had been in. It was even harder not to beg him to unlock his chamber doors and pretend everything else did not exist.

"I missed you," Lachlan said into my throat before pulling away from me.

"I missed you too," I said.

His eyes lingered on my lips before looking down the hall to the Council Room doors. "Perhaps we can catch up after the debrief?" he suggested, his voice pained. He did not want to go. He too wanted to go back to his chamber.

"I'd rather catch up now," I blurted out. I blushed immediately. I really needed to sleep; I would be unable to sensor myself otherwise.

Lachlan pushed a hand through his hair, the other gripping me a little more tightly. "As would I," Lachlan practically growled. "But we would not be given privacy unless we debriefed first." He kissed my cheek, and my skin was set aflame again, his hand slipping into mine. He motioned to the Council Room door and we both regretfully walked towards it.

Discussions were held with heaviness and the time spent within the Council Room was long.

"The Keepers of Temple Ilona will be sending birds out to warn the other Temples of the insight we received form Delilah, if they have not already. However, we cannot rely on them to do all the paperwork, nor assume that those birds won't be intercepted," Theone stated. They yawned then poured themselves some water from a pitcher filled with dried oranges. "We should also send owls out informing Temple's of the assassination attempts. The massacre at Temple Samu can be linked to this. It is all connected. We should have known it was only a matter of time."

"Already on it," Nerice said. Nerice was fully dressed, as was Bellamy. I wondered if they were already awake before our arrival.

Bellamy was busy writing things over parchment, leaning over the table with a flustered expression on her face. She was clad in more armour than I was used it, her expensive, gold-leafed leathers tied over chainmail and a helmet sat next to her ink pot. Her hair was tied in a thick braid around her skull and was decorated with gold chains as I was accustomed. I refused to imagine her fate in the future. I had to pull my mind from those thoughts. Lingering on them would get me nowhere, but it was hard not to look at my friends and see the people they had become.

"This is important. Making sure the Temple's are safe means less refugees of war," Bellamy noted. She quickly rolled the piece of parchment she been writing on. Lachlan moved a glowing hand over it, drying the ink instantly. "We cannot let more people retreat into the trees, not like the others…"

There was a moment in the night that itched the back of my mind. We never stopped riding the horses, but the pace was slowed with the sun gone. Screams in the darkness kept rousing me and Cathal kept shushing me because I would gasp, frightened. We moved in single file, our silhouettes barely depictable against the already dark night. The snow barely gave any light with the thick cloud cover.

When we had made it back to the only road leading to Blackwick, winding carefully up the mountain, something large moved through the thick brush beside us. Cathal pressed against me, his breath was steady and deep, but his body stiff and on edge. He rested his chin on my shoulder and whispered, "Close your eyes."

A branch crunched loudly and horse behind us, Vice's, cried, frightened.

"Move!" Theone commanded.

The pace picked up, the horses flew through the path like the wind.

"Keep your eyes closed!" Cathal instructed just as I was about to peak.

The mountain air was sharp against my face. I was hungry and felt my heart beating as a more inhuman cries called out from around us. I could have sworn I heard my name amongst the screams.

When we had reached the edge of town, where the soldiers bell perimeter sat and the torches were wedged into the snow every few feet, a couple night guards hailed our approach. Theone had yelled something at them, and I opened my eyes just in time to see flaming arrows whistle past me and into the dark, very early morning.

Cathal had been impressed we made it.

"Unfortunately many believe the forests are safer than anywhere else. Taking in the mage refugees is our chance to prove to them wrong," Lachlan urged.

Bellamy handed the rolled parchment off to scout who quickly ran from the room.

Theone yawned again then dumped their glass of water over their hair. Their makeup smudged slightly but their expression remained determined as always. "We need to plan for that dragon," they said.

"How do we defend against a dragon?" I asked. I sat leaning on the large table. My eyes flickered over a large map of the known world. I spotted where Blackwick was, so isolated from many other towns and cities. I held my head up with my hands, still exhausted from the trip.

Lachlan let out a huff. He shifted uncomfortably. "There is little we can do." Lachlan looked at me and I recognized the look in his eyes from when I had watched a version of him look back to me through large doors before his death. The admiration. The fear of not seeing me again until the After. Again, I brushed the image from my mind. That world did not exist yet. It never would.

"We should plan for evacuation, not a fight," Lachlan said.

"There is nowhere to go," Theone said. "Not this far in the mountains. Not in the winter. All the village knows is to flee here."

Everyone was quiet for a moment. A hand on my back startled me and my eyes shot open. I had not realized I was falling asleep against my hands. It was Nerice.

"We have written down what you prophesized," Nerice said. "Do you have any more information? Perhaps dates?"

"Afraid not," I yawned.

Nerice sighed.

"Maybe if you meditate with Priestess Mirna when she arrives, she could help connect you more with the spirits," suggested Bellamy.

"I could actually just use a good night's rest," I said. I glanced over at Lachlan. His bed *was* closer to the council room than mine.

"We must organize our troops and prepare for the new refugees, but I'm sure we can do that while you sleep," Bellamy said.

I returned to my chambers. Lachlan accompanied me, his face lighting up every time he caught me glancing up at him on our walk through the Tabernacle halls.

A fire was lit in the hearth of my room and the smell of spiced tea and bread warmed it. How I missed that bed. I went inside then leaned against my desk, fearing I would fall asleep the second I hit my bed, and watched as Lachlan looked around the space.

"You made this place cozy," he commented.

I looked at my embroidered curtains, my stacks of books and tarot cards on barrels and shelves, my green sweater hanging on a sanded antler acting as a hook. "I'm glad you think so, I tried to make it home."

Lachlan nodded approvingly then returned his attention to me, walking over to lean on my desk beside me. "I umm…stayed here before you. It was my room for a long time, but I never needed this much space. After seeing your memories, I wanted nothing more than for you to have it."

I felt his hand move onto mine.

A temptation fluttered into my mind, the possibility of sharing a space with him, seeing him every morning and every night, getting to know him more intimately. "There's enough space for two here," I said.

Lachlan made a low groan and angled himself to face me, his hand giving mine a little squeeze. "We are…I…" Lachlan groaned again this time seemingly frustrated with himself.

I looked at him. Seeing him next to me, nothing else seemed

to exist. The life before this one was fading quickly.

I missed Earth. It bothered me that I could not call my friends and invite them over for cake and video games and movies. It bothered me that I could not have a weekly video call with my cousin so we could catch up. It bothered me that I could not shower as often as I liked. It bothered me that I was now *very* behind on many different television shows and missed the release of a video game I had been looking forward to for years.

I had grown comfortable here. I liked helping in the kitchens, making pastries and bread, chatting with the laity. I liked that I had become a trained warrior. I liked that I knew magic. I loved how magical everything was. I loved how this world was untainted by pollution. I loved my new friends. I loved…

Lachlan leaned in close to me, his hand moving from mine to hold my cheek. "We are in a middle of a war. I feel emotions I didn't believe I could allow myself to experience during such trials and tribulations, but I wanted to and here you are testing me while I try to lead these people." His eyes focused on my lips, and I felt a shiver run through me as excitement brewed again. Lachlan leaned closer, enough that I could taste his breath, smell the coffee on it and the cedar on his skin. He lowered his voice to a whisper, frightened someone else might be listening to us. "I am afraid for the first time in a long time, not for my own life, but for yours. I do not think I could stand to lose you. If I stayed here, in your room, I don't believe I would let you sleep."

"Would that be so bad?" I asked quietly.

His lips were on mine, his hand moving from my cheek and around the back of my head to twist into my hair. I moaned, riling Lachlan up, making him kiss me as though he was starved. He moved from the desk, effortlessly lifting me up to the tabletop so he could move between my thighs and press closer. I wrapped my arms around his neck, my mind swimming, drunk off the taste of him. My insides warmed with the longing to have more. I felt a hand move up to one of the straps where a pauldron was attached and then his hesitation. Lachlan pulled away from me and I whimpered trying to hold onto him, craving more. He put a finger to my lips, and I opened my eyes to see him smiling the most delicious smile I had ever seen.

Lachlan traced my lips with his finger, and I nipped at it, making him chuckle. "Let me consider your offer. It is…something I want, Delilah, it is." He swallowed. "But I need to make sure I can both protect these people and give you the time I want to." He kissed my forehead then leaned back onto the table, letting out a slow breath. He took my hand into his again. "If events were different…If we had met before I became Commander…" He looked frustrated and slowly I saw exhaustion come onto his face. He leaned close to my ear, his lips brushing against my skin. "I will worship you like no other, that is a promise," he murmured before kissing my neck.

I moaned again, clutching at the back of his head to try to keep him there but he gently pulled away and kissed my hair before stepping from the desk and heading to the door.

"I won't keep you from resting." He smiled a truly seductive grin. "For now." Lachlan turned to leave, but I scurried over, pulling him back to steal another kiss. He obliged me, the door thudding back closed as I grabbed hold of him. His hands were full of me for a few more blissful moments before he pulled away, laughing at my enthusiasm. His lips hovered close to mine, brushing teasingly around the skin. "Quit tempting me, you might win." As I melted from his words, Lachlan saw his chance for escape. He kissed my cheek quickly and opened the door. "Enjoy some sleep, Delilah."

*

It was early morning the next day, the sun casting beautiful colours over the horizon. Vice's potion had done wonders, especially with a chaser of spiced tea. I planned to go make lemon squares in the kitchens with the laity cooks then bring some to my friends. I also hoped they would act as an excuse to tempt Lachlan back to my chambers. The rest would be a special treat for the refugees who we

241

expected any hour, also taking the trail we had.

The laity in the kitchens were excited by my return, even more so when I told them what I wanted to make. They got busy with the usual. Bread was kneaded and baked, bacon fried, porridge was stirred with winter berries and cinnamon and dried orange zest. The kitchen was hot, coffee was boiling. I had slept well and felt content back within the kitchen. The laity and I took turns singing something while we worked. I was grateful that Nerice had not come to find me to pick up my usual schedule, the coming army more important.

A few hours passed when something close to existential dread washed over me. Theone had found me, bringing a cup of mulled wine Bellamy had made, when the Tabernacle bells rang out throughout the village. They echoed loudly over the mountains, silencing the kitchen as we worked. The morning and evening bells were always soft. With these ones I could not hear myself thinking, they were so loud. Theone dropped their cup of mulled wine mere seconds after handing me mine, horror in their eyes.

I did not need anyone to tell me that the bells were a warning.

"Wait here," Theone instructed before rushing out of the kitchens. I swallowed and breathed slowly, trying to calm myself from the building nervousness inside me. I took a slow sip of the mulled wine. I could taste chocolate, and it seemed Bellamy had had fun mixing her hot chocolate with mulled wine.

The bells kept going for several minutes causing me to not enjoy my drink the way I wanted to. When they stopped the laity cooks went back to work, kneading bread for later, cutting vegetables, murmuring quietly amongst themselves instead of singing jolly tunes. The air had changed from one of delight to one of concern, the same feeling that had hung here in the months, and probably years, before I appeared.

I pulled the lemon squares out of the stone oven, one of the other cooks had the floor icebox opened for me and looked expectantly at them as I lowered them down. I had been so excited to eat and share the squares, a whisper of summer in this never-ending winter. Already three other batches sat in the icebox.

As I rearranged the icebox to make sure the squares sat flat next to other food, there was a scream from down the hall leading to the kitchens. Swords and shields clashed. The familiar unsettling *swoosh* of a blade running through leather and skin was too loud. Younger laity skittered to the far end of the kitchen and an older man, who had been a warrior in his youth rallied for help in push a workbench up against the kitchen door. The bulky man who often washed dishes and I ran to assist. We pushed the bench firmly against the door just as someone rammed into it, trying to get in. Everyone grabbed a weapon of some sort. A knife, a rolling pin.

The older cook pulled a dagger from under his apron. "Fuck," he said under his breath.

Everything was back in my chamber; my armour, my weapons. I ran to an iron rack hanging from the ceiling and grabbed an iron skillet. One of the younger girls squeaked my name and when I looked at her, she slid her butcher's knife across the floor to me from cowering in the corner with a couple other laity.

All the cooks knew I trained with the troops, all of them knew about the power I held; my eye was a dead give away. I could feel my heartbeat in my ears, and I swallowed again, willing the tears threatening to prick my eyes away. I would not let these people know I was scared.

"The bench wont hold," the older cook said, gripping his dagger tighter.

"I know," I said.

There was only one way out of this kitchen.

We were trapped.

The door continued to shake and splinter as whoever was on the other side slammed against it, trying to break through. I stepped beside the door, with my back against the wall. I lifted the iron skillet high, gripping the knife with the dull end of the blade against my wrist. I nodded to the other two near the door, while the rest tried to hide behind counters and in the pantry. I swallowed and the door burst open the work bench nearly flying clean across the kitchen. I swung the skillet with my whole weight and hit the soldier coming through with full force. He fell on his ass then three more came storming in after him. The big dishwasher jumped one soldier and the older cook hooked another soldier with his shoulder, tackling him to the dirt floor. I stabbed the butcher's knife into the back of the neck of a third soldier who was distracted by his comrades being attacked. He dropped.

A huge crash sounded, glasses shattering and wood cracking. The dishwasher had been thrown into the pickled vegetable shelf and a big gaping hole had replaced it. The laity man groaned and the soldier he had been fighting turned around, staring me down. I heard as the older cook was hit with a killing blow and one of the laity members behind a counter yelped, trying to hold back a scream.

The soldier sneered at me and I held the skillet up again like a small shield. He spat on the ground then charged. I only had street clothes and an apron on. The dishwasher was struggling to get back up after being thrown through a shelf and I held my now bloodied knife up by my face, above the skillet. The soldier tried to strike and I knocked his sword away with the skillet. I sliced my knife forward narrowly missing the soldiers face as he dodged out of the way. I ducked and dodged him until I crouched and smashed the skillet against the soldier's knees. He screamed out in pain and collapsed as I popped back up to hit him over the face. The soldiers helmet flew off and black blood splattered out from his mouth. I pounced him, smashing the skillet into his face again and again until he stilled, dead. With only two soldiers remaining, the one I had originally knocked back and the one who killed the old cook, the rest of the kitchen fell upon them. The dishwasher finally got up. He was sliced and bruised but was able to stand. He grabbed the boiling coffee pot and dumped the contents over one soldier and while the others swarmed the last soldier like angry bees.

"There's a tunnel back here," the dishwasher coughed. While bloodied and boiled corpses laying strewn across the dirt floors, the other laity peered through the gaping hole in the wall. It was dark and cold, centuries of dust gently moving in a soft breeze.

A soft breeze.

An exit.

"I need one of you to out these bodies in the cook fire. The rest of you go down there! I bet it's an escape route!" I commanded, my chest heaving. I gazed over the bodies of the fallen soldiers and my eyes caught the emblem on soldier's chest plates as the laity scattered. I recognized it as the same insignia that was stitched or carved into the armour of the soldiers in the Stills, and the ones in the dark future. Even the guards Adder had all bore the same symbol.

No.

Logo.

"Holy shit," I whispered.

I watched a torch being hurriedly carried down the long tunnel. The dishwasher was dumping cooking grease on the bodies of the soldiers before hauling them into the massive hearth. No other soldiers seemed to be in the corridors that led to the kitchen, but a trail of bodies, both soldiers and laity, littered the cold floors.

I had to *move*.

I took off, knowing I would need my armour and weapons if I were to stand any chance in the coming onslaught. Laity were running around panicked in the halls through pools of blood. I smelt smoke, heard screaming outside.

I tore through the lower corridors of the Tabernacle before flying up the stairs. As I turned a corner I plowed into Theone, and we bounced off each other. Theone grabbed me, panic in their eyes.

"Thank the gods, you're safe! We must get to the gates for orders!" Theone exclaimed, already turning in the bloodied hallway to head outside. Their armour, which they always wore except when they slept, was splattered with fresh blood; both red and black. Their sword was dripping with carnage and their golden eyes were sharp, reminiscent of the day I first met them. "I shouldn't have left you behind, I am sorry!" they cried.

"No, don't apologize, I was fine. What's happening?" We began running together through the Tabernacle, in the direction of my chambers.

"The dragon!" Theone said. "Dozens of soldiers dropped off it and wreaked havoc as it lit the village on fire. It flew off but we're sure it's coming back with more soldiers."

The village had no time to prepare for the attack. We had thought we had more time, but the future was not set in stone, and by coming back through time we must have accelerated the dragon attack. Blackwick had been safe here for decades and now the war had found it.

"Have the refugees made it here yet?" I asked.

Theone closed their eyes and whispered, "I don't know, Andreja guide them." Their hand gripped their sword tighter, and I realized they did not have their shield. Their eyes shot back open. "Get dressed. I'll meet you at the gate."

Tears welled in my eyes. "Andreja," I whispered. "If you're real, please...*Please* keep my friends safe."

I was never sure what I had believed in on Earth. I just existed. Yet now, I wondered. I wondered how this world was affecting me. There was something slowly blooming in my spirit. Something that felt like faith. Faith in my friends, faith in myself.

"I'll be right behind you," I said to Theone as they took off down the hall.

I rushed to my chambers, heart pumping, and scrambled to put on what I could. I was acutely aware that I did not have enough time don all my armour, not if I wanted to help. I fastened some lighter pieces on my body over my commoner clothes after pulling my bloodied apron off and fumbled with the straps before I ripped open my storage chest to grab my daggers.

Durin appeared in my open doorway. "What a fucking season," he growled jogging in. I heard him fiddle with the mechanism he had been working on for his wrist. I gazed at the beautiful daggers Gwen had made for me and fastened them to their places on my hips.

"Is Theone already gone to the gate?" he asked.

I nodded, making sure everything I had put on was secure.

"How did you miss them?"

"I came through the side entrance, by the trebuchet," Durin said. "Shorty, look!"

I had not noticed when I had run into the room, too distracted by wanting to get my weapons and some armour on. There, sitting on my bed next to my sweater and pajama top, was a helmet. I walked over to my bed. At the brow, was a small flying dragon chasing an owl up the forehead. I picked it up to examined it further. It was lightweight, but the metal seemed strong. Underneath the helmet was a note.

To match your tattoo. Gwen.

Another gift.

Durin took the note and tucked it into one of my pockets as I held the helmet in my hands. "You know, I saw Gwen pestering the quartermaster for a while. Didn't realize it was for you," Durin said, impressed. "Dragons are supposedly creatures of Andreja. It's why they were hunted for so long -because if you could conquer a dragon, perhaps you could conquer the gods. I heard rumors they were her children, but Lachlan never confirmed that he saw his grandpa with wings." He glared up at the roof, as if looking past it to sky above it. "Vice was right. Something is wrong with this one."

I felt my eyes well further, and I rubbed my nose. I could wait to cry. Gwen had always believed I could be the best. I had to remember to thank her when this was over. I'm sure she would be disappointed that she was unable to witness my face upon first seeing her gift. I had not had the chance to say hi since my return. She had made me a surprise.

I put the helmet on. It fit perfectly.

Durin and I met Theone and Vice at the gate. Theone was getting a report from Lachlan, nodding attentively. Vice wore armour on his arms and a chest plate. Even during our journey to the Stills, I had never seen him wear this much armour.

This was *bad.*

"There is a colossal force coming over the mountain. We

cannot see it yet, but it's only a matter of hours according to the scout report," Lachlan said.

Bellamy and Nerice were there too. Bellamy looked terrified, wearing a thick fur cloak over her armour, her breath puffing quickly in the cool morning air. She wore it often when she was on night watch, but somehow, she looked smaller in it this morning. I saw the shine of a dagger at her hip, a quiver full of arrows on her back and a bow in her hand. She had confessed to me once, when we were chatting after a meditation and stretch session, that she had not actively trained since coming to Blackwick. She enjoyed playing diplomat. Blackwick was away from the Northeastern Province and Bellamy had hoped not to see the war here; not to fight. Despite her talent as a Rider and warrior, she was like me and did not enjoy having to kill to stay alive.

"Do we know what banner?" Bellamy asked, her tone obviously frightened. "Southern?"

"We don't recognize it," Lachlan said. He too wore more armour than I was used to. An actual weapon was on his person. I could not believe it was possible for him to have more things covering his body.

"You're *unsure*?" Bellamy breathed, the nervousness in her voice threatening to worsen. She pulled her cloak tighter around her body. The Northeastern Province was hot. Mountains in the winter were not Bellamy's element.

"I know the banner," I confessed. "It's from Earth."

Everyone's eyes landed on me, all their minds quickly catching up to whatever implications my information gave them. That seemed to be enough, for now. There were more pressing matters before us.

Cathal came jogging down a side path, his axes stained in black blood. It was the same path Lachlan and I had strolled once. Cathal put one axe into a loop on his belt and held his hand out to Bellamy when he reached her. "I'm getting you back to the Tabernacle, Bells. Your mother will gut me if you get hurt in this," he said. Bellamy shakily took his hand. Cathal looked at Lachlan.

"Commander."

Lachlan nodded to Cathal to leave but then there was a pounding at the gate and several scouts went to arms. Bellamy squeaked and moved behind Cathal, a hand reached behind her to grab an arrow. Nerice cocked a brow at her Second. Most of the troops had been within the village when the bells went off, getting their breakfasts. There was only a couple dozen outside of it, still on the job. "Open the damn gate!" a nervous, voice begged from beyond it.

"Asa!" Vice exclaimed.

Lachlan motioned to a couple soldiers. They opened it only enough for someone to squeeze past, but Vice pushed through it. I chased after him and Lachlan followed behind me. Several corpses were strewn by the gate baring the logo of those who invaded. One still stood with his back to us. Enchanted daggers had skewered him in place and slid out of his back while we watched. When he dropped, Asa was revealed behind him. The daggers disappeared into the air from Asa's hands, and they panted, looking up from the body to us. Relief washed through me. The refugees had made it to Blackwick.

Asa hunched over heaving as they tried to catch their breath. Vice rushed to their side and held their arm. I spotted mages cowering by the treeline. A couple of Nerice's scouts were already setting bodies on fire. Florence came jogging from the treeline, their arm bandaged and bloodied as she waved to us.

"My…father…" Asa coughed wiping their mouth, blood staining the leather of their glove. "He escaped." Asa slowly straightened, chest still heaving. They looked like they were in a lot of pain, but I could not see any physical wounds on them.

Florence came beside us and waved at the trees. Keepers emerged from the treeline, motioning for the mages to move towards the village. "The night was chaos, Mum," she said. Nerice had appeared, her arms crossed and eyes attentive as Vice ushered Asa through the gate. "That bastard blasted us while we were on the road and disappeared. Those *things* came out of the trees. We lost half the refugees. We would have lost more if not for the Keepers, thank the gods," she said.

I glanced over my shoulder as Florence continued to debrief Nerice and Lachlan. Vice was talking to a soldier at the gate and caught Asa right before they collapsed into the bloodied snow.

"I have you, it's alright," Vice cooed.

Asa looked up at him with thanks in their eyes and leaned on Vice for support. Lachlan whistled at the gate and pointed to Asa. "Get them to the Tabernacle," Lachlan instructed when two of his troops pushed the gate open further to look at their commander.

Vice carefully, and almost regretfully, handed Asa over to the troops.

"Seer!" Asa said as loud as they could. They coughed again before spitting a thick wad of spit and blood out to the earth. Asa's voice was strained when they said, "*Cifarelli Salvatore.* That can't be a man, can it?" One troop picked Asa up into their arms while the other trailed behind them.

I paled.

I did not know how this was possible.

"Its magic is deeply tainted!" Asa's voice called from beyond the gate. "It consumes his followers! They couldn't have resisted it if they wanted to!"

"Commander!" a soldier screamed.

We all turned.

The dragon.

The beast landed far in the hills, its roar loud and terrible. My eye sung at its presence. I stared at it. Though it was kilometres away, it stuck out against the snowy mountains, and I could almost feel what it was feeling. Its rage. Its *pain.*

Something else hummed inside me. Something that felt familiar, but I could not quite place it in the chaos.

"Time to go!" Cathal said. He knelt, pulling Bellamy over one shoulder, and charged to the fence line.

"Everybody to the Tabernacle! Save who you can!" Lachlan commanded. "Blackwick is not a fortress! Retreat now!"

The refugees started running towards the gate, many already

wounded, fear covering their faces. Caoimhe's Keepers accompanied the refugees, making sure they were through the gate before them.

Lachlan drew his sword and nodded to me before turning to the troops who backed us, all hurriedly dressed into their war armour, just as I, and armed as best they could. "Only engage if you absolutely must!"

Troops scattered. I swallowed and drew my daggers.

It seemed like hundreds had made it ahead of the main force, all air-dropped from each pass of the dragon in the skies. I was astonished Florence and the others had dodged the entire force safely, despite being attacked by what prowled the forests. Every other word out of Theone's mouth was a curse, expressing absolute rage against yet another betrayal by Adder. Theone burned with fury, and no one stood a chance before them. They fought harder than I remembered they could, and it was a long time into combat that I realized I was fueled as they were.

Bodies fell by our blades, my mind unscathed by the death.

That snake had been trying to get me arrested for months and he had known what was going on the entire time. He reported back to Salvatore. He had faked remorse. If the former deacon had been successful in my arrest, I would have never made it back to Blackwick. Instead, I would have been handed over to his master and dead. The future I saw would be set in motion.

The *audacity*.

As Asa had said, the army we fought against was infected with tainted magic. That much was clear. The taint did not weaken the opposing force as it had with my companions in the alternate future. Instead of leaking from the corners of their eyes like tears or from their nose, the blackness inside them consumed their eyes, their veins dark rivers against their skin. They were blind to what was right and wrong. I had not fought opponents like this when we travelled through the Stills. I would have remembered their *eyes*.

Though there were few buildings outside the wall, we still

checked them while other recruits attempted to hold a line on the path leading to the village. Abruptly the marching ceased, but then chanting echoed over the hills. We could see the huge line of soldiers coming through the mountain as the army waited for their next command. Only a moment passed, a single heartbeat, when we heard it.

Theone waved at us in a hushing movement, hissing at nearby troops as they slaughtered soldiers near them. "Quiet! What are they chanting?!" Their expression was concentrating, eyes squinted, listening intently to the words echoing through the mountains.

Vice paled. "It's a summoning spell! We need to go to the Tabernacle *now*!" he exclaimed.

A vicious sound, the one I remembered from when Vice and I were sent forward in time, echoed through the mountains and everyone was silenced in fear. An enormous shadow swept across the bloodied footpaths of the village. The rising sun was hidden by the darkness. A ball of fire collided with one of the buildings near us, shattering flaming debris outward. Not enough people were able to get away from the building in time, and those who could, excluding myself and my three companions, ran.

"We cannot face that here! Go!" Theone commanded, breaking the silence. Their voice expressed the fear I knew we all felt. We had to take cover. We stood no chance against a dragon.

As we ran through the trashed village filled with corpses of both our own and Salvatore's troops, I could feel my anxiety building again. There had to be some way this would not completely end in chaos and death. I needed to save these people...*my* people. There had to be a way to turn this around.

I was rushing past the tavern when I heard the innkeeper curse. We were almost to the ledge that overlooked Blackwick, the steep staircases leading up to the Tabernacle in sight, when I slid to a halt. I sheathed my daggers.

"My husband!" he cried as he kicked a large crate that blocked his door, debris from the building next to it piling on top of it. The innkeeper was old. I could see he had been through a duel before we got there, fresh cuts on his arms and torso to prove it. I diverted to help him.

"Seer!" he said with relief. "My husband wasn't in the Tabernacle, he has to be here!"

The crate looked too heavy to lift on my own, or even with the innkeepers help. It was huge, practically the size of myself. My companions had kept running when I had spotted the innkeeper and I did not want to leave him, or his husband, behind. "Clear the top and help me push it!" I instructed.

The innkeeper and I moved left of it, trying to force the crate out of the way, but it barely budged and the smoke from the fire in the building next to us was thick, choking us out. I almost called for Theone, they could not have gotten far, when two blades came crashing down onto the crate, crushing it.

The innkeeper kicked the contents and shattered boards of the crate out of the way of the tavern's door. Once open enough, he squished through. I heard a voice behind it that was not his, happy to see him.

"Thank you!" the innkeeper called from inside. "Thank the gods!" I waited outside the door until the innkeeper pulled his husband from the building who wept with relief that his partner had come back for him. The husband was younger, clutching a small, framed painting in his hands while he and the innkeeper ran past me.

I nearly knocked Gwen over as I threw my arms around her after.

"Delilah, we can save this for later," she said urgently, though I could hear her smile breaking through her words, I wished I could see it, but her helmet protected her face just as mine did. "I heard you needed some assistance, but I see you are doing well on your own." Her tone was teasing.

"We need to help anyone left! Help me check the buildings for stragglers, okay?"

Gwen nodded to my orders and put a hand on my shoulder, reassurance flowing through me, the building anxiety silenced. Gwen clicked the pommel of her dagger to the edge of my helmet. "Of course! Nice helmet you got there," she said, a smile very clear in her voice.

"How are you so calm!" I laughed nervously.

"Someone's got to be. Trust me, you will be alright," she said. She began to hum, her voice beautiful in the sounds of collapsing buildings and crackling fire. She disappeared into the smoke.

I wondered if Gwen's confidence was warranted or if was she faking her demeaner to make me feel better. I stared at the shattered crate. The innkeeper and I could barely move it, but she had crushed it easily.

What a woman.

I let out a hard breath and pushed forward.

The fires were spreading through the village quickly and I sensed the return of the dragon. Something else hummed along with it, familiar like I could feel it under my fingertips. Another blood-chilling screech echoed through the mountains and the great beast swooped overhead, casting the village in darkness. My ears rung from the sound of its roar and my bones felt the chill of winter and death in the air. It pained me, hearing the dragons anguish.

The looming possibility of not making it out alive hung heavy. I felt hyper-aware of where the dragon was, how it felt. Its will was not its own, just like many of the soldiers.

Everyone must have felt so lost. Their haven was breached. Their homes were on fire and falling to pieces. A great army was coming to kill them. I shook the feeling off, I had to focus and help. There still had to be a way.

The dragon had set many buildings on fire, some of Salvatore's troops had broken through the wall and began to reap what was left of the village. I looking for Gwen and worry panged my thoughts every time I did not see her. I knew she was helping people but the longer I went without seeing her, the more unease I felt. Few troops lingered in the streets, knocking on doors, opening them and yelling for villagers to leave if they had not already. I had seen several a few times as they zigzagged through the cobblestone streets to help villagers, but not yet *her*.

Nuns, the refugees, and many others were inside the Tabernacle by the time we made it there. Lachlan stood at the doors, waving people inside. Villagers ran in for safety deep within the halls, past the wooden exterior and into the carved out stone tunnels of the mountain where fires kept them warm. Nuns and mages helped the wounded.

Just as I made it inside, making sure no one else was in eyesight of the Tabernacle doors, only the sounds of the dragon and crackling fire outside, I watched Priestess Mirna collapse. She had come in with Florence and the refugees to oversee High Priestess Caoimhe's Keepers. I had been happy to see her, that she made it, until she dropped. Vice caught her and two of the Temple Sisters gasped, running to her side. She was wounded. I could only guess she must have been caught in crossfire somewhere between the forest and the battle. Adrenaline had kept her going.

Vice helped her to a chair. "One of the tainted found her. The blade was sharp in both of them..."

"Aye," Priestess Mirna said, a soft smile on her lips, entertained by Vice's recount. "Tell everyone how violent I can be." Part of her chasuble was askew, revealing the trousers underneath that were usually covered by her black robes. Strapped to her thigh was a large dagger. I looked at Priestess Mirna's hands, the gloves covered with dark blood. I remembered that Nerice was also a priestess, and I remembered how violent she had been in the future. Priestess Mirna had won whatever fight she had been in, but just barely.

I frowned. Mirna was a sweet woman, I did not want her to die, but the blood staining her robes widened with each passing second. My stomach stung and when I pressed my hand to my side, blood stained my palm. I looked down seeing blood wetting the wool between my armour and skin. *When had I gotten hit?* "Shit," I hissed.

One of the nuns aiding Priestess Mirna took a strip of fabric off her own robe to applied pressure to the Priestesses side. The blood seemed to be quelled, and Priestess Mirna signed in relief. I saw many villagers on the floor, leaning against the Tabernacle walls and pillars, all exhausted and wounded. The dread inside me attempted to grow. People wept and cried for help from the gods.

I had to do something.

I knew I could do something.

"Seer!"

I turned.

Lachlan jogged towards me, relief on his face seeing I had made it until he noticed me trying to hide my wound. "*Delilah!*" He came close to me, ripping his gloves from his hands as he tried to check my wound, but I flinched away.

"I'm fine!" I said.

"Let me make it nothing!" Lachlan begged.

Vice eyed me from beside the Priestess, he was helping the nuns tend to the Priestess, but I could not see what they were doing. Their bodies blocked my view with their fussing. I did not see my other friends. I winced and moved my hand.

Lachlan discarded his gloves to the floor and dropped to his knees. I saw the burn scars on his hand, and the blood in his hair. In the shadows of the hall, he hovered a glowing hand over my side. A few moments passed before he pulled his hand back. "It could be worse, thank Krix," he breathed. He pressed his hand to the wound, and I felt my skin pull itself together as it stretched and itched to heal. I hissed, squirming under his touch. "I'm sorry, I'm sorry," Lachlan whispered, looking up at me with shiny eyes. When he finished, he grabbed his gloves back from the floor and put them back on. He stood, pulling me into his arms.

"This isn't looking good," Lachlan said softly. "We're likely to die." He squeezed me tighter.

"Salvatore's army doesn't care about us. He wants the Seer," Asa croaked. I pulled away from Lachlan only enough to find where Asa was. When I spotted them, their eyes stared at me almost apologetically as they pushed themselves up on their elbows from laying down. They had been resting against some pillows I recognized from one of the prayer rooms. Several other wounded folks were resting on some too.

Vice had handed the Sisters a potion vial for Priestess Mirna when he heard Asa speak. He spoke softly in the Bygone Speech to the Sisters then hurried over to Asa. "You need to rest," he urged to them.

"Why does he want me?" I asked.

What the fuck, what the fuck, what the fuck.

Asa gently lay back down with Vice's assistance. "I don't know, sweetheart," Asa frowned. "I'm so close to the After now. I can hear them *speak*." I could feel Asa's eyes on me still.

"You are the only one untouched by the forest," Vice observed. He had sadness in his voice. His eyes were concerned for his young friend as he wiped swear from Asa's face. I remembered how he held Asa's husk in the future, the agony he experienced with me. I could only hope he was not remembering them in that state now.

Asa smiled at their friend. Their nose was bleeding, but they did not seem to notice or care. "The trees cannot take what they already have." Asa's voice was *so* quiet, and they looked back at me. "I believe in you, Seer. I believe you can stop this and be the leader this world needs."

Vice stroked Asa's matted hair from their face before cleaning their nose with his sleeve. He looked at me with a pained expression. He knew something I did not.

"Seer —*Delilah*," Lachlan's voice pulled me back from the tunnel I was slipping into. "I have no plan to make this survivable." He looked helpless, and for the first time since I came here, he looked *young*. "We could have tried to turn the only trebuchet to the mountain, but it was damaged by that damned-"

"We're already overrun, and you want to bury us?!" Theone cried. Theone, along with Cathal and Durin, jogged towards us. Theone's eyes looked wet, everything within them wanting to cry but they desperately held it back. I could not imagine how they felt.

Theone had lost their mother, their Temple, and now their village was about to be destroyed.

"Our people are already dying, Theone," Lachlan said, his voice pained at the thought of burying the village his great grandfather built with a goddess. He put his hand briefly on Theone's shoulder, though Lachlan still stood close to me. I felt his breath on my exposed skin, warm against the cool air within the Tabernacle. My hand moved to pull off my helmet, but in the quiet something stopped me.

Vice, still by Asa's side, was watching Priestess Mirna as she struggled to stay conscious in the arms of her Sister's. His expression softened as he gently passed a hand over Asa face, sticky with sweat.

Mirna looked at Vice, then at me. "Where is your spymaster? My fellow Sister…" Priestess Mirna coughed again and one of the other Sisters wiped the spittle from the corners of her lips with tender care. She looked drained, like so many others.

"Nerice!" Theone boomed. Nerice appeared from around a corner, several of her scouts on her tail, papers falling from their arms as they fumbled to sort them and pack them away from her office within the Tabernacle.

"Colonel Theone," Nerice said with a force smiled, her eyes wide, almost irritated, before her eyes found Priestess Mirna on the floor with the other nuns. Her smile fell and she sprinted over to her, kneeling.

Priestess Mirna took Nerice's hands into her own, her voice was strained as she spoke. "The kitchen, there is an old passage. Not many know it's there. You can evacuate through it, and it will lead to the other side of the mountain. It has probably been unused for at least a decade…" The Priestess squeezed Nerice's hand. "You just need time."

"There's a back entrance through the Tabernacle?" Lachlan asked.

Priestess Mirna smiled and her eyes closed as she slowly nodded. "For emergencies. The Mother would have known." She fell limp. I prayed she was only unconscious.

Nerice moved the Priestess's wrist, her sharp fingers pressed against it for a moment before relief washed over her expression. "Who hasn't been down there?!" she snapped, looking at her scouts. "Find that door!" The scouts bolted and softly Nerice said "Hand her to me," to the Sister who held the Priestess in her arms. Carefully they exchanged Mirna's unconscious body.

"A shelf covered it!" I interrupted. "It broke open when soldiers…" I looked back to Lachlan. I knew now what I had to do. They had to make out of here, they needed time. "I will buy you time."

Nerice stood, holding Priestess Mirna in her arms effortlessly while the other nuns scrambled to their feet. She started her way to the back end of the Tabernacle, stepping over villagers who groaned on the floor. There was barely any room to walk. "Bellamy!" she shouted. "Get everyone downstairs!" I heard Bellamy respond somewhere in Bygone Speech, but I could not spot her in the sea of people.

Lachlan seemed to know what I was intending. "You aren't going alone," he stated.

I had never really thought about death. I assumed I would never die this young. Admittingly, I also never thought I would die protecting people from an evil army in a magical, medieval realm.

"I won't let anyone else get hurt," I replied.

My heart tore in two seeing the hope in Lachlan's eyes fade; how much he wanted me to make it through this, the underlying grief that he too did not want me to die. I slipped my hand in his, knowing he would feel me shaking. He squeezed it before bringing it to his lips to kiss my fingers. His eyes connected with mine through my helmet trying to convey how much more he wanted; and how much he wanted me to live. I reluctantly let go and turned away to head back out of the Tabernacle, knowing if I kissed him, I would not leave. Behind me I heard Lachlan barking orders and people moving, getting up or helping others from the floor to evacuate. I was not entirely paying attention to his words.

"Everyone! Follow Mother Nerice to the kitchens. We're

getting out of here."

I put my hand on the smaller door beside of the main entrance to the Tabernacle ready to leave. There was a simple set of locks there rather than a large board to barricade the large main door. A recruit stood beside me, unlocking all the bolts.

"Delilah…" Lachlan's voice reached me, and I peered back to him.

"I pray you all make it out, Commander," I threw my voice loudly so he could hear. I went to turn to leave, but I saw Lachlan heading in my direction, checking the straps on his armour, pulling his sword from its scabbard.

"We will buy them as much time as we can," Lachlan said.

"We?" I questioned.

"Yes, we're coming with you," Theone said sternly. Vice and Durin stood next to them, nodding in agreement. I saw some bandages wrapped over one of Durin's knees and Theone had a bruise darkening on their face.

"No, I can't ask you to do this. You're not risking your lives for me!" I exclaimed. "Not again, not like this. These people need you."

"We would not have it any other way, Shorty," Durin said, he smiled encouragingly, the same smile I recognized when he would recite tales of Lachlan to me. "Besides, Cathal is probably halfway through the mountain already. Have you seen him run? He is like the wind."

"These people have Nerice, Bellamy and Cathal," Lachlan assured me. "They will take care of the village. They're some of the best we have."

I could feel tears in my eyes again. I felt strong with my friends by my side, but it was not their time. "No," I said again. I swallowed, my body shivering with fear. My life was not worth theirs. "As your Seer, you will go with Blackwick to safety and I will protect *you*, for once."

Durin's smile dropped, and the air actively shifted as the dynamic between us changed. Theone nodded at the instruction. I knew a Seer was the highest point of authority in the church, and I had accepted it before them at the trial and again here. Theone exchanged looks with the others, they spoke Bygone Speech in a hushed tone before saying. "You heard her. Let's help the wounded move," Theone instructed.

I stared at them suddenly skeptical of their compliance, but I brushed it off.

Vice gripped his staff firmly before leaning in close to me as Theone and Durin returned to the help people up, passing them off to able-bodied individuals. "Remember what I said in the Stills, Delilah," he said before joining them. *You want something bad enough, it will happen. The gods will hear you.* I heard his words clear in my mind. I remembered the power he wielded before me there. The Bygone Speech he spoke. I opened the door.

Blackwick was consumed by flame, the fire so hot it burned blue. The snow had melted and given way to the streets below. The smoke from the flames rose so high it blocked out a good portion of the sky. The dragon had set fire to everything, not one building untouched by its scorn. I could still feel it, its torment. Dark magic-tainted soldiers laced the paths that many once walked without fear. The corpses of villagers I had known, and our enemies scattered the ground laying in pools of their blood boiling and sticky from the fires.

I drifted in and out of the shadows, keeping twisted, angry soldiers away from the Tabernacle doors. Something sliced into my back, and I hissed, disappearing into the shadows again so I would not have to pull out whatever had embedded itself there. It hurt. I appeared again behind the tainted soldier and with one clean slice of my dagger, I removed his head.

The main army had to be close if not already here. I moved with ease and without fear. Nothing churned in my stomach, promising to leave me sick. No headache pounded within my skull. My tears were dry. Somehow, knowing I was protecting people I loved was enough to keep my personal demons at bay.

I had to give everyone time.

I was a time traveller.

I could do that *one* thing.

Any other day I would have been overwhelmed, but I refused to be now. Hours had passed since the beginning of the invasion. The fires were hot, and for the first time in months I was sweating. Bodies were piling up at my feet, buildings continued to crumble.

The dragon screamed in the sky above me, returning to finish what it started. It turned towards the overlook of the Tabernacle, gliding closer and closer. Its throat swelled, readying to its final strike. It flew in close, buzzing with familiarity, and let loose its flame. I tried to avoid it. An explosion next to me sent my body hurtling. I was winded and something was broken inside me, but I got my barring's back quickly, pushing myself up from the bloodied earth. I coughed, trying to find my breath again.

You want something bad enough, it will happen. The gods will hear you.

My ears rung from being thrown. The ground shook underneath me as the dragon landed, growling so deep I felt the vibrations in my bones. I prayed everyone had made it to safety as I now faced smoke and darkness and unholiness. In the thick smoke puffing up from the village below, two shadows slipped from the dragons back.

I watched a twisted figure walk through the black smoke towards me, unphased by the chokehold the smoke was starting to have on my own lungs. The familiar sensation picked at the back of my mind again and I rubbed at my eyes, focusing on who strolled beside it.

A man.

Adder.

The jagged form looked thrown together. Pieces of grey flesh were stretched thin as paper over its body. Large slices of polished metal pierced out of its flesh, forming thick spikes along its legs, its arms. Sharp fins stuck out of its shoulders and back. Its hands resembled that of the long, hellish claws the demons had at Machine crash sites. A monster had forced its way out of a man, if it had ever been a man to begin with.

Adder moved with a smug gait beside it.

How I wanted to wipe that look from his face.

I sheathed my daggers knowing I could not use them, not against *this*.

"This is your end," boomed the creature.

"Not yet, it's not!" *Lachlan's voice.*

My eyes shot around, trying to locate him. The whistle of arrows shot through the smoke. The former deacon yelled out in pain and the creature beside him disappeared into the shadows. *This* was how it had escaped the explosion. One of Durin's arrows was embedded in one of Adder's triceps. He clutched at it, cursing a colourful array of words. He had barely any time to react before Theone tackled him to the bloodied earth.

Vice ran to the two of them, saying something I did not catch.

"You okay, Shorty? Durin asked. I looked beside me and Durin reached down, lugging me up, my hand in his before I realized I put it there.

"What are you doing?!" I demanded. "I said to go without me!"

Durin smirked. "We'll take it up with the gods when we meet them. Let's get this thing."

A shrill scream echoed and rumbled around us.

The dragon.

Lachlan ran towards us, his sword aflame, and slid to a stop beside Durin, his eyes on the dragon.

Theone pulled Adder, now bound by the wrists, to a stand and Vice tried to take him from them, "I will detain him, go!" he said. Theone reluctantly released the former deacon to Vice and drew their sword, it too igniting as their eyes landed on the dragon.

Adder laughed, almost manically, through the blood spilling from his teeth and nose. Theone had to have tackled him hard for him to already be so wounded. "You will never win, Seer! You can't command a dragon like *He* can-" Vice punched the former deacon directly across his face and Adder went limp in his arms. Vice rolled his eyes.

"You believe *you* are chosen? That *you* can control these people?" a disembodied voice he growled. I clenched my fists. I remembered the creatures skin stretched over sheets of metal, *familiar* metal. The back of my head tickled again.

No.

"I'm not scared of you, asshole," I growled. "Show yourself!"

The creature reformed next to the dragon, his skin so colourless, so thin, I could see each vein in extreme detail. His expression changed in the smallest degree from before, like he recognized something in me. "Do you think you can intimidate me?" the creature growled. "You stopped my demons, but you will not stop *me*! You will revere me. I am *Cifarelli Salvatore*, and you will kneel before me!"

I looked closer at the metal sticking from the creature's form. Like the pieces of Machine scattered at the Stills shores and amongst the mountains, this creature wore them as a part of him. I looked at the mountains around us. I could feel the heat coming from the dragon and burning village. I heard the marching of the army's approach. There was so much snow waiting to become a mass grave. Maybe even the creature with its stolen technology.

"You will resist. They always do," the creature snarled as I ignored him.

The dragon, rageful and cursed, roared in response. Black sloped from its eyes, crying out the blight it contained. Its chest heaved, struggling to breathe. Despite its anger, fear was in its eyes, its spirit. I remembered when Vice had said something was wrong with it, when Durin agreed. I could see it now. I fully understood. The taint, the dark magic.

How did Salvatore control it?

"Give me that *Eye*," Salvatore snarled.

Flaming arrows hailed down over Salvatore from Durin and again he disappeared into the air once more.

The dragon roared, our ears stinging. We turned our attention back to the beast and charged it, but I was wrenched back. I involuntarily screamed out as I was thrown to the ground. Salvatore stood over me, glaring down at me with the same expression I had seen on Adder's face many times before.

"Delilah!" Lachlan shouted.

"Focus on the dragon! I got this!" I shouted back.

Salvatore stretched out his hand, a determined expression on him as he whispered a spell. A headache threatened behind my gifted eye, and I felt the warm sensation of blood trailing from its corners.

"Centuries of preparation and suddenly you think you can stop me?" Salvatore growled. His clawed fingers hovered to my face as he said his spell again, frustration evident in his features. I fought against his will. My eye felt like it was on fire, but I made no sound to indicate the pain. I refused to let this abomination think he would win this. I heard my friends fight the dragon behind Salvatore, their swords connecting with its flesh, felt the heat of the dragon's fire.

"Your gift will be mine!" More pain shot through me and the creatures hand began to glow red, his black nails looking sharper.

I swallowed, grabbing a dagger from my side. "It's mine!" I yelled. My eye instantly stopped hurting. When it did, I shoved the dagger through Salvatores outstretched claws. I popped up from the ground, renewed with energy. Salvatore screeched and I ripped my dagger through his palm, driving it straight into his eye. The dragon roared as Salvatore did. My attention went to the dragon. Blood seeped from its his front claw and its eye, matching the wounds I had given Salvatore.

"Centuries of my work! Undone because of a *girl*!" The creature roared. Black blood seeped from his eye socket, leaving trails over his clawed hand as he stared down at me. "Centuries of effort lost!"

I looked at him and steadied my voice. "Priestess Katerina did not die for this chaos!" I hissed. "She died so your reign would end!"

This close to him I could see the dark magic twisting beneath his skin, wanting to pull him apart. His monstrous body was scarred from battles long past. He smelt like he was rotting from inside, corrupted, just like the demons. The metal sticking out of his flesh was worn from years of weathering. One piece caught my eye, blinking at me.

A red light.

My eyes widened.

Salvatore threw his hand down, his eyeball discarded on the ground next to him and his skull gushing with blood. He stared me down. "I once saw the Other. I wanted the old gods to explain *everything* to me after years of suffering in this decaying vessel. I wanted them to grant me something if I had journeyed there, a mortal in the world where the gods could walk. I deserved that much! All I found was their empty thrones and promises. I spent years watching my body rot for nothing..." The creature sneered, seemingly far away for just a moment. "I was confused; cursed. But now I stand before you, having gathered the will to correct this damaged universe. Pray that I succeed."

"Your mother is disappointed she raised someone who turned out like you," I hissed.

Salvatore roared, disappearing into the air once more. This time I could not feel his presence, I could not feel the Machine on him. I was almost relieved until I remembered the dragon.

My friends screamed, and I went to them. I could see hundreds, thousands of troops marching into the village below. We were running out of time. It would be mere minutes before they made it up the steep stairs to the Tabernacle overlook.

"Get away from it!" I screamed. Vice and the former deacon were gone, but Durin, Theone and Lachlan still fought against the beast, shields and armour blackened by fire, swords dripping with the black blood that infected it. "Now!" I screamed shooting my hand out towards the dragon.

A portal opened, reminiscent of the ruptures I created for weeks to send demons back to the Other. This one was *big*. Wind stirred around us like a storm. The smoke from the village snuffed out. Clouds had covered the skies, a blizzard ready to burst from them.

My friends scrambled away from the dragon, and it tried to claw at them from where it stood before realizing what was behind it. I could sense the gate into another world, one I had opened. The portal spun inward like whirlpool trying to suck in everything around it. Wind grew stronger, throwing debris around and pulling at the giant beast. Theone thrust their sword into the frozen ground and reached their hand out grabbing hold of Durin's arm as the portal tried to drag them in with the dragon. Lachlan's hand glowed with magic and he grabbed hold of the broken trebuchet, his eyes looking at me with fear. I was not close to anything to hold on to.

The dragon cried out struggling against the pull of the portal. It wanted to stay on this plane. It screamed feeling its imminent death calling to it from the other side. It thrashed with fear, uncontrolled now, sick and confused. I could not let it stay here. Not when Salvatore was still *somewhere*.

A mechanism unfastened from underneath Durin's sleeve, and several bolts unleashed controlled explosions by the dragon's feet.

The dragon's eyes zeroed on me.

A final strike.

I was too close.

The beast bit down on my leg as I tried to move away from it and my body was pulled from under me. With my concentration broken I could feel the portal starting to close before its purpose was served. I screamed out, the wind slowing, the pull of the portal less aggressive. Lachlan reached out with his free hand, a struggled groan escaping his throat whole he tried to hold the portal open with me.

I shrieked. All I could hear was my own voice echoing through the village.

"Delilah!" Theone shouted.

A sword went into the dragon's other eye.

The dragons grip loosened on my leg. At least, I thought it did. The beast backed up in attempt to get away from Theone's blade, though it remained in its socket.

By retreating, it got too close to the portal.

It was sucked into a void, its will to fight forgotten.

The portal snapped shut around the dragon's neck. A final gust blew out around us. The only thing left of the beast was the bloodied severed head in snow and dirt and ash. Blood dripped from its eye where Theone had left their sword. The base of its skull dripped black sludge and crimson onto the earth.

I was loud.

The sound of my scream was all I could hear.

I wailed. I had believed the pain my eye caused me was bad. This was worse. I dared a glance to my leg, only to see that below my thigh was completely gone. The tissue was shredded like cheese. Blood poured out onto the dirt from what was left of my leg.

"Holy fuck!" I screamed.

Lachlan dropped beside me. He fumbled through his pockets searching for a potion, panicked. I heard the voices of the others, but I could not focus on anything besides the pain and the gore left behind in the dragon's wake.

Seeing the state of my leg, I screamed harder until Theone embraced me from behind, pulling me up onto their lap while they tried to soothe me, their body rocking mine back and forth. Theone's arms clutched my body, their hand stroked through my hair, my helmet having been taken off at some point in the chaos and I could hear their voice trying to calm me through my screaming. They were trying to sing.

"We gotta get out of here, Blondie!" Durin's voice was thick with caution while trying to keep himself level-headed.

I heard several more explosions. I was lifted into the air and my vision started to drift in and out. I screamed again, tears rushing down my face. I felt weaker by the second. The whole right side of my body pounded in agony. I felt cold.

Doors slammed, barred.

Vice was suddenly there, holding a bottle to my lips. "Drink, Delilah, you need to drink this." I screamed more, and Vice's voice became tense. "It will slow the bleeding!" he snapped.

I looked up, the familiar carved stone of the Tabernacle was above me, beautiful images painted on the ceiling. Manoach was depicted flying in the heavens, his wings that like a bat.

I was being carried and we were running.

"You need to cauterize it!" I blubbered out. I don't know how I managed to spit out the words. I had to live. I could not go down this way. Not after everything else I had lost. I still had to defeat Salvatore and a world to bring to peace for my friends.

"We need to what?" Theone asked as calmly as they could.

"Use your sword and press it to her leg to stop the bleeding! Do it now!" Vice hissed. I heard more words from the others. Another door slammed open, it was daylight again, the air bit at my skin. There was a huge smokestack in the sky. I continued to howl.

Vice pressed a potion bottle to my lips again. "Delilah! Please!" I drank the potion and coughed some of it up. The pain that flowed through me made me want to vomit. I almost did as the liquid trickled down my throat. We slid to a stop, and I was set gently to the ground. Someone's arms were around me. My leg still throbbed. I saw Theone in front of me, their eyes wide. Their sword ignited into flame.

Who held me?

"I'm sorry," Theone said, pain in their voice.

Shadows blurred in front of me against the brightness of Theone's flaming sword. I could hear my heartbeat, my breathing slowed. My head flopped towards the mountains, and I saw Durin shutting an old iron door connected to a red rockface. I looked to the higher peaks beyond it, covered with decades of snow and I reached out to them with the same will as I did when I opened portals.

That army would never leave these mountains.

"*Snežni plaz,*" I said into the wind. The deep snow began to fall from the stone, rushing towards the village and us.

"Gods hurry up!" Durin shouted as the ground began to shake. The mountains snapped, echoing for miles as more snow released from the peaks and raced towards us. The expanse of snow cracked again and again as more slid down the slopes. Blackwick and the army would be buried underneath it.

The potion Vice gave me began to kick in, sending waves of calm through my body. I could still feel the bite and the pit of my stomach turned at the carnage that lay where my leg once was. Theone pressed their flaming sword against my severed thigh, and it happened quickly, the new pain. The hot sear against a part of me that was never meant to be touched, and pain was brought anew. I screamed, the last thing I heard was my own voice echoing through the mountains, louder than the crashing of the approaching avalanche. Then there was silence and darkness.

I was dreaming. I always knew when I was because it usually peaceful, save the demon nightmares I occasionally got.

This dream was different from what I was used to.

I still felt safe. I stood on the deck of a grand ship. The smell of the saltwater seas strong in the air and the sun hot and high in the sky. The air was warm and blew heavily, pushing the ship swiftly through the water. I looked around seeing members of the crew, *my* crew, smiling as they worked, laughing, and talking to each other. I knew them, though I did not yet know their face, or maybe I *did*. My feelings were conflicting.

As my eyes lay on each different face a name would come into my mind.

I knew them!

They were not only my crew, but my friends. I continued to scan the deck, and saw Cathal steering the ship, his hair bleached brighter from years of being at sea in the sun and skin tanned as dark as Bellamy's. He noticed me looking at him and smiled a small, close-lipped smile before returning his attention to the seas ahead.

"Captain."

I turned, a smile on my face because I knew the voice and it was a victory to hear it say my title. My mind drifted before I saw who addressed me.

Time passed.

Chapter Eleven
I Don't Know What Day It Is

How much time had come and gone, I was unsure. Again, I was lost to the exhaustion, to the trauma, to the recovery. I drifted from one brief moment of consciousness to the next. The first I remembered was my boot being removed. I lay heavily on someone's lap, too weak to move, furs wrapped around me to keep me from the sharp winter air. Someone's warm skin pressed to my own, our heartbeats feeling as one. I heard Lachlan's voice crying closely and felt my hand being clutched as if letting go of it would mean I would die.

"Please stay…Oh gods, I want you, I need you. Oh, please. *Prababika prosim.*"

He sounded so *sad.* Lips pressed against the top of my head, and I drifted away.

The second moment was a little longer. I saw the tops of coniferous trees pass above me, the occasional snap of a branch in the distance and whispers to ignore the sounds. I felt a heavier presence of something old amongst the spirits of the familiar. The sun was rising.

I was *so* tired.

I was *changed.*

"Hello?" I croaked out. My voice was pitched and almost lost to the pain in my throat. A hand squeezed my mine. Figures surrounded me.

"Delilah! Thank the gods!" *Lachlan.*

I smiled as I fought to keep my eyes open, just to see try to focus on who was around me. Lachlan stroked my cheek with his bare, warm fingers and I passed out again.

Somewhere in the darkness I could hear my name being called. It was not my friends who said it, but rather thousands of different voices. They called out from shadows, yearning for me to follow them and fall deeper. Rapid memories scraped at the edge of my mind. Screams from the forest, my name murmured on horseback, bell parameters being tested, glowing eyes just beyond the gate of the refugee camp down the mountain.

When I finally awoke, I did so with a gasp.

I could hear arguing and tired whispers carried on the wind. The warm glow of sporadic campfires brought light to the dark night. We had made camp.

Theone jumped up from a crate by the foot of the cot I lay on and rushed to my side when they heard me. "You're awake!" they shrieked.

I leaned against my elbows, propping myself up. For a moment, I had almost forgotten what happened.

"The gods have truly blessed us…"

I startled, turning towards the soft voice of whoever had been beside me. Priestess Mirna, alive and well from whatever wound she had suffered back in Blackwick. I was relieved to see her sitting on the ground beside me, a fur on her lap for warmth. "As soon as your breathing became stronger, the Commander went to rest, but it appears he is awake now. You, however, should continue to sleep."

"How long have we been here?" I asked groggily, looking around to gather my bearings. I sat up completely, my body aching as all my muscles tensed. It felt like the first day after training with Gwen. I felt weak and could feel sleep pressing itself back into my mind. I must have been out for hours.

I gazed across the dark camp that had been set up. We had settled in a clearing, though it was not anywhere I knew. Massive trees and brush surrounded the makeshift camp. Bells attached to strings put us on display for the trees. Snow had been shoveled into a small foot-high fence line underneath the string perimeter. A couple taller snow walls were built where there were no tents for privacy. It was snowing.

Lachlan, Bellamy and Nerice stood a hundred yards away around a tall fire. Tired scouts stood by them, watching the flames and listening to them debate. Nerice's back was turned to us, but there was an extra shroud of something covering her that did not surround the others. I did not see Durin, Cathal, Gwen or Vice amongst the tired crowds, but I saw villagers who had escaped and troops and Keepers tending to the wounded. I thought somewhere heard Durin curse.

"We have been here for about a week, Delilah. Please don't move!" Theone's voice was heavy with worry as I went to turn and sit on the edge of the cot.

I heard heavy footsteps against the icy ground thudding quickly from behind one of the only canvas tents. Cathal and Durin practically tripped over each other coming around the corner.

"Shorty!" Durin said. "How're you feeling?"

Cathal held out a large flagon that smelt of straight liquor in his massive hand. "You're going to need this," he said holding the cup out to me.

I looked at Theone's pained face then glanced over to Priestess Mirna whose eyes suggested I could do what I pleased, but I may not like the result. I frowned, and that was when it all came rushing back.

I yanked the furs from over my legs, or what was left of them. My right leg was gone, only the stump of my thigh wrapped in bloodied linen bandages remained. I felt my lip quiver as I tried not to break into tears.

Cathal urged the flagon towards me. "Take it," he pressed.

I took the mug from his hand but did not drink. I only stared at where my leg was supposed to be. The emptiness.

Theone sucked in a hard breath. "Adder is under watch by Caoimhe's Keepers at this time across camp. You are on bedrest until you are completely healed," they explained softly. "We were waiting for you to wake up before moving again. We have all been praying for you."

"I found a carpenter to build you a nice prosthetic, so you have something to work with when you're ready," Durin said motioning to what was missing. "She's done prosthetics for the whole town. The surgeon said with time you could walk easily and possibly have little pain. I'm sure when Blondie has the time, he will make sure it wont hurt."

I could *almost* feel my leg; a phantom itch or pain, the stretch of a muscle consumed by teeth and fire. I took a sip of the alcohol as I continued staring at the empty space on my cot. The alcohol was harsh whiskey, Durin's favourite, and I let out a big sigh after swallowing. "Well, this fucking sucks," I croaked. I chugged the rest and Cathal's brows rose high, impressed.

"I'll get you another," Cathal said disappearing back into the camp.

"I'll get the Commander," Theone said, knowing Lachlan could probably get my mind off the loss.

Priestess Mirna put a hand onto my own, bringing my attention to the present. I looked at her. Durin stood close, a cup also in his hand. He looked defeated, tired. His brows were pressed close together with concern for me.

"The enemy was buried," Mirna told me. "Your Council has been reviewing the documents young Asa took from their father. We are closer to the end of this war because of you and your companions."

I lay back down, turning onto my side to face the heated voices, seeing Lachlan and the other council members stand by a fire, their motions exaggerated in argument. Theone approached them. The Priestess pulled the furs back over my bare lower half. The snow that had fallen on me melted cool between my skin and the blanket, waking me up a little more. I focused on the conversation across the camp.

"We must plan our next move. We cannot stay in these woods and expect to remain safe forever!" Nerice hissed, her voice carrying on the wind. There was an extra dark note in her tone. I was not used to her sounding like this.

"The obvious escaped me!" Lachlan snarled back. His tone, though also tense, was not nearly has upset as Nerice's seemed to be.

"Do you hear yourselves!" Bellamy broke in. Her voice wavered and I got the impression she had been crying prior to whatever argument they were having. "We will be left in shambles if you continue to fight like this! We are a *family*!" She stepped between the two and they seemed to defuse with her hand on each of their chests. They all were dressed in the garb they had been wearing during battle, except their appearances were much more dishevelled.

Lachlan's voice was calmer when he spoke again, careful with his tone. "We had a base, we had safety. I realize what we are making our people face out in the open like this, but we could never have prepared for an army of that volition to make it this deep into the mountains. Not even with the knowledge they were coming. Blackwick had been safe, do not blame me for not having a plan for a *dragon*!"

I sighed and returned my attention to the Priestess. "Do we know what happened Salvatore after the battle?" I asked. It hurt to talk. My throat felt stripped, like I had been coughing a lot, the icy mountain air tearing into my lungs harshly. All my screaming after the dragon bit my leg off was probably a culprit to the soreness.

The Priestess pulled more blankets over top of me then handed me a small wooden cup, taking the flagon away. She lifted an iron kettle that had steam drifting from the spout then poured the contents into my cup, the smell of lemon, mint, and honey wafting in the air around my hands.

"So far there has been no sign of him, this Salvatore. Know your avalanche caused that monster's numbers to be greatly depleted. We are sure of it, but Mother Nerice has not sent any of her birds to reach out. Your Council decided it would be best to stay quiet until we find a place to settle again."

My chest felt tight, and I peaked down at my body underneath the covers. Bandages were over my torso, my breasts bound beneath stained linens, and blood dried against them. My skin stung as the cold hit it and I pulled the furs tighter around me. The mountain air was unforgiving without clothes. I took a sip of the tea and sighed contentedly at its warmth. My throat felt instantly better.

"I should help them. Make sure they wont start bickering again. I can't let poor Bellamy stay between them," I said quietly.

"Let them work it out themselves, Shorty. This is the first

time the camp has been lively in days," Durin said. He plucked the iron kettle from where the Priestess had set it and poured himself a cup. From a pouch on his hip, he produced a flask and dumped some of the contents in with the tea. A beard was growing out from his usual stubble, bright orange clashing with his sandy blonde hair.

"We survived the cold wrath of these mountains so far. The people believe it is because their Seer watches over us. There have been whispers of you for so long. How blessed are we that you finally arrived and saved them when the war came to their doorstep," Priestess Mirna said. "How can anyone truly know the gods are *not* with them, when you stand amongst us with their gifts?"

Speaking with Priestess Mirna, I was reminded she was a holy person. I was reminded how she was really in her calling. I was reminded of all the times I sat in on Nerice's sermons and that she too was a revered member of the Temples. I wondered if there was ever a time Nerice comforted someone the way Priestess Mirna did to me now.

I sipped the tea again, letting her words sink in. "I believe *something* is with us…" I admitted.

The arguing had completely stopped. Glancing back to the large fire where my Council had been, they now looked in my direction. Theone with them, the news of me being awake delivered. As soon as my eyes met with Lachlan's he moved to jog over. I sat up again to meet him and Durin and the Priestess removed themselves from the area to let us be alone together, or at least as alone two people could be in a camp consisting of a village.

"You're really awake?" he asked, his voice soothing.

"I am…" I replied. "How could I not be with all these heated words between my friends…"

Lachlan knelt, his knees crunching into the snow below, and hugged me around my waist. He held me so gently, mindful of my wounds and aches. I could smell the sweat in his hair, the faint hint of coffee on it and I was calmed. When he pulled back, his eyes darted over my face assessing injuries again. "How could this have happened to you?" he asked.

"A dragon tried to eat me. That's how," I said. To think such a great battle had taken place. To think I finally saw the full extent of the war and thought the battles in the Groves were bad, but *this*. This could never have been prepared for.

"I'm so-" He took my hands in his. "*Everyone's* so glad you made it, Delilah."

I ran my thumbs over his leathers and metal bracers, wishing I could feel his skin on mine. I wondered if he could feel my touch beneath the layers. "I'm glad I made it too," I said.

Lachlan dipped his head and kissed my cheek, lingering there. My body flushed with warmth by his touch. He kissed my forehead, lingering there too then slowly moved away, his eyes looking beyond me to the rest of the camp.

Most of the camp was awake. The night was dark and still, but it seemed every able-bodied person there was doing something, too anxious to sleep deep within the woods. Content with what he was looking for, Lachlan's eyes came back to mine, something different within them. He smiled contagiously. "By the way," Lachlan said low and raspy. His lips came to my ear, teasing the skin around it. His voice no louder than a whisper and his breath was hot and enticing. "Only *I* am allowed to eat you."

I felt my cheeks blush deeply and I gaped as Lachlan kissed my cheek again. He was such a nice distraction. "Okay," I squeaked. He chuckled and stood back up.

"May I lay with you?" he asked. I nodded, laying back down, careful not to bump my thigh. I watched as Lachlan unhooked his plate armour and kicked off his boots before carefully climbing behind me. He wrapped his arms over me and nuzzled his face into the back of my neck. I warmed from his touch and tried to push myself closer to him. Lachlan kissed the back of my head, warming me up despite his cool leathers.

We lay in silence for a long time. I watched shadows of villagers and Keepers and soldiers bustle around the camp. A few campfires were put out, the atmosphere quieted. Eventually everyone slowed down and only a few recruits stood on watch as they circled the perimeter, watching over us. It stopped snowing and clouds started to peel away to reveal two almost full moons. The constellations were clear and colourful. I picked out one to pretend was Earth.

"I haven't told you how I got my scars," Lachlan said quietly. I jerked in his embrace. I had thought he had fallen asleep. He rubbed my arm reassuringly and kissed the back of my head.

The camp was nearly silent now. The Council had disbanded for the night, amongst the last to find a place to rest.

"You might have a lot of scars," I noted.

"You know which one's I am referring to," Lachlan said. He moved my hair, his lips teased the skin on my neck and threatened a kiss.

Other villagers in Blackwick, refugees from the war, troops in the army, amongst them many had scars, big or small. A lot had prosthetics or were deaf or blind from explosions in the field. I now joined them with my missing leg, but I never saw scars like Lachlan's. Healed burns so deeply embedded over his handsome face and hands. I had assumed he had been in a fire when he was younger, or maybe a mage had an altercation with him during a fight at some point. I never thought to ask him.

"Go on," I said.

"When I was a boy, a dragon had come over the Tabernacle where I was transferred to train as a Keeper…I was one of the only survivors, thanks to my magic."

I fell asleep that night with Lachlan beside me. He admitted how he wanted to sing to me, knowing music helped with my anxiety, Durin or Theone's meddling no doubt, but he did not dare wish to haunt me with his terrible voice. Instead, he played with my hair, lulling me to sleep regaling stories of his youth. Some were one's I had heard from Durin before.

I dreamt of a castle, a mighty fortress protected by the mountains on all but one side. Its city overlooked endless rolling hills and was protected within a hidden valley only those who lived there knew about. In the winter, the open side of the basin would fill with snow, hiding them away for months as the people lived there in peace. I watched as city folk came and went through grand doors of the Keep and moved in and out of shops. I walked amongst ethereal beings and greeted the townsfolk like long-time friends. Magic wisped around them granting wishes of abundant crops, safe passage in the seas, a healthy pregnancy, and wine better than their competitor's shop.

I felt myself smiling, feeling the peace this place offered. I passed by a shop window, and in the reflection was a tall woman with blind eyes holding hands with another woman with hair long and raven dark. The tall woman leaned down to the other.

I said, "Thank you," to the raven-haired woman and when we stopped holding hands, the dream went black, and I awoke.

Something trickled down my face where my gifted eye was, and worrying it was blood I wiped at it. Blood did not stain my skin, but instead it was wet with tears. Something told me I had witnessed a memory. I had not felt pained by it. I felt I had been gifted it, just like the Eye. I looked off in the distance, a deep feeling in my gut telling me where to go.

We had to head back towards our ruined village. We would find a hidden path. We would find a new stronghold and it would be there that we would live out the rest of our lives.

Lachlan had already gotten up to start the day, but Priestess Mirna was back at my side.

"Can I help you dress, Seer?" she asked gently. I nodded, grateful, the pains in my muscles slowly resurfacing as I became more and more awake. It was a slow and careful process, but eventually I had pants on, the amputated pant leg tied in a knot so it would not dangle. I had a donated jacket on and was left bundled up on the cot surrounded by furs as everyone packed up to move again.

Vice approached me about an hour after I awoke and pulled the crate Theone had been sitting on the night before close to me. "May I speak with you, please?" he asked.

I was bored sitting here, watching the troops carefully put

away what made up the village camp. They folded the few tents available, loaded a dozen or so crates onto one of the three wagons. I saw there were several injured folks on stretchers made of old branches and bedrolls or sacrificed tents. Laity paired up to help carry them. I had not thought there would be a lot to pack, since the evacuation had been rushed, but it seemed there were enough supplies that a week of camping warranted a slow and meticulous repacking. I was relieved to have someone to talk to, since everyone else was preoccupied. "Aye, you can," I said.

Vice set his staff to the ground between us and looked at me fondly. "While you slept, we all had a lot of time to theorize the things Salvatore said back in Blackwick, and what you said. Nerice and Cathal attempted an interrogation with Adder, but he wont talk." Vice let out a long sigh. "High Priestess Katerina possessed powerful magic, as any member of the Holy Order does. We know she caused the explosion at the forum, in attempt destroy that monster Adder claims as his master. That much magic is overwhelming for even the most talented of mages. We do not yet know how Salvatore survived it, but it is clear he possesses equally powerful magic to our Divines. I know you must be tired, and the others are hesitant to ask, but do you have the mental space to tell us anything else you may know?"

I could see the tiredness in Vice's eyes. The same exhaustion that darkened everyone else faces pleaded with me. I sympathized, knowing that I would have eventually been approached.

"I know how he escaped Katerina and Blackwick," I told Vice. He cocked a brow expectantly. "It's the same magic I apparently possess." I looked down at my hand, willing it to disappear into the shadows cast down from the naked trees above then return to physical form again. "I do not know where I picked it up. Maybe Gwen tried to teach me, those early days are a blur and this eye was painful."

"Shadow magic. Impressive," Vice said. "It is rare to see it in the modern era. We are lucky Andreja chose you and you accepted her."

"How do you know I accepted her?" I asked.

Vice looked up at the sky where it was clear, almost warm. One could pretend there was no war below the mountains, that we had not all just run for our lives. Voices talked to each other, birds made songs inspiring spring to come. Vice clasped his hands together, still thoughtfully looking up to the heavens. "There are some stories of the gods when they walked with us. If they were to take human form, they sacrificed a piece of themselves to hold some of their magic and immortality. If they had kept it, they would have to return to the After sooner. It is said that the Eye at Andreja's Temple, was once one of Andreja's physical eyes during one of her incarnations here. In many stories, Andreja often sacrificed one or both of her eyes. She is the goddess of adventure, among other things, and she could see our world from the After just fine while she was there; what an adventure her life would be if she could not see while here, right? These pieces left behind by the gods become foci, used to channel ancient magics in times of need for the Chosen. Only the Divine's were allowed near them. I have seen many of these over the years. Old memories of even older magic. Salvatore may have thought he could take it for himself. Especially since the relics at Samu's Temple were destroyed. We know why that is now, of course.

"It is *your* magic now, until it is time for you to go to the After, when it will return to Andreja." Vice tapped his eye, mirroring where my gifted eye was. "Also, it stopped bleeding when you cast magic, which is an easy tell." He smirked.

I could almost see my reflection in the shine of Vice's ruby eyes. The sharp, disconcerting pupil where my eye settled glimmered back to me, and I refocused on the conversation.

"I have more to tell you," I said. The connections were undeniable to me now. The people here did not believe in coincidences, and the culture was something easy to lean into when magic was so real all around me.

"Alright," Vice said. He did not seem surprised or curious by my words.

"Salvatore has Earth technology embedded in his body."

Vice waited for me to continue. The trees ached in the wind

and the camp was nearly packed up. I smelt grass and dirt on the wind, coal and copper on the passersby.

"When I faced that *thing* in Blackwick, he had Machine pieces all over and inside him. The kind of Machines my people used to travel through space and time. Adder he said he got the piece for his spell from Salvatore. and…" I watched Vice's expression shift, evidence coming together for him as I spoke, like everything was lining up in the theories he had been mulling over for months.

"Time magic," Vice said. "Like Andreja's."

"That's over-simplifying it," I said.

"Maybe it is your people who are over-simplifying it."

I was taken aback. Vice shrugged then sat straight up, looking around as more and more people cleared the area.

"This is valuable information. If this metal is indeed the kind your people use, it could offer a solution to his defeat as well, no?"

"Maybe." I did not know how I could figure that out on my own. Perhaps if I had stayed in school longer, Travelled more, a solution would be clear like Vice suggested. I had to stay focused. "His name though. I recognize it. He wasn't a good man on Earth. This places magic, the power he now possesses has made him much dangerous," I was exasperated just thinking about it.

Lachlan approached us then. When my face lit up seeing him, Vice took that as a reason to exit. He nodded to me and my thoughts fleeted.

"Are we leaving?" I asked as he took Vice's spot on the crate.

"We're trying to," he said. He had dark circles under his eyes, and I wondered if he had actually slept since the battle.

"I know where we need to go," I told him. "Back towards Blackwick. There is a path we would not have noticed coming from the direction of Blackwick, but we will see it from this one."

Lachlan leaned forward to kiss my cheek. "Back to Blackwick? We were going to search for an alternate route towards the Stills. Nerice sent owls with a request to occupy early this morning. Returning to Blackwick could compromise the people who remain in our care."

"Trust me," I said.

Lachlan searched over my face and a soft smile settled on his lips as he realized what I was really saying, what I was *seeing*. "Always." He leaned back and scanned the area nearby before he spotted a scout. He called their name, waving them over. He spoke to them in Bygone Speech and then turned his attention back to me when the scout took off to, I guessed, tell the rest of the Council to organize the route. "What will await us back towards Blackwick, *Seer*?" he asked, his tone playful. A hint of the smile he used when we were alone breathed against his lips. I was reminded of delicious things he had said to me, promises not yet followed through with. Before us I could see memories that would last lifetimes, tales that would extend the millennia after millennia. I could see a place where I, and the rest of our people, would never have to worry about war again and my heart was full with that knowledge.

I told him, "Home."

Lachlan stayed with me as the last of the camp was broken down. Fire pits were covered, the bells were wrapped up and carried in small packs. Even some common walking areas were brushed over with needles, hiding our tracks from things lurking around us. The cot I was on had to be packed up and Lachlan plucked me off it, supporting most my weight as I stood shakily beside him. He helped me to one of the wagons, where Cathal lifted me into the bed, his movements steady and gentle, unexpected. After he placed me amongst the furs and bags set there, Lachlan hopped in to sit beside me.

"Need anything else, Commander?" Cathal asked.

"That's everything, Major. Thank you," Lachlan replied.

Cathal saluted him before carefully climbing out of the bed. He turned to me, saluting me as well. "Toots," he grinned. Bellamy joined beside him and Cathal patted her on the back. Seeing them next to each other, I could definitely tell they were related, though they seemed closer in age like siblings than uncle and niece. I watched as the two melted into the crowd. An impressive feat for someone as large as Cathal and as extravagant as Bellamy.

Lachlan kissed the side of my head over my matted hair as I got comfortable. "I will always wonder how a man that loud is so graceful," Lachlan said to himself. "I'm glad to have him on our side."

People bustled about, a new excitement in their step since I gave Lachlan a direction. I could not have fathomed the fear they felt prior. I had seen a lot of people I recognized, but knew many had not made it to this camp. I could feel it in my bones, and I wanted to know the damage. The wagon started to move, and I winced, the ground much more uneven than I expected.

"Lachlan?" I said adjusting my position. My mind told me the trail they decided on was right, I would not have to speak up about it again.

Lachlan turned to me, thinking I needed help to reposition, but I put my hand up to stop him before he tried.

"How many did we lose at Blackwick?" I asked.

A shadow covered his face as Lachlan took in my question. Things around us seemed quieter. I knew it would not be good news, but his expression made my heart sink. "*Maybe* half of our people made it out, it could have been much worse," Lachlan finally said after letting out a long breath. "I, umm, was hoping to have this conversation somewhere more private with you."

Oh no.

Lachlan angled towards me, his voice lowering to make sure no one else could hear us. "We were lucky that those who made it out did without proper time to evacuate. Thanks to you and your companions, the drills our troops ran to make sure we could leave as fast as possible..." He swallowed. His hand gently rubbed the knee that was still there through the furs, a comfort before bad news. "But, of the people who made it out of Blackwick, I'm afraid your mentor Gwen was not among them..."

He felt me tense up from his words and Lachlan's hand moved from my knee to my hand, and he grasped it tight. "My deepest condolences, Delilah, I know that the you of two were fond companions. She was a very wonderful, brave woman…”

I could feel as the pain in my heart intensified, as my breath became harder to catch. My eyes overflowed with tears before I could stop them. I had wondered why I had not seen her. I had felt something was off. I had not let myself believe. “How….? Who can confirm…? I don’t- I can’t-,” I stuttered. I stared straight ahead, watching as others trailed behind our wagon. There was a whimper in my voice. The rest of the world started to disappear and sorrow only existed.

“One of the laity at Blackwick -she had been giving final prayer to an elderly woman in town. She was there still during the second attack and got trapped under debris from a fallen beam. She said Gwen came into the flames and pulled her out of the rubble and…told her to run. The nun was surprised she herself made it out because the moment she stepped from the house it collapsed. She did not see Gwen after that. I have personally checked with every single person here, Delilah. I have barely slept since we left the village. No one has seen her…I’m so sorry Delilah, I’m so *very* sorry.”

Lachlan’s voice faded from my mind as I wailed. My heart broke. A piece of me had been taken from this plane.

I never knew loss like this.

I was finally becoming myself here, the anxieties from my former life were dissolving. Someone who had been helping me through it was *gone*. I heaved, breaking down into Lachlan’s embrace. The movement pulled on the stitches of my residual limb and more pain shot through me. The world was darker without that Gwen in it.

“No!” I wept. “No, I refuse to believe she’s…She can’t be!” I could not bring myself to say it. I cried harder, the crisp chill of Lachlan’s armour burned my cheeks. Gwen had been invincible to me. I had watched her dozens of times with other troops, and she handed them their asses on a silver platter each time. I had heard her stories from when used to go out on missions with other scouts, and everyone would always come back without a single wound each and every time. She had split open that crate at the innkeepers home as if it was simply an egg and freed his husband.

How could she be dead?

Lachlan held me. He stroked the back of my hair like Theone would on the field. I sobbed harder, clawing at his chest plate to have something to hold onto and his hand found mine, allowing me to squeeze as hard as I could. His voice reached me through my sobbing, through the darkness that consumed my mind. He pressed his head against mind and spoke gently against my hair. "I'm sorry, Delilah, I really am. She was one of the best. You will meet her again in the After. I know she will wait for you."

"She was my best friend!" I cried.

Lachlan squeezed me tighter to him. "I know," he said softly. "I *know*."

For a while, all I could do was cry. I suppose I was a crier now, but this felt more than warranted. Everything did. I desperately sought anything to distract me from Gwen's passing. Lachlan stayed beside me, in silence, supporting me when the pain would hit me all over again. The town travelled through the rolling hills of the mountains, bumpy with frozen foot trails from days before and unforgiving in the winter weather. Fridged air sunk into our skin, my tears froze quickly when they left my body.

It had taken hours to become coherent after Lachlan told me of Gwen's fate. Lachlan assured me that as soon as we settled somewhere safe, troops would go back to the ruins of Blackwick to find those left behind. They would dig them out and burn their bodies to release their spirits to the After. He assured me that the second they found Gwen's body, I would be notified and could send her spirit to the gods myself.

Others cried over their pain, their loss. Everyone mourned their loved ones as I did. I heard many crying, saw more sad faces than I could count. I wanted to be stronger than my grief. Lachlan assured me I was allowed to be upset, that no one would think any less of me for expressing my feelings. We were one in our grief and, somehow, I found comfort in the togetherness of it.

When I started to calm, I noticed Nerice, her face puffy and eyes tired and shiny. I wondered if it was her position in the Temples that caused her to mourn such a loss in her people. I wondered if it was *someone* she grieved for.

The mountains were scenic through the unforgiving winter. Under other circumstances, I would almost think them romantic. Fresh snow dusted the red rock-faces and trees glittered in the sunlight. No clouds hung in the sky. The days went on and warmed, the air longing for spring. This part of the world was untouched by the war, and it was a sliver of beauty after a terrible storm. I wondered how far we had travelled from the village since I fell unconscious and how close we were returning to it.

The smell camomile, ginger, and mint floated around as tea was passed around by the surviving nuns of the Tabernacle. The smell was soothing mixed with the cedar and pine of the mountain trees. We trekked for two days before setting up camp again. How anyone was able to stay awake that long without falling to exhaustion, especially Lachlan, was beyond me. If I was not crying, I had drifted in and out of sleep within Lachlan's arms.

Scouts that were sent ahead to find a place to camp eventually sent word back of an old, unnoticed path that seemed to be promising. They had not seen it on the way out since they were not looking for a way out of Blackwick, not back towards it. Nerice told them to keep going, leave markers for the rest of us that were promptly erased as Nerice found them. She wiped her eyes often. Once Bellamy tried to comfort her, for whatever she was upset over, and Nerice brushed her off, asking to let the subject drop.

On the evening we settled down, I tried to distract myself with the scenery. We made camp in a clearing carved out of the mountain. The stone wall that was exposed through the dense trees was almost perfectly round and on the south side a small glacier waterfall poured into a pond where everyone refilled canteens and barrels that once held food. The space seemed unnatural though it had grown wild from years of no guests passing through it. Whoever had carved this place out must have taken a very long time to do so.

My friends situated me with a bedroll and several pillows donated by villagers next to a fire that Cathal and Durin made. Lachlan finally fell asleep on a cot he had originally set up for me a few feet away. Cathal patted my back as I shifted next to him.

"How are you doing, Shorty?" Durin asked. He was oiling his bow. Freshly sharpened arrows sat next to him in a leather quiver, now damaged with scorch marks.

"Could be better," I sighed. "I keep thinking I can feel my leg. I keep waiting for…" I could not say it.

"I'm sure once you're cleared for a prosthetic, you'll feel a lot better," Durin said confidently.

I remembered feeling Lachlan's body around me. His warm hands trying to soothe me in my crying. Durin was probably right about him helping with the healing process. I thought I would have been experiencing more bleeding, but it seemed under control. Of course I had been, once again, unconscious for several days before I was fully awake, and I dared not ask how bad the carnage was before then.

After the night I woke up, the nights had been clear, and I had watched as the moons grew full. I had not seen Vice, but knew he had to be around. Anytime I would wake up during the wagon ride, there were potions waiting for me in case I was experiencing pain or nausea from anxiety. Maybe he had been with Asa until tonight.

"How long have you known Vice?" I asked my friends as Cathal handed me a cup full of warm broth. We were almost at the end of the supplies that had been taken out of the kitchen as Blackwick fled.

"Oh, maybe a year or two. Vice just showed up one day saying he wanted to help. I imagine it was because he had enough of Adder's shit," Durin shrugged.

"He rubs me in the wrong way," Cathal commented.

We looked at him.

Durin laughed and set his bow down beside his quiver. "He's peculiar, for sure," he said. "Especially for an Amaranthine. Everyone knows Nerice is Amaranthine, but you can almost forget she's one sometimes. With Vice…"

Cathal had a cocked brow at Durin. "What's wrong with Amaranthine's?"

"Nothing, you just don't see them often. All those stories…the *trees*," Durin shrugged again.

Cathal shifted, mumbling something to himself before returning his attention to spooning broth into cups quietly. In the future, Cathal's eyes were so *red*. They were grey now, flecks of blue scattered in the iris like shattered stained glass. He caught me looking at him.

I knew another secret.

So did Vice.

"What is it?" I asked Cathal. "That hits you the wrong way?"

Cathal shook his head. "I haven't figured it out yet." He kept my gaze in a way to suggest he knew I knew something; whether it was his secret or Vice's, I could not be sure. A wolf howled, it sounded close, and Cathal jerked in surprise. Durin stifled a laugh.

"Vice has never not been odd, at least for as long as he has been with us. No one knows him from before, except for Asa and Adder, but we can't judge him for Adder, and we only just met Asa. He is a wise man, a good healer, and Blackwick has benefited from his presence. That's what matters," Durin said.

I nodded and Cathal offered me some dried meet, which I nibbled at as conversation began to pick back up and the rest of my companions joined us. Bellamy, Nerice and Theone came to the fire after some coordination with Nerice's scouts. Nerice cuddled up next to me, drinking from a bottle of what I assumed was wine, and Theone kicked Cathal from his spot so they could sit near me. Bellamy looked dishevelled for the first time in her life, her hair barely restrained in its golden pins and chains and her boots were caked in mud. She sat delicately down to the log Durin sat on and pulled her furs tighter around her before Cathal passed her a cup of broth. She smiled gratefully to him.

"It's growing warmer, don't you find? The further into the

mountains we go. This is unusual," Theone commented as we watched the flames. "I wasn't expecting spring for several weeks still."

Bellamy finished her broth quickly then stood to wander behind me. "It is definitely a little warmer," Bellamy agreed with Theone. "May I put braids in your hair? Idle hands…" she asked. I nodded and her gloved fingers began to braid my hair after she brushed it with a golden comb she pulled from her hair. It must have been among the things she grabbed during the evacuation. She was a lump of fur capes behind me. Having used to live by the sea and accustomed to the warmth there, I could not imagine how she was dealing with camping. I wondered if she had asked to braid my hair to give me some familiarity, because for a brief moment her hands felt like Gwen's fingers were in my hair instead of hers. I let myself pretend they were my late friends and that she was safe with us.

"It is strange," Bellamy continued. "Blackwick was most definitely colder than here, and a week could not have transitioned *this* much weatherwise. I believe I will stay cozy until we have a more permanent location. I cannot risk shedding layers while this air bites me."

"There is magic here," Cathal said simply. "Can you not sense it, Mother?" Cathal looked from Nerice, still cuddled against me, over to Theone. "Colonel?" They were silent. "It's everywhere, all over these mountains. It's been getting stronger since the battle."

Everyone looked at Cathal as if this should have been clearer to them sooner.

"I suppose you're good for more than just a good time and medicine, eh Cathal?" Durin commented. "Vice wouldn't have said anything to us about it. So, few can sense it these days who aren't Keepers. Caoimhe's are so preoccupied with the injured they probably haven't even thought about it."

"We're going to find a fortress," I said. Everyone looked at me, Bellamy's hands stilled for only a second, our conversation silenced. "I dreamt about it the other night. I told the Commander to go back in the direction of Blackwick. I…I think we will be safe there."

The silence hung for a few more moments and Nerice sat up from leaning on me, suddenly more awake. "Antore," she said after swallowing a heavy drink from her bottle. Attentions moved to her. This was her first real words outside of giving orders to her scouts and the argument with the Council nights before. Several lights lit in my friends' eyes at the word she said. "It could be still standing. Perhaps centuries of snow had hidden it."

"What a sight to see if it was," Theone said, dreamily.

Durin and Cathal exchanged looks, surprised as I was to hear Theone have a voice so uncollected, youthful.

"What's Antore?" I asked.

Cathal seemed the most interested in answering my question, while the others began to speak amongst themselves about a castle. I felt as Bellamy finished braiding my hair and she patted my shoulder to indicate she had. She walked around and sat next to Cathal on his log, and he wrapped his arm around her to help keep her warm. He seemed like he would be a good cuddler, always warm and comforting when he was not flirting with other recruits. Bellamy was definitely grateful to have a family member with her through all the chaos.

"When the gods still walked with us, they often congregated at a mighty Keep, called Antore. It was lost eons ago. Many believed it was just a myth," Cathal explained.

I thought about my dream. I thought about the blind woman in the reflection. Vice had said Andreja would often sacrifice her eye or both to walk with mortals. "Theone," I said turning to them. "Who in the Patheon was Andreja's best friend?"

Theone faced me, their thoughts being brought back to the present after letting their imagination wander. "Andreja was never best friends with anyone in the Patheon. She views them more as siblings. Her friends were always mortals." They looked thoughtfully up to the sky and smiled. "If we consider their time in Antore," Theone's smile turned into a satisfied smirk. "Her best friend would have been *Shamira*."

The following day, when we packed up and started our journey again, I could hear Theone's enthusiastic voice echo far across the mountains as they discussed the possibility of reaching a legendary Keep with Nerice. Nerice appeared more like her usual self, but if I caught her gaze, I could still see the pain she carried. I heard Durin laughing at Theone's excitement and Cathal would chime in every once and while with Bellamy or Florence, imagining what it would look like.

Lachlan had set up an area in the back of our wagon again, amongst the crates holding the almost depleted vegetables and supplies. We were enveloped by pillows and blankets to make me as comfortable as possible and villager voices sounded refreshed, excited, louder. The caravan went far, carefully picking through heaps of melting snow and old rockslides. The scent of spring grew heavier with each passing hour and the anticipation of a world without ice and cold wind seemed to revitalize our people. I could smell fresh grass carrying on the wind, crocuses were forcing their way up through thinning layers of snow.

As the sun crested the mountains, readying to set for another night, one of Nerice's scouts came running at full speed from up the path towards us. His expression was full of excitement. "Commander! Seer! We have found something! Something incredible!" he said panting.

"How far?" Lachlan asked eagerly sitting forward, excited to see an end to the journey. He still had dark circles under his eyes, despite starting to sleep more often. When he occasionally dozed off against my shoulder throughout the wagon ride, I was given the opportunity to stroke his cheek or play with his hair. How I wished I could do this every night.

"About five klicks ahead. Stay on the path! My eyes are still in disbelief! I have left markers, as ordered!"

"Spread word, immediately!" Lachlan instructed. The scout nodded and ran to the group trudging behind us. This morning our wagon had been one of the first to leave, leading the way behind a couple Keepers who marched ahead in case of an ambush. Their clothes were dirty and needed some mending. No one had had a chance to change since the battle.

Behind us Nerice yelled "Finally!"

Lachlan motioned ahead, a playful grin on his lips. "Want to see?"

"How?" I looked at my healing thigh, covered in warm furs.

Lachlan called out for Cathal, who appeared by the side of the wagon within moments.

"Yes Commander?"

Lachlan gently untangled himself from me, stretching his arms before pulling himself up. "Pluck the Seer up for me, please. You and I are going to have a race."

Cathal boomed with laughter as he patted the seat next to Durin who led the horse pulling our wagon. Durin halted the wagon and people began to move around us, an entertained grin on his face.

"Five kilometers with you unencumbered?" Cathal asked. "Easy." Cathal thumped up into the wagon as Lachlan climbed out. Lachlan stretched and Cathal carefully lifted me into his arms. "Are you doing alright?" he asked. I felt so small in Cathal's arms.

"Whatever Vice has been leaving me is a godsend," I replied.

Cathal carefully adjusted me before hopping back out of the wagon. He kicked the wheel when he joined beside Lachlan on the path and the wagon continued moving forward with the tired but excited crowd. "Good luck!" Durin laughed.

"I'll be gentle," Cathal purred to me before taking off ahead.

I heard Lachlan yell at him, his tone equally surprised and unsurprised by Cathal cheating in their race. Peaking around Cathal's shoulders, I saw Lachlan chasing behind us. We rushed up the path, my laugher echoing through the mountainside with the voices of other eager travellers. We ran through a bottlenecked mountain pass, only wide enough for a cart to pass through it. Its walls looked carved out, years of effort scratched into the sides, moss and small plants creeping out of cracks and edges searching for sunlight through ice.

Despite the setting sun, the passage grew warmer the longer we ran. Ice thinned out, snow became easier to step in, Cathal moved faster, and Lachlan began to catch up to him. While we raced, my heart felt full with the joy of camaraderie. I was shown a glimpse of what life could be when the war was over. How I wished for my friends to see its end.

Time passed quickly, listening to the Commander and his Third throw playful words at each other. When the corridor opened up, we were welcomed with a view overlooking something wonderful.

Below was a deep basin, protected by the mountains on three sides. The fourth side was empty, looking out over the rest of the mountains. Cathal set me down, supporting me on a plateau that faced the basin. Lachlan slid beside us, panting, and took my weight on him so Cathal could walk further to the edge. They both stood in awe, gazing into the valley's depths and taking it in as the evening fog began to settle into it. From this angle, it looked as though a cloud sat within the valley, perfectly hiding it from the rest of the world.

Towards the center of the valley I could make out a wide trail dotted with the scouts ahead of us. A large, sparkling lake lay within the center, the winters ice ready to break open. Thick luscious green coniferous trees surrounded it. The trees and brush that had gone to sleep already showed signs of waking up with small buds cresting the branches. Near the edge of the basin, where the mountains opened to the setting sun *there* it was.

Everything that we had gone through, all the lives lost and pain, had been worth it for this.

The place I had dreamed about. A great, ancient, and forgotten castle stood tall and unopposed with a great wall the colour of mist. Old, abandoned homes were nestled around it, their thatched rooves caving in and forgotten. There was a whole city waiting to be lived in and there was more than enough room for the people of Blackwick to be there.

"This is incredible," Lachlan's voice was winded, but his eyes were full of possibility.

"I call the castle," Cathal joked, a big, excited grin on his lips, his sharp teeth shining in the light of the setting sun.

People spread throughout the Keep, into dilapidated farmhouses around the exterior wall, old shops with apartments, and many other spaces in long forgotten places. There was ovation as everyone entered the valley. It seemed exactly what we had hoped for, and the cheering and clapping sounded for hours into the evening.

"How could this place have been forgotten?" Theone mused as we walked through a mighty archway. It was the entrance to the castle grounds, and Theone's hand brushed against a symbol I recognized as a sign of Keepers. I had not known the Holy Order was so old and I got the impression Theone had not known either.

Lachlan looked at it thoughtfully and squeezed my hand, his brows furrowing, confused. We were back in our wagon, having waited for its arrival on the ledge leading to the valley. "My parents never mentioned this place. I would have thought *prababica* would have said something to them. She had to have known this was still here."

Theone traced over the stone carving, the repose they often showed put on in times of pain or illness during my early days of adventuring now on their face. "The things these walls must have seen…" they mused.

Nerice pushed through the thick crowd in the main courtyard. Her crimson-coloured eyes appeared more alive than they had been in days, and she looked around with wonder and excitement.

I looked up at the arch, amazed it endured hundreds, maybe even thousands, of years between the last person who walked these grounds and us. The arch stood taller than the Tabernacle in Blackwick, and even larger structures stood proud within the walls of the ancient city. Overgrown with plant life, it waited to awaken from a long winters sleep. I was filled with the absolute certainty that this was *home*.

Nerice pointed to a tower at the far end of the city walls after pondering each corner for several minutes. "Mine," she said simply.

No one objected. Everyone else was too preoccupied with

directing villagers and refugees. Keepers were sitting after a long journey, holding hands and murmuring prayers of thanks into the wind. The laity from Blackwick sat near them humming a song filled with happiness as Priestess Mirna whispered blessings over their shoulders. Bellamy kindly spoke to recruits and groups of villagers, directing them to carefully pick a space to sleep for the night and more permanent plans could be made when everyone was rested and fed.

"Bring me my birds!" Nerice practically screeched as she started to walk in the direction of the tower.

I felt Lachlan jerk in surprise at her raised voice. A scout clicked their tongue somewhere. A horse pulling a small cart piled high with caged owls and crows sped past us. The ropes strapping the cages together were ready to snap and mud spit up from the wheels in the carts wake. He had clearly been waiting for Nerice to call for her beloved pets.

We explored.

Within the walls of the ancient stone city stood towering buildings, reaching into the sky like trees. Decrepit shops were built on top of each other and family apartments crowned them as nests in foliage. Laneways made of brick marked wide streets and alleyways. Broken signs hung from sidings or lay in front of weathered doors marking what shops used to flourish here a millennia ago. Smithies, silversmiths, alchemists, and ancient market stalls painted a picture of this place once thriving, just as it did in my dream. Watch towers stood in the four corners, and the tallest point of all, the Keep in the center. This place was once completely self-sustained and would be again.

For hours into the night I stayed with Lachlan and Bellamy as they directed people to safe areas the scouts had found if people had not already discovered a place for themselves. I sat perched on the edge of a wagon watching as many tired people came in, crying with happiness. They all would pass us, coming to touch my hand and thank me for bringing them here. Eventually, when the moons had risen high into the night sky, everyone had all made it inside and voices quieted.

Theone, having made a full round several blocks in the first few kilometers of the city with Florence and Cathal, returned just as the last of the villagers and soldiers shuffled inside. "We will need to rebuild the gate here," they said.

Lachlan nodded in agreement and pointed to the towers near the archway. Above us was a rusted portcullis, pieces of it eroded away, the rust eating at the stone around it. The towers above it had seen better days and parts of the walls were missing, lost to time. I could not see the tops of the towers. They were covered by the mist hanging over the city, a cool blanket in the night.

"We will put a watch in those towers. They look large enough to house the Keepers and some of the soldiers. I'm sure they will be thankful to stop tenting. The other towers can act as barracks and perhaps even Nerice's scouts could house up there."

Theone nodded approvingly. "Well thought Commander." They closed their eyes, taking a deep breath then sighed it out. When they finished, Theone turned to face us. Like everyone else, they were exhausted, something I knew they would not have let on if they had a choice. Theone's hair was slick with dried sweat and their makeup was almost completely rubbed off after days of being unable to clean their face or reapply. "I have directed Bellamy to a nice manor that one of Nerice's scouts found. It has less rubble than most of the explored areas. I had meant her to set up a space for herself there, but I believe she is creating a place for the Council to meet instead. I should go stop her."

"You should rest, Theone," I encouraged.

Theone nodded. "There is so much to be done. You two should find someplace too, before all the good corners are taken," they suggested, motioning towards the castle. "No one has really explored there. *Maybe* Cathal, but I have not seen him in hours. Everyone has been surveying the exterior structures, working their way inside. There is a lot yet to discover."

Lachlan's face lit up with the promise of adventure and he

gave me a gentle shove, his armour clicking against my pauldron, the only piece of armor I donned. "Shall we?" The smile on his face was one of excitement, of anticipation. He looked relieved to have a place to settle and the fatigue on his face was softer than it had been in days, or even hours, prior. Lachlan's smile was contagious, and I felt myself beaming back at him, taking his outstretched hand into mine so he could help me into the castle.

Amongst the rubble and fallen beams, the castle seemed full of numerous rooms and endless corridors. It would be weeks, if not months, before the entire Keep and surrounding grounds was completely uncovered, repaired, and rebuilt. Lachlan patiently walked with me, supporting most of my weight as we moved to wall sconces, lighting them with our torch. As more light illuminated the latest room we were exploring, it was obvious it had once been a grand ballroom, no doubt able to entertain hundreds of people or announce important rulings. At its center a massive fire pit sat with ancient coals, overturned benches that once circled it lay discarded near the decorated, dusty walls. A collection of thrones backlit by the foggy moonlight sat untouched by time at the head of the hall. They were positioned in front of a massive stained-glass window depicting scenes and stories I had yet to learn. Lachlan's eyes settled on the glass a moment longer than mine and I could see recognition in his expression. He focused on the faces of the people coloured in the glass.

"Do you know them?" I whispered, afraid that speaking would shatter the art in front of us.

Lachlan made a barely noticeable nod. "A part of me does. This is a tale lost to time. Perhaps if I meditate, I could recall."

One of his past lives knew this place.

On the walls leading from the entrance to the thrones were many doors. We were interested in the ones closest to the thrones. Where most of the doors were plain, wooden, desiccating, these ones were barred with iron and wore the Keepers sigil. I indicated to the left one and Lachlan helped me sit to one of the thrones while he tried the door. Moisture and age wedged it sealed. After gently trying it a couple times Lachlan took one look at it and rammed it through with his body from a running start, the wood exploding to dust and wild boards on collision, the iron clicking against the castle floors.

I watched him as he came back from the dark corridor to retrieve his torch and help me go further into the castle. Beyond the door lay more hallways and doors and two staircases. The stale castle air started to lift after years of closed chambers. "We could get lost," I said to Lachlan as we picked a way to go.

He brought my hand to his lips, my heart fluttering with excitement at the anticipation of his affections. Lachlan brushed my fingers against his lips while he spoke. "Being lost with you would not be terrible." He kissed my fingers then lowered my hand back down. "Besides, Nerice would find us eventually."

We chose to go up the stairs. I did not yet have a prosthetic or a crutch to lean on and could not go with him, but Lachlan had a good feeling about where the stairs would lead. "I'll make sure the stairs are safe then report back?" Lachlan proposed. I agreed, leaning against the stone wall.

The old wooden stairs creaked angrily as he worked his way up. I heard the snap of a board echoing down after a minute of his ascent followed by Lachlan's sharp cussing. I laughed a little.

"It's fine! Nothing happened!" Lachlan hollered down.

I laughed again, hearing embarrassment in his voice. "Whatever you say!" I hollered back.

Upon his returned Lachlan described a beautiful, almost untouched bedroom chamber at the top of a tower. "It's miraculous," he said enthusiastically ten minutes later. "Only cobwebs and dusty furniture lie within it. Almost as if someone had only left it alone within the last year." He believed it was one of the highest points in the Keep. Lachlan told me since I was the highest ranked in the church, I should take the chamber. That way I could watch over the valley and our people within it.

When not in mortal danger, I found it difficult to remember

where I stood with everyone here. I knew, to them, I was a sacred figure. I could not deny the power I now possessed, the hope and faith everyone had in me. I knew I accepted it and could not ignore that I had saved a village and buried an enemy with a simple command to snow. But just like when I was given a bigger room at the Tabernacle in Blackwick, I thought I did not deserve it. After some urging, I agreed to take the room. I grew tired and hoped for a soft thing to lay on.

Lachlan helped me sit back into one of the chairs in the throne room so he could find someone to help him with me. He wanted a few people present in case another stair gave way.

Several troops and Vice returned with Lachlan to help me. Lachlan carried me up, though not with the grace Cathal possessed. One recruit in front of us tested the stairs and one walked behind. Vice and a third soldier waited at the bottom of the stairs for a worst-case scenario. When we reached the top, Vice came up to wait with me while Lachlan went to arrange a visit from the surgeon to get my leg assessed at earliest convenience.

Inside was almost perfectly preserved just as Lachlan had described. The room was bright from large south-facing windows with the moons shining in big and brightly. I glanced at Vice, scared of something happening and he held his hand up in dismissal. "The worst of it is over, do not worry," he assured me. His eyes glowed in their light.

The windows stood floor to ceiling on the opposite side of the entrance door. Beautiful tapestries sewn with gold and vibrant colours hung on the walls telling more lost stories I knew nothing about. Upon closer inspection I saw an embroidered figure with long raven coloured hair, just like the figure I had seen in my dream. Her name whispered in my mind: *Shamira.*

A large carpet covered nearly the whole space. The edges of it frayed with age. Some sections seemed more worn than others, a clear common walking path marked from whoever use to live here. A grand desk was set near some bookcases filled with petrifying books by the corner where the windows were. A large column bed was positioned near the door with a nightstand on either side of it, the polished wood dark and dusty. On one stand was a faded jade sculpture depicting the sun and two moons all squished close together. When I lingered on it, Vice told me, "A symbol of Krix, often representing his three children."

"Krix only had three children?" I asked curiously.

"Yes. Just three. All with the same mother. I imagine Priestess Mirna would love to have this piece in her collection while she and the laity rebuild a chapel for the townsfolk," Vice said. He brushed his fingers over top of it briefly, leaving a trail in the dust that had caked on it. "I could take it to her if you like?"

"Please," I said. I did not intend to go back down those stairs until they were reinforced.

The only thing that showed this room had not been lived in for a while was the copious amounts of cobwebs and dust over everything. A sheen of grey coated every piece of furniture and dust floated in the air, caught in the torch light. Vice handed me his staff for support and stayed close to me so I could look around the room freely.

I pretended it was a princess's bedroom out of a storybook and smiled with the potential this room had for me, for my future. I noted a large standing mirror and was unwilling to look at it, afraid of the reflection I would see staring back at me. I limped to the windows where I saw a latch to open them. Dusty brass hinges clasped the glass together and I realized part of the window was built as a door. I unbolted and opened it to a balcony. A spring breeze rushed in around me, disturbing the dust in the chamber. I felt like I had finally stopped holding my breath after a long time of doing so and Vice sneezed.

Vice took the relic off from the nightstand, cradling it in one arm like a baby as he joined me outside. I leaned on the stone railing of the balcony without noticing I had shuffled out onto it. From this view, I could see almost the entire valley below. The moons' reflection in the lake, the torchlights of villagers making homes in the outbuildings, fireflies in the trees, the battlements that enclosed the

Keep with scouts already patrolling them. The big dark emptiness of the one side of the valley stretched out to the rest of the mountains and world below. It was a sight to take in and I was excited to see it in the daylight.

"Many eons ago, before most of our recorded history, this place was home to knights," Vice began. "The Temples were first establishing themselves in this world and these knights acted as the Tabernacle's disciples, spreading the word of the gods, as Keepers do now. The Tabernacle began because, several decades prior, demons had begun to run rapid on the mortal planes with the gods. They grew bored with their homes in the After and instead of a few occasional possessions or hauntings because of spirits gone mad, they all flew out of the portals the gods gave them and caused chaos. The Temples offered refuge to those who turned their obedience over to them. The only safe havens were the Temples, protected by people trained by the gods themselves.

"The knights encountered a witch, claiming she could bring a solution to a world where the gods refused it. They brought her back here to address the Patheon. She said she could temporarily take the demons away since the gods refused and the world could return to what it had been before: peaceful. Despite her efforts, she did not have enough power to completely imprison them, but she *did* have enough to create a place to put them: *The Other.* She believed they did not deserve to be in the After with the gods, that they should be punished. The witch said one day the demons would return. She foretold a great evil would ravage our world and in the final days the skies would fall. The demons would rage upon our home again.

"She said that this would be when her power had grown strong enough to return, but she would not help us this time. It would be someone else's turn. Instead, this person would be brought forth with a gift bestowed from the gods and through them they would be the one to trap the demons away once more, saving our home. Only the oldest, darkest spells could release them again. Only the most tormented of souls would become them. .

"Keepers were birthed from the knights, and everyone

eventually left this castle behind when its purpose was no longer needed. It was forgotten. The whole world has been expecting this to happen, even if their spirits had forgotten. Then *you* dropped out of the sky."

Vice rubbed his fingers over the relic again, carefully cleaning it from its grime with his flesh. His expression was far away, as he looked at it. Despite the retelling of this story, it felt more like he had been reminiscing with me. I did not pry. I thought it better to stay on subject.

"This witch…she was Shamira. *Shamira's Avowal.* Because she said it would happen. Theone had asked me if I heard of it when I first woke up."

"Aye," Vice said.

"How poetic that this demon thing kind of began here and it will end here," I said, hopefully.

Vice smiled, his attention moving from the relic to me once more. "I had hoped you would look at it that way."

Vice walked back into the chambers, and I slowly followed him to examine it closer, note how much I would have to eventually clean, how I would arrange it to make it my own. It felt so cozy, despite the spaciousness of it. It felt like I could really make a life here.

"Before coming here, I never stepped foot inside a castle and now I have been in two," I admitted. "The entirety of my old house could fit inside just this room." I made it to a large table and leaned on it as I continued to speak to Vice. It was wooden and thick, a pane of grimy glass topping it and with stacks of dusty books. "This world is so magical." I looked around at the room, to the beautiful tapestries, to the intricately carved columns of the bed, to the relic in Vice's hands.

Overnight this world had become everything to me. It was mine now and I could not deny that to myself.

Vice nodded and smiled a wolfish grin. "You have no idea, Delilah. The world *is* magic. Every world is. Including yours, even if you do not believe it." He looked around the room. "I never would have imagined things to turn out like this, but I'm glad of it." He looked back at me, still cradling the jade carving. "You are destined for remarkable things. You and every one of your companions."

"Durin said you joined a year or two ago. You were accepted because of your wisdom, but why not make any friends?"

"You are my friend, are you not?"

I paused at his quick response. I had hoped to have more of a glimpse into his life before us. Before the army. "Of course!"

"Well then I made at least two friends," Vice smirked. "You and my dear feline companion back in Blackwick." He looked sad. Aside from several horses and Nerice's birds, I had not seen other animals during journey here.

Vice gripped the relic tighter in his arms.

"How did Shamira have so much power? She was not even a god. Could a witch really possess magic like that?" I asked.

Vice perked back up at my question. "She was a *Seer*. Like *you*. I do recall you were accused as being a witch by Adder when you first arrived," he teased.

"Don't remind me." *How did he know that?*

Vice chuckled again then sobered. "I imagine he accused you because Adder knew the power you held at the time."

"What's the difference between a witch and a mage anyway?" I asked.

"Mage's typically have a moral compass and code they stick to. Witches are outside of that."

"But what made Shamira so special? What made the gods and knights listen to her in the end? What made the people trust her?" I asked.

Vice's wolfish grin returned, though he had fought it at first. He seemed like history was a favourite subject of his. I had to remember that. "Because Shamira was Krix's mortal wife," he said. He paused and looked down to the relic in his arms. He traced a finger gently over one of the moons on it. "I should bring this to the Priestess."

Vice disappeared very quickly after that.

After everything that we had gone through, the exhaustion, the death, I found it hard to grasp that this could be all part of a prophecy, millennia in the making. I looked at the tapestry again, fighting sleep in the torch and moonlight while I waited for Lachlan. The woman I imagined was Shamira stood at the center, her arms up casting magic with leaves encircling her and cats sitting at her feet.

"Delilah?" His voice was tired, but Lachlan had finally returned. It had been such a long journey. I yawned, thankful I had not fought my sleep for nothing. How relieving it was to finally have a place to rest. To have a space of my own again. Delight mingled into my fatigue and part of me wondered if he would stay here with me, like he had every night on the trails.

"Admire this pretty room with me some more," I said.

Lachlan slowly approached me as his eyes scanned over the room, impressed by its grandeur. "Are you going to claim this as your chambers then?" he asked.

"Only if you claim it with me," I replied.

Chapter Twelve
Spring

In the days and weeks that followed our arrival to the forgotten city, restoration went quickly. Those who had not acquired any injuries during the battle and evacuation were intent on returning Antore to its former glory. Thick vines so deeply tangled together were peeled off stone walls like a thick layer of wallpaper. Saplings were cleared from the main courtyard and streets to make walking easier yet older trees so wide and tall they rivaled buildings were left alone on the overgrown roads. Mason's and carpenters planned to rebuild around them, faithful that we would be grateful for their presence once the summer heat hit the city. Thousands upon thousands of lilac bushes bloomed and their perfume carried around the streets with the freshness of other budding trees.

The most amazing sight of all, was the view of the city from my balcony in daylight. Lachlan had been right; it was the tallest point in the Keep and I could watch all the goings on below from my tower. It blew me away that a metropolis that rivaled the size of Toronto was hidden within the mountains. Between the rooftops and emerald tree canopies people moved around full of life.

I even had a view of the gap in the valley from my room. After further exploration, I was told that through it one could look down to the ruins of Blackwick.

It had been me.

I had pulled centuries of snow from the mountain and buried an army with a *word*.

I had uncovered a place for these people to thrive.

Lachlan, Cathal and a few other troops left on a mission soon after our arrival to Antore. They would return to and recover as much as they could from Blackwick. I was left to decompress and heal.

Even though only several weeks went by in their absence,

the city was transformed, and I got to watch it grow from my chambers. A lot of work had to be completed to bring Antore to its once great splendour. Rubble was cleared and refugees quickly became townsfolk finding their own homes within old houses and apartments throughout the city. Farmers were planting crops, and Bellamy was sending orders for livestock. A glimmer of what this place had been began to show and the spirits of everyone within were lifted with every passing day.

The day Lachlan returned was beautiful and warm. After a stormy night, the sun shined brightly. I had often left the glass doors open to not just let the stuffiness out of the room, but also feel the spring air and sunshine on my skin. I was so happy to feel the warmth on my skin after spending so long being cold.

Today the open windows welcomed the smell of a rain shower on grass, and I found contentedness in such a simple scent after the cold, harsh winter. Since I was stuck in my tower until I was cleared for my prosthetic, I spent most days resting. I would read in bed going through delicate books Vice found in an ancient library just days after arriving to Antore. I would lounge in the sun meditating. I would sing lyrics to old Earth songs, summoning them to my mind from a life when I would pick them at my radio job.

I had a lot of time to come to terms with my missing leg. I cried and I mourned it, just as I mourned for Gwen. I missed the days I would wake up to cook the village and Tabernacle breakfast, then train and play with my best friend. I missed her teasing. I missed her gentleness when I had a bad day. I missed just hanging out. My friends must have sensed the torment my heart felt because in the afternoons and evenings, I was often joined by one of them. Nerice visited me the most, giving me an unexpected comfort through my grieving process and the Priestess in her shined through with the same comfort and calmness that Priestess Mirna had.

I was exhausted over everything I had been suffering. Every time I thought I could start to pull some semblance of myself together, allow myself to live in this place as I did on Earth, something new magically materialized to quell my peace. I found myself asking if this world was testing me. I wondered if something was trying to make me surrender. After all the trials and tribulations that I had gone through in mere months, after weeks of mediation, and support from my friends, I convinced myself it all was a small price to pay for my life and I grew grateful to just be alive.

Lachlan entered my chambers holding something in his arms. A scout followed behind him carrying a crate. The surgeon sat on the bed with me, having arrived only minutes before to check my condition. I was thrilled with Lachlan's return, eager to feel his lips on mine again. We had only one night together before he left, and it was spent sleeping cuddled up against him before he could even undress. He kissed me when I was half asleep the morning he departed, and I fell asleep before I could plead with him to stay longer.

"Lachlan!" I exclaimed. The troop behind him jumped a little then said something to Lachlan quietly. He motioned towards the ornate, glass top table and the troop brought the crate there before leaving. I opened my arms wide, waiting for Lachlan to come embrace me. The surgeon waited patiently for us to greet on another.

"I have a surprise for you," Lachlan said as he came to my bedside. I eyed the crate on the table then looked back to see what Lachlan held in his arms. The dust had been cleaned from the room, fresh linens were donated from makers, and I had been the one to shine the table clean, uncovering a beautiful floral design in the wood under the glass. The glass had to be strong because it did not crack with the thud the crate made against it. Lachlan knelt, moving his arm to reveal a small orange tabby cat.

I lit up. "A kitty!" I knew this cat. I had seen her around the bunkhouse Vice had lived at in Blackwick.

Lachlan's expression matched mine, pleased with my reaction as he pet the creature with his thumb. "This little peach was amongst the ruins in Blackwick. We were surprised she had lasted so long out there by herself. I fed her a few times on our way here, but I thought you could use the company."

I pet the cat's head with my fingers, and the loud, happy rumble of purring filled the room before Lachlan set her down. She wandered the room, investigating it for mice or a place to sleep. She settled on a sunbeam. I looked forward to Vice visiting and seeing her. I knew he would be happy she made it out.

Lachlan greeted the surgeon before settling on the bed beside me. It was the largest bed I had ever slept in. Bellamy and I had shared it a few times in his absence, and I would forget she was there with me it was so spacious.

The surgeon inspected me. She asked me how I felt, what I had been taking for the pain. I explained that I had been using potions Asa had made for themselves but gave to Vice to give to me. Since arriving to Antore, Asa had been on bedrest, their illness having put them in a chokehold. Vice spent a lot of his days with them. Most of the time Asa was asleep during his visits, but Vice would be there regardless and would treasure his time with them when they were able to keep conversation. I had not been sure what was in Asa's potions, but after I said it was made to help them with their infection from the forest, the surgeon understood.

She had prepared several herbs for teas to take in case my pain worsened and some to help promote the healing. She then carefully removed the stitches and put fresh bandages around my stump to act as padding. Afterwards, she presented the prosthetic leg Durin had commissioned for me. The surgeon explained how to attach it and said to take my rehabilitation easily; it was already impressive that I survived the dragon. The prosthetic was two solid pieces of wood with a hinged lock where the knee could be so I could unlock it to sit and lock it again while standing and moving around. It was delicately carved into a feminine leg. Whoever carved it, was a talented craftsman.

Lachlan kissed my forehead while the surgeon packed up the soiled bandages and cleaning implements. I could tell Lachlan was having a hard time on my behalf with my missing leg. He had been quiet as the surgeon rebandaged the residual limb and discussed medicines and care with him.

"I'm a mage," Lachlan said when the surgeon mentioned it would be easier to have a healer on standby for me. "I've been studying the body and have a talent for magic thanks to my *prababica*."

The surgeon nodded and opened a tome from the bag she had pulled her supplies from. She went to a page with some drawings of the lower anatomy and showed Lachlan the images. I could not make out the words on the page, but there were pictures of plants next to extremities and symbols I could not place. "Your *prababica*? Was she also a talented healer?" the surgeon asked as she wrote down a few notes for Lachlan to refer to on a fresh piece of parchment.

"She was a god."

The two of them eyed each other for a moment, the surgeon glanced at me, right to my gifted eye, before continuing to write down information for him. The surgeon then explained the tome she brought with her was filled with old spells. She was not a mage herself but carried the spellbook with her in case she came across one to share with. When she finally left, Lachlan pushed his hand through his hair and looked to the ceiling like he was gazing at the heavens. When he looked back, his eyes ran over my legs. I had not been wearing a proper pair of pants for weeks, but my breeches covered my upper thighs just enough to almost cover the bandaging over my missing leg.

"I could have lost you," he said softly. "I…How could I have gone on?"

I reached out for him to come closer, and he took my hand in his. I was unsure how to respond. I knew we had feelings for one another. I wanted nothing more than to spend my days with him and learn more about his life. I longed to taste his lips and feel his skin against mine. I knew in my heart how much love we had to give to one another. I was not used to a man being so straight forward with how he felt. He kept surprising me.

"You didn't loose me, I'm still here…Well, *mostly*." I looked longingly at the space where my leg used to be. "Not a day passes that I am not grateful that you and the others didn't listen to me when I said to evacuate with the rest of the village."

Lachlan kissed my fingers, his nose resting on my knuckles as he took a deep breath, drinking up my scent. I treasured his touch.

Right now, the world faded into only him and I. Lachlan looked over at the orange cat, sunning herself happily.

"She's not the only thing I brought back," Lachlan said nodding towards the crate. "Let me grab it for you."

"No, help me with my leg, I want to go see myself," I insisted.

Lachlan plucked my prosthetic from the end of the bed where the surgeon had left it. I had not been out of the bed yet today and I was excited to be cleared after weeks of being inside my room. It took a few minutes for us to get it right, but when the prosthetic was on, Lachlan pulled me up off the bed.

I carefully moved towards the desk while Lachlan held my arm in case I tumbled.

"Do you want to sit back down?" he asked, worried, when I hissed at the pressure between my bone and the wood.

"No, it's just a sore," I said between teeth. The pressure was heavy and uncomfortable, but bearable. I hoped it was just a matter of getting used to it. "It's just very different."

Lachlan took a step away from me but kept his hand on my arm. "You can do this," he assured me. "I have troops with missing limbs. If they can do it, you can."

When I reached the table, I noticed Lachlan trying to conceal his excitement for what lay inside the crate. I pulled the lid off. Sitting inside it was my sweater and pajamas, mended, washed and ready to wear. I never thought I would see them again. I felt my eyes prick with tears and I snatched my sweater out of the crate, burying my face in it to take a long sniff. A piece of Earth. A piece of someone who I was slowly letting go of. I dabbed my eyes with it to push the tears back.

"We tried to uncover what we could for you." Lachlan swallowed, a concerned look on his face. He put his hand on my shoulder and squeezed it. "Unfortunately, we did not find Gwen's body. We dug up a lot of remains of those left behind to release their spirits, but the area we believed Gwen to be was only burnt beams. We must assume her body burnt in the fire. She's at peace…"

I took another deep inhale of my sweater, feeling my eyes fight against me as I was reminded that Gwen was gone. The lye soap was still fresh on it and something that reminded me briefly of the way Lachlan smelled ignited my memory too. I did not know if I was saddened or relieved that Gwen's body had not been found. That it was assumed already burned. That she was in the After. I set the sweater to the desk, grateful to still have a piece of Earth and saw a little embroidered dragon over some singed wool. Underneath my pajamas there was pieces of my armour that I had not donned before battle, my bag of rings, and water-damaged tarot cards and the little collection of rocks I had been working on. Lachlan had found almost everything I left behind.

"Thank you, Lachlan," I said, smiling up at him. "This means *so* much to me." I appreciated everything that man did; for me; for our people. As the leader of the army, he had made it his duty to go back to the destroyed village and do what he could for everyone else who left it behind. I was sure he had brought back many other recovered belongings to members of the growing city while there, but a deep feeling said that he mostly had gone back for me. I hugged Lachlan, tightly. I tried to mold into him, but his layers of metal and leather and furs made it difficult to find his form underneath. I heard the *clink* of my earrings hitting his plate armour before I felt the cold of it on my cheek. "Thank you so much."

Lachlan hugged me back, resting his cheek on the top of my head. I could smell his morning coffee still clinging to his furs and the campfire smoke from the night before. Again, I tried to hold him tighter and feeling my attempt, he gave me a big squeeze.

"I cannot stand seeing the light in your eyes fade, Delilah. I had a lot of time to think while I was away," Lachlan took a deep breath, "your eyes are the light in my darkness. If anyone does not believe in the gods, they should gaze at them in my...my..." Lachlan trailed off.

Wow.

My cheeks reddened. My entire body warmed by his words. He made me *so* happy. Happier than I thought I could be, especially after all the trauma in the wake of the war. I wanted everything that I was to be shared with him.

"May I call you mine?" Lachlan said in a low voice, as if speaking any louder would scare me off.

The word *mine* sent thrills through me and I nodded excitedly at his question. "You are my light too," I told him.

Lachlan pressed his lips where his cheek had been. He kissed the spot a second time and I could feel his lips smiling against my hair. "Then you can call me yours," he said.

We continued to embrace until Lachlan stroked my cheek, coaxing me to look up at him. My heart pounded. I peered up and he kissed my forehead, holding his lips there for a long, blissful moment.

I kissed his unshaven chin, a beard now wearing his face from weeks away. His breathing deepened, anticipation floating around us.

Time felt slow.

We caught each other's gaze, and he angled his head towards mine. With a charming grin on his lips, he grazed closer. We breathed each other in and then his hands were around my waist, pulling me in for the hunger.

His lips were soft against my own. His tongue expertly moved with mine as a tender kiss turned ravenous. Lachlan held me closer against him so there was no chance of escaping. In one smooth motion, his hand slid down my thigh and pulled my leg up as he spun me around, lifted me to the desk, and moved his body between my thighs. His kiss deepened and my appetite grew. I wrapped the leg I could control around his waist, pulling Lachlan tighter and he growled approvingly.

We pulled away at the same time, staying within a gasps distance of one another. He brushed his lips against mine, promising a delightful treat now that he had returned to me. His breath was intoxicating, and I wanted to drink him up. We smiled at each other, his eyes hooded and seductive, luring me in for more. We moved in to kiss again, and then-

A knock at the door.

Why was everyone knocking all the time?

I untangled my leg from around him and Lachlan stepped away. He licked his lips and took a deep breath, gathering himself.

"Seer?" It was Theone.

Lachlan cussed under his breath. He spoke quietly, mostly to himself, and all I could make out was "if they were a just soldier ..." *What would have happened if Theone wasn't here?* My imagination ran wild.

"Theone if I have to ask you one more time to call me by my name, I will not make you that dessert I promised!" I hollered to the door. Bellamy had a source in the Northeast Province that supplied chocolate for the right price. It was where she had got her hot chocolate and where I would have the means to make cake. Bellamy had ordered it mere days after our arrival to Antore when I mentioned having a recipe that I could share. She had been chatting with me about the contemplation of getting her family to move to the mountains from the sea. We had just finished some stretches in bed to keep my muscles strong during my recovery. She quickly told the other Council members of the possibility of cake and Theone had been thrilled.

Theone stepped in with a bunch of sealed and neatly folded letters. Their eyes were focused on them, making sure not to drop the large stack they carried. "I apologize, Deliah, but Bellamy wanted you to review these thank you letters before-" They looked up seeing Lachlan a mere step away from me. I still sat, flushed, on the table. "Commander Lachlan," Theone stated, their eyebrows raised in surprise. Their lips rolled inwards as they carefully chose their words. "I did not expect you to be here yet."

Lachlan coughed and scratched the back of his head, standing straighter, as he usually did when addressing anyone in public and took another step away from me. "We returned ahead of schedule. I...umm...brought her back the items our mission collected from Blackwick."

Theone nodded, their expression brightening by his words. "Success?"

Lachlan nodded, only now looking Theone in the eye having

avoided it prior. His expression changed a little and I watched as some sort of conversation happened between them. "Aye," he said.

"Well done, Commander." Theone set the letters to the small nightstand that used to have the relic on it. Centuries of sunshine bleaching the wood made the spot where the relic stood evident by the dark spot its absence left behind. "You get to these when you're able, Delilah," Theone said. They nodded to Lachlan who nodded back to them. "Commander." Theone left, the door closing tightly behind them.

Lachlan took my hand in his and kissed my fingertips. "I should go," he said softly, his tone disappointed.

"Says who?" I asked, hopeful, not letting him release my hand.

I saw something cross over Lachlan's expression; something greedy. He grinned briefly, his eyes on my lips, then bit it back. His grip on my hand tightened a little more. "I appreciate you saying that, Delilah. You have no idea how much I do…" He sucked in a breath, and I watched a thousand different considerations go through his mind in a matter of moments. Lachlan knelt before me, his face close to my stomach, a smirk still on his lips, before he lifted my tunic only enough to reveal the jagged, healing scar on my side that was forming from whatever stabbed me back in the battle. "How about I help the scarring on this, hmm? Go sit on the bed." He let my tunic fall back around my hips and stood up, his eyes moving over my face longingly. I did as he instructed, and he climbed on the bed in front of me, removing his gloves.

"Lie down and lift your tunic for me?" he asked.

I lay down and attempted to make my voice salacious, tempting. "Are you sure you wouldn't prefer it be removed completely? You could take it off…"

Lachlan bit back another smile and shook his head, regretfully. He made a noise, fighting opposing thoughts within his own mind. "Don't entice me," he said. "Your tunic, please."

I lifted my tunic to expose the scar there. Lachlan looked at me, then my side again. "This shouldn't be a problem," he said confidently. He wiggled his fingers playfully and then he set both hands on my waist. They were warm, and a tingling sensation reminiscent of pins and needles tickled me as his hands pressed slowly over my skin. When Lachlan's hands moved to my hips, the tingling travelled into my thighs and grazed down to a part of me that burned for him. I gasped with excitement, but as fast as it touched me, it retreated, and I groaned. Lachlan smirked and slowly moved his hands back up my waist to my ribs and they revealed soft, perfect skin in their wake, the scar completely gone.

Our eyes locked and I wanted to lean forward to kiss him. Kissing him was all I could think about and whatever magic he used for healing…whatever caressed and teased me…I swallowed and inched closer to him on my bed. I could hear as his breath slowed, his eyes moving all over me, before frustration covered his face. "I need to check on a few things," he said regretfully. "Could I come back later?"

I deflated, but an idea popped into my mind. "Of course, this is your room too after all." We smiled at each other some more. "I think with this new limb and your return, I might make some dinner for everyone. Celebrate our health and our new home. Would you be kind enough to inform the rest of the Council and I will tell Durin and Vice?"

Lachlan smiled. "And where will this dinner be?" he asked. "The tavern of course."

The stairs to my tower were rebuilt during Lachlan's absence, though I had not been able to use them until now. The tavern had been established quickly and the innkeeper from Blackwick had sent me a letter saying I would always have table at the tavern as a thank you. I knew old kitchens were unearthed and the laity started up their village meals again. All I really needed was a stool to rest on so I could prep, but I had the rest of the afternoon to find my way to a kitchen, make something delicious for my friends, and get it to the tavern.

Whatever Lachlan had done to me on the bed made me feel

better than I had in weeks and the space between my residual limb and the prosthetic was not as tender or heavy as it had been when I first stood up.

Yes, my friends and I would have a splendid evening.

I walked the scenic route of the city with a small map Bellamy had given me. I was excited to finally tour it and enjoyed the long stroll seeing the leaves and flowers in bloom. Ivy and vine still crept up the stone walls, though not quite as thick as they had been when we arrived. The common streets were cleared and busy with townsfolk, excited with their new lives in the beautiful city.

With Antore being settled into and tensions easing from the battle, Nerice's scouts were going back out into the province for surveillance and recruitment. They were giving refugees directions to Antore, clearing the areas with heavier bloodshed for civilians, making sure they could live as far from the war as possible. Scouts made it to the Stills quickly, meeting up with the ones who were not in Blackwick when the army hit. We knew through correspondences with scouts stationed around the province that the Temples had heard of the ex grand deacon's betrayal, and we were thrilled to inform them we still had him in our custody. How he hid his deceit for so long was beyond everyone, but now they ramped up their security in case of other breaches within their ranks. Nerice, though I knew she was just as upset as Theone over Adder, hid her attitude on the matter. Something told me she had something planned for him if he did not talk soon, and it involved leaving him in a locked room with Theone and a sword.

It would take time to establish the influence the Council had hoped for across the province. Now, with the Temple's approval, all we had to do was wait.

When I had finished cooking, the laity in the kitchens were happy to help me take it to the tavern. Especially since I had made extra for them and the innkeeper. The tavern was tall, like many of the buildings in the city. The bar had a collection of seating areas on the entrance floor. There were two staircases leading to the several other floors above it and a river rock hearth sat in the middle of the main area. The hearth was similar to the fire pit in the Keeps throne room, perhaps made by the same mason as a reflection of it. It warmed the tavern with a loving atmosphere and when I stepped through the doors it seemed this place had never lost its guests.

When my friends collected in the tavern that evening and I carried a chocolate cake topped with whipped cream to our table, Theone had stars in their eyes from excitement. I placed the tall two layered cake at the center of the table between a big pot of fist stew, thick with tomatoes, paprika, garlic, fried potatoes. Honey and thyme read rolls, and a dandelion salad accompanied the food and there were at least six large bottles of wine on the table. When I caught a look at the innkeeper, chatting happily with his husband and several patrons, he smiled widely at me. The wine was another thank you.

Every seat at our long table had been taken except for mine which was open between Theone and Lachlan. I flopped into it, tired from moving around all afternoon after weeks of lounging. My hip hurt on the side with the prosthetic. I may had overdone it, but the looks on my friends' faces were worth it, especially Durin's. His memories of eating stew together by his tent in Blackwick or on missions were definitely coming to mind, because they were what inspired me when I had decided what to cook.

"Oh Delilah, this looks amazing!" Theone exclaimed. They drew a large dagger from their belt and began to cut themselves a thick slice of cake. "Thank you!"

"I'm sure everything tastes amazing," Lachlan said, looking directly at me. I flushed from his implication and Durin, who sat across the table from us, poured me a tall glass of wine with a shit-eating grin on his face. When I looked at Durin to thank him for the pour he winked at me and I took a deep sip from the glass.

Serving my friends was like making plates for family dinners on Earth and I got the impression that, even though these people were my friends, they felt excited to be served by the highest rank in the church. Especially with Nerice there and Theone considering taking High Priesthood, their mothers ring a shiny, constant reminder to everyone. It only felt like a few minutes had passed when I realized at least two bottles of wine were already empty by the time everyone had full plates.

Everyone was engaged in colourful conversation. Nerice flirted with Cathal, who seemed thrilled about it. She licked gravy from his cheek when he missed it with a handkerchief and when she finished, he playfully bit at her nose with is dagger teeth. Bellamy was the biggest lightweight in the group, a detail I had forgotten from our slumber party in Blackwick. After one glass her cheeks were redder than raspberries and she giggled at every terrible joke and pun the others made, even when nobody else did.

The deeper into the wine we went, the more touching I observed at the table.

Durin tossed grapes into Theone's open and awaiting black-painted lips from across the table and he held their hand with a loving expression as they said something in Bygone Speech to him. Theone cut a second slice of cake for themselves with their dagger after finishing their first serving of stew, their eyes dreamily watching Durin with their walls down from the wine. Cathal licked Nerice back while she was not paying attention and when he did, she climbed onto the table to escape him, laughing, beckoning him to chase. Cathal boomed with laughter and slapped her ass as she still crawled over the wood. Nerice situated herself between Bellamy and Vice, trying to convince Vice to kiss Cathal while she watched. Vice, almost choked on his wine and declined, but when Cathal laughed harder, Vice smiled. It was nice to see him happy, after all the worry I knew he held for his ill friend.

Lachlan leaned in close to me as I watched Nerice pat Vice's back, thrilled to see him show emotion around her for once. Lachlan had shaved since I saw him this morning, but I felt stubble had already grown in and it tickled my neck. "I think they're going to get married," he whispered.

"What?!" I whispered back.

He responded, "Durin and Theone. They've been courting and worshiping since before I joined the army. With us settling here, I think they're comfortable enough to take the next step." His eyes flickered between our friends, and he moved a little closer to me. "Everyone else seems to be having sex with each other too. Maybe not Colonel Bellamy, but…" He shrugged, not finishing his thought.

My jaw dropped. "What delicious gossip!" I giggled to him. I never would have expected him to be so blunt and the others did not seem to notice what he said.

I smelt the wine on Lachlan's breath, hints of chocolate and coffee laced in with it and I was instantly intoxicated by him. His hand moved over my inner thigh and gave it a small squeeze. "I think you would be delicious," he said before returning his attention to the table, moving his hand moving away. I had trouble concentrating on the conversations I held after that. Lachlan appeared unphased by how much he riled me up and emptied another bottle of wine into his glass. He watched Durin and Theone making eyes at each other, smirked, and threw a bread roll at Durin's head, hitting square between his eyes. Theone instantly glared and Lachlan laughed like an amused schoolboy.

Durin looked at him with a challenging smile and uncorked another bottle of wine that had been hiding under the table. "Do you need more wine, Blondie?" he asked Lachlan.

Lachlan shook his head and took his fork, scooping up a large bite of the cake from the center of the table. "No, I just wanted to bother you," he said playfully.

Durin laughed and followed Lachlan's lead by taking his own bite from the cake. They started talking about a memory they had from years before, and their laughter was contagious around the table. When Theone noticed the two of them were eating straight from the cake rather than cutting slices, they made a fuss about sharing and then sliced themself a third piece. Theone then moved from beside me to beside Bellamy who was carefully arranging her second bowl of food into a visual masterpiece. I looked at my friends and how close we had all become. Vice spoke to Nerice and Cathal with a smile, Bellamy giggled and danced in her chair with enjoyment of her food and Theone leaned on the table, happily eating their third slice of cake, watching Durin with the same stars in their eyes as they had at the sight of the cake.

I took another bite from my own plate.

This was what family felt like and I loved it.

After dinner Lachlan walked me to our chambers, gayly telling me how tonight reminded him of a dinner he once had over a decade ago with his Keeper friends and Durin. They had a delicious meal "Though not nearly as good as this one," he assured me. He told me how the night before he led his team to storm the Gods Wall, they ate meatball soup seasoned with mint and cumin. They pushed back the opposing forces then proceeded to finish its construction. It had taken them three days and they did not sleep the entire time; fueled only by the dinner they had shared that night. "This dinner could have probably fueled us a week," he said enthusiastically as we made it to the chamber doors. The stroll back had been slow, my body catching up to me for using it so much after all my rest. I smiled up at him with anticipation. His words from dinner having never left my mind, allowing to me wonder what our night would bring.

"You flatterer," I said smiling up at him.

Lachlan put a hand up on the doorframe leading to our room, leaning close to me. My body heated, awaiting his touch. His free hand gently tucked under my chin to angle my face towards his. He kissed me *so* softly. His breath still tasted of dinner and wine and only furthered my appetite for him. I held on to a piece of his chest plate, to taste more of him, and his kiss deepened with the same urgency I had. We stood there for while, and I found myself luxuriating in the simplicity of an evening tongue session. To my dismay, Lachlan eventually pulled away.

"I bet the others are worshiping tonight," I whispered as his lips lingered.

Lachlan chuckled and moved his lips to my throat. "The question is: is Cathal with Nerice or Vice?"

I gasped. "Nerice doesn't care that Cathal is with someone else?" Nerice never came off as the sharing type to me.

Lachlan shrugged. "Nerice hasn't really been monogamous

since-” He paused. His lips moved from teasing my throat, and he searched over my face making sure what he said next would be okay. “Gwen. She hasn’t been monogamous since Gwen transferred from the scouts to the front line. I assume she wouldn’t be upset with Cathal if she isn’t monogamous herself. Besides, I think she likes women more.” He watched me for a moment, gauging my reaction.

“I never knew they were together,” I said.

“I never thought they wouldn’t be. I believed Nerice was planning to marry and grow old for that woman, but then Gwen requested the transfer about a month before you fell out of the sky and their fight over it was so explosive Nerice broke up with her.” Lachlan seemed more sobered by the conversation. “Sometimes I wonder if Gwen knew the transfer would cause Nerice to leave her and just wanted it to be Nerice’s choice to leave, not hers. They really loved each other.”

Gwen had never mentioned her relationship with Nerice and vice versa. I never would have guessed they had such a terrible breakup either from the way they interacted at my slumber party. I now understood why Nerice was so upset on our journey here, why she helped me mourn Gwen. She was mourning her too. *They had loved each other.*

Silence hung for a few moments and Lachlan released his hand from above me. He kissed my cheek, and his voice lowered in a wonderful way. “Good night, Delilah,” he said turning to leave.

“Where are you going?” I asked.

He smiled reassuringly at me. “To sober up. I’ll return soon.” He descended the stairs, disappearing into the dark tower.

I sighed and went inside the room. I took off my clothes and put on my pajamas then lay on top of the blankets, staring at the faded frescos on the ceiling. After imagining the people who painted it and remembering the months with Gwen, the rest of the castle slowly quieted and went to sleep.

I thought about the war. According to history books I read it began almost a thousand years ago, and I still tried to grasp how something could have gone on for so long. It started in the South

Province. I had read about it recently, a text saved during the evacuation in Blackwick that a nun had. It talked about a single star falling from the sky, birthing a river in its wake. It was within a century of the fallen star that the war began. Many now believed falling stars were omens of destruction. How scared everyone must had been the night I arrived.

I was relaxing on the bed several hours into the night. The cat slept on the balcony in the moonlight, a bowl of milk sitting by the desk, no doubt something Lachlan had done when I was cooking. I was content reading, surrounded by my nest of pillows. It was late when the chamber door's latch moved, and the door creaked open. I set a book down, a story about when the gods first walked the world. It was another Vice had rescued from the library; one of the only surviving copies amongst thousands that turned to dust by breathing on them. According to the book, those who were born with magic, and were not taught it, were descent from the gods. The gods really loved to have sex, and it made me laugh considering it was not much different from myths on Earth. It made it more surprising that the first god, Krix, only had three children, let alone with the same woman, Shamira, while other gods had children by the tens of thousand.

As I rose to go to the door, I almost thought it may be one of my friends coming to talk as they often did in Lachlan's absence. Bellamy would gossip about what she heard recently, mostly about nobles from other province's who were still unaffected by the war. Sometimes it was things she overheard from Nerice about catching scouts fooling around in forbidden or dangerous places. She would stay over on those nights. Nerice would come to describe the stories she made up about the goings-on of her owls, right after she updated me on the days work and delivered any reports that she felt I needed to know about between guided meditations and, what I now knew to be, two friends grieving over a loved one. Theone would air grievances they had over disputing troops or Durin, then listen to me as I expressed my anxieties and worries about the world. I had been thinking I would fall asleep after I was done the chapter I had been reading, hoping Lachlan would wake me up when he returned. Now I was curious about what my friends had to say, especially after such a vibrant dinner. Maybe Nerice clocked Lachlan's flirting. Maybe I could ask if she was comfortable sharing memories with me about her and Gwen.

Surprise and excitement reawakened me as Lachlan stepped into the room. I almost did not recognize him. His armour was completely gone, the copious furs that layered his Commander's uniform shed. No gauntlets, or steel boots, or perfectly kept hair. He did not even have boots on. He wore a long, lose tunic and wrap pants. He looked sleepy and vulnerable, but his eyes lit up when I met him there.

"I didn't think there was anything under all that armour, except for more armour," I teased.

Lachlan chucked. "Aye, in fact there is a person hiding under all of it," he quipped.

"Did anyone see you come this way?"

"Nerice, but she sees everything," Lachlan said with a shrug.

"Oh, I hope not *everything*," I giggled as I kissed his cheek. I sometimes wondered if Nerice ever slept.

As soon as I closed the door behind him, Lachlan was upon me. His hands set themselves to my waist and I was against the wall, his lips buried in my neck and teeth grazing my throat, begging for a taste of me. I gasped and he pulled away at the sound, a wicked grin on his lips and his expression promising great reward. I pulled him into kiss.

We fumbled to the bed, and he covered me, feeling my whole body under his hands and my hands running over all of him. I snaked my hands up under his tunic and felt scarred flesh I imagined matched his hands and part of his face from the burns. Underneath his skin, the man was nothing but solid muscle and…*gods*.

All those months of longing for him…

I craved his hands to explore my body. I pushed his tunic off to see his naked chest.

Lachlan had more burn scars with some spots growing a thin

layer of hair after years of healing. His stomach looked like it had a puncture on it from long ago and he did not cringe away when I grazed it with my fingers curiously. I gave him the option to remove my clothing, and his lips took a long, delicious moment on mine before hovering above them, teasing me, giving me life.

"If I have you now, Delilah, neither of us will be leaving this room for many days." He grinned then pulled himself away. Lachlan rolled off me and lay on his back, patting his chest. "Let us calm ourselves…We can wait until your leg isn't so sore, and when it is not so late."

I propped myself up and pouted at him. I wanted him *so* badly. He could read it in my expression.

"I've been trying to hold back, trying to remember there is a war happening and there is *so* much paperwork," Lachlan sighed. "Tis why I left you earlier. Wine…can loosen my control and my memories." He bit his lip, looking me up and down. I felt heat raise within me again at his starving gaze. "Let me experience you sober, Delilah, and remember every inch of you. *Every taste.* How I regret not having before your trial…" He leaned forward, his lips once again almost on mine, his voice lowered. He teased me, drawing me in for a kiss but would not let me have it. "Please?" he whispered.

I bit my lip and swallowed, trying to gather myself, to show the same restraint he had. "Are you saying you have a habit of blacking out if you are all liquored up?" I teased.

Lachlan laughed and lay back to the bed. "Aye, I *can* have the habit of forgetting important details from drunken nights. Why else would I walk away from you earlier?"

"Well, Commander, I will oblige your authority," I said, cuddling into his chest. Lachlan gripped me a little closer, his hand skimming down my back and over my ass before settling around my upper back and relaxing. He kissed the top of my head. When Lachlan was on top of me, I had been graced with a preview, a torment, of what awaited me underneath his trousers. My underwear was soaked, and I knew Lachlan was very aware of their state.

"Thank you," Lachlan whispered.

The world flourished with life. The trees glittered with millions of tiny emeralds. Wild vine had all but consumed the stone buttresses of the castle and I came to understand why such a thick layer had been removed when we first arrived. Nature was still very much the owner of Antore, and the people did not seem to mind. Carefully curated farmlands formed around the outer wall of the city and once lost homes were now loved and cared for. Houses and shops that could not be saved were dismantled to use in structures that were in better condition. The Keep continued to be restored and updated. Murals once dulled with age were repainted. The portcullis became functional, the crumbling barracks rebuilt. The hum of voices was a constant song that soothed my soul, and it felt as if I always had company.

Lachlan woke me gently as the sun barely began to shine into our room. He gave me a kiss, my body igniting by his touch, and he smiled victoriously as I wrapped my arms around his shoulders. He pulled me into a sitting position and gave me another kiss before telling me he had to attend to his duties. Bellamy had cleared an office for him while he was away as one of her projects and he told me where I could find it on the grounds. He left with delicious promises for me.

Soon after his departure, Vice arrived with a tall ladder and paints. He expressed a need for a distraction. Asa had experienced another bad night and insisted Vice take some more time outside of their chambers. I could see the stress on Vice's face as easily as his pointed ears. He was deeply concerned for his friend, but Asa said they loved the mood Vice had returned with yesterday evening. More time outside would be good for him and Asa wanted to see their friend in a good mood again before days end. Vice decided bringing the colours of the frescos on the chamber ceiling to their former vibrancy would be something to cheer him up. He had already painted the ceilings in Asa's chamber and assisted with other beautiful pieces around the Keep when he was not visiting with them.

Vice reacquainted himself with the orange tabby as she brushed up against his legs. He still held the ladder under one arm and a plate of paints in the other when he noticed her there. A small smile settled on his face as he said "Hello, old friend," before quickly starting his restoration project on my ceiling. Vice's delicate eye was impressive. I never knew he was such a talented artist.

I spent a good chunk of the morning watching Vice paint. I sang a few songs hoping that, despite my average voice, Vice would find solace in it like I did when anxious. Around lunch, I left him to continue on his own.

I visited the laity in the kitchens, who were excited to see me up and well, and decided to make some bread with them. When the bread was out, I put together a tray to bring to Lachlan in his office, unsure if he had breakfast. I arrived at the end of a heated discussion Lachlan was having with Cathal and Theone.

There was conflict on how to deal with Adder. I could feel the intensity when I entered the room and from what I understood, contact had been made with the Temples on the matter, but they only responded with official renouncement declaration of the former grand deacon and a notarized parchment to hand over to him. They trusted us to deal with him at our discretion.

Since his capture, Adder had been very resistant to any interrogation. He had been convinced that Salvatore would come and save him from our clutches, like he had between my trial and the battle in Blackwick. Time went on and Adder slowly realized he was wrong, and Salvatore had abandoned him. At first, he was shocked at our defeat of the dragon and that I still lived. Then he had become inconsolable. When I arrived at Lachlan's office, it was then that I discovered he had recently requested that if he were to say anything, he wanted to say it to *me*. The argument my companions were having was how to approach the situation.

I learned Lachlan and Nerice had put Theone in charge of Adder's interrogation, with Cathal there to make he would not be killed. It was a test, to see if Theone could handle this professionally and set their personal feelings aside. I was not sure how I was supposed to interrogate the man, especially after all the grief he had given me and our people.

"You can do it," Lachlan encouraged. "I heard about the way you handled yourself in the Stills before the time debacle. It will be just like that."

"That was different. I wasn't as traumatized or angry," I paused and took a deep breath. I could do this. All I had to do was talk to Adder. That was one thing. I could do one thing. I set the lunch tray down to Lachlan's desk. Boiled eggs, jam, thick cut bacon, buttered herb sourdough and coffee sat on it and the smell made my stomach grumble with hunger even though I had eaten a bunch of fresh bread and jam in the kitchens. *I could do this.* "But, if it helps our situation, I will talk to him."

Cathal put his hand on Theone to steer them from the office, but they batted him off, before following him out. Theone was definitely frustrated having to deal with Adder.

"I will assess him later this afternoon. If he doesn't review well, I will have him sit in the dungeon for another day and discuss with the Council follow-up actions," Lachlan said. "If he seems palatable, we can take you to him this evening, if that is alright with you."

I nodded as Lachlan turned and leaned back on his desk, smiling down at the plate of food and fresh coffee. "I know you mustn't enjoy the political side of this, but your voice matters. You are our Seer. The gods have given you a gift and you have an unbiased opinion in all matters. Your judgement will be just and fair. People will listen to you, if not Nerice or I." He scratched the back of his head and poured some coffee into a cup, lifting it to his nose to smell it, a pleasant and satisfied smile lifting his lips as if the coffee could right all the wrongs in the world. He took a drink of it.

"I wouldn't call myself unbiased. I think Adder is a dickhead," I said.

Lachlan almost spit out his sip at my words. When he managed to swallow, he laughed a little setting the coffee back down. "Oh aye, but you are better than him, are you not?" He smirked at me. I liked to think I was, and Lachlan knew it. When I stayed silent, he picked his coffee back up in one hand and a piece of bacon in the other. The stresses of his job returned to his face. The safety of an entire city and army was a lot to carry on one's shoulders.

"Do you want to go for a walk? Take your mind off everything for a little while?" I suggested, spreading some jam on a piece of bread for him.

Lachlan took another big breath from the coffee cup and took a sip, smiling contently. "No, I just want to eat," he said looking at me, his eyes scanning over me before giving me a seductive smile. "Perhaps I'll have some dessert later."

The former Grand Deacon was being held in the old dungeons below the Keep. Underneath the main hall of the castle were the kitchens, and below them were the once rusted cell blocks that now held sobering drunks, and Adder. It was cool in the dungeons. The sun illuminated most of the space, shinning in through large windows carved out of the rock of each cell. I imagined the views looked out over the side of the valley that opened up to see the rest of the mountains, maybe even see over our old village. Prisoners could easily climb out of the windows to escape, but no one would, because to escape would mean to fall and parish.

The dungeon was quiet, save the snore of one person loudly sleeping off a hangover from the night before. It smelled like wet rock, tea, and fresh bread when I arrived, a snack having recently been served to those who resided there. A few sconces flickered with candles lighting up the dark corners of the dungeon and a single recruit sat while reading a book at a table with two chairs.

A plate of bread, cheese, and pears with a cup of tea sat at the entrance of Adder's cell. It had not yet been touched. The former grand deacon stood leaning against the large window, looking out over the valley, pretending he did not exist while we arrived. He was not wearing the religious garb I was used to seeing him in. Instead, he wore simple linens, and I thought there were tears on his face.

Theone pulled the free chair from the area the recuit was

reading and set it beside me. Cathal's deep voice echoed loudly in the dungeon hall. "Adder."

When he turned towards us, he looked as if he had not slept since his arrest. His eyes were bloodshot, sad. Cathal motioned for him to approach. I sat down with Theone, Nerice and Lachlan around me. I let out a long breath, preparing myself for whatever conversation was about to take place. The former deacon had a cell at the end of the dungeon, several empty cells between him and the sleeping drunk.

Adder looked down to my prosthetic leg then back to me. "You killed it," he stated.

"I had help," I replied. Cathal patted my shoulder and then took a few steps away to make a round of the dungeon. Now that Nerice, Lachlan and I had arrived, he did not need to police Theone's temper.

The former grand deacon looked around his cell for a moment then dragged his own chair from the corner. His space was simple. There was a bedroll on a stone slab carved from the mountain to act as a bed. A small wooden table with parchment, a quill and two books on it sat left of the window in the corner where Adder had dragged the chair. A bucket sat on the opposite side of the cell as the bed. I could only assume it was used as a commode.

Adder glanced down at his snack plate, his expression suggesting this was the first time he was noticing it. He took the tea into his hands, though it seemed to have cooled since it was served.

"It had taken decades for Salvatore to charm that beast. It was to help him show his power and acquire all the other godly totems from the Temples around the provinces. He was going to overtake this world and make it better," Adder began.

"What was wrong with it before?" I asked.

So many different replies crossed over Adder's face before he settled on the right one. His brows were furrowed, concerned by his own thoughts. He continued.

"Most of us alive today do not know a time where this world wasn't at war. Salvatore's words were honey in a world that handed us ash and coals to eat." Adder took a sip of tea. It smelled of apples, lemongrass, and vervain; a mixture I recognized as a sleep aid the kitchens made. It had been a comforting drink in my early days in Blackwick once I used up all my herbs originally gifted to me from the laity. I could see on Adder's face that he regretted not getting to his tea while it was hot. "I have had time to meditate and reflect on what I've done. The betrayals. I am guilty of envy. I am guilty of pride. I am guilty of greed. I wanted what the High Priestess's had with the old- with the gods, but it is rare for a man to take a position such as theirs's. My parents were in the church. My parents hid a lot from my *sestra* and I while we were growing up, but as soon as we were able to enter Temple ourselves, they told us of a new god and how he was going to change everything.

"My *sestra*…She dove straight into the new evangelisations. She climbed quickly through the Keepers, but the dark magic Salvatore had opened up to us had driven her mad. She…killed herself for him."

"Who was your *sestra*?" Lachlan asked.

Addar's eyes were shiny, ready to cry again as memories flooded him. They darted between Lachlan and I. "Persephone." Adder's voice cracked as he said her name.

"Grand Deacon at the Gods Wall in South Province," Lachlan confirmed. A missing piece of the puzzle seemed to fall into place for everyone.

Adder's lip quivered as he tried to gather himself. "I felt cheated from her death." He looked at Lachlan knowingly. "I know you did what you had to." He let out a long sigh before he resumed. "My parents and Persephone had dedicated their lives to Salvatore and his promises. They had been making attempts to change the Temples but were only successful in the South Province. I thought I could do more here. I had been making a pilgrimage to Samu's Temple after Persephone's death, when Salvatore came to me. He promised me many things and it was exciting. Years of being with the Temple and I knew I would be no higher than a *Deacon*. All other positions were filled with young, thriving people and I was too old to do anything but what I did then. He promised he could bring her back…He promised he could save my child. I could have my family again.

"That was a year before he started targeting the Temples. I helped Salvatore plan. He introduced me to higher-ups within the Temples around the province that he had manipulated and to many others that he had sunk his claws into. I was convinced I would rise in his command, achieve what I had always wanted from the Temples. He made me believe I could have everything," Adder took another sip of the tea, sighed, and then set the cup back to the stone floor next to his food. "I know now how wrong I have been, and many have suffered because of me. Gods forgive me."

The former deacon looked down to his hands, I could see the regret in his eyes, hear it in his voice. I looked to my companions, my council. This was not exactly something I was familiar with nor what I expected when they told me he requested to speak with me. I did not know what I was supposed to do and yet he spilled a confession to me without prompting. Theone, though they were still clearly upset by him, nodded for me to speak.

"Why me? Why not talk to anyone else?" I asked.

I watched as a tear slid down the mans face. Adder had lost his way a long time ago and wanted to find himself after he had betrayed everything that he once believed in. His jaw worked while he found the right words to say.

"Because unlike me, unlike that *creature* creating ruin in our beautiful lands, you were chosen *Seer*. I see that now." I could tell he was focused on my eye, tethered to the gods, an obvious indication to their presence in the world. "*You* are destined to stop Salvatore. He is the reason for this war. Stop him and you can end it. His army is nothing without their leader." Adder sat straight and wiped his face, though tears continued to trail out of his eyes and down his cheeks. "I have the names of those in league with Salvatore at my office within the Tabernacle of Blackwick. There is a hidden compartment under the top of my desk. They're there. I know my Asa had forwarded you a lot of information, but they would not have found *that*. These other officials corresponded with me and each other, plotting each move for the next several years," Adder explained. "You stalled us from attacking the next Temple with the stunt you pulled in the Stills, but I don't know how much more time you have before Salvatore moves again. I don't know if you will be able to uncover anything in Blackwick. My memory…It's why I had everything written down, so I could give the illusion to Salvatore that I was still as sharp as I had been in my younger years. He will attempt to kill another member of the Holy Order soon. High Priestess Saoirse, I believe she is next. Save her."

Nerice looked at Florence, who had appeared at some point during Adders confession. Florence nodded, knowing what Nerice wanted and disappeared down the corridor. Cathal left with her.

Adder went on. "I claimed to be a holy man, and I was once. I think I was." He looked down in shame. I scanned his cell again, listening to his words. I noticed the clergy robes he used to wear, resembling those that Priestess Mirna, Nerice, and the other monks and nuns had. They were neatly folded and tucked under his desk. His golden septum ring shined in the light on the pile next to the official parchment from the Temples denouncing him. By being denounced, Adder knew he was no longer worthy of wearing them.

"I remember months, perhaps years before Salvatore came to me another deacon had approached me with word of a new god, just as my parents preached. This new god claimed that the gods had truly abandoned us and said He would recreate this world in his image, where men can be most holies. It seemed unreal. Then when I met him…" He shook his head as he relived the moment. "This power he commands, the extension of himself, all those sharp pieces keeping him alive. They are not of our world. I never understood them, but I feel like you might, *Seer.* It had been so long since the gods were with us. I did not know what a god was supposed to look like! To see this creature in front of me…I believed…" Adder coughed trying to catch his breath as he worked himself up. The shame he held in his words. Tears ran down his face more freely as he put his face in his hands.

"My *prababika* was Andreja! How could you disbelieve?!" Lachlan boomed. I had not thought it would be Lachlan who snapped first. Theone held the back of their hand in front of Lachlan's chest, holding him away from the bars. I heard Lachlan's heavy breathing as he huffed and calmed himself back down.

Adder shook his head in shame and whimpered, "It is so rare now to have the gods here. Even when Andreja was with us, she was the last to be seen for centuries. There had been none in the South Province for hundreds of years, even before Salvatore's arrival there. It's why they stopped believing, why the sands took them. Your *prababika*…You are the only one left alive to have met her. Not even the elders who lived in Blackwick had known her, how was anyone to believe *stories*?"

"She was private in her last years," Lachlan growled. "Blackwick was smaller then! And I was but a baby, but I *knew* her. You should have had faith!"

Adder nodded, agreeing, and looked up at me. "Forgive me. I know now I will be forsaken for my sins. It will be a miracle if I am granted any mercy in the After…It will be centuries before I can see my loved ones. I beg of you, forgive me and maybe I will be able to see them one day again. I made a mistake. Have you never made one?"

"I never betrayed my own people," I stated.

Adder coughed again then wiped his face. "*You* could be more, Seer, I believe that now. Forgive me, *please*." He held the iron bars, slipping one hand through them and reaching out to me, just like Antore's people did to me when we arrived here; a hope for a blessing, for luck, forgiveness. I was not a god, but these people believed me to be something more, just as Adder said. I heard as Theone's hand moved to their sword, the small click of metal threatening to be lifted from its sheath. Lachlan shook his head at them. Nerice crossed her arms and sneered, rolling her eyes at his gesture.

I slowly stood. It took everything in me not to shake, not to show that this whole conversation did not rattle me. "Only the gods can forgive you, Adder," I said.

As we left the dungeons, we left to the sounds of the former grand deacon weeping.

I took a break from climbing all the stairs from the dungeon in the main hall. It was being worked on by a few carpenters, but they retired for the evening. Now only laity members were within in, scrubbing the floors to clean even though they would have to do it all over again tomorrow when the carpenters returned to finish with the support beams in the ceiling. I flopped into one of the nine thrones by the windows and Lachlan sat next to me while Theone and Nerice walked off to discuss what they had learned.

"How do you do this every day?" I asked him. "The strength you must have to endure this!"

Lachlan let out a single, entertained huff. He stretched his hand out from his throne to mine and I took his fingers. No longer did he wear the full set of armour as he did in Blackwick. With the valley heating up, he chose not to wear his leathers and instead sported only a few statement pieces of chain or plate armour, claiming so long as he stayed out of the sun he would not overheat. This meant no gloves and I could feel his skin against my fingertips.

"I'm exhausted by strength," Lachlan admitted. "I dream of a simple life amongst my friends. I long for peace and softness. I desire a day that I'm not praised for how well I do my job, in fact one that I am not praised at all."

I could empathize with him.

The only thing that kept me from completely burning out on Earth was going on vacation.

Now I was here. Here I could not stop. No one could. Not until this war was finished.

What was life here without the war?

"What will you be doing in this simple life, Commander?" I asked.

Lachlan leaned over the arm of his throne, bringing my hand a little closer so he could kiss my fingers before releasing them from his lips. "Aside from you?" he asked.

I blushed, and he smiled, entertained, then leaned back into the throne, though he kept my hand with his.

"I think I would enjoy fishing. I've always loved the water," Lachlan said. He looked at me fondly then back over the darkening hall. Laity still cleaned the floors, but sconces on the walls were being lit. I could not tell who, but one of the nuns were singing.

"The night you fell from the heavens, I had a dream about a lake," Lachlan's voice was reflective. "Growing up I often dreamt of water, rivers, the seas. That night, I dreamt of a lake, and I floated in a small boat at its center. I was night fishing, when suddenly I saw someone below the surface of the waves, drowning. I reached in to pull them out. Just as I was about to see who it was a scout burst into my room telling me the sky was falling. We left immediately to assess the damage along the route to Blackwick. Search for survivors if they were caught in the flames." He looked at me almost quizzically. Thoughts turned in his head. "You were soaking wet when we found you surrounded by flames…"

He sighed then stood. "I should join Nerice and Theone back at the Council Room. In Bellamy's manor. Do you need help up the stairs?"

I shook my head. It was only my second day with the prosthetic, and I loved the independence it gave me, even if I was sore at the end of the day. I thought about the advancements Earth had. How much comfier artificial limbs had to be compared to straight wood and linen padding.

We parted ways and I headed towards our chamber.

The conversation with Adder had shaken me. Confrontation had never really been a favourite of mine, hence why I had found jobs that I worked mostly alone. Living here was showing me how much more I was capable of. Something about that thought excited me. A longing within me stirred. The call for a greater purpose still hung in the air after months of feeling it for the first time. I wanted to answer it.

When I reached the top of the tower where our chambers

crowned, Vice sat on the last step before the door. His head on his knees, his braid was barely held together, his hair disheveled. The atmosphere around him felt somber.

"Hey," I said. "What's wrong?"

Vice's face looked up quickly, startled. His eyes deeply red and shiny with tears. His trousers were darkened where the tears had shed before I reached him. "Asa is gone."

My heart broke for him. I carefully lowered myself to the stairs beside him and held my arms open for a hug. "Vice, I'm so sorry." He came into my arms, sobbing into my neck and squeezing me tighter than any hug I had ever experienced before.

Chapter Thirteen
Morning and The Days That Followed….

There was a place of interest marked on the map of the Keep. The scout's had not explored it for they could not get past it. After a night filled with tears and hot chocolate, I was drawn below the tower where my bedroom was. I carefully minded the old wooden stairs below as they gradually turned into stone steps. Slowly, the sound of the Keep and outside world drowned out. The stairs were steep and awkward for me to navigate with my new leg. I underestimated the number of them, but eventually I reached the bottom and was met with a large door. According to the map, it was guessed that behind it led deeper into the mountains. However, this one was not a wooden door like many around the Keep. Nor was it broken or splintered with age.

This door was made of stone.

"Put your hand here."

I jumped, spooked. Turning, Vice stood next me, his hands resting on his staff as if he had been here the whole time, his soft voice echoing around the chamber.

"Holy shit, Vice!" I hissed. He was not in our chambers when I awoke, and I thought he had gone to rest. I suppose he had come down here instead and I had somehow known where to find him.

He handed me his staff for support, seeing I was a little winded from my descent, then grazed his hand across a carving on the door, the colour of all the artwork on it long faded. The carving resembled a long exotic flower; amaranth.

"Where does it go?" I asked.

The light down here was so dim I could barely make out Vice's pale form. Just the reflection of his shiny eyes. "Put your hand on it, Delilah."

I raised the hand that bore the pink scar of a hand grasping my own then put it over the flower. The door began to creak and ache. Stone scraped against stone and the age of the place echoed and ached up through the tower. The door opened revealing a dark, long corridor behind it. I blinked, trying to make my eyes adjust to the darkness when suddenly torches on the walls caught aflame. One after the other leading down to the other end ignited. Magic hummed around us. The walls on either side of the tunnel were covered with carvings of lives long passed. The stone had been carved in such detail that laugh lines were included on the faces of people it depicted. People working their crops, praying to the heavens and worshiping, the paint as colourful as the day it was done. We followed the hallway, taking in the beautiful art. Vice, though I sensed he was not much better than last night, seemed to have his spirits lifted a fraction from this discovery. When we reached the other end and met a wooden door, I opened it expecting more art, or even another armoury or chapel.

Instead, I stood there in shock.

More torches caught aflame, illuminating the large circular cobblestoned room. A dozen different doors leading in different directions sat on the outer walls and in the center, completely misplaced, was my Machine.

My mouth fell agape. My heart sped up.

"My…" I slowly approached it, not believing I was really seeing what was before us. It was nearly as perfect as the day I left on vacation. It felt that day had passed years ago, yet as I stared at it, I longed to step inside and have the controls at my fingertips.

"Such an interesting little cottage, to be built deep within a forgotten place…" Vice looked at me knowingly. I looked at him, still unable to comprehend what I was seeing. He urged me forward.

I felt my eyes well with tears, excitement. "Did you…?"

Vice shook his head. "I did nothing."

I pressed my hand against the front door and felt the low vibration of my Machine. It was still working, still alive. "Do you know what this is, Vice?" I asked.

"What I know is everything is connected."

I ran my fingers along the top of the door frame and felt the key box. I slid it open and found my spare Machine key. "This is *my* Machine. Do you want to see the inside?"

His expression lightened. Vice's academic mind intrigued after months of seeing pieces of them all over the area. He wiped at his face, still puffy from the night before, now grateful for a new distraction. "I would love to."

I could feel his presence very closely when I turned to unlock the front door. Somehow, I knew he was analyzing the key. The ones here were old-fashioned in nature, by Earth standards, long and thick pieces of weighted iron that had to be held in the whole hand. They were nothing like the tiny piece of metal I used to unlock my front door. I was never a fan of the coded doors. They malfunctioned more than Machines were lost.

I unlocked it and let the door swing open. Since the generators were still going, I flicked the lights on.

"Wow," Vice said looking to the ceiling as the lights appeared. "This looks nothing like what we've found around the province." He was impressed.

"That metal is inside the walls. Everything that makes these vessels livable burnt up in the atmosphere or the explosions. They aren't meant to crash, let alone fall out of the sky."

How was it in such pristine condition?

How was it sitting in the middle of a castle?

I had to show the others.

"Stay here, Vice," I said. "These switches on the walls turn on the lights. That room," I pointed to the open door closest to us, leading to the control room, "is unlike anything you have ever seen. I will be back soon."

Vice nodded then carefully moved further into the cottage. He flicked on another light switch and looked approvingly up at the fixture. With the lights on, his attention quickly found one of the bookcases I had. Books had fallen from its shelves, and he picked one up, kneeling to look at the cover.

I left him there and moved through the corridor as fast as my body would allow. When I reached the bottom of the tower, I took another deep breath to hurry up the stairs. My leg screamed with revolt.

"Lachlan! Lachlan, help me find everyone!" I exclaimed when I reached his office.

Lachlan stood up from his desk, some papers falling from its surface in his surprise. "Is everything alright?" he asked. The urgency in my voice must have worried him.

I leaned forward rubbing the area where my prosthetic connected to my thigh. "Yes! I need you to help me find Theone, and Bellamy, and Nerice! Meet me at the bottom of our tower. I opened the door!"

"Amazing!" Lachlan said enthusiastically.

"I have something to show everyone!" I started rushing back through the door. "I'll find Cathal and Durin!" I called back.

I knew I would be able to find Cathal or Durin in the tavern. Durin had put in another appeal of resignation as a lieutenant when we arrived, this time he was approved, and he had been celebrating daily since his release. Lachlan had increased the training with Cathal as his Third, and Theone's Second should Lachlan pass on before the end of the war. Cathal made it his personal mission to play *hide and seek* with his Commander most days. He would hide in the tavern and another recruit or Bellamy would find him there.

Durin enjoyed Cathal's company and spent a lot of time telling tales for extra coin when the bard at the tavern was taking a break. I found Durin at the bar, sipping honeyed tea and whiskey. He downed it seeing my urgency as I yelled his name from the entrance of the Tavern.

Cathal was not there this time. Instead, Durin said he was tending to people in the new infirmary. His people were advanced in medicine. Often a surgeon was a Fury, or descent from one. Cathal used his skills as a field medic throughout the war and I fully understood why Bellamy had originally come to train the Northwestern Province; she was going to learn from her uncle. It was Cathal's extra care Lachlan had seen in the same battle Nerice spotted

Bellamy that made him decide to take Cathal in under his personal training. Cathal, despite his brutality in battle, had a soft spot for anyone with even the smallest of wounds, including a papercut. His connections were just a bonus opportunity for the army, just as Bellamy's had been.

I knew the mages who practiced healing were doing their best, but as Lachlan stressed, recovery for anyone was better when there was a team behind them. I recognized Cathal's whole crew in the infirmary working along side the mages and a couple Keeper's and laity. Cathal left with Durin and I after making a joke about being found faster than usual.

My companions met at the stone door, though Nerice was already in the tunnel admiring the carvings. Lachlan put a hand on my arm, a concerned look on his face while I panted from running around. I considered maybe I had got out of shape in the weeks I healed, but I remembered that I was literally hauling ass around a city and castle and needed to be easier on myself.

"Are you *sure* you're alright?" Lachlan asked.

I nodded at first, but then shook my head. Lachlan could clearly read me easier than a book. "I just have something to show everyone." I was both nervous and excited to show my friends this discovery.

I led them down through the corridor, all silenced with either concern or curiosity. Cathal and Nerice paused a few times to look at the stonework of people worshiping. Cathal seemed extra impressed by the artistry and the two made suggestive eyes at each other. When we reached my Machine, they were all curious to why a stone cottage was built within the depths of an ancient castle.

"It's not completely a cottage," I explained as I brought them inside.

Vice was still there. He had cleaned up what books had fallen from the shelves, and I noticed pieces of shattered plates in the garbage tin along with broken glass from a shattered window. Vice had clearly made himself comfortable, for he sat on my old leather couch and was reading through an atlas I had.

Of course, he had found the atlas.

"What a strange little house," Nerice said. "Very cute. Very colourful." Vice closed the atlas as the others came inside and set it to the spot next to him before standing. Nerice started wandering around immediately. "It doesn't seem nearly as ancient as-"

"This is my home," I blurted out, cutting Nerice off. All eyes were on me. "Well, I lived in it on Earth."

"I don't understand," Theone said, stating what everyone else was thinking.

Durin pulled out an antique DVD from my collection on the wall. "Is this a book?" He popped it open. "Nope." Durin slowly closed the DVD case and put it back where he found it.

Their eyes continued to watch me.

"Remember all that debris around demon sites? The vessels I mentioned?" I tried explaining. "Inside these walls are the components that allow my people to travel through space and time. This is where I lived, on my planet." An idea popped into my head. "Maybe with this, we can find Salvatore. Maybe…" I did not say the rest.

Seeing my Machine, standing inside its living walls, I could not deny that returning to Earth crossed my mind again, but I did not long to go back as I once had. Instead, seeing it gave me a reason to stay and help in a way I knew I could. If Salvatore had Machine embedded into his body, I could track it with my own vessel.

Vice existed the control room where he had roamed. "An interesting place indeed," he said. He motioned towards the room. "This place is different."

"That room controls the Machine. It can find *other* Machines. If I can get any readings from it, we could potentially find Salvatore within moments," I explained.

Nerice looked at Bellamy then Lachlan. "We could put our resources elsewhere and plan an attack against him!" she said.

Lachlan kissed my forehead. He put his hands on my shoulders as he leaned his forehead on mine. "What magic have you been hiding?" he teased.

"It's not magic, it's science," I said.

Everyone explored, looking at my art, my books. Bellamy found my closet and dug through it with vigor. I went into my control room, some books still on the ground from the malfunction, though Vice had piled them neatly. I gazed over the control panel, reading the screens and settings, the confusion my Machine was experiencing. Where the location screen was, the word *unknown* blinked on the dashboard. I would have to take a more detailed look into the manual again, refresh my memory on the details. Seeing it, I knew my Machine would not be ever able to leave this place.

If the Machine was confused, you were lost, *forever*. There was no going back. Some theories suggested the missing Travellers had been lost because of malfunctions. With Machine's broken and dead across the province, Earth would never know what really happened. Surely, not all of them had ended up here.

Surely.

I looked back to my friends and watched as Durin and Lachlan read the backs of books. Durin tucked one into his jacket. Nerice picked through my kitchen cupboards, pulling out canned goods and piling them on the counter before opening the fridge and promptly closing it. The stink the food within reeked of long rotten meat and vegetables, scaring her off.

"Durin, would you like to hear Earth music?" I called from my control room.

"Are you going to sing?" Durin called back. I turned back to the dashboard of my control panel, gently grazing my fingers over the keys as my former life whispered memories to me. I turned on my stereo and went back into the main area seeing wonder in my friends' eyes. Music played from speakers in the walls.

Everyone seemed charmed.

Nerice danced leisurely along with the beat that played on the speakers and ripped a can of applesauce open as easier than biting into a piece of fruit. She was happy with the contents inside and spooned it into her mouth with her razor fingers.

Cathal flopped onto my couch. The sound of its legs crunched, breaking under his weight. He sunk down and made a face as he pulled the atlas out from under him then tore into a bag of ketchup potato chips he took from the counter. "Oops, sorry," he said, not getting up but getting more comfortable into the cushions.

"Look at this painting," Nerice said with a mouth full of applesauce. "It's Antore!"

Durin, Lachlan, Theone, and Bellamy, her arms full of clothing, gathered before the painting. Nerice danced away from it, still swaying gently to the beat and shovelling applesauce into her mouth. Cathal sat up to look.

"Gods give me breath, it is," Theone said, shocked. As I joined my friends to look at the painting, a sharp shiver went down my spine. It was one of the castle paintings I had bought off the previous owner of my Machine.

"How could this be?" Bellamy asked. Everyone looked at me as I continued running my eyes over the painting.

I did not understand.

I looked at the signature.

It was not the previous owner's name, but I knew the last name.

"Lachlan," I breathed. I put my fingers on it.

Lachlan shook his head as he focused on the name. "Russell Blackwick isn't anyone I know," he said, confused. His eyes widened a bit as he took the rest of the painting in. "The date!"

The date read thirty-seven years in our future.

I was dazed, wandering back to the control room.

Someone from here had made it back to Earth.

How?

I studied the dashboard as I was so used to doing a lifetime ago. Something caught my eye that I had not noticed before. On the screen next to the word *unknown,* I saw the Machine serial number I had manually typed in before my journey. Blinking red, like the light I had seen submerged in Salvatore's petrified skin, the word *found* flashed. Somewhere, within the hundreds of thousands of miles that this planet had to offer, Salvatore's stollen Machine was alive.

Theone, Bellamy and Nerice, arms full of canned food or clothes, left to return to Council business. While Cathal, after downing the bag of chips, returned to the infirmary and Durin to the tavern. Lachlan remained behind with me. I wanted to stay in my Machine for a little while.

Even though I stood within it, I was having a hard time grasping it was alive and well. I was particularly thrown off by the painting, which, after inspecting the others I had purchased from the previous owner, were also other places around the province according to Lachlan. All were painted by the same man.

After closing the door behind Vice, a pile of a half dozen books he liked from my collection at hand, I looked at my broken window. The rest of the windows had cracks in them. I considered tapping one, my hand hovering before the fractures on the glass. I thought better of it then sat heavily to my newly broken couch. I unhinged the lock on my prosthetic by the knee so the leg would not stick straight out, and my skirt draped over my legs. Lachlan sat next to me, his eyes still full of wonder.

"I'm trying to comprehend someone making it back to Earth," I admitted.

Lachlan put his arm over the back of the couch as he leaned back. "Sometimes it's best to leave those questions to the gods," he looked at me, "as hard as it may be to achieve. It's easier on the spirit and sometimes you get answers in the After, when you can reflect on all your other lives."

I turned to look at him. Lachlan stroked my cheek with his free hand, his gaze kept drifting to my mouth.

"Do you remember anything from your lives before?" I asked, breathing in his scent.

We were finally alone, and he was offering me a distraction from my troubles.

"There is no sense on lingering on the past. It's why we're reborn," he said simply. His voice was low, seductive.

I felt a fire spark in my belly has the hand that stroked my cheek moved into my hair. He pulled me closer, and gave me a deep, satisfying kiss.

As his hand released my hair, the one along the couch gripped my shoulder. He dipped to kiss my throat, working his way up my neck to nibble at my ear. Perhaps he was right, there was no sense on lingering on the past. That mentality could also be applied to the future, to whoever had made those paintings. All that existed was the present. Right now, his hand moved over my thigh, and I ached for more. I opened my legs, allowing him easier access if he so chose to do so.

"I'm only curious," I swallowed. He felt the heat between my thighs. He grazed my breeches with his fingers, tempting me for more. "It's not something that is common where I'm from."

Lachlan pulled away, now interested in the conversation.

Damn it.

"Oh, well, umm, I can remember a little. The more you accept your new life the less you remember of your old ones. In the After you can remember them all because you are not confined to a mortal body, but with each incarnation you can meditate to try to summon who you once were back ."

I turned to him, putting his hand back to my thigh. "Did you love someone in your last life?"

"Not the way I love you, Delilah. I never married, as far as I can remember. Never cared to until..." He smiled softly, looking away from me almost embarrassed. If my hand did not hold his, I thought he would have taken it away again.

"The last few years have been trying," Lachlan started. "I found myself praying to Andreja, asking her to give me a reason that would make it all worth it. Then I saw *you*. I saw you with my *prababika*'s eye and suddenly everything made sense. Have you ever felt that way?"

"You love me?" I asked.

Lachlan chuckled. "Of course, Delilah. I thought it was obvious."

"I love you too," I blurted out.

Lachlan smiled wide and kissed me, his hand squeezed my thigh, the same pleasurable tingle he teased me with a couple nights prior spread from his touch, awakening me, urging me to spill over the edge.

"I'm glad to hear that or else this would have become very awkward," Lachlan joked. He kissed me again, hungry, aching. His hand hooked the bottom of my skirt, lifting it so he could find his way between my thighs again. I wanted to reach out and touch him but there was so much armour in the way.

Two fingers grazed me again and I sucked in an anticipated breath. He had yet to touch me this way and I craved him. His hand continued to stroke and tease me. I withered to his touch as he leaned his forehead to mine, his eyes happily watching my expression as he pushed me closer and closer…

His voice remained alluring as he spoke. "Do you want to stay here or move to that little bedroom I saw?" he asked. He moved his hands under the waistband of my breeches. Two fingers slid inside me and moved slowly, caressing me right where I needed them to. I built up quickly, the tension making me squirm and want to grind against his touch.

"I want you," I breathed.

Lachlan nodded, eager to give me what I wanted, what we both craved. His fingers slipped out. He untangled himself from me to remove some of his armour, key pieces to free himself only enough to access me. I struggled to pull my breeches off under my skirt, but when I was successful, he pulled me on top of him, pushing my skirt out of the way. One hand snaked between us to help himself inside while the other gripped my hip. As I slowly lowered overtop of him, he groaned with fierce satisfaction. Lachlan looked over my face, remembering every detail of this moment. The bliss.

Satisfying with how I fit, he settled his other hand on my side. I took his face in my hands to kiss him. He slowly lifted me and guiding me back down. I moaned against his lips. As Lachlan sped up, the pressure built, and everything disappeared, but him.

After the discovery of my Machine, the surrounding doors in the circular chamber were explored. Nerice's scouts discovered many different passageways leading all through the valley. Nerice concluded the passages were made for the advantages of the people who once lived here; and now us. Doors led deep into the mountainside and out to old, overgrown cave entrances for a safe escape. Some opened to the lake. One door led to a smaller cathedral than the one being restored in the main city. Within it there were old statues of the gods, dusted and webbed, hundreds of years since their last visitor.

Bellamy and the rest of the Council finished the office where they would meet for coordinating the army and its influence, moving all the maps and letters from priests and Temple nobles directly to that area rather than one of three offices around the Keep. Before that room, running around was chaotic, and I would always hope I would run into Nerice, rather than anyone else, to ask where to find somebody. After all, she saw everything. The corridors within this one room, made moving through the city easy and quiet. The Council and I were grateful. The only downside was all the stairs.

Soon I found myself spending most of my time in my Machine. I began a new routine. My mornings were spent in the kitchens, the smell of bread and bacon clinging to me easier than perfume. My afternoon and evenings with Vice while we put all our concentration on the hunt for Salvatore. My nights were my favourite, with Lachlan between my legs.

I was convinced Vice was using the research as an opportunity to distract himself from his grief, and I could not deny him. He had collected local and provincial maps. He convinced Theone, with the help of Lachlan, to give up the single world map the Keep had. It was a piece of parchment very rare to come by. Nerice and Bellamy had been indifferent on the matter, busy coordinating with Temples and the scouts on the field.

Vice rolled out the maps on my dining table, weighing them down with random objects he found around my Machine. Objects like tiny porcelain cats, action figures, and cups that had not fallen out of the kitchen cupboards and shattered were all keeping the maps from rolling back up.

I looked at the screen where my Machine told me another was present. I selected it, but a red X flashed over the screen and a disappointing, hard beep sounded out in rejection.

Right.

The Machine did not know where it was, so it could not tell me the location name of where the one Salvatore had stolen was located. I sighed heavily then grabbed the Machines thick, heavy manual. The last time I held it was the day I had travelled here. It felt strange in my hands now, so neatly printed and bound better than any book I had read in months. This was a luxury.

I was confident there were other settings I could find on the control panel that would give me distances or general direction, but I had not used those settings before, not since school. The Machine had to give *some* information, despite how it fought me. When I sat in my chair to open the manual, Vice came into the control room. He had been helping me tidy in addition to finding Salvatore. A lot of things were out of place from the rough arrival. The control panel was caked in dirt and dust, and I had not cleaned it yet.

"You believe Salvatore has pieces of his Machine keeping him alive?" he asked curiously. We had been exchanging theories for hours.

"It's not his, he stole it," I said flipping through the manual, trying to find location instructions. My head still reeled with the thought of having another part of Earth back. My photo albums, my clothes, a childhood stuffed animal that would guard me while I slept, all within my grasp once more.

I tried to recall the day I had come here. The things I did before I dropped out of the sky into this new world. The brief sense of familiarity standing in my Machine, though it was nice, also felt somewhat alien. I had grown used to my new life and now I had a huge piece of my old one.

I spent most nights within my Machine, knowing it would be easier than climbing all the stairs every day to the top of the tower. Lachlan happily obliged sleeping on my comfortable Earth mattress. When we first discovered my Machine, it smelt stale from all the months of dust, sitting there waiting for me. I planned to have my blankets and clothes brought up with my books. Everything else would be donated. The glassware and plates that survived, the furniture; others in Antore would have more use for them than I. No longer would I be able to watch DVD's, not unless I rigged something with the solar panels, but I felt the panels could be used for something more useful. Instead, I planned to make a wall of DVD discs into an art piece for the tower chambers and the cases could surely be used for something else.

Vice had said everything happens for a reason. My Machine was here for a reason. I just had to figure out what that reason was.

I continued flipping through the book. How to troubleshoot, routine maintenance checks, information on the self-destruct, reselling instructions, programing the filters for well water, how to find other Machine's.

There.

I began reading.

Machine Locator: while searching for another Machine, you must have the Machines serial number to add into the locator.

I raised my brows.

My assumption on other Machine's crashing. My fear of it being each missing Traveller from Earth. My heart felt tight. I took a pencil and stuck it into the spine to mark the page. Flipping to the back of the book, I searched for the pages with serial numbers. My manual had been a new addition when I purchased it and there were old numbers printed in the back, but I had filled in more since I became a Traveller. Hundreds of numbers and names, maybe thousands, all recorded in the back: Missing Travellers. I walked to the panel and typed in one of the more recent numbers in the back of my book.

Found.

I typed in the number of someone who went missing around the time I first started Travelling.

Found.

I flipped back a few pages to the numbers printed with the book. The first person to go missing:

Found.

"Holy shit," I said dropping the manual to the floor. I had been *right*. Never in my life had I wished so hard not to be. "Vice, did you see a newspaper somewhere?" I squeaked.

"A what?" Vice asked, picking up the manual and flipping it to the page I had marked. He scanned his eyes over it. "There are a lot of words here that I don't completely understand…" he said curiously, a smile growing on his face at the possibility of learning something new. "You must teach me."

"Right." My brain had begun to reset. I was in a familiar place. My thoughts had returned to not watching the way I worded things. "A large parchment. Black and white. Maybe some coloured images on it. It would have lot of other pieces of parchment with it. Like a large, delicate book."

Vice nodded. "I have seen that." He went back into my living area, manual still in hand, and returned moments later with the newspaper. "More instructions?"

"No, it's a collection of articles keeping locals up to date on what was going on in their country and around the world. Instead of updates from messengers, letters, and owls, it's all collected into a daily parchment delivered to your door." Among other methods.

"Sounds convenient," Vice said handing it to me.

"It can be." I flipped through the pages, searching. I remembered the sweet old man who used to walk the paper to me every week, the smile he would give me. I never asked him his name. "Also read through that manual. It has a lot of information about Machine's in it and I have several other scientific books on my shelf there," I motioned to the bookcase with a dried-up plant and several of my old school textbooks. "Those are the texts I read while I was in university and training to captain my Machine. If you have questions,

let me know." Vice wandered briefly to the shelf I had indicated and selected a book on mechanics; the book had a lot of visuals in it which would be helpful for him. That as when I saw it:
MISSING: THIRD TRAVELLER IN SIX MONTHS; COINCIDENCE?

I pointed to the title on the paper. "Here! I read this before I left." It was a flicker of a memory.

Vice came behind me, the mechanics book in hand on top of the manual and read the page as I did. We saw the name at the same time.

Cifarelli Salvatore.

"Fuck!" I said throwing the paper. "I was hoping that I was wrong!"

"Well," Vice said. He moved quietly around me, seemingly unmarred by my outburst. He picked the paper back up and moved it to the page we had been looking at. A photo of Salvatore was printed on the page and underneath the photo was the Machines serial number that he had stolen. "This is just a man. He looks nothing like what we saw in Blackwick," Vice observed.

I sat down, my heart pumping. My mind raced as it had on our journey through the Stills.

How did all the other Travellers end up here?

How did Salvatore get here?

How had he changed into that creature?

Did he know who I *was?*

Vice read over the article again. "He disappeared from your world before you did it seems," Vice observed. He made a face. "But why would any of the gods bring that *thing* here. The timing is off. Salvatore has been here for centuries. This indicates he had disappeared rather recently before you arrived, correct?"

"How did his Machine even get here?!" I blurted out, my eyes far away. "Did he get here on his own? Willingly? Or…" I shook my head. The metal sticking out of his body, the light blinking under his pale skin, his flesh trying to pull itself apart. "I think…" I began, my mind was far away, pulling the memories back from the battle. Puling memories back from closing ruptures and seeing the aftermath of a crashed Machines. I thought about the falling star a century before the beginning of the war, carving a scar into South Province.

Vice could see the concern on my face, the growing terror trying to take hold of me. He put a hand on me, bringing me back to the room with him. "What do you need?" he asked.

I could feel myself begin to cry, not for myself but for all the missing Travellers. Vice folded the newspaper and set it on the control panel. I watched as he tried to find words to comfort me. He looked over the dashboard and pressed the button for my stereo. A favourite artist of mine clicked on and music sounded throughout the Machine.

I deflated, wiping at my face.

How did everyone end up here. I took the manual from Vice's hands, opening it back to where I marked it. I read through it as fast as I could, scanning for key words then went to the panel. The singer on my speakers howled and hummed, her voice a sirens song. She had died only a year before I was born at ninety-three. She had been a favourite of my great-grandmothers. My great grandmother was the reason for my love of oldies music. I was instantly soothed.

I changed 'location' to 'mileage' on the dashboard and input the Machine's serial number associated with Salvatore. The screen flashed the numbers *6834* over the word *kilometres*.

I exited the control room quickly and went to my dining table, looking over the world map. I found Antore on it and pointed to the surrounding mountains. "What's six thousand eight hundred and thirty-four kilometers from here?" I asked.

Vice came beside me. "That's a precise number," he said. He pulled the provinces map close, over the world map. "I would say, somewhere between this point and this one," he said pointing to two areas with a long finger. I felt his eyes on me, waiting for my next move. I could feel his worry.

"That's far from *us* at least, thank the gods." I slumped into a dining chair and looked over the map again. "Adder said he would be trying to assassinate High Priestess Saoirse. Is her Temple close to that marker?"

Vice pulled another chair out from the table and sat next to me. "No, but perhaps you should bring this to the Council, Delilah. They can send scouts, request specific information from Temples nearby and work from there."

I swallowed and leaned my face into my hands as my elbows rested on the table. "It doesn't make sense. If he was here centuries before me, the Machine shouldn't have survived. There is no way…" I shook my head, speaking through my hands. "I can't help but feel this is somehow my fault," I admitted. "All those people…"

Vice gently took my arm in his and moved one hand from my face so I would look at him. He was deeply hunched over, so big in a space so small. "Delilah, he disappeared before you had. How could you possibly be blamed?"

Our eyes connected. I could tell he was doing his best with reassuring me. He did not have a soft voice like Durin or Theone when they would comfort me, but I recognized he wanted to help in his own way. He had figured out the music. He was doing a good job. He was a good friend.

"You're right," I sighed, leaning back in my chair.

Vice moved his hand away. "Aye. With the knowledge you have, it just proves further that you came here with a purpose to help this world. With this new knowledge it could lead to Salvatore's defeat."

"You have a lot of faith," I said. "Everyone seems to."

Vice nodded. "You can choose to live with or without faith, Delilah. Living with faith is a far better life than one where all you can see ahead is darkness and despair because you have lost the faith that kept you going in the first place."

"How profound," I said.

Vice shrugged. "I suppose. But if you have lived for as long as I have, and seen what I have seen, it's hard to not carry it. Especially when a woman from another world falls from the sky and *lives*. I grew up on the prophecy that someone would do just *that*."

I smiled. "Thank you, Vice."

Vice grinned, satisfied he pulled the frown from my

expression. "Of course." He grabbed his over-jacket to put back on. I had turned on the heat in my Machine to keep the coldness of the corridors surrounding us out. Despite the growing heat outside, the deep caverns were as cool as an autumn night. "Let us call in for the rest of the day. You can give your findings to the Council and plan from there."

I nodded. He was right.

Just one step at a time.

Chapter Fourteen
Summer

After the months of residing here, many parts of the Keep remained undiscovered. Nerice's scouts went into the depths of the stone walls day after day and kept finding new passageways and rooms. Old dungeons with cell keys still hanging on the walls, living quarters with beds still made awaiting their holder to rest. There were several armouries and a large forge with the weapons and armour rusted, but intact. Walls wore sculptures with brilliantly carved stories of people who walked the halls long before us and tapestries hung frozen in time, no one to gaze upon them for centuries. Old houses and apartments were restored. A second inn and tavern was built into the caverns below the city. More people were coming in every day hoping to escape the warring lands below the mountains.

It was the warmest day I had experienced yet when I decided to step into a Council meeting. It had been a while since I had, and I felt I should as Seer. I had put it off, thinking they would ask me to go back into the province to deal with more demons. I was a little scared to leave the safety of the valley since Blackwick's destruction, yet no one brought it up.

Today was the first day I saw Bellamy wearing a single layer. She had a glass pitcher of cold tea on the thick table, and I was greeted with a glass to refresh me. "We're finally having beautiful weather," she said happily, handing me an updated map of the known tunnels below before returning her attention to the rest of the Council. "Thanks to the grand former deacon's confession, we have made a lot of headway."

The days had stayed hot for weeks. I had always thought Bellamy was a beautiful woman, but she had always dressed modestly, and I never fully took in the body she had underneath. Now, in the heat of the summer, she wore barely anything at all. Clad in a thin teal silk dress, it cascaded down and exaggerated the curves of her body. She wore golden sandals that glittered in the sunlight, an accessory to match the chains in her hair and the rings on her fingers. Somehow, she smelt more like sunshine than usual, a delicious lemon pastry.

Nerice elbowed me as she walked next to me.

I had been gaping, *whoops*.

Nerice smirked and returned to discussing our options. "Aye, but we still must unearth those names. With the melt, it will be easier to access and search the ruins at Blackwick, but there is no guarantee they're still intact." The other's had dressed down as well. Nerice wore a lace navy robe, untied to reveal a knife strapped to her thigh and a linen tunic embroidered with the symbol of the Temples at the neckline. She had her hair tied back for once and I could see sweat bead around her hairline.

Theone donned only a breastplate and gambeson. They too had a blade strapped to their side and the dark makeup around their eyes was smudged from rubbing sweat away constantly. Their lips were still impeccably painted black.

Lachlan had his gambeson on, but it was unfastened exposing the linen shirt underneath. The belt around his waist holding his sword was loose and his hair was slicked back with sweat. His gloves were not on, exposing his scars and he wore sandals and loose trousers to keep himself aeriated. The condensation on the pitcher made a small puddle where it connected with the table.

I wore a pair of shorts from my Earth collection and a sheer blouse I only tied up halfway. Every time I looked at Lachlan his eyes darted back to the table, away from my exposed cleavage. Bellamy had braided my hair earlier in the day and I was grateful to have it out of my face.

"We know that Salvatore is planning to lay siege at the Temples. It's only a matter of time after the first two. We have it on good opinion that High Priestess Saoirse is next, but after all the deceit Adder lay on them, the Temple's need more than just his word and I agree. We need to uncover those names. At least we can track Salvatore in the interim." Lachlan looked at me to continue and explain.

Eyes were on me, and I felt self-conscious. This was the first time I felt like I actually had something valuable to add to the conversations with the Council. I did not want to seem foolish when presenting to them, even though I knew my friends would not make me feel that way. They knew most of the information anyway, as I was sure Lachlan shared anything I told him regarding my Machine with them.

"I have strong reason to believe Salvatore still has the device that he came here with. It's like mine." I tried to keep my statements to the point. "I'm confused because the lifespan of these vessels are short if not taken care of. Our technology cannot last for *centuries*."

"Perhaps a spell is involved. Ancient magic older than the war," Nerice suggested. "In the library we uncovered, there was a pile of burnt books. One title was still visible and after some digging, we believe all the books on necromancy within the library were the ones burned. It's possible *he* got those grubby claws on them. Necromancy combined with your Earth magic could give him some sort of edge. Longevity. Whatever. Bad people have ways of doing bad things in my experience."

"Necromancy? Impossible!" Theone scoffed. "*Shamira* was the only recorded successful necromancer."

"Yeah. *Recorded*," Nerice said with a cocked brow.

"He was just a *man* on Earth. Not a good, but a man. He could not have learned necromancy!" I said in disbelief. "Whatever Salvatore did to become what he is now it's-"

"Dark magic," Theone said. "We all know it."

"*Necromancy* is dark magic," Nerice hissed.

"Let us calm ourselves," Bellamy said holding her hands up. "We begin by uncovering the former grand deacon's letters. We get the names of those within the Temple that we need to, we intercept their correspondence, we present the evidence to the Temples. People will get arrested. Salvatore's resources will begin to dwindle. They *did* increase security around other Divine's since Adder's confession, and we have been granted more Keepers to protect Antore and our Seer, but more needs to be done. The will of the gods have not been *this* present in generations." She began to pour herself a glass of tea, then moved around the table where our own glasses sat empty, pitcher still in hand. "So far everything aligns with the future you saw in the Stills. We were lucky with the dragon attack. Small blessings."

"I have a team ready to search," Nerice said. "We can pray everything is dry now."

"Your best chance to search Adders office is to go into the Tabernacle through the passages we used to escape rather than digging it out."

"I already thought of that," Nerice said.

Lachlan sighed. "Of course."

Nerice smirked.

"Continue the research you're doing Delilah. We have sent scouts out in every direction with a distance you gave us. They will send owls with anything suspicious or of note," Bellamy assured me.

I nodded. "On it."

*

I walked along the console of my sleeping Machine and sighed heavily. Soon the power would run out if I kept it on for the whole cottage. It had gone into hibernation in my absence as it was programed to do, but the power could only go so far without a fuel resupply or sun to recharge the solar panels. It would die without power to regenerate it. I glanced down to my wooden leg, saw the beauty carved into it. If I had lost my leg back on Earth, I would have been fitted with a bionic leg. I would be more comfortable moving around.

I had an idea.

I *had* Earth technology and brilliant minds all around me.

I turned to Vice whose eyes were memorizing the dashboard, in love with the science of it. "Do you think you'd be up for a project?"

"Of course, what do you need assistance with?" he asked. Vice had been running his fingers over another section of my console, his eyes thoughtful after reading all the textbooks I had from

360

school ten times over. Engineering, mechanics, history, the Machines manual, all absorbed by his curious mind. He barely asked me to elaborate on what the books said, and he had made many notes of his own in a blank book he bounded. It was easy, having a second person to research and help with the controls. Two minds on the screens meant we could try to find Salvatore two times faster. He had a better understanding than anyone else here and I was sure he could help me with my idea.

"I'm going to disassemble my Machine," I told him.

Vice moved his staff from one hand to the other, leaning on it, his expression intrigued. "Do you not think it can help us further with finding Salvatore?"

"The opposite. We won't need to keep coming down here, and I will be able to move more freely."

"You want to become one with your Machine, like your theory with Salvatore and his stolen technology," Vice stated. I could see the interest he had in my proposition, the potential with it.

I nodded. "Aye, if Salvatore can become one with the Machine, so can I." I looked at the lights and switches and screens of the console, still grimy from the dust that had accumulated in my absence. It had been a used older model when I bought it and now its age really showed. Underneath the console and throughout the walls was endless metal, wires, and technology. With it, I could create a smaller version of my Machine's power. Still fit to track Salvatore but also containing the technology to work with my body, compacted into my own special prosthetic.

"I'm going to need a smith and the surgeon."

"Those are interesting requests," Vice said.

"And you can help me with the configuration." I pointed to a small metal door high on the wall behind Vice's head. "In there is the source that keeps this place running. It's going to die soon if I keep this whole place going without refueling it. If I give it something smaller to control and dismantle the tiles on the roof that use the sun for life, it can potentially last much longer."

"Smaller?" Vice repeated. "How are you proposing to

incorporate it?”

I motioned to my wooden leg. I had figured out how to walk, even run, with minimal pain. Save the large climbs up and down the stairs of the Keep and my small limp as the leg was a little too tall, I could almost move normally. Though phantom pains still haunted me when the weather was going to be bad, I was proud of the progress I made. I was confident that with Vice’s mind and my own, we could figure it out in no time.

“We’re going to make me a new leg,” I said.

“Hmm,” Vice said intrigued. “I will be glad to help.”

*

Proceedings going forward progressed quickly. Nerice’s scouts uncovered the letters Adder had mentioned, though the words were a little smudged from being buried under snow for so long. Her Third, Captain Florence, led a team to scatter over the province and intercept correspondences between traitors within the Temples. Multiple owls were sent out to make sure the proof would reach the Holy Order.

“We have invited Priests and Priestess’s from Temples to witness the letters and confirm the truth of them to their Divines,” Bellamy said. “It is only a matter of time before we have their full support and complete access to Keepers. I’m certain.”

“I like that confidence. We need a win like this,” Lachlan said. He wiped sweat from his forehead and pointed to several locations on the world map we had brought back up from my Machine. “These are the areas we suspect Salvatore to strike next, if he decides to alter his plans. He most likely knows we have Adder. These locations are within the distance Delilah gave us and according to her sources, we suspect he has not made a move yet.”

The number on my locater had not changed in months. Though word came in from others preaching his will, things had seemed calmer with his smaller provincial numbers and no dragon to wreak havoc.

After designing the lower leg with assistance of the surgeon, making sure I had the anatomy right and measurements would be accurate to my body, I sent the design to the same smith who had made my daggers and helmet. It was her wife that carved my wooden leg. When the smith gave me the metal prosthetic back, with the hinges, compartments, and gaps where I had asked, Vice helped me integrate the technology into it.

I had a limited idea on the technology within my Machine, since I never built one. Vice had never worked with anything like it before, but we worked through trial, error, and several electric shocks. At first Vice was intrigued by the *magic* that revolted in our work. Then, after several weeks, he became irritated by each misstep he made, cursing in Bygone Speech and glaring at whatever piece of technology he was working on. Luckily, however many centuries Vice had been alive, it had given him the ability to easily adapt, and he had an uncanny understanding for most components after little review.

We spent days in the tunnels below Antore, carefully constructing the device by candle and mage light to conserve the power in my Machine. To make sure everything would last long enough to rig the solar panels up for charging, I was afraid to use any more energy from the generator. If the heart of the Machine died, I would not be able to revive it and there were no Machine specialists here, at least no living ones.

There were several nights when I woke up on the dining room table, jerked awake by my head colliding to the wooden surface. I would see Vice, unphased by my disruption, carefully working away on the new leg with small tweezers and ten books open around him to make sure he could do what we were hoping for. Lachlan's soft snores would sound from the bedroom and a cold cup of tea sat beside me that I assumed Lachlan brought down when he came to bed. Other instances I awoke in my old bed, the low voices of Vice and Lachlan speaking to each other. Slowly Vice was opening up to the rest of my companions and he was becoming fast friends with Lachlan. I had a hunch they were playing with spells to try to coax the wires into submission, but I doubted the Machine would listen to their charms.

When it was finally time to put the heart from my Machine into the prosthetic, everything slowed down. The feeling of a significant moment on the cusp of occurring buzzed, and I had gooseflesh. I felt good about this, like something had been leading me here from the start. I stressed to Vice that we had to be careful when handling it; the power cell was hot and unstable. Vice and I wore thick leather gloves as we opened the small metal door on my control room wall. Nerice had snatched a pair each for us from the smith after I told her we had been electrocuted a few times. Now staring at the humming, glowing piece of my Machine's heart, I felt a breath of sadness. Everything this was meant to do, was going to change. *My Machine would never Travel again, and it would never see Earth. At least it would still have me.*

"Moment of truth," I said, holding my breath as I carefully plucked the heart from the wall. All the walls had been torn open to expose the innerworkings of the Machine. Wires and cogs were ripped out to find the right pieces to incorporate into the leg. My control panel was carefully picked apart to make a simple command pad. Whatever remained of this place when we were done would be used where it could in Antore. It was all I could offer to this place, without working in the kitchens. The Machine made a creaking noise as the life left it, the sound of it powering down forever, becoming just a little skeleton of a cottage in the middle of a giant fortress.

Vice could see the pain it caused me, taking it apart. "Antore is your home now, my friend. We will always be here for you. For as long as you will have us."

I turned and Vice carefully took the cell from me, looking at it in awe. The light it emitted pulsed in his hands, glowing a bright blue colour. "This looks created by the gods," he said. I could see endless possibilities within Vice's gaze, enthralled by the cell. "I can feel it grow warmer in my fingertips."

In the years I had been in school, in all the textbooks I owned and discussions I had with professors and fellow students, even the woman who sold me her Machine, not a single person had an answer to how the fuel cells were made. There was some big secret hiding it. A patent claimed Machines were made accessible to most families, so long as the secret was never revealed.

Vice blew gently onto the cell, a motion similar to blowing out a candle. "Be soft, little thing," he told it, and the cells light dulled to a warmer glow, instead of a sharp cold one. I stared at him, still analyzing the heart in his hands, hundreds of ideas crossing his expression every second.

Perhaps there was magic involved.

"It's very beautiful," I said remembering the first time I saw the cell of my Machine. How captivating it had been, just a tennis ball-sized orb seemingly magnetized between intricate metal rods. Vice carefully positioned it into the new prosthetic as I sat on the stool next to him. It clicked into place and the sound of a small engine starting whirling. The leg lit up with life, lights blinking, wires vibrating. My eyes widened, eager. My hope, with the new leg, was that it would be as flexible as the bionic ones on Earth and move with me as an extension of my mind. We had spent weeks configuring it, praying it would connect with my life force and my heart would become one with its own. This was not a replacement of something I lost, just an aid to make my position as Seer more accessible and hopefully less tiring. I even incorporated an on-off switch, so at night I could save power and a plug to attach it to the solar panels Cathal and Vice and had carefully secured to the roof of the tower. I think that was when Vice really started to open up and Cathal let his opinions drop of him. Vice had lost his footing and Cathal snatched him out of the air, securing him safely back beside him. Vice had seen how we all cared for one another and Cathal decided he was just a regular guy, and a glimpse into his own future.

I prayed the leg would last into my old age, if I was lucky. After all, the fuel cells were meant to power a Machine for at least a year without refilling the power, and longer when recharged. Not once had I heard of a retired Machine. None had been disassembled and used as spare parts for other Machines as intended. Hopefully something that could power a whole time-travelling machine could handle one leg.

Vice motioned to my wooden leg still strapped to my thigh and waited. I unstrapped the leather in a hurry. The wood was now carved with the names of my friends, each one engraving their name. Nerice took the opportunity to carve a penis to the bottom of the foot one night while we had another slumber party filled with wine and pastries. I looked forward to her not asking how my dick was feeling every time I entered a room with her. That was…if this worked.

Vice took the old prosthetic and helped me fix the new one to my thigh. I could feel the familiar vibrations that used to be my Machine move up through my body and then slowly dissipate as it synced to my heart. The few lights blinked along with my heartbeat and the leg was silent, waiting. Vice let go and looked me in the eye, his expression hopeful while he closed hinges, shutting the armor plates over the leg to protect the technology beneath.

I swallowed and moved the foot of the leg.

I moved the foot of the leg.

My eyes widened in excitement, and I stood. Vice jumped up, knocking his staff to the floor with a big smile on his face to match my own. "By the gods, we've done it!" he exclaimed. I spun around and took a few steps through the now dark, dead Machine. The leg pressed against me like the wooden one had, but I did not notice it. Before I had a slight limp, but now it was as if I had never lost the leg in the first place.

"We've done it!" I repeated. I practically danced from excitement, and I hugged Vice. He took me happily into his arms.

We did it.

We ran up the corridor and into the Keep. Vice and I had no idea it was early morning, having worked all night on the final configurations of the prosthetic. When I turned a corner, I ran straight into Bellamy. In her hands she held a tray of bread, preserves and tea; the usual breakfast she brought to us during our science experiment. The food and tea tumbled everywhere, and she yelped with surprise. "Delilah! Krix's breath! Are you-" She looked down where the prosthetic was, only a long tunic on my body and the leg exposed, shiny in the torchlight of the corridor. Vice slid to a stop beside me, and he put his hands out toward it as if presenting a prize.

"Oh, Delilah!" Bellamy screeched with delight.

"Look at it!" I screeched back.

She grabbed my hand and bounced giddily, covered in tea and jam. "We must show everyone else!" she exclaimed.

Lachlan, who often slept with me in the Machine, had moved back to our chambers in the tower the night before. He slept, looking absolutely at peace in our bed, having dragged my Earth mattress up to replace the ancient one we had been sleeping on before. I jumped onto the bed and Lachlan sat up, ready for battle, a dagger appearing in his hand from cloud of black smoke. "Who goes there!" he boomed before pausing, realizing it was me. "Delilah!" He discarded the dagger, his face lighting up at the sight of me and his smile warming my heart.

I swung my legs around so he could see just as Bellamy and Vice flew in the door, wanting to see Lachlan's face at the news. "Look!"

Lachlan looked down and his smile reached his ears. "It worked!" he exclaimed.

"It worked!" I repeated.

*

It felt good, to be back into my old routine. I had found balance between working in the kitchens and training with my friends. With my new leg, I felt rejuvenated, and I found one of my favourite activities were meditating by the lake rather than in my room or the new Tabernacle. When I wore pants or a full set of armour, it was easy to forget one leg was made of metal and Machine parts. I felt strong, unstoppable. I resumed training and I did not tire easily. I would spar with Cathal and Theone, and both gave me praise for the comeback I made.

"That leg packs a punch, toots," Cathal said, rubbing his side from where I kicked him with my prosthetic.

"It does?" I asked, my hands still up, ready to defend myself if he chose to attack me again.

"Aye, it's as hard as being hit with a war-hammer," he said, bringing his arms back up to match my stance. I could see him flex his muscles, challenging me, waiting to strike.

"Maybe all that rest has made me stronger," I swung at him, but he jumped back. Before he hit the ground I tried to push-kick him, but Cathal grabbed my leg and smirked as I nearly fell over.

"Maybe," Cathal said. He pulled me forward by the leg and dropped it so I could catch my balance. His hands grabbed my face in his large palms. His teeth we *so* sharp with his mischievous grin. "Or maybe you were always this strong and just needed a boost of confidence." He kissed my forehead then released me, taking a step back. "Get your swords." I watched as he turned to grab a large axe leaning against one of the stuffed training dummies. The blade on it was the size of my thigh and Cathal laughed as he watched my eyes widen by the sight of it. "Theone is coming in an hour, and they are not going to show mercy to you, as I have." I had barely drawn my daggers when I turned and saw Cathal was running at me in a full sprint, axe in hand.

*

People were not frighted of the trees here. The uneasiness that shadowed everyone beyond Antore lifted as soon as you crossed into the valley from the mountain pass. There was no curfew. People did not rush out of the forest as the sun set to the safety of their houses. Shelter veiled this whole area. Life never felt fragile since moving here.

I could hear laughter often and children ran around and played without fear. The world was bright and warm and the heaviness that the war had loomed in the air all those months ago seemed like an age long since passed. Times were good. The army was growing, and our influence was high with owls returning telling us Priests and Priestesses were trying to get to Antore by autumn.

Under the old growth trees of the valley, the final weeks of summer grew refreshing, the heat more manageable and sweat no longer coated everyone's brow. Crops and livestock were plentiful, and I was told many times by both the Council and townsfolk that that no one had experienced comfort as they did now in the safety of Antore. People could breathe and the worries of the world could not reach us here.

The troubles of the war were not forgotten. As word continued to spread of our survival from Blackwick, of a Seer from the gods who had defeated a dragon controlled by evil, our safe haven away from all the bloodshed filled with more people seeking shelter. Antore grew quickly from crumbling ruins to a flourishing city. Every day more refugees arrived, and the renovated quarters began to run low. Able-bodied carpenters and masons could not keep up with the demand of housing and tents filled the side streets as they had in Blackwick. The walls separating the city from the valley held makeshift shacks and multiple families lived in single apartments.

Larger cities sent news of great tragedy, and it kept us humbled. Though we thrived here in safety, other cities, like Purrdemore and Zol were falling into ruin. I could still see the sadness in the eyes of those who lost their homes and families to the horrors I had not seen in months. We could not ignore that there was a war out there, and no one pretended to. Though there was a blissful period of peace for the people in Antore, it was not long before reality of the war hit us once more.

One day Zaanthru, the eye of the world, sent pleas of aid. The shores surrounding them had been under siege for weeks and the only reason we received their letter was pure luck. Keepers from the island had been sent out over and over since Salvatore's forces first arrived but no one made it very far until the single young Keeper got through. He was barely alive and in tears, having been brought in by the latest group of refugees. He begged us to save his city, and to let him stay with us until it was taken back. Temple Krix was there and despite its Keepers being amongst the highest trained in any province, their fleet was beginning to struggle against Salvatore's forces.

"Priestess Mirna is in shambles," Nerice said. "I saw her this morning. Temple Krix is where she grew up."

Chapter Fifteen
The Giving Day

Music droned in my mind. I had wireless earbuds in my ear, having fallen asleep listening to the music I had downloaded to my phone months before on Earth. There were only eight hundred songs on it, and I kept it charged through the hookup I installed to my prosthetic. I wore them daily, during training sessions or while I hung out in my chambers alone. I knew it was only a matter of time before the earbuds or my phone's technology failed and fried, but I wanted to get as much out of them as possible. The music helped me sleep, not that I had much trouble, but it gave a soothing comfort that kept me attached to my old life.

The morning sun was just starting to peak over the mountains surrounding the valley. There was a vague memory of Lachlan telling me he had some important business to attend to in the early hours of the morning before I fell back asleep. He had kissed my cheek and disappeared, the music lulling me back to sleep for at least an hour before I sat up. The air whispered that autumn approached, and I pulled the earbuds from my ears, stopping the music.

I learned autumn was the favoured time of year for everyone, and today I would see why. There was a tray on the desk with a pot of spiced milk tea still steaming and a plate of fried eggs, bacon and potatoes beside it. The smell beckoned me to breakfast.

I grabbed my prosthetic from leaning against my bedside, and it hummed to life as it connected to my thigh. I slipped my feet into a pair of knitted slippers from Earth, even if one foot only had the memory of being cold. Having the slippers were another nice reminder of the life I used to live and would serve me for years after my phone died. My cousin had knit them for me mere months before I dropped out of the sky. How grateful I was to have this piece of her.

I had been trasnformed. That *call* grew stronger with each

passing day, and I was connecting with *something*. As I sipped my tea and ate my breakfast, I wondered if this was what other Seer's had felt before me. If they too were moved to answer it. Months had passed and I made the decision that I had to leave the safety of the Keep. I was ready for whatever this world had in store for me. I had begun attending sermons weekly with Lachlan and felt moved with the ones speaking of grief and loss. Still, I could sense Gwen somewhere within my heart and I found myself hopeful to see her in the After. Through the months of meditation and discussion with Nerice and Priestess Mirna, it was as if I could reach out and touch whatever power was gifted to me and my connection to the gods.

Still, was really chosen to do this?

The direction felt right…

Once dressed and fed, I made my way to the Council Room, where I heard the usual heated voices, discussing movements of scouts, plans for moving the army or how the last interception had gone. When I entered, they quieted and Lachlan walked over to kiss my cheek, his features softening when he spotted me. By the time I made it there, the rest of the Keep was awake, and the sounds of a lively city were ensued.

"Delilah," Theone greeted. They stood next to Nerice who was hunched over the new grand table, carved with the map of the known world, a long-running project finally finished. Bellamy tucked a piece of paper behind a pile she had in her hands and huffed as her eyes scanned something else. The room was tense.

"We've been debating about the situation at Zaanthru and decided to send Commander Lachlan with our largest legion out into the province. Cathal, Neice and Florence, will be accompanying them. Colonel Theone, being Commander Lachlan's Second, will stay behind with myself in case things go sour. At least then we will still have people to help run whatever remains of the army and Antore," Bellamy told me. Her eyes watched me to gauge my reaction, but when I did not comment she continued. "From our interceptors, we believe that Salvatore still has his intentions on High Priestesses. His army is being redirected from Zaanthru, though many remain at the shores on the Southern and Northwestern provinces to keep the islanders isolated. If Zaanthru falls, he can take it and will likely win this war. It's one thing to destroy two Temples, it's another to take Temple Krix and everything within it. We must already be out in the province if we intend to cut him off before he acts, not in Antore. There are four other Temple's between Salvatore's current location and Temple Krix. He will likely hit them along the way to Zaanthru. Any one of the relics within Temple Krix could give Salvatore the ability to turn this war in his favor and people who are at the cusp of following him could be turned if he has them. We think Salvatore will hit Temple Virág first, since that is what Adder suggested."

"The nun's and monks there know of the possible impending disaster," Nerice said. "There is not much more we can do until we get our forces out. The scouts who delivered the message's have stayed with them. We are going to need everyone able to join us to take this fucker out."

"I'll go too."

The stillness that came over the room was unsettling, but the tenseness that was there when I entered disappeared.

"You'll go?" Nerice confirmed. She looked at me with tired eyes, her ginger hair obscuring some of her gaze.

I nodded. "The people need me, even if it's just to see me there with them. You said you need everyone able."

I watched as the four of them exchanged looks and Theone walked around the table to me. They pointed to Zaanthru and where Virág's Temple was located. Both were far, much farther than I had travelled before.

"It will be at least two months journey to reach the Zaanthru, and we will be travelling through many battlegrounds to get there, hopefully removing Salvatore's troops as we go. We should be able to make it with our numbers, but we cannot guarantee a return." Theone's eyes searched over my face, analyzing me in case I did not grasp the situation. I caught their gaze. I knew they could see the fear, but I hoped they could see something else there too: my determination to help our people. After a few long moments Theone nodded. "Okay."

The main cathedral in Antore acted as the local Tabernacle. Priestess Mirna, along with other Sisters and Brothers, had chambers within it and held services for the faithful and vigils for the fallen often. Within its walls were beautiful frescos, brought back to life by the nuns and others who had an eye for art. They depicted the story of creation, tales of valor from the knights who once lived here, and scenes portraying other lost cities in their prime. At the front, stood the eight life-size stone statues of both men and women, or people who presented that way. They were statues of the gods, found in the chapel below the Keep, but now they were housed where everyone could see them.

The statues stood tall and proud, some ready for battle, holding swords, shields and axes, while others held items of the home, baskets full of fruit and grains, a gardening trowel in one hand and a cat in the other, an anvil and hammer. The one holding the cat was my favourite and reminded me of the cat Lachlan had brought back from Blackwick and now followed Vice around the city.

I thought it wise to visit before our departure, not because was pressured, but because it was hard to ignore the gift I have been given and wanted to thank the gods for it. My ability to cast spells, the strength I had built, relationships made, every time I had escaped death... All the moments that led me to this place made me feel grateful and alive and it was because of *them*.

Often my companions would tell me who they left offerings for when they visited. The way they spoke about the gods was as natural as someone talking about the weather. I never approached the statues during my visits until today and did not think to bring an offering. I almost felt guilty I had no gift to return to them. As I stood in front of the statues, I was moved in a way I did not expect.

Andreja, the goddess who supposedly chose me and birthed Lachlan's grandfather, held a bow and arrow at the ready and a smirk that warmed my heart to look at. I stood in front of her form, contemplating the comfort her smile brought me.

"Does she speak to you?"

I jumped, spinning on my heel to face Priestess Mirna. I did not know how long I had stood before the statue of Andreja, but apparently long enough for the woman to sneak up on me. She gazed at the statue as I had been before, love and admiration in her eyes. I could sense the distress she held within her for her city. Each of her sermons would end with prayers for them. Right now, she disguised her worries with a serenity I wished I could have in her position.

"I guess, in some way, this statue does," I said looking back at Andreja's form.

The Priestess tilted her head as if examining the statue closer. "You know that was not what I meant, Seer."

I looked at the other gods that stood before us. It was remarkable that their forms were left unscathed for centuries. Thanks to the books Vice had given to me, I knew which statue was which.

Dagr, the god of the rivers and seas, day and night. He was depicted with a spyglass, carved with constellations on the handle. According to the books, he controlled the weather.

Samu, the god of thieves and commerce, patron of travellers and guide for the dead. He was written as good friends with Manoach, the god of death and rest. Samu would walk with you to the After. It was only those who were truly called, were met by Manoach in death. Samu, was also the messenger to the gods. He was said to carry everyone's prayers to whatever god they prayed to. He held a scroll and quill, so he could write down everything someone said to him, nothing would be missed. I remembered Adder and Nerice served under him.

Gyula Jozefa was the god of marriage, love, fertility, life, and the afterlife. They ruled over sickness, health and medicine. Their form was beautiful, holding herbs in their hands for healing and a tome with the word *vse* inscribed on the cover.

Imrus, the god of fire, forges, crafts and the patron for smiths and weavers. He was the one who held and anvil and hammer. He was built like a bear, almost like Cathal, but was depicted shorter than the other gods.

Ilona, the goddess of wine, ecstasy, celebration, sex, and beauty, held a bottle of wine in one hand and an axe in the other. She was the reason why the people called sex 'worshiping' for the act of consensual sex was literally an act in favour of the god.

Virág was the goddess of harvest, famine, seasons, nature, protection, handicrafts, and agriculture. She had been the statue I enjoyed the most, aside from Andreja, holding a basket full of bread, berries, and vegetables in one hand and a cat in the other.

Manoach stood simply with his fingers touching in a triangle. Whereas other statues looked forward, watching those who stood before them, Manoach looked over his shoulder, watching the other gods. Vice had told me Manoach was Krix's best friend amongst the gods.

"Why is Krix not depicted here amongst the others?" I asked.

Priestess Mirna turned to me and shrugged. "Most of these were probably carved when the gods still walked amongst us. The Commander comes by often; he has expressed that Andreja's statue has the likeness he remembers though she was older when he knew her and thought some characteristics of her were different here. They share the same smile, I think.

"This statue depicts a goddess with the sharp eye of a hunter. When Andreja was last in her mortal form, she was completely blind in one eye for her entire life. I don't believe they appear the same with every visit, but they tend to pick certain characteristics. Now we can only hope to see them in the After. Krix had last walked with us many eons ago. There are a selected few who believe he never left our plane and is just lost to time. He was the first of the gods to disappear, after the last of his children died."

"How did his last child die? Do you know?" I asked.

"I believe old age, but he had suffered for a long time with lycanthropy. What a heartbreaking condition," Priestess Mirna said with a sigh.

It was quiet between us, and I looked over the faces of the gods again.

"What do you think he looks like? Krix?"

The Priestess shrugged and handed me a cup of tea. A pot was always brewing within the walls of the Tabernacle, I was told, but that could be said about anywhere within the city. The tea in Tabernacles was meant for healing and calming, and I enjoyed a cup every time Lachlan and I came for a sermon. "I bet he is very handsome," Priestess Mirna said fondly.

I looked at her and she smiled, nodding to me before turning to go back to her duties. I had heard from Lachlan that they were trying to campaign for Priestess Mirna to be the next High Priestess of Samu, since Nerice denied wanting the responsibility. Theone was still contemplating stepping up for Andreja's Temple. However, the vote would be long for Priestess Mirna with the war going on. A High Priestess or Priest usually would name a successor before their death, but Temple Samu's had not, as her death had been so sudden, and many had expected her to live a long time before a successor was named. The Temple's had been lucky I had been there before Katerina's death. She had known she was going to die and named Theone as her successor to me. She had only been fifty-three years old. Samu's High Priestess was even younger. Now, to elect a new leader of Samu's Temple, the other High Priestesses had to come to a consensus, one of which came from recommendations of other officials around the world. It was a tedious process. Many feared more Temple leaders would fall before a final vote.

It had been months, and we knew Salvatore was going to make a move soon. We were leaving tomorrow.

I turned back to face the statue of Andreja, and I took a sip of the tea. I looked into her stone eyes, seeing a twinkle of something there. I could imagine the colour of her hair and eyes. I could imagine the way her voice sounded while she laughed. It was then I noticed the eyes of each of the gods. They looked like the one I had been given, the pupil sharp like that of a snake or cat. I felt the purpose within me bubble and almost boil over.

Salvatore would not win.

I would not let him.

It was the first day of autumn and the Giving Day had arrived in full swing around the city as I left the Tabernacle. I loved the smell of fall leaves in the crisp air, reminding me of autumn back on Earth, except *fresher*. Pure. The anticipation for this day had been building the last few weeks and I was excited to be a part of it. The day was a celebration commemorating when Krix breathed life into the universe. People would celebrate everything good to happen within the last year and, no matter what time you were born during the year, this was when the people collectively got *older*. From my understanding, it was also the mark of the new year. It was the only reason we did not leave immediately to seek Salvatore. Today was the most holy day these people could have.

My birthday had been in the fall on Earth; the leaves would be almost all gone, and I would look around believing my part of the planet was going to sleep until spring. I had no idea when it would be in this world, there was no way of knowing if there were the same number of days here as Earth. Each season felt longer than it did on Earth, but I could not be sure considering this was all new to me and the passing of time was marked by the moons and seasons, not days of the week or months. If I had managed to keep count of the days, maybe then I would know. Regardless of the time of the year, for me to follow their customs, to be part of their community, today meant it was my thirtieth birthday.

Antore's streets were decorated with garlands of dried fruits, autumn flowers, and leaves. Inside the kitchen pots of hot apple cider and mulled wine bubbled, leaving a warm spiced scent floating around, reminding me of Nerice, who always smelt *so* good. Silk runners dyed red, gold and orange brought warmth and life to the usual grey walls that did not have tapestries or frescos on them. I witnessed children painting the bare walls surrounding the city, creating floral murals like the ones in Blackwick. Their parents lent encouraging voices their creativeness. Some were even covered in paint and joined their children in the designs. I had seen more movement than usual in the days leading up, many vendors coming in with barrels of wine, spices, sugar, and herbs I could swear smelt like marijuana. While most people decorated for today, some soldiers finished packing the war wagons and fed the horses their last large and nourishing meal before the long journey through the Stills.

I walked from the Tabernacle through the market laneways back into the Keep. I strolled into the grand hall, where people were almost done decorating. A remarkably fast set up from when it was empty this morning. I could hear a local bard exercising her voice on the platform where the nine thrones sat. Something large was covered in a tarp behind her. She had a lovely voice.

Her song called me back to my days with Vice in my Machine. The nights I played different songs from my stereo, getting what I could of my old world before settling on hearing it through the earbuds until their technology failed me. How I would miss listening to my favourite songs on the stereo or in concert.

Throughout the morning, I had noticed many people walking around in their best clothes. Each outfit displayed the fanciest and cleanest garments they owned. Now with the sun high in the sky it seemed everyone was wearing formal clothes. Businesses hung closed signs on their doors and townsfolk poured into the Keep for the party.

I felt a pang of envy within me, wanting to wear something pretty too.

My bridesmaid dress.

I looked in the mirror for the first time since the hand mirror. When I peered at the glass, I was greeted with a dirty and tired reflection, spooking myself. I had streaks of grey in my hair, from the stress I had experienced early on in this world and my eerie, godly eye stared back at me with hundreds of stories yet to be told. I was scarred, I was fit, I had a prosthetic leg made by a medieval quartermaster and an immortal, magical werewolf filled with time-traveling technology. I did not completely recognize the reflection gazing back at me, but the tattoos were mine, the piercings in my ears and nose were mine and the rings on my fingers were mine. This place had changed me in more ways than just physically and as I stared at myself, long and hard in the mirror, I knew that it had been for the better. My reflection was no longer scary. It was just me.

I eagerly put my bridesmaid dress on. Though the style was not exactly local, I thought if I put a shawl around my shoulders and let my hair flow freely, it could blend in well. The fabric was matte and soft, and I told myself people would just think it was a very expensive piece from somewhere far away.

"Woah, Shorty, what a dress!"

I turned from looking at myself in the mirror, having noticed my shiny scar on my face glinting in the sunlight coming in from my windows. Now dressed and clean, my hair was combed after thirty minutes of getting it to submit to an acceptable texture. I had put on some makeup, probably for the first time since my cousin's wedding.

Durin stood halfway between my door and the stairs behind it. In his own best clothes, he had gold on his fingers and around his neck to match the many piercings in his ears and his golden tooth. His hair was braided back tightly to his scalp instead of just his long fringe tied out of his face or several small, beaded braids on one side of his head. His tunic was slate grey, and his boots looked brand new. He had cleaned up his face from the usual stubble and he looked younger and rested.

"Oh! Thank you! It's been a while since I've worn it." I had lost a lot of weight since living here. Though I felt stronger and could see the muscle definition that had not been there before, the dress fit better when I was fuller.

"The Commander is going to love it." Durin looked beyond my gaze and down straight to my ass. "Aye, he's definitely going to love it," Durin said approvingly, a cheeky grin on his lips. He waved me to take his arm. "Come. We have a surprise for you."

I took one last look at myself in the mirror. My dress was red with a sharp slit over my prosthetic leg. The shawl was a black lace I had traded my couch for a week ago. Wearing it meant covering my dragon and owl tattoo on my back. I decided to discard it. I looked at myself with the dress and my shiny leg. My godly eye stared back at me with the snake-like gaze. The red of the iris matched my dress. This reflection was who I was. I took Durin's arm after slipping my feet into some sandals Bellamy had given me and smiled down to him as he happily walked me from my chambers.

We entered the grand hall, now restored to its former glory. The tapestries had been sewn where moths and age had eaten at it; the colours more vibrant. Silk runners were hung from the ceilings, candles alit like stars carefully placed so nothing could get set on fire easily. A new carpet had been made to cover the cold floor and the hall smelt of spices and wine, erasing the smell of old wet stone and moss. Tables were set up with plates of roasted meat and vegetables I had helped prepare the night before. Boards of salted meat and soft cheeses, bowls of fresh pomegranates, apples, and berries, and tiered platters of cakes and pastries were piled halfway to the high ceiling. There were large pillows and cushions placed along the edges of the hall and people were pilled into them with plates of food and pints of drinks and pipes at hand.

And the *music*.

At the end of the hall, where nine thrones sat, was the skull of the dragon that ate my leg decorated completely with flowers. I could not hold a grudge to a creature that was being controlled. I could only be impressed that people dragged it up from Blackwick.

Dancing around the skull was a large group of musicians playing a variety of instruments. The bard from earlier sung, her voice haunting and beautiful as a song I knew deep in my bones left her lips and echoed throughout the hall. My friends appeared around me, all dressed in their finest garb and excitement on their faces.

I was without words.

People danced to the music that enchanted its away around the room with ease.

"Earth music," I whispered.

"Vice figured out your weird house and was able to replay music while you slept. Durin came to listen and write down everything he could about the instruments and lyrics," Lachlan said. "Cathal bribed the bard."

"It helped that some of those not-books had little books filled with the lyrics inside them. I took them to record in my free time." Durin shrugged as if it was nothing.

"I *love* this one." When I closed my eyes, it was as if I was standing in a concert venue and not in a castle on a whole different planet. The bards voice echoed effortlessly around the room. A couple mages had charmed it, making sure no corner would go unheard.

Nerice pulled me into an open space excitedly and began to dance with me. What seemed to be the rest of Antore danced merrily around us, the joy on their faces showing no fear for the future. Nerice spun me under her arm and caught my hip with her pointed fingers as I twirled into her. I saw Theone and Durin take to the dancefloor and Bellamy and Cathal made for the tables of food with Vice in tow by Cathal. Vice did not seem to mind his hand being held and Lachlan made himself comfortable in one of the piles along the walls, a pomegranate in hand. He watched Nerice and I dance, content to see his city and friends happy.

Nerice's smile was sharp and delighted as she expertly led our dance. She wore beautifully embroidered navy trousers. A golden-beaded gambeson clung tightly to her form in a flattering way. It looked like she had combed her hair since this morning. We glided around the dance floor, moving around friends and strangers. She bumped playfully into Theone and Durin, who moved their hands to ours and we were a little spinning circle until Nerice took me away again.

I felt new and alive and like this was where I was supposed to be. I loved these people more than I could have ever imagined loving anyone.

How could I have ever denied this world when everything, no matter how scary, was so extraordinary?

We danced for a while. The bard had mastered many of the songs from Earth. I saw as the music, new and enthralling to the people of Antore's ears, brought fresh life to them. I felt as tears fell from my face, joy lifting me to a place I thought out of reach for a long time, but again and again I was surprised, and it was magical. Nerice wiped a tear from my cheek with the cuff of her gambeson, at first looking concerned, but seeing my smile she realized I was happy. The music beat eventually changed and let me go, bowing then motioning to the comfy pile of pillows and silks that Lachlan sat. A bowel full of pomegranate seeds that he had carefully removed from the flesh and two cups of tea sat near him. I curtsied to Nerice, and she cheerfully wandered to a food tables.

The whole day continued with celebration.

I drank wine and ale and spiked tea. I ate more pastries than I could count. I sat in the softest, most comfortable pile of pillows that were lovelier than my bed. With Lachlan's arm around me, he periodically glanced over to me with love in his eyes. He told me about other Giving Day's in his life and his lips found mine or my throat making me forget everyone around us.

Soon words were lost to us, and his hand made its way between my legs. At first, I was worried someone would notice, but as I glanced around, I saw everyone was too involved with themselves to notice their Commander having his way with a prophecy. I groaned as his fingers found what they were seeking, and his kisses grew hungrier against me. I let myself fall under his spell, my eyes closed, my only focus on the movement of his fingers between my thighs. Quickly, Lachlan moved behind me, his legs on either side of mine and he let me lean back into his chest, one hand working me up and another firmly on my breast as he whispered all the things he wanted to do to me later. I opened my eyes to look at him, only to see a woman wearing a flowing rainbow-coloured dress, smirking down at us, entertained. I tapped Lachlan's cheek, and he looked up before jerking his hands away from me. He put the two fingers he had been using into his mouth, before wrapping his arms over my shoulders, his posture relaxed.

The woman giggled. "Oh, don't stop on my behalf," she teased. Long black hair, shiny in the candlelight, made her features almost cat-like within its shadows. She smelled of rosemary, moss and mead and her eyes were the colour of burnt caramel in a golden bowl.

Every inch of her dress was decorated with swirls of multicoloured beads, making it look like the most expensive outfit here. She was the most beautiful woman I had ever seen. In her hands she held a vial of ink, a needle and a small heavy dowel. "I like your tattoos. Would you more, Seer? I would love to add you as a customer. It would be fantastic for business."

It took a moment to gather myself, to switch my brain from Lachlan's magical touch to socializing, but I plucked my rings from my fingers and put them in a small bag Bellamy had given me an hour or so ago to stash trinkets townsfolk had periodically brought me throughout the day. I stuck my hands out, palms down, towards her. "Go crazy," I instructed. I never had a stick and poke tattoo before, but I was a fan of the art.

The woman was very talented, creating a beautiful abstract design of a flame on the tops of my hands and triangles on the bases of each finger. It only hurt a little, which was impressive. "You'll need to keep the skin clean for several weeks as they heal, Seer, though I can retouch if you return."

Lachlan looked my hands, his lids low as they usually were when he watched me. "No time needed." Lachlan hovered his hands over mine as the artist finished and gave a little flourish when his fingers began to glow. I felt my skin heal, the tickling sensation familiar from his *talent*. I looked over to where his head now rested on my shoulder, his lips leaving my cheek from a kiss. All the soreness from the tattoos were gone and I could put my rings back on.

He looked at the tattoo artist, holding his hands out to her from around my body. "Me as well, please."

The tattoo artist grinned and examined his hands. She pointed to the parts that had his burn scars. "I can't go over this tissue, but I can make something similar for you."

"Perfect," Lachlan said.

When she finished, Lachlan brought his freshly tattooed hands up to eye level, letting me have a closer look. "Blow on my hands," he instructed.

I did as he said and watched the tattoos heal perfectly before my eyes. I looked at him in shock. "That was you!" I accused.

Lachlan chuckled and gave me a big hug. "Aye, but you helped." He kissed my cheek again and pulled me tighter against him. After Lachlan threw a small coin pouch to the woman, a few other people at the party approached her and she disappeared into the crowd.

Nerice jumped into our pile with pastries, having disappeared for several hours after our dance. At some point she had removed her shoes, along with her fancy gambeson, exposing exceptionally perky breasts barely concealed by a crocheted bralette. Her hair was now messy, and her mouth was full of fresh bread. She made an "ooOoo" sound as she looked down at us laying in the pillows cuddling.

"Are you two going to have a little *godly* fun tonight? Looked like you were in front of everybody before the artist stumbled upon you." Nerice smirked before shoving one of the powdered pastries that fell from her plate into her mouth. Her face was covered in icing sugar and jam.

I sat up from laying against Lachlan's chest and shoved her. "That's none of your business," I laughed, trying not to blush. *Of course she had been watching.*

"Everything is my business," Nerice said through her pastry. Lachlan sat up behind me and snatched a pasty of his own from Nerice's plate before she could move it away from him, laughing through her full mouth at my embarrassment. The hall had grown warm with the fire at the center and all the people dancing.

"Are you envious?" Lachlan asked, taking a bite out of the jelly filled cake he swiped.

Nerice cackled in amusement then swallowed what was in her mouth. She scanned over me with a glint of something both dangerous and inviting in her eyes. "Obviously!"

I swatted at Nerice, and she laughed harder before she ruffled her hand in Lachlan's hair. Lachlan bit at her hand, but she moved it before his teeth connected. "You two have fun. You might not get the privacy again," she said putting more delicious treats into her mouth. I reached over to the plate to take one for myself and Nerice let me take one willingly.

Bellamy came scurrying over as Nerice got up, letting out an excited squeal, each hand holding a large bottle of wine. "Is this where the party is?" she asked plopping down beside us. Her hair was loose, and she wore indigo, sheer fabric over her pants and tunic. Her eyes immediately went to Lachlan and I's almost matching tattoos and her smile widened. "You two are lovely, I'm delighted you found each other."

I looked at Lachlan, who had already been looking at me, a satisfied smile on his handsome face. "I am too."

Bellamy had been socializing with Durin and Theone previously, having ditched her uncle to socialize with as many people as she could. She found us after our other two roamed away together. I could hear Cathal's laughter boom through the hall, almost louder than the music being sung. When I spotted him in the crowd, surrounded by his team, I saw Vice sitting at a table next to him, a dreamy smile on his face. It was such a merry day, and I was thankful that a world at war could still find joy like this.

Lachlan kissed my neck, whispering "Would you like to wander away?" in the most appealing, silky tone.

Chapter Sixteen
The Next Day

Donning my armour after so long without it was a cool drink on a hot day. A breath of fresh air, a warm cookie out of the oven, it felt good and right to be wearing it. My helmet, the one Gwen had given me, tugged at her memory as I put it on, ready to leave. Today we marched.

Thanks to the tunnels below Antore, I was able to move within the depths of the growing city without many interactions or distractions. Often, when walking the grounds, people recognized me and approached, requesting to touch my hands or my shoulder or ask if I would wish them to be watched over by the gods. At times, it was overwhelming, and any walk would take twice as long to get where I wanted to go. In the tunnels I could avoid the distractions. Many did use them, the troops and scouts, kitchen staff and Temple laity, but amongst the city folk, the tunnels were not common knowledge, and I was grateful. The circular chamber where the skeleton of my Machine lay dead had doors leading to the kitchen, several armouries, the small cathedral and Tabernacle, and many other escape routes and places like the Council Room. The circular chamber was a shortcut, cutting out the many twists and turns of the city above.

When I entered the Council Chambers, the electricity there was hot, and I knew something had changed since yesterday. Nobody was speaking, just looking at the map and frantically sorting through papers. Except Nerice who sharpened her nails with a glass nailfile, grumbling in Bygone Speech.

"What's going on?" I asked. It was early in the morning, and many still slept off their hangovers. It had still been dark outside when a scout had knocked at our chamber doors, requesting we dress to leave and head to the Council Room. Lachlan tried to shoo the man away, but in hushed whispers the scout had said something to Lachlan that changed his mind, causing him to dress quickly and go ahead of me.

"We received important news from further inland. I'm afraid this is a bad development," Theone said, fighting yawn. Their makeup looked hastily done, but somehow it made them look more threatening than usual. They too must have rushed to the Council Room, their expression serious and concentrating as they read whatever report was in hand.

Bellamy rubbed her eyes with the back of her hand, her cheeks flushed and breath slowing. I had the feeling she had beat me here by moments. Cathal stood leaning against the wall, his eyes closed, and arms crossed. I wondered if he had fallen back asleep there.

Nerice seemed to be the only one wide awake.

Everyone was fully clad in layers of armour, weapons strapped to them.

Nerice tossed the nailfile to the floor and unrolled a long scroll, laying it out onto the table. Florence was at her flank. Usually, Florence and Bellamy acted as separate pieces of Nerice's ever watchful minions. This morning, they were her right and left hands as Bellamy moved to the opposite side of Nerice as Florence to read through the scroll.

"Bad development is an understatement," Nerice said. "High Priestess Saoirse of Temple Virág has been assassinated. Her death, along with the deaths of those within the Temple and our watch outside of it marks the next move from Salvatore. At the time of this report the surrounding area was in flames, hopefully releasing the dead. Our letter indicates mage Keepers are trying to hold what's left of the Temple and are guarding the relic there. We must push to reach them before Salvatore's army breech the hold, if they have not already. We only have as long as it takes for this creature to get the relic at Temple Virág."

I looked down at my metal leg as everyone continued to tiredly speak amongst themselves, planning what to do, going over every back up plan. I pulled my pant leg back and lifted my leg up to the table, so I could see the tracker I installed to watch Salvatore 's stolen Machine. *723* blinked on the screen. My brows furrowed. He was closer than he had been yesterday. *Much* closer.

"How far away is Temple Virág?" I asked.

"About twenty sols, weather and travel conditions permitting. By the time we get there we will be lucky if Salvatore's troops remain, and anyone is left alive. This is the closest he has been to us since Blackwick. Why do you ask?" Nerice said.

"How many kilometers is it?" I confirmed.

"Close to seven hundred, perhaps a little more," Lachlan stated.

I looked back at my leg. "He's still there. As you said, we need to go. Now. We can continue to track him on the move."

The others did not question me. None of them tried to understand the science behind what my Machine was and decided it as a perk to me being a Seer. Though Vice had done his best, and learned the mechanics of it, he still claimed it magic.

The Council nodded as Bellamy looked over the scroll again. "We must assume Temple Krix in Zaanthru can fend the troops off for now and will remain safe." She sighed heavily. "There are still three other Temples between him and Temple Krix at this time. Hopefully Salvatore will move to Temple Imrus, Dagr or Gyula Jozefa before bringing his full force back to Zaanthru. I will keep watch here…" Bellamy looked at the others then set her eyes on me. She tried to smile encouragingly. "You all make sure you come back, alright?"

"We can't promise anything," Nerice said. She turned to Florence and said something in Bygone Speech that sent her sprinting from the room. "I will bring my fastest owls with us, and we will coordinate."

Lachlan nodded. "One hour everyone, then we move out. Get everyone in the forest into the walls. Lock the gates behind us, notify the city. No one leaves or enters until we return. Put a watch at the entrance to the valley and at the break in the mountains. There are enough stores to last through the winter in case of a siege. If that creature finds this place, go to the caverns below and lead them out of the mountains north to Fury settlements. Cathal has sent his team to his village to notify them about possible asylum. There is a Tabernacle there that can assist."

Bellamy nodded and took out a fresh sheet of paper as she began to write the order. "Aye, Commander."

I could feel my heart pumping with nervousness, conversations quieted in my ears as they continued their coordination. I pulled my pant leg back down. Theone put their hand on Lachlan's shoulder, and he responded in kind. The two put their foreheads together, their eyes closed in silent prayer for each other. I could see the pain both were experiencing and the fear, the possibility, of not seeing each other again. Lachlan was Theone's mentor, their Commander. The two were friends.

"I will protect them, Commander," Theone said. "Bellamy, and I will protect them all."

Lachlan gave Theone's shoulder a firm squeeze. "I know you will, *Commander.*"

Theone's eyes snapped open and caught his gaze. Lachlan smiled proudly at them. They nodded and Lachlan nodded back before they let go of each other.

There was a deep hope cast over us that there was a way to succeed. There was no other choice. Between all the intel from Adder's letters and my technology from Earth, our understanding of Salvatore was more than anyone had since he began the war. All we could do was pray it was enough.

This was it.

Cathal, Durin, and Vice stood at the front gates of the city, each donned in their armour and weapons, packs on their back. There was a pack at Cathal's feet ready for me. Cathal placed a heavy hand on my shoulder, sharp smile on his lips. "It's good to see you go out with us, toots," he said. "You and a little luck will surely grant us victory!"

Durin gave me a strong pat on my back, making me step forward as Cathal released me. "Agreed!"

Cathal picked up my pack and tossed it to me with ease. As I caught it, I nearly dropped it from its heaviness, and he laughed.

"Thanks," I said, lugging the pack over my back, and securing it.

One thousand troops left Antore.

Husbands and wives cried as they parted from their loved ones. Foragers and farmers tossed care packages onto the wagons that rolled through the gate to leave. We would walk until nightfall and take a break until an hour before first light then repeat until we reached whatever remained of Virág's Temple. Lachlan said if our army moved quickly, we would make it sooner.

Every few hours, I would climb a wagon to check my leg if Salvatore had moved. So far, he remained. We would have no other tell. The owl we had received with news of High Priestess Saoirse's assassination was one of dozens sent out as indicated by the number on its message. It was the only one to make it to Antore, just as the young Keeper was the only one to make it past the blockade surrounding Zaanthru. I could only assume that was why Nerice had been so sour in the morning. She loved her birds.

Though I had walked through Antore's gates many times with my friends to walk to the lake or in the valley's forest, this exit was different knowing there was a strong likelihood it would lead to my death and many others. I swallowed, following behind hundreds of troops.

Lachlan was near the front, coordinating with Cathal and Florence. I moved beside a wagon piled high with bedding.

Vice came up beside me and I looked up at his stoic face. I could still see the sadness in his eyes from months passing between Asa and now. I wondered if my friends could see the same thing in my eyes over Gwen. Vice glanced down to me, his red eyes something I could never truly get used to. "The moons will be full while we are away," he stated.

I nodded. "Okay." I looked ahead, following behind the wagon. Durin was at the front, steering the horse. He had volunteered to go out, even though he had resigned from his position. He was reluctant to leave Theone, but he also did not want to wait to find out if his best friend was not going to come back to him.

"I said it will be *full moons*," Vice continued, his voice softer now.

I glanced up at him again but this time he did not meet my gaze. He kept his eyeline forward and I could see his brow cock expectantly for my reaction.

"*Oh.*"

"Aye."

"Did you try to get out of it this time?" I asked.

"No." He yawned.

"Are you going to be alright?"

Vice struggled to find an answer for a few moments. When he found the right words he leaned down, his voice low in my ear. "It's a lot of people to be around, it *might* be a problem."

"Have you told Cathal? Nerice? Maybe they could help," I suggested.

"I get the feeling neither will be helpful on the matter, especially Cathal," Vice said simply.

I did not press and glanced up at the trees towering over us. The leaves were turning. It was hard to grasp that I had been on this planet for almost a year. I had not seen autumn on this world yet, and I was looking forward to it, if we survived. I let out a long sigh before taking in another deep breath of the crisp autumn air. Death whispered around every tree trunk and mountain ridge.

The landscape had changed dramatically since last winter. A clear path had been cut through the mountains from Antore. What had once taken over a week in the thick snow, carrying the wounded from the attack, now took until sunset. Our first camp was made in the ruins of Blackwick, over a light dusting of snow. What kept the snow from meeting Antore, I did not know.

Setting up our tents, I knew everyone was uneasy outside the safely of our valley. To the north, I could see the divot in the mountains where I had pulled at least a century of snow down last year. From this angle, no one could tell a city thrived tucked away even deeper within the mountains than Blackwick. I soaked in what was left of my former home. Some burnt buildings still clung to their frames and rotted from two seasons of rain and weather. Storm season would be upon us, and the rage of the Stills would extend far over most provinces, sogging what was left of the village. Lachlan said he would be surprised if we found anything remaining of the village after next winter. I could almost make out where some of the more rotted buildings used to stand, imagine the life the village had before the battle. None of the beautiful artwork, painted by generations of villagers, existed anymore. Only drying weeds lived where wild leeks and other herbs and vegetables had once grown. I wondered where the building was that Gwen had perished in.

I sighed, having forgotten the discomfort that the world held beyond Antore. A large string perimeter of bells was set up as people settled for the evening. I glanced beyond the firelight and thought I saw something move in the shadows. A form darker than the trees, the almost human shape with horns growing as branches. My name was carried on the darkness, voices not quite right, and I returned my attention back to the camp, knowing better then to let my eyes linger.

People spoke of what they expected in battle, what they expected in the After.

All I expected was to march with our troops and meet the lunatic who started this war. I could not leave my people to do this alone or the world would fall into Salvatore's claws. I had to be with them. I had to help. I had to stop him.

There was already frost within the mountains beyond Antore, though winter had yet to arrive. People murmured softly with the darkening night and tents went up expertly as many turned to rest immediately. I had been used to the socialness of the city; it was never completely silent there, but in the ruined village, the only sounds in the night were those on watch and the occasional screams from deep within the trees.

After farewells, the march leading out of Antore had been next to wordless. Occasionally, people would speak. Comrades would talk about their favourite memories of Antore, or which god they were most excited to meet after battle. Lachlan had made a lot of conversation with Nerice and Cathal and coordinated with Florence. Periodically, I would be updated.

Firelight brought a haunting glow to Blackwick's ruins. I glanced towards the collapsed and rotting Tabernacle, where I had hosted a slumber party with my friends, with Gwen, right before everything really started to get hectic.

You will be alright.

Gwen's last words to me, rang through my mind. I let out a slow breath and turned to see Lachlan and Nerice once again speaking with Cathal and Florence, looking over a map laid out on a table set up by a massive tent where I would sleep with them tonight. Nerice put a pointed fingernail to one spot, tucking some hair behind her ear with her free hand. They spoke in Bygone Speech, and I turned back to the fire before me when I heard the word for *afraid*.

Durin had set up a fire in, what he insisted was, his old midtown camping spot, and though it had not been cleared of debris, it had enough space for Vice to set up their tents. I dumped dehydrated vegetables and meat into a hot pot of water along with a package of seasoning I took from the kitchens. Juniper, thyme and apple mixed into the soup, the vegetables plumped, and the meat softened. Durin pulled a loaf of bread out from a sack on the wagon he had been leading. He too had swiped some items from the kitchens.

"Doing alright, Shorty?" Durin asked, bringing my mind back from the smell of food. I spotted movement outside the treeline. I saw something in the shadows, this time closer to the bells, and returned to stirring the soup. I knew that spirits supposedly did not linger when their old bodies were burnt, but it felt as if something was watching us, and it was hard to pretend it was not there.

"I don't know," I said honestly.

Durin began to pull the bread apart into even sections to share. "You know it's okay to not be alright," he said putting each piece into wooden bowls.

I nodded and stirred the pot, the smell of everything starting to come together wafting up satisfyingly into the autumn air. "I appreciate you saying that," I said. "I just don't know how I'm going to react when everything is happening. I haven't seen the war in a while. I don't know what anything looks like out there anymore. How bad has it gotten? How many more people are dead? How many are waiting to be burned?" I asked. I took a deep inhalation of the soup and for a moment the building anxiety lifted. I could almost imagine I was back in the kitchens at the Keep.

Durin nodded and sat on an old burnt beam Vice had dragged near the fire. "We won't know until we see it. Let's try not to think about it." He picked up his bow that had been leaning against the beam. He took an oiled cloth from his pocket and started to wipe it down. "It's best not to dwell on what we can't control, Shorty. All you must worry about is watching your back when blades start swinging."

I nodded. "You're right," I sighed. "It's just hard not to think about it."

Durin nodded and continued to examine his bow.

Cathal sat heavily beside Durin, a wine bottle in hand. The beam crunched beneath him and Vice came around the tents with a pile of salvageable wood to keep the fire going. "Tell me about it," Cathal huffed. "I'm *very* excited to get back out there. I've been feeling all pent up."

"I noticed," Vice quipped. The two of them exchanged looks and Durin's brows rose. Though his eyes kept to his bow, I could almost see him try to hide a knowing smile.

"Your team has been going out. Why not go with them?" I asked pulling my boots off, replacing them with my Earth slippers.

"I wanted to stay behind, in case my best girl needed me," Cathal said with a sharp grin, eyeing me with a ravenous look I usually only saw Lachlan use on me. "Also, with events thickening, I needed to be on call for the Commander and Colonel Ward. They already almost lost me once with that fucking demon onslaught at my docks. It's *apparently* difficult to find people who want to lead." Cathal paused and looked out into the distance. "Fuck, I hope my ship is okay out there."

I threw my stirring spoon at Cathal, but he caught it before it connected with his face. Again, I was met with a ravenous, toothy grin, daring me to try it again. He licked it then tossed the spoon back to me with the gentleness I lacked in my throw. "I hope you're kidding about staying for *me*," I said. "There are more important things out there."

Cathal shrugged and started setting the bowls Durin made out in front of everyone so people could serve themselves when the soup was done. "I know it may not seem like it, but I am a man of faith and that means," he connected gazes with me before he continued, his eyes moving back to the bowls and bread, "I believe you were sent by the gods, and I don't want to miss a single moment of it."

I rolled my eyes. The camp only had a few whispering voices amongst the thousand who were among us. People pacing the perimeter on watch, some making dinner like us, others asleep, and the last few discussing tactics for the not-so-distant future, all quiet. "But what if I wasn't?" I asked.

"You really believe, after everything that has happened to you, that you're not?" Vice asked.

"I get conflicted," I started. "Being a prophecy is a lot of pressure!"

"A woman falls from the sky and survives. That same woman survives a siege of demons, blasphemers, and a dragon!" Cathal boomed enthusiastically. He leaned forward, catching my gaze again, hungry and enticing. I imagined him a couple hundred years from now, when his storm-filled eyes turned blood red in the wake of his Amaranthine lifestyle. How terrifying of a man, he would be. The *teeth*. "Woman, I will follow you for one thousand lifetimes. I believe in you as easily as I breathe." He leaned back, uncorking the wine.

Vice smirked and pulled a piece of his bread portion off to eat. I knew I believed in this world, in its people. *Fuck*, I even believed in their gods. I had accepted that something more powerful than anything I had ever dreamed of somehow chose me. Though here I sat, still blown away by the faith and support these people had for me.

The sun had not broken over the horizon when Lachlan gently woke me up, his voice tender and soothing. I blinked awake to see him already fully clad in his armour and furs. "Everything except this bed is packed. We must go," he said. I looked around seeing the shadows of the trees and a hint of light glimmering beyond them cresting the mountaintops. The tent had been packed up around me. Troops were kicking out what was left of fires and wagons were already on the move. A few yards from where I slept, Nerice looked up from a scroll and caught my eyes. She winked then walked towards one of the wagons rolling away with Florence, who was nodding attentively to whatever Nerice was saying to her. I sat up.

Lachlan passed me with my pack after helping me into my armour. A troop packed up the furs and cot beside us. As Lachlan stood behind me, fastening a cloak to my shoulder plate, I sensed anxiety in his movements.

"Did you bring the metal that makes your leg magic itself to you? What did you call it?" Lachlan asked.

"Solar panel, but I only need to charge it every few months. I turn it off at night, so I should be able to keep using it without any issue until we get back, if I remember to turn it off. I left the panel at the Keep."

Lachlan nodded and finished fastening the cloak. Today was cooler than the day before, breath puffed out of everyone's mouths making the season change more obvious. "I just wanted to make sure you were able to…" He lowered his voice, and I felt his lips on my ear. "I just wanted to make sure you were able to get out of here if you had to."

I turned around. The bed had been disassembled quickly and I saw the remnants of it being pushed onto a wagon. Lachlan held my hand. "I'm not leaving you. Not until the end," I told him.

Our days continued rather repetitively for two weeks. We travelled until the sun was almost gone, camp would unpack, and people slept or watched the perimeter in shifts. My companions and I shared daily dinners around the fire, cups of wine poured deep to make sure we slept through the night and its terrors. The sense of something watching us turned into something following us and I found Nerice and Priestess Mirna saying blessings over the bells every evening before they slept. Leaves continued to colour, and the weather carried a crisp bite on it with every passing day. The army moved through the Stills, its sheer mass deterring many of the on-going battles there. Rain begun to wage its own war on us as we drew closer and then crossed a large road between two lakes. I caught Cathal praying a few times, not for us, but for his ship, hoping the storming waters would be kind to it.

According to Durin, we were making good time. Storm Season was usually the time of year battles were at their weakest but proved difficult for those aligned with the Temples to free spirits.

"If we continue as we are, we'll make it to the Temple soon," Durin yawned. "I think I heard a scout say that we will take an extra long rest to make sure everyone has enough energy before battle. A final time to make peace with the gods. We can't go rambling in like undead and hope to win." The troops were definitely being affected by the long journey. We had been pushing to move through the province fast and our food was starting to run low.

Nerice dropped to the ground beside me by the fire, crossing her legs and nodded in agreement with Durin's words. "You head correct. We are taking a long rest tonight in fact. We'll stay until mid afternoon then walk through the night. Should reach the Temple before morning the day after tomorrow. We want to attack under the cover of darkness, take as much advantage as we can."

Durin tossed Nerice a green apple as I stirred a pot with a rabbit Vice had brought me an hour earlier. Wild carrot root and swamp potatoes boiled in water and wine beside it. I did not ask Vice how he caught the bunny. The moons were practically full and the memory of his body twisting out of a wolf was hard to forget.

"Good idea," Duin said. "I could use a twelve-hour nap."

Nerice took a large bite of the apple. "For some of us, or

perhaps all of us, this will be our last night before we meet the gods. We must make the best of it." Nerice glanced over at me and looked me up and down. "I'm sure the Commander wouldn't mind sharing if you asked nicely," she smirked.

My jaw practically unhinged it dropped so quickly. I shook my head, in disbelief of her words. "Nerice!" I screeched.

"Not even a kiss?" she asked optimistically. "Kissing is good luck!"

"Don't bullshit me, Nerice," I laughed. I took a deep breath of the stew and smiled at the satisfying smell. "Tell you what, I'll let you grab my ass before the battle so you can bring that memory with you until the end of time."

"No, Shorty, she isn't lying. Kissing *is* good luck. I'd take one from Lachlan if it meant winning this. I'd even kiss Sir Academic or Major Danger over there, if it assured us a win."

I looked at Vice, who was helping Cathal set up tents. Nerice cackled in laughter.

"Cathal isn't *that* dangerous!" I said, entertained.

"Delilah, *you* haven't been in his bed," Nerice said, cocking a brow at Durin.

Durin's eyes widened, and he stopped fidgeting with his wrist mechanism. He had two now; one with a blade and one that shot small bolts. "That is not what I meant! Gods have mercy on me!" he exclaimed. "You ever see Cathal when he's overwhelmed? Blades start reeling and you better not be caught in them!"

The three of us laughed together, entertained. How I loved my friends.

"You know what?" I said playfully. "Hold on." I motioned to Durin to come stir the soup pot then rushed to the main tent where I knew I would find Lachlan. Inside he was once again looking over maps at a large table, Florence was with him, writing on parchment, nodding as he spoke. One of Lachlan's lieutenants were on the other side of him, and I imagined a time where Durin stood there instead of the man who did now.

"Commander Blackwick?" I said, my tone beckoning, sultry.

399

It was one of Lachlan's favourite ways for me to talk to him.

He looked up, trying to hold back a smile he only made when we were naked. "*Seer*," he replied.

I approached him. Florence and the lieutenant took a couple steps back to give us space.

"Nerice asked if I could give her a kiss for luck tonight and I wanted to know if you would be amicable with that. If you were, maybe others would enjoy one as well?"

Lachlan grinned, his hand snaking around my waist to pull me flush against him. "Aye, of course, if it keeps the morale high for what lies ahead. I believe a couple musicians are taking out the war horns and drums tonight too to play some music, spread some joy. It will be a nice reprieve before the storm." Lachlan leaned down to my ear, his voice low and sending shivers through me. How quickly he could make me ache for him. "And if it keeps *my* morale high, perhaps later I can kiss you between your thighs and the gods will favor us in the battle?" I swallowed and Lachlan kissed the side of my head before he released me and turned back to the table. He coughed a little bit and said something in Bygone Speech, summoning Florence and the lieutenant back to his sides. They undoubtably heard our exchange because Captain Florence was biting back a smile when she glanced at me.

"I'll see you later, Commander," I said, my voice higher than I intended.

"Have a nice evening, Seer," Lachlan said, a smile in his voice.

I made it back to the fire, but not before grabbing my old cell phone from my pack. I had been charging it with the solar panel and listening to it with my quickly dying earbuds. They did not know what to do without regular updates. I had not listened to any of the music since we left Antore, but I had grabbed my phone, a small clutch in case I felt too uneasy over something. With my friends, it was easier not to need it and it was difficult to think I had once carried it everywhere with me.

Cathal and Vice had joined our group upon my return.

"So," I said as I plopped myself next to Nerice. "I had a couple ideas." I lifted my pant leg to expose part of my prosthetic. I turned on my phone and then pressed a button I had integrated into the leg to connect my phone to it. It had been an easy modification Vice and I worked on. I initially had deigned it as a way for me to listen to my music after my earbuds eventually died. The blinking light on my leg indicated Salvatore had still not moved from the Temple and we were closing in on him. Those poor people there must be wearing thin now, if they had not already perished.

I tried to stay optimistic.

My leg beeped and I smiled, selecting it to shuffle. The music started to drone out, the drums played a thrilled heartbeat, the guitar far away and promising something delicious. Cathal and Durin's faces lit up when they realized what I was doing, always lovers of music.

"You keep surprising me," Cathal laughed. He eyed my leg, impressed by its *magic*.

"I surprise myself sometimes," I replied. I then turned to Nerice. "My other idea: I asked Lachlan for permission to give out some luck to everyone and he said yes."

Nerice's jaw dropped in surprise as a smile itched at the corners of her lips. It was a very amusing expression to on her face. The woman was hard to surprise. "You're lying," she said in disbelief.

"I am not." I kissed the air in her direction.

"And *you're* sure you want to give it out?"

I nodded.

Nerice tackled me to the ground and kissed all over my face. I giggled, her lips soft and tickling me. She was a lot lighter than I thought she would be for being so tall. She sat up after a minute, leaving the smell of lavender and apple cider around me. Still in a straddle, she tapped her cheek with a sharp finger. "It must be reciprocated, or it doesn't work," she said before she looked down at me, her eyelids lowered seductively and her smile triumphant.

I laughed and pushed myself up on my elbows, kissing her delicately on one corner of her mouth. She kissed me as I did her, then rolled off. She held her cheek while I sat back up.

"I will never wash this again," she looked at me. "Or a least not until we have water to spare, and you kiss me on the lips because then my lips will never be cleaned."

I giggled again then looked around the campfire. "Anyone else interested?" I asked as music continued to reverberate from my prosthetic. The beat was the perfect medium between fast and slow, the voice dry and longing, singing about their crush and their *need*, for someone else. The satisfaction that was promised. In another life, it had been a regular rotation when I brought someone to bed. My phone really knew how to choose a song.

Nerice grabbed the bottle of wine I had used for the soup, taking a drink of what remained from it.

I looked at Durin and he smiled then shook his head, declining. "Theone and I agreed our last kiss would be all the luck I need. I promised to marry them if I make it home and I don't want to meet the gods knowing their lips weren't the last I had on mine."

My heart melted.

"The Colonel wouldn't even know if you did," Cathal pointed out.

"Oh, they'd know," Nerice said, her lips still on the wine bottle, a little bit of liquid escaping from the corner of her mouth.

"Besides, you're basically my sister, Shorty. Kissing my sister on the lips isn't something on my list of things to do before I die."

"You *love* Theone," I said.

The sweetness in Durin's voice could never be rivaled when he smiled and said, "So much."

Cathal caught my gaze, beckoning me with a large finger. He still wore his armour, which included gauntlets that had fingertips pointed like claws, reminiscent of Nerice's fingernails. "I'll take one," he said with a purr in his voice. He looked at me. In his grey eyes I saw all the months of our friendship, and his secret.

I wondered what kept him from telling the rest of our party and how Nerice did not know. Maybe he had only become one in the future where I was believed dead, but I remembered the shock on

Vice's face when he saw Cathal's changed eyes. How it seemed that it should have been obvious to him. I remembered the disappointment in his face when he had not known. Cathal and Bellamy looked very close in age. I did not know the logistics of how one became Amaranthine, but I knew he was not born one.

Cathal rolled his lips in and then back out as if he contemplated something while we watched each other for a few seconds. I crawled across the small circle by the fire seeing Cathal's sharp grin grow wider at my approach. Durin scooped soup into bowls and Nerice's hand collided with my ass while I passed her. She was *strong*.

I remember there was a point in my life here that Cathal's sharp teeth, along with Nerice and Vice's blood-red eyes, left me with a little bit of apprehension. It was so unusual from everything I had known before, but now I saw those features as a part of my friends, *and only a little menacing.*

I sat on my knees in front of Cathal and leaned in to kiss him, pausing, waiting for him to lean in as well. His hand suddenly seized my jaw between his forefinger and thumb, angling it up for his lips. We connected and I tasted his tongue and the wine on it. He lit a fire inside my belly, reminding me of what would come later when I crawled into bed with Lachlan.

I pulled away and looked at Cathal in disbelief. He had been one of the better kisses I had in my life, and I did not know what I expected from him. Cathal licked his lips then kissed my cheek before releasing his grip from my jaw. "You taste like strawberries and mint, and I love it," he said in a deep, appealing voice before smiling his sharp, smartass smile.

Nerice shoved Cathal playfully. "Don't worry, he's just trying to get a threesome, or foursome, out of you with his honeyed words. He told me I tasted like chocolate and smelled like cider. ext thing I knew my pants were around my ankles and I was bent over a desk in my tower."

The night moved on.

Blankets and pillows were brought out to make the campfire

cozier when a cold wind blew in and clouds filled the sky threatening another rain. A few more people joined us, enthralled by the music from my leg. The soup was eaten quickly, and the last of the wine bottles were emptied. I gave away a few more kisses to some scouts and a couple troops who inquired, as Florence had gossiped to her friends about my request to the Commander. *Everyone* was exceptionally good at kissing.

Not knowing I had fallen asleep, a soft cough caught my attention, rousing me. I was laying next to Cathal's tent. There was a lantern inside, but thankfully I could not see silhouettes moving with the sensual whispers inside. I turned over towards the dying fire, and saw Vice squatting next to me, his hands on his staff and expression concentrated. He watched me intently and I could see what light was left in camp reflect in his eyes, shining like a wolf in the night. The camp had quieted except for a few murmurs surrounding other dimming fires. I could imagine the only few left awake were those who were on watch and whoever might have found someone to love for the night. I could hear Lachlan's voice in the distance as he spoke with Nerice and Florence. I wondered who was in the tent with Cathal. I took in Vice's tall, thin, but formidable, form. I thought about seeing his naked body those months ago when he turned back into a man from a wolf. The waxing moons longed for him.

"Vice?" I said, suddenly awake. "What's up?"

Vice slowly put his staff down and leaned forward bringing his knees down to the dirt beside me. "I was hoping I could return…for the luck," he said quietly.

I nodded and rubbed my eyes. "Yeah, okay," I said drowsily. I looked up at the sky and saw the roundness of the moons, the clouds having given us some grace for the night. Blood pumped through me knowing what they meant. I began to sit up, but Vice moved quickly, leaning forward on one hand, and pressing the other lightly to my chest. I looked at him, my mind on high alert. He firmly, but gently, pressed me back down into a laying position to the pillows I had been snoozing on. I felt the air rushing into my lungs. My heart beat faster with feeling his hand on me. My eyes were on his, a tension building like a cord pulling tight. ready to snap or storm clouds filling up, the first clap of thunder moments away.

He looked like he was straining to find words to say to me. His expression was concentrated, almost pained. "I don't want to do this if it frightens you. I'm barely holding myself together, Delilah. If you move too quickly or get too excited…" his words drifted away, and he removed his hand from my chest, his fingers clenching, realizing he had touched me. He was so close to my face, my breath change must have been obvious. The cord pulled tighter, and I watched as Vice took *very* steady breaths.

My brows furrowed and I nodded, understanding.

Vice squeezed his eyes tightly. "Your heart is beating…*so fast*," he stated, the last to words he said in almost a whisper; as if savoring them.

"Aye, there's a werewolf struggling to hold his person form hovering over me," I whispered.

Vice moved quietly. If I did not see him in front of me, I never would have known he was there. "I want to give you something," he said.

"Not a bite, right?"

Vice opened his eyes and made a face, unimpressed by my joke. "You are so powerful, Delilah, but you could harness more, if I give it to you."

"What do you mean?"

"I want to give you *my* magic, with a bit of luck," Vice smiled softly, almost painfully. The wind blew a sharp gust of autumn air around and I thought I heard something whisper on it.

Vice had hundreds of years of magic behind him. "I can't let you do that, Vice," I said.

"You can. It is my gift to you. I do not need it anymore. I could never use it again, but what a waste it would be. Why not give it to my *friend.*"

I thought about what he said to me. He was more than just a mage. "But how will you survive the battle tomorrow without your magic?" I asked.

Vice glanced up at the sky then looked back at me as if the answer was obvious. "The night isn't the only time I can change, Delilah. It only makes it harder to hold this form."

He was going into battle as a wolf?

"Holy shit," I said.

"Does that mean yes?" Vice confirmed.

"Will it hurt?"

Vice shook his head. "Gods, I hope not." His lips came to mine, pieces of his hair that had escaped his braid dangled on my face. I was suddenly very awake and felt renewed; *fierce*. All the worries in the world left me, fresh air filled my lungs. Warmth covered my body, magic filled it. A feeling deep set in my bones recognized the energy being passed over, hundreds of years of training, of knowledge. Just as I started to get into his kiss, Vice pulled away from me. His hand stroked my cheek, his eyes squeezed tight in great concentration, his chest heaving. He kissed me again after his face relaxed then leaned his forehead on mine.

"Good luck tomorrow, Delilah Golding," he said softly. And then he was gone. He disappeared into the darkness as if he was never there. I sat up, looking around for any trace of him. Even his staff was gone. My heart still raced. I felt free and my mind rushed with ideas, solutions, and outcomes to every scenario that laid before us.

"Holy shit," I breathed, scrambling to my feet and running towards the big tent. Someone, I guessed Vice, had turned the music off on my leg. I ran into the tent, out of breath and excited. Lachlan and Nerice looked up from the table. Florence nodded to me, a welcome to the discussion.

"Someone is finally up I see," Nerice said with a smirk. "Did you have a nice nap?" She glanced quickly at Lachlan and smirked before looking back to me.

"I did! I really did. I need to talk to you two. I have an idea."

Chapter Seventeen
The Final Day of War

Months ago, at a time that I had just barely gotten to know this world, a magic spell sent Vice and I hurtling forward through time. I remember finding my dear friends trapped in a cell and shackles being tortured by dark magic and the men who followed Salvatore. I remember learning about the further assassinations of the Holy Order and how it was the last straw before Salvatore ruled and ravaged the world. He had succeeded in his war for power and so many had died. In the future I had witnessed this world suffering because I had not been there to stop it.

I remember for months I was frightened, and anxiety ridden, mourning the life I used to live. How strange it felt to think of now. I stood in the camp a woman transformed. We were getting ready to march out, leaving the wagons and tents behind with a skeleton crew of people to watch over and, if things went south, warn Antore. Hopefully we would reach the Temple while the night was still young.

There was a tent set up at the outskirts of camp housing totems to the gods. Priestess Mirna sat amongst them, her hand placed over the small carving of a dragon. Her eyes were closed as she murmured in Bygone Speech. I had witnessed many troops come and go from that tent over the last couple weeks and I felt it was my turn.

"Priestess Mirna?"

The Priestess removed her hand from the totem. She had insisted on accompanying the army on the journey to battle, even after the pleas from the nuns for her to not go. Nerice had agreed to let her come as far as the last camp. She would remain here awaiting the wounded and dying and connect to the gods as she saw fit. She looked over her shoulder at me.

"Seer," she said, "it is good to see you. I noticed you are feeling strengthened this morning." I wondered what she may know about the goings on around the camp and if all priestesses had the same seeing eyes that Nerice seemed to possess. Mirna motioned her head towards the totems and returned her attention to them. I recognised one as the statue from my chambers when we first discovered it. The sun and two moons now polished a deep and beautiful green. There must have been so much dust on it prior, that its colour was so dulled. "Have you come to pray before you leave? The Commander was in earlier, speaking to his *prababkia*, hoping for good favor."

I walked across the tent, taking in the black silks, embroidered pillows, and patterned, carved candles. It was a pleasant oasis, the illusion of the war gone within its space. I smelt sandalwood and lavender, and my mind eased away from *what ifs*, solidifying the confidence I gained the night before.

Priestess Mirna did not wear her usual robes. Though her hair was still wrapped in its scarf and a ritual shawl draped over her shoulders, she wore shiny armour and leathers that reminded me of the armour I saw on Andreja's statue back at the Keep. It was odd to see her in something other than the soft, billowing fabrics I had come to associate with her and the other laity at the Keep. I sat on my knees, next to her, my hips on my heels, and looked at the different totems of each god. An Owl, a cat, a wolf, a squid…

The priestess motioned to the helmet in my hand, the dragon carved into it, then looked back to the dragon totem she had been praying to. "Andreja," she said softly. Andreja's totem was the only one that was a magical creature amongst the wild and domestic animals. Each one was placed on empty crates draped in silver embroidered silks. Dried flowers, cups of tea and wine, and incense sticks were carefully placed around them as offerings.

I smiled, thinking of my friend who had given me my helmet and daggers.

"She speaks to you every day," the Priestess continued. "Through your memories, through her great-grandson. You might not think to listen, but she chose you. Did you choose her?"

I looked at the dragon and then back to my helmet. I thought about the statue in Antore and the comforting smile on it. I thought about my *eye*. All my friends had such faith in the world around them. In me. "I did," I said.

Priestess Mirna smiled, satisfied, and put her hand around my shoulders. "Everything will be alright."

*

The Temple was a three-hour march. Night was on the cusp of taking the lands when we left and as we got closer, the sound of bloodshed got louder. I looked to Durin who adjusted the mechanisms on his leather gauntlets. It looked different than the ones I had seen him fiddle with before. His hair was pulled back completely, the braids tucked into the tie to keep his eyeline clear. He concentrated on the gear, letting his peripherals lead him while we followed Lachlan and around a dozen troops. The rest of the army was spreading out.

"New toy?" I asked.

"New toy," he said. "Theone had Nerice acquire a new one for me. She wanted to make sure I have every advantage. How's my bow looking?" Durin asked. I glanced behind him where he had his bow secured to his back, his quiver hanging on his hip.

"Shiny," I said.

Durin smiled. "Good."

The troops disappeared into the forest to surround the moors that the ruins of Virág's Temple lay within. The ether of the forests near the destroyed Temple were not as scary as they were in other places. Whatever magic Virág's Temple had extended far into the surrounding areas. I still felt watched, followed, but tonight it was not the sense of being hunted. It was a sense of anticipation, or curiosity. I did not dare look into the trees, nor behind our group when we separated from them. I could not let my curiosity from the forest extend to me, as it often tried to do.

There was a hope that the remaining Keepers were yet alive in the lower sections of the Temple. A Temple Mother would have magicked the entrance sealed, but if they faltered even a little, Salvatore would break through. It would have to be a strategic and

409

tiring defence. We knew whatever relic inside, lay with the people below and those people were drained. How they had held off for so long, was a miracle.

Our troops surrounded the ruins that centered a half a kilometer of bog terrain. It rained and thundered, the storms lending us additional cover in the night. Dozens of groups moved around the perimeter, waiting for the signal. Once the farthest division reached their location, a flare would be sent up and others would follow. We banked on the lights acting as a distraction to Salvatore's followers below and a guide to us. Hopefully it would be enough time for me to start the music from my prosthetic. Music that I prayed Salvatore would recognize, even after one thousand years away from it, and just maybe, he would be distracted himself long enough that we could get through a decent amount his forces. He had remained at the Temple, laying siege with the rest of his men for weeks. His need for the relic inside far outweighed his care for his men, if he ever had any to begin with. The stubbornness of his old life still stuck to him now, unable to grasp that Temple's would no longer go down without a fight.

The sound of the rains was loud. Loud enough not even our clanking, metal footsteps could be heard. We crouched at the crest of the surrounding hills, looking down over the devastated Temple. Small fires dotted around the crumbling building showing us where Salvatore's soldiers camped. I could hear bells swinging in the breeze, a warning for what followed us. Despite our differences, they still feared what lay beyond the safety of the moors.

There were countless bodies among them, all rotting, the stench lifting into the hills where we waited. What remained of the Temple was immense, the columns raising high as the ancient trees this land carried. They marked where the entrance would be. Viscera of both Virág's disciples and Salvatore's wet the statue form of Virág that once stood proudly on a pedestal. Now pulled down, her head was cracked off. The gardens that once bordered the Temple were destroyed, dug into trenches by the opposition. I could see the beauty it once had, and it devastated me.

Stone walls that still stood had words of hatred and

defamation, renouncement, painted in blood or carved deep into the sides. Stained-glass windows were shattered in the muck, the encampment loud with rageful curses.

Salvatore's men fought amongst themselves hungry for more death. Demons were born before our eyes, ripping out from inside living beings. I tried to focus beyond them to what remained inside the Temple. I sensed those trying to hold the doors, the fatigue, the pain. I could feel the last of their magic dwindle, their protective shield coming to an end as they finally reached their limit. We had been granted to witness the final moments.

Hopefully the music would be the sign they needed to know we had come for them.

Lachlan came beside me as I stared down to the Temple ruins. "I spoke with the best mages we have, and they will be ready at the signal. I will project to the north end, and they will move it east and so forth. The troops were warned that it will be *loud*."

I nodded, still looking out towards the Temple, seeing rubble and blood. Seeing the hordes of people and demons trying to smash their way into something cherished by their ancestors. Something stirred inside me, deep and ancient. How dare this creature do this to such a wonderful world. I scowled, felt hardened and ready for what was to come. Salvatore never got what he wanted on Earth and nor would he here.

"This is the advantage we need to get close," I said.

Just like when we danced on the Giving Day, an enchantment to cast music around the great hall for everyone to hear, everyone would hear this music. Lachlan kissed the side of my head and followed my eyeline. I could see how the war had affected him over his life, how close to an end it could be, how much he hoped.

"May the gods watch over us," Lachlan whispered.

"May the gods watch over us," I repeated.

The flares went up. Bright, sparkling blue lights shot into the sky, shooting out in spirals once they neared the raging clouds. One after the other hurtled upward on each corner of the battlefield, illuminating the dark, raining night so brightly it was as the sun was out. I fingered down the side of my leg until I felt the button to turn on the speaker. I had put it to full volume before we left, and the music blared out of my leg. Lachlan let out a large breath and touched my prosthetic before rubbing his hands together. He looked out to where he knew our people hid within the hills, his arm shooting towards the north, hand glowing brighter as he sent the sound towards the other mages. His free hand grabbed his sword.

"Charge!" he roared.

The music reverberated around the valley getting louder each time it connected to a different mage. The music moved inward, shaking the ground with help from the onslaught of our army. My thoughts were deaf to me from the volume of it. All I needed to do was get down there and to Salvatore. I could do two things. I drew my daggers and dashed down towards the Temple. A wave of people ran over the hills as the blue mage lights fell over the battlefield, dying fireworks in the rain.

I felt the fear spread through Salvatore's army for the first time in his reign. Our army had grown immense compared to what it was back in Blackwick. Many had come to Antore not only for shelter, but for pilgrimage, vowing themselves to me and our cause, wanting nothing more than to be a part of finishing this. The avalanche had disposed of a good portion of Salvatore's army, the waters surrounding Zaanthru had wore them thin. The army before us was large compared to other legions around the world, but now we had one to match it and Salvatore's forces knew the end was near.

Whatever magical barrier that held Salvatore out of the Temple broke. Amongst the many, I spotted Salvatore's monstrous form at the doors of the crumbling Temple. His long claws scraped against the once beautifully carved entrance, and his twisted, tainted body turned, his eyes zeroing on my approach. Our gazes connected across the battlefield. I could feel his rage, I could feel his stolen technology. Two people, connected.

"*You*," he growled, his voice clear in my mind. His expression curled into a sneer before throwing his claws up against the doors, shattering them like ice. He disappeared into the darkness of the Temple.

Armies collided.

I narrowly blocked a sword between the blades of my daggers. I push-kicked the man holding it back and my blades found the temples of his head in one smooth movement. Blood poured over his cheeks while my daggers crisscrossed in his skull. I ripped them out before running forwards. There were hundreds of people to push through. I dodged and tumbled, advancing to my best ability. I blocked and sliced. Black blood dripped over my blades. My feet sloshed through mud and guts and blood. Demons screeched all around me. I watched more soldiers transform, their bodies tarring open as demons ripped their way out through bones. Someone fell against me, and I thrust them away.

I felt my friends around me though I was not sure where they were. There were so many people and so much more blood. The music still blared. It was hard, moving through the bodies, both alive and passed. I had already lost count of the men who came between me and the Temple. All I had to do was make it inside to Salvatore. I could make it. I just had to-

A *scream*.

A sound both unnatural and unnerving making me spin around and see a blade deep in Nerice's belly. She stood several yards from where I paused and dropped her bow to the ground, shocked. She stared down the man who held his sword inside her, a wicked grin on his face. My eyes widened in horror.

"Nerice!" I shrieked.

She did not hear me. Her expression changed from disbelief to fury to…hunger.

Just as I knew not to linger my gaze on the trees, I knew to stay away from Nerice. I stayed locked on her and the rival soldier, my heart speeding up. Nerice and the soldier stumbled apart from each other as she shoved the man back. Something about her became unnatural as she pulled the blade from her belly, screaming from its sharpness moving through her flesh. When she recovered her barring's, blood stained her beautiful battle robes and poured down from her belly, Nerice crouched low to the ground like an animal. The man shook his head, shock on his face from watching her. He noticed her eyes, realization dawning on him. Nerice lunged at the soldier, her movement smooth and cat-like. Her legs wrapped around his body as she ripped the helmet from his head. Her nails dug into his throat as he yelled, "Get off of me, you demon!"

Her pointed nails sunk deeper into his neck, and I heard him scream louder, terrified. I heard him scream *no*. I watched as a mist of blood floated out of him. His body shrivelled and thinned to a desiccated, grey corpse within layers of armour. The body collapsed to the ground and Nerice breathed in deeply as the blood flew into her nose, still straddling the corpse on the ashen earth. She let go of him, the man aged fifty years and dried up like he had been long buried. Nerice's eyes were redder than I had ever seen them. She stood, kicking the man's head. It tore from his shoulders, flying into the battle. Nerice walked back to grab her bow. Though blood still stained her leathers and robe, she no longer had a deep wound in her belly. She raged forward, drawing an arrow from the quiver on her hip.

I was tackled.

I moved my dagger, ready to attack, but stopped inches from Durin's wincing face.

"Nerice can handle herself," he grunted before rolling off me. He had the tip of an arrow sticking out through his breastbone, blood spurted out every second. Durin clutched at his chest, flinching as the arrow snapped between him and the ground. "Go!" he demanded as he raised his other hand, and a bolt flew from a mechanism on his wrist past my head. I heard a grunt and turned, seeing a soldier drop mere feet behind me, a sword ready in his hand and Durin's bolt clean between his eyes. "GO DELILIAH!"

I stood and spun back to face the Temple. I ran as fast as I could, watching as mage light continued to shoot into the sky for light over the battlefield. I jumped over corpses and dodged around people who grappled with blades at each others' throats. Somewhere I heard a wolf howl, and knew Vice had let himself loose on the soldiers.

"Seer!" I looked up and saw Florence on an armoured horse charge towards me. "Grab my hand!"

I sheathed one of my daggers as I reached out to her. Her hand connected with my forearm, and she lifted me on the horse in one clean sweep.

"I will get you to the doors," she said, drawing her bow. "Hold on until you can't anymore." Florence moved quickly through the battlefield. As her horse sped forward, she was suddenly standing on the stirrups, tall, readying an attack of her own. She held in her hand three arrows. The horse ran through flames and Florence dipped them down to catch the fire. They sizzled. As she released them ahead, explosions went off and people were thrown from our path.

"Durin," I yelled over the music and warring screams. "He was hit!"

Florence drew three more arrows and nodded. "I will go back for him. My priority is you, Seer." She let the three arrows loose and three men before us fell, one landing in the flames she made prior. The horse pushed through the battle. We got closer to the door where a big gaping hole lay in Salvatore's wake. Florence was fast and her arrows were faster. This was why she was under Nerice's command. I could only imagine how efficient Bellamy was.

Florence dropped back down to the saddle and pulled the reins, halting the horse just as we were about to collide with rubble at the Temple entrance. The horse whinnied and she turned to face behind us, drawing more arrows. "Move it!" she commanded.

I slid off the horse redrawing my sheathed dagger.

Something had changed since the battle began. Something felt off, wrong. I paused at the entrance of the Temple, looking out over the thousands who warred against one another. I saw a red blip hovering in the battlefield, like a piece of stray lightning. I felt all the demons, both new and of those who perished from their crashed Machines. A loud thunder rolled over the moors and many cringed at the sound that was louder than the music. I saw the piece of stray lightning move through the fury and rip open something that had wanted out, now freed. A gigantic demon, different from any of the others I had seen before it stepped into the combat. As it connected with the earth below, the ground shook. It stood fifteen feet tall, hunched over and shiny like metal. It had a mouth full of jagged, thin teeth that dripped with the sticky black ooze other demons had. Its body rippled with thick, bloodied muscles and its grey, rotting skin slopped off its body revealing black bones and maggots feasting on tissue. The demon laughed manically as it surveyed the people around it. "Oh yes," it rumbled.

I had never heard one talk before.

I could not leave my people with it.

I had to open a rupture. It would suck that *thing* and every demon around it back to the Other.

Black ooze dripped from the corners of its mouth, and it licked its lips drinking it in, staining its lizard-like tongue. Part of its skull was exposed, its one eye where its bone protruded was empty of life and its other shined from the mage lights in the sky. Several rusted, ancient swords were stuck in its back and legs. Flesh pealing from the massive horns on its head. If I concentrated on where its bones were exposed, I thought I saw live wires beneath its flesh. It clenched and unclenched its fists then roared as it began to swipe at those closest to it, Salvatore's troops included.

Our soldiers attacked the great beast. *Take them back*, I thought, concentrating on Virág's broken statue. The huge demon stepped with great force, nearing the statue as it raged forward. I willed a rupture to open there, the words to the old spell leaving my lips. A portal flickered, its magic fighting to open. This would be the most demons I would send back, and the portal had to be big. Finally, the rupture in space and time opened, a soft sunset glow shining out of it as it grew larger than the portal I had opened on the dragon. The rains started to slow in its wake, and everything tensed.

You will take them back, I thought forcefully.

Demons screamed, tortured. They clawed at rotting corpses and soldiers and rubble, trying to fight against the pull of the rupture.

The large demon roared out in pain and fell to its knees, gasping for breath. Its chest heaved. Our people furthered their attack, giving their all on Salvatore's soldiers who were distracted by my magic. Hundreds of flaming arrows berated the great demon from every direction, singeing its flesh.

Lessor creatures burned up to ash without so much as being touched by a blade, the portal no match for their will. The big demon screamed, electric pulses shot out around it. A big axe landed in its neck, Cathal's no doubt, and it finally released its grasp on this plane. It got sucked up, the final creature to be called from my spell and I released the portal, red light shining out from it, a wave of wind washing over the battlefield. The fight turned in our favour.

I could move on and turned back to the Temple. I went inside.

A trail of fresh bodies littered the front hall of the Temple. Adults and children, massacred.

"Cifarelli Salvatore!" I called into the darkness. "Come here you bastard!"

Inside the stone walls were still intact, but the beautiful paintings were now stained by blood splatter. I could not tell how many soldiers followed Salvatore inside, but I could only hope it was enough I could handle.

I stepped carefully, the corridor darkened by closed, barred shutters and candles tipped over and slowly catching aflame on old tapestries depicting scenes of Virág and her people tending to crops. No sounds of the battle could be heard within these walls, and I turned the music on my leg off to quiet my approach.

"Seer," someone coughed. I whirled around and I could see High Priestess Caoimhe laying propped up against a hallway alter, two armoured nuns draped over her, dead. This was how they survived so long. Caoimhe had come and protected what she could.

I rushed over, sheathing my daggers before I dropped to my knees before her. "My Divine," I gasped. "You're alive! Why are you here?!"

The High Priestess smiled half-heartedly. "Aye, barely alive," she croaked. "That creature is sloppy." She moved her head to face down the hall before looking back at me. "Saoirse was my *sestra*, I could not leave her defenceless. I came with my Keepers months ago and did not tell anyone I would be here." Caoimhe pointed weakly down the hall. "It went that way." An armoured hand grasped my fingers, and she pulled me with impressive strength towards her. "It wants our vestiges. In the lower chambers, my monks are protecting it, but I don't know for how long they can continue. Help them."

"But you," I began.

Priestess Caoimhe's other hand went over mine, pressing something into my palm. "If the gods have decided it is my time, they can have me. *You*, will be the successor to my *sestra* and Priestess Mirna mine." She let go of my hands and leaned back against the wall, exhausted and dying. "Now go."

I looked at what she placed in my hand. Two rings. An antique gold ring with a purple gem and an emerald ring bounded in iron sat on my palm. I slipped them on my fingers, over the leather, and stood, heading in the direction Caoimhe had told me to go.

I moved through the darkened corridors, the smell of swamp water and incense mixing with the thick copper scent of too much blood. I followed a trail of gore, led by a *pull*. That same pull that I now recognized as *Machine* steering me. I had sensed it at the battle in Blackwick with Salvatore moving around us, I sensed it calling me as I stared at my old Machine within Antore. *This* was Salvatore. His blight and sourness put a bitter taste in my mouth from following him. Bodies begun to dwindle as I moved through the Temple, a déjà vu of something I had experienced before. A flood of memories washed over me with each step. I was reminded of walking through Andreja's Temple. I could hear High Priestess Katerina's screams, her pleading voice telling me to run as she passed me her ring for Theone. I remember seeing Salvatore for the first time, knowing now that the jagged metal sticking out of him was stolen Earth technology and he had forced his being into some sort of ancient undead, demon creature. My insides churned. I would never understand why he would do that to himself.

I paused, kneeling to check the locator. It flashed quickly. I was close, within a kilometer. Around the corner was a shadow shrouded staircase. The memory of Andreja's Temple feeling dark and frightening fluttered in my chest, but that was because I did not know where I was. Virág's Temple was dark, and the copper scent of blood hung in the air making it thick and angry, but I did not feel fear *here*. The spirits of those who had not been released yet hung heavy. I could feel them. The bereavement from all the souls desperate for the After.

Most of the Temple lay underground, like the seed waiting to be watered. Virág's Temple was dug deep into the earth, built resembling roots and going on for miles. The sound of dripping from the wet moor's leaking in echoed with my footsteps. I descended the staircase. As I got closer to the lower chambers, light still glowed from torches on the walls. There was no sound of swords clashing, or people enacting spells.

What I heard was laughter.

I followed the sounds through twisting hallways. I saw the occasional body of a nun or monk leaving a direction to the final chamber. Intermittently, there was a fallen follower of Salvatore, their skin blackened by burns, crispy and freshly singed. I peaked around corners of stone archways leading to storage rooms or sleeping quarters. I saw army men ransacking chests, pulling drawers out and fabrics discarded, not good enough for looting. They did not notice me as I crept past them.

I continued forward until I reached a huge chamber, the size of a farmer's field held up by wooden columns made of the old growth trees that once stood where the Temple had been built lifetimes ago. The walls were painted like the inside of a feast hall, scenes of hundreds of people eating and crafting together through the seasons. The ceiling was that of the sky, painted as daylight, transitioning into night with stars that sparkled back at me like the real night sky. There were overturned tables and chairs, the remaining nuns belonging to High Priestess Caoimhe thrown against them either unconscious or dead. At the far end, stood Salvatore before an enchanted door. The door looked exactly like the one in Antore, the one at the base of my tower.

Salvatore's claws slowly scraped over it, longing for its contents, before he sensed my approach. He looked different than I remembered him at Blackwick; older, weakened. Perhaps the weeks of attacking this Temple had taken an unknowing toll on him.

"You think you can stand against *me*?" Salvatore growled from his gnarled teeth. He looked over his shoulder. "A *girl*?"

"You underestimate us all. Just like you had during your campaign. We learned from our past transgressions, *you* fled from them," I hissed. I watched Salvatore's expression hitch in the smallest degree, a memory from eras long past. He turned to face me. Slowly he walked across the chamber, the heels of the massive boots he wore clinking loudly against the marble floors. The metal sticking out of his form glinted in the torch lights. I could see the red light on his shoulder blinking quickly, in sync with the tracker on my leg. I lifted the cuff of my pant leg enough to reveal the prosthetic I had fashioned from my Machine. *Found* blinked brightly on the screen there and Salvatore bared his teeth, revulsion in his eyes.

"You are from *Earth*." His fists clenched. "I should have known. How did you survive?"

"I am *chosen*. Unlike you who claims to be to be a false god. *My* people know where I am from, and I gave away your secret to them."

Salvatore was quiet for a moment then scoffed. He looked around the chamber, to the massive mural of the feast hall, its people celebrating Virág's accomplishments with the world. His hollow eye returned to me, the other now covered with an eyepatch from my handywork. There was not a human piece left of him. His voice was clear and loud from across the space. "Oh? How will the rest of this puny planet understand those words? Aliens from another world, wreaking havoc in their home?" I knew the tone he had in his words. It was the same when he spoke during campaigns, interviews. He really believed he was right.

"Where you poisoned this world with your greed, I became

one of them. I don't belong to Earth anymore. I belong to Alhan, and you *never* will," I hissed. I threw my hand out before me, sending Salvatore's monstrous body careening into the chamber door leading to where I expected Virág's relic to be. The room echoed with the collision and dust fell from the ceiling. "I am not just a girl to them. I have been sent here by the gods to stop *you*." I clutched my fist and could hear bones break and metal bend beneath Salvatore's skin. He let out an unnatural, ear-piercing sound and I charged towards him. I released the grip in my hand and Salvatore staggered back to his feet.

"You learned their magics quickly," he snarled.

"I barely needed to. I just had to harness what was already there," I said. "Andreja gave some of her power to me when you tried to steal it. My friends gave me the confidence to control it. This authority you tried to take, this world you attempted to make in your own image, is the same pattern you had on Earth. What made you think it would end any differently here?"

Salvatore raised his hand, trying to cast magic on me, but nothing happened. He tried again and a third time, his face twisting in frustration. Black blood oozed from his nose with his concentration, but again, nothing. I shot my hand out towards him as he cursed my name, my shadow moving faster than light across the walls.

"Don't you know everyone always gets their comeuppance?" I hissed. I stretched out my arm and my shadow wrapped around Salvatore's body to hold him still. He squirmed beneath my grasp as I pulled him towards me. "How does it feel?"

"You are not special," Salvatore snarled. "How could you believe such nonsense!" I was close to him now, still holding firmly to the magic that bound him. Before me stood the man, the *creature*, that caused so much death and chaos. I remembered all the tears I cried, not just here, but in my other life. "I told you before and I will tell you again, their gods are dead, their thrones empty. I spent lifetimes trying to find my place here and when I could not, I made it. They need a leader!"

I stared at him in disbelief, unimpressed by his attempts to bate me. I squeezed him harder, and he hissed.

"Earth no longer served me-"

"You're an asshole, and you stole a Machine to get away from the repercussions of your actions," I said matter-of-factly. "You got caught and you didn't want to live with the consequences. Now you corrupted this world with your selfishness, again believing you could get away with it!"

"People on Earth did not understand my vision! Earth could have thrived! Everyone is always so resistant."

"Your vision is outdated, just like you are," I growled.

Salvatore's words poured from his lips, his anger trying to cover the growing distress as he realized he could not free himself from my grasp. "I wanted a better world. I tried to create one on Earth! When the people there could not appreciate me, I wanted to go back in time to create a place that would! Except I ended up *here*. My stupid, blabbing ex-business partner had not roused from our fight to tell me how to use the Machine. I raged, smashed the controls, and the Machine revolted knocking me unconscious. I woke up, crashed in this place. The betrayer was tangled in the electric wire of the Machine that had cut a scar into the South Province. I did not know how I survived, until I realized I had not. I watched my body rot, be chewed on by scavengers.

"Years went by. I grew mad. Everything I had known on Earth was wrong. As I screamed into the nothingness, I was sucked into the desiccation that was left of my bones and meat and I rose again, mangled and repulsive. My heart did not beat, no water could satiate my thirst.

"I crawled to the Machine's pieces and pulled apart what I could. The solar panels, the power cell clinging to life within it, just to make my body strong enough to not break beneath my weight. I wandered deeper into the lands of this world and found a Tabernacle, asleep in the cold night that I could not warm from. A monk saw me wandering the corridor and tried to burn me alive. I was lucky enough to stab him with a knife I had carried with me from the Machine wreckage. I took his clothes and wandered the halls there, found their written texts.

"I hid in the Tabernacle for months, killing anyone who found me. Eventually they abandoned their holy place, deeming it haunted, unsanctified. They tried to burn it down, but I escaped, ancient scrolls in hand. I learned of their world; I learned their magic. I found my way onto a ship. That was where I found my first devotee. I baited him at night, tricked him into trusting me. I told him about my power, what was just tricks I could use from the Machine I built into this vessel you see before you. I told him of the world I envisioned, and he loved it. Everyone loved it. They were tired of all these *women* running the world. How could anyone let that happen!" Salvatore spat a black, bloodied wad to my feet. "Then I found the gods' castle. I found their necromancy. There are so many more dead than there are alive."

"This planet was a world at peace before you showed up!"

"It was a world full of idiots and I enlightened them!"

I took a deep breath, the words to open a rupture to the Other filling my mind. I spoke the words quietly at first while Salvatore tried to continue to talk to me, stall me, hope for his men raiding the rooms around us to find him. I watched as his eyes widened when the realization of what I was doing dawned on him. I spoke the spell louder.

"You cannot put me there!" he roared. "I will find my way back, I *swear* it!"

The portal opened and wind picked up around us as the portal ached to suck something up inside it, still starved from all the other demons I had fed it in months past. I could feel the creatures on the other side wanting out, ravenous. I willed Salvatore's body towards it, ready to give the Other what it wanted. I felt his eyes scorning me and I locked mine onto his. "For as long as my spirit lives you will never *ever* win. If by some gods-forsaken reason you make it out of the Other, I will put you right back."

"I will never stop," he boomed.

"You will die every one of your lifetimes regretting your choices, I promise you that, you fucking heretic." I released his form, and the portal swallowed him up. Salvatore shrieked in terror, and I watched ancient, unholy things tare at his body, the screams of both Salvatore and the beasts surrounding him echoing loud in the chambers. No doubt anyone nearby could hear it happen. The portal closed and for just a moment the world was quiet. I inhaled deeply then let out a slow breath. I could breathe. It was over.

Rushed footsteps approached, the soldiers Salvatore gave empty promises to coming to investigate the horrors they heard. In the far corner of the chamber, I heard a groan.

Shit.

I rushed to a nun, roused from unconsciousness, her head bloodied, but otherwise unharmed. Her robes matched that of High Priestess Caoimhe's. "Sister," I said, grabbing her hand.

She groaned again, her eyes struggling to stay open.

"Sister, my name is Delilah, I am your Seer."

"*Seer?*" she croaked.

"Are there any laity left? Any Keepers?" I asked, softly. The footsteps were getting closer.

"Behind the door. Most Holy sealed them in. Me and the others stayed out to protect them. No one can open it unless…" She coughed, rubbing her head.

I looked back at the massive door, its carvings now changed from the claw marks Salvatore had left on it.

"I will get you inside. You stay in there, okay?"

She nodded and I hauled her up, her arm limp around my shoulders as I practically dragged her over to the door. I pressed my scarred hand to the flower there. The violet and emerald rings on my finger glimmered in the torch lights.

"Divine Caoimhe…" the Sister whispered. She tiredly looked at me as the door ached open, gasps of the others beyond it echoing out.

"Take her," I ordered when my eyes connected with a monk. A young boy barring green robs, the same as others I had seen fallen here, cowered behind him.

"Of course," the monk said grabbing the nun as I passed her to him.

"You!"

I looked over my shoulder, seeing the other forces gathering.

"Stay inside!" I said.

The nun moaned again in the monk's arms as he held her, carefully bringing her near to the back of the chamber. I saw a rusted trowel on a pedestal and at least twenty laity cowering, daggers at hand.

I shut the door, and it clicked, locked once more, a heavy sigh leaking out between it and the frame. A shadow of tiredness crowned me. Killing my way through Salvatore's faithful, opening two ruptures, wading through the corpses throughout the Temple to find an end to the war, it took a toll.

There was no trace left of Salvatore as the first of his men came into the chamber. I drew my daggers as they cursed me, realizing who stood before them. One demanded to know where their leader was.

"Don't let me out of your sight," I said.

"What?"

I melted into the shadows and moved through them like water. Music hummed in my mind, calming me, while I drifted in and out of the reality before them. Gliding into physical form long enough to slice through the back of an ankle or tendon causing soldiers to collapse. I threw a dagger across the chamber, hitting someone in the throat, only to disappear again and reappear next to them. I ripped my dagger back before they collapsed. Black blood splattered against my skin. The soldiers scrambled further into the chamber, trying to get a hold of me.

I continued to tire.

The shadows were getting harder to control as I went on. More soldiers poured inside surrounding me. I wondered what it looked like outside, if my friends were still alive. I knew I could not let these men make it back to the surface. They could not continue Salvatore's tyranny on their own. Even one less asshole was better than none.

I made it to the entrance of the chamber. Everyone who had

been looting the place for its riches, greedy and prideful in their plundering, now here and preventing me from leaving. The bodies of at least a ten of their comrades lay behind me.

One soldier moved to kick me, and I grabbed his foot pulling him forward then pushed him back, knocking him off his balance. I dodged out of another soldier's grasp and countered, shoving a dagger straight up from base of his jaw. It jammed there and I abandoned it in his head. A soldier grappled me from behind and I grabbed his arms, forcing our bodies forward, flipping him over my shoulder. I drove my armoured foot into his face when he hit the floor. The sound of him squelching underneath my weight and his blood spilling over my boot, engraved into my memory. I panted, I sweat. More tried to take me, more fell by blade.

How many were here?

How many more were at war outside of the Temple?

I lost my other dagger in the chest of a man who charged me with no weapon, just rage. I was surrounded. At least four had their arms on me, trying to wrestle me to the floor and hold me still to make a final blow. I could not melt into the shadows again. I was too concentrated on not choking to death. I did not know if I had been stabbed or not, or if I was already dying.

I made the decision quickly.

These men would not make it out of the Temple.

If I was going down, they were going down with me.

I strained to reach down to my prosthetic leg, allowing whoever had their arms on my neck to get a full grip. I felt pressure in my face and ears as I gasped for air and forced myself to search for a button that I never thought I would press.

If you don't think you can get out of something, that button will make sure history won't change because of you.

I wrenched my prosthetic leg from whoever held it, their voice cursing. I freed it long enough to bend it into my reach.

The self-destruct button.

It was contained in a metal box with a small hook lock at my calf. I could not figure out how to disengage it safely and instead opted to use the levers and wire surrounding it as other core pieces to the prosthetic. I had not thought that it would come in useful.

With every Machine it was built in. A recourse in case you were cornered by a dinosaur or *in the middle of a war.* If the captain could not travel and knew they would die, the number one thing we could not do was leave our Machine behind. No trace could be detected, in case it would alter history; the very thing Salvatore had tried to do. Some Travellers had messed up before, petrified pieces of Machines were found over the centuries and until we made them, there was no scientific explanation that archeologists could settle on with the fossils.

How human of us.

If we could not live, no one could and I would make sure history wound not change further because of *him.*

The explosion would end everyone around me, within the surrounding tunnels, maybe even anyone on the upper levels of the Temples. I fully understood why High Priestess Katerina had done what she did. She had tried to stop Salvatore, tried to remove the chances of him coming back. She had known his power before any of us did.

Being connected to Andreja as she was, I wondered if Katerina had known what the future would be when she gave me the Eye. Salvatore was gone and hopefully the majority of his followers were about to be. I prayed for the Temple laity in the stone chamber with the relic. I prayed that whatever magic sealed them inside would save them.

With all the time, swords and blood I had gone though, I knew it was all worth it to save them. My people would be alright.

My fingers connected with the button, and I closed my eyes, pressing it. I had done what I set out to do. I would see my friends again the After. A light shined behind my eyelids and then red enveloped me into oblivion.

Chapter Eighteen
After

I stood at the top of an extremely steep set of stairs that descended from the skies around me. Stunning pinks, purples, reds and oranges swirled around in a loving manner, a perfect sunset or sunrise. I felt calm. I felt safe. I took a deep breath smelling the fresh air around me and it smelt like the plot of land I rented on Earth.

"Seer."

That *voice*.

I turned, and Gwen stood there, her blind eye restored. She was clad in the armour I remembered her last wearing. Or at least, close to it. The difference was it looked like it was made of dragon scales.

"Gwen!" I screeched in excitement, lunging at my friend and wrapping my arms around her.

Gwen laughed, lifting me up off the ground as she embraced me. When she set me back down, she smiled lovingly, proud. "I told you, you would be alright," she said. Her hands moved down to hold mine, giving them a firm squeeze.

My cheeks already hurt from smiling at her. I looked over her body and then beyond her to the endless warm skies around us. My smile fell, awareness about the situation settling in.

"I died," I said. A deep sadness fluttered through my belly, but it did not take root. I was with my friend, and I knew the world would be safe.

Gwen shook her head. "No, I wouldn't let that happen. Not yet anyway." She smiled meaningfully at me, as if there was a joke that I missed the punchline for.

"Excuse me?".

"You're still alive, my friend. You're just knocked the fuck out."

"I'm hallucinating?" I asked.

Gwen laughed, a sound I had missed dearly and it warmed

my heart fully by hearing it again. "Also no," she said, entertained. She lifted our hands between us, eying the big purple and red rings High Priestess Caoimhe had given me. She smirked at them then looked back at me. "I have given you so many gifts, do you think you can do me favour in return?" I looked at the way her smiling lips sat on her face, the familiarity past her being my friend. I found the statue in Antore. I found Lachlan.

Disbelief washed over me. "No way," I said.

Gwen continued to smirk then let go of one of my hands. Her fingers motioned beside us, plucking a large sapphire ring out of the air. The band was thick, and the stones were clasped in a silver owls talon.

"I need you to deliver this to the Temples. I know there are politics going on down there, but after what you did, appearing with this will seal the deal. You, tell them that together with Theone and Mirna, you will pick the next High Priestess for Samu."

My mouth was agape as Gwen placed the ring into my hand and closed my fingers over it. A tear ran down the side of my cheek. "I miss you," I said.

"I know. Tell Nerice I'm sorry and tell Lachlan his mom approves of you. How couldn't she though? I picked you," Gwen teased.

"You could have stopped everything. So many don't believe the gods are with them. You could have-"

"I was in a mortal incarnation. Time works very differently for me than it does you, but that does not matter. Only life matters. I picked you, I was born, I lived, I joined the army in Blackwick, you fell from the sky as planned and I watched my *pravnuk* fall in love with you." Gwen sighed from the reminiscing.

"Why me?" I asked.

"Because out of the thousands I yanked out of time and space, you were the only one who answered Katerina's pleas." She grabbed the back of my head and brought her forehead to mine, smiling wide. "We'll see each other again."

Tears rolled down my cheeks and I put my free hand to the

back of her head, trying to keep her with me for just a little longer. "We better," I whimpered.

"I will be with you forever, whether you like it or not."

I closed my eyes, trying to drink in this moment with my friend.

She was gone.

I blinked awake, my ears ringing. I lay prone on cold, cracked marble, my fist still clenched around…something. I brought my hand in front of me and plucked a sapphire ring from my grasp.

Gwen.

I took a gasping breath, as if I had not been breathing and looked around. I saw flames and the burnt forms of those who had attacked me crumbling as their ashes flaked away in the wind. There was sunlight, the roof above me was blown open from the explosion. I heard voices shouting. I could hear my name being called in the distance.

I was tired.

I closed my eyes.

*

I smelt cranberry tea and coffee. Woodsmoke mingled with fresh linens. I was warm. When I opened my eyes, Vice looked up from staring at his folded hands. His eyes widened seeing me looking at him and he stood, moving so swiftly out of my line of sight that I thought I imagined him there in the first place.

"Commander," his voice was urgent. "Lachlan, she's awake!"

I looked to where I had heard Vice's voice and saw as Lachlan shot up from a lying in a pile of furs on the ground. Vice was crouched down next to him, now looking at me over his shoulder. Gratefulness washed over his expression.

"Delilah!" Lachlan said. He scrambled to his feet and rushed over to me, almost tripping in the furs and over Vice as he ran. His hand gently took mine. "My deepest love."

I looked around, feeling tired, disoriented. Vice had

disappeared, perhaps to give us privacy. I croaked Lachlan's name.

He smiled, relieved, and his lips pressed against the hand he held. "I'm here. You're here." He kissed my hand again. "We won."

"We won?" I repeated, strained.

He squeezed my hand. "The Temple exploded. When the smoke settled, the *trees* dragged what was left of Salvatore's forces out of the moors. There are reports coming in from every province of Salvatore's army surrendering, if not dropping dead. Those who haven't are retreating in the South Province beyond the Gods Wall. The killing has stopped. The bloodshed is over. We won!" I could hear Lachlan's voice waver as he was about to cry. I looked at him, I saw his eyes were shiny with tears.

"I'm alive," I said softly.

Lachlan nodded, holding my hand to his mouth and kissing my fingers again. "The gods protected you. We found you surrounded by ash, your leg was on *fire*, but the rest of you was as untouched as you were when we discovered you at Andreja's Temple."

"I saw her," I whispered, my voice scratching. "I saw Andreja…the rings…" I looked around observing that I was in the tent where I had been sleeping in throughout our march to the Virág's Temple. The maps, privacy curtains and caged owls were gone. In their place were several more cots and bedrolls on the ground. The wounded lay under blankets being tended to by laity. I thought I recognised one of the nuns as the one I had plucked off the Temple floor and put in the vault. She sensed me watching her and looked over at me from the bedside of a wounded soldier. Her lips mouthed the words *thank you* then she returned her attention to the soldier.

Lachlan patted my hand, drawing my attention to it. Both Caoimhe, Saoirse and Gwen's rings were on my fingers. "You saw her?" he asked.

I nodded fighting heavy lids as sleep craved me. "Where is everybody?" I croaked.

Lachlan's eyes saddened. "We lost a lot of people in the

battle, but no where near as much as we expected. Cathal is in the surgeon's tent. Someone snuck up behind him and some other mages. He took them out, but not before three people died. Nerice has been brought to the dungeons in Antore and meditates. She, umm, took a lot of lives and must settle before coming back to the Council. Bellamy is acting in her absence. Durin is…" The hesitation in Lachlan's voice lingered a second longer than normal. His voice as he said, "in the After."

"The After?"

"As many before us, it seems we both lost our best friends to this war. Captain Florence pulled him from the battle before the explosion. She ran him back to camp for a surgeon or healer, but he passed away before anything could be done. An arrow struck an artery, the surgeon could do nothing. Florence stayed with him until the end. Theone is heartbroken once more." Lachlan looked so miserable. The sorrow I recognized on his face was my own after Blackwick. I felt a tear escape my eye. My heart broke for Lachlan, for Theone, for me.

"He saved me," I said softly. "I had gotten distracted before I made it into the Temple, and he took the arrow for me. I wouldn't have made it without him."

Lachlan tried to smile, the tears in his eyes escaping as well. "That man was always saving me too." He climbed up onto the cot I lay on and cuddled behind me. His arm held me tight, his face nuzzled into the back of my neck. "I did not know why I needed so much saving until I met you."

I cried with him.

Vice did not return.

*

It had been a slow journey back to Antore. Those too unstable to move were left behind at the last camp. Scouts were sent ahead to retrieve more healers. I spent most of the journey asleep in the back of a wagon, struggling to stay awake and eat.

Nerice had been amongst the first who rushed ahead to

432

Antore. Every part of her bounded and gagged on the back of Florence's horse. The blood lust was too much for her. Something I did not know about the Amaranthine's was that those who were young enough could lose control. I did know what *young enough* meant. According to Vice, she had taken too many deadly blows moving through the horde and as a result siphoned too many lives to heal. I wondered how Cathal was doing, though from my understanding he had been covering one of the ranged groups. Not as many came for them as those in the main battle. He saved who he could and had remained in camp to help tend to those effected from the battle.

When I asked how old Vice was, he replied, "Older than Nerice."

Between him and Lachlan, the two monitored my vitals. Though I had not showed any wounds when they found me, when I had first awoken in the tent, it had been several days since the battle. *Surprise, surprise.*

When we made it back to Antore, Theone and Bellamy greeted me. They had tears in their eyes, and Theone's dark makeup was smeared suggesting they had been crying before our arrival. We all hugged and once we settled, we made our way to the dungeons where Nerice sat patiently, on the opposite end of the dungeon where Adder was. This side of the dungeon did not have windows. Bellemy brought a basket of sugared croissants and fruit tarts filled with lemon curd and blueberries. The four of us talked between the bars. It *almost* felt like a slumber party. Nerice's eyes were *incredibly* red, and it was almost disturbing the way she watched every movement we made. She was a bird of prey, caged.

While we ate together, a scout brought us tea and wine to share. Theone expressed their disappointment in not being able tell Durin something but said they had whispered it to his ashes when Lachlan handed the urn to them upon our return. Durin now sat in his old room at the Tavern, beside a bottle of his favourite whiskey and Theone's bed. Theone had decided to move forward as the next leader of Andreja's Temple after our return. Preparations were already underway for ceremonies to crown them, Mirna, and I.

Afterwards, we would choose the next High Priestess of Samu's Temple with the rest of the Holy Order.

Bellemy had fallen asleep against Theone's shoulder after hours of chatting. She talked about everything except the war, trying to keep our minds on something full of light. She described in great detail how the vegetables were doing in her personal garden, how her husband was getting use to the life of a farmer, rather than a duke, and her excitement for the announcement of three new High Priestesses in the coming months. Theone carefully lifted Bellamy's sleeping body and carried her back to her house down the road from the main market street.

Nerice kissed her hand then pressed it to the bars, smiling softly at me after I watched Theone leave. "You go sleep. I should feel better in a few days, a week at most. You still smell *so* good to me..."

I nodded. "Gwen says she's sorry by the way," I told her as I stood.

My emerald ring shined in the torchlight, and I watched the hunger in Nerice's eyes subside long enough for her mind to drift to our friend. She squeezed the bar of the cell and nodded. "I forgive her," she said quietly. I left, leaving what remained of the pastries close to the bars so Nerice could eat them.

Vice stood waiting for me beyond the dungeon doors.

"I didn't get a chance to tell you yet, but I am glad that you lived," he said.

"I think your magic helped," I replied.

Vice smirked. "Maybe you're right."

He walked with me back to my chambers, though it was a leisurely stroll for us. The prosthetic we made together was ruined in the explosion. Lachlan had said they removed it, worrying the flames would burn me, but there were no scorch marks on my skin. The shell of it was still intact, but the technology within was beyond repair. It was on its way to Temple Krix, the latest relic to add to that with the gods. I was back to using my original prosthetic leg, Nerice's dirty pictures carved into it and all. With this prosthetic, I felt phantom pains there once more, but the pangs of discomfort just reminded me of how far I had come. I would have a carpenter sand it down and the pain would dissipate, and I would be back to walking without a limp.

"Can anyone just give their magic away, Vice? I asked.

"It is a blood magic spell, but many know the magic well. Just as lovemaking can bring great favor from the gods, magic can be given through luck and a kiss." He smirked again, motioning for me to continue up the stairs of my tower. "Besides, who better to give it to than a Seer and High Priestess?"

I looked up at him. His red eyes looking down to me with a certain shine. I was several steps ahead of him on the stairwell that led to my chambers, but he still stood tall above me. "Thank you," I said.

"For the magic? No need to thank me-"

"No. When we first met you told me to thank you when this war was over, and I was still alive. Well, here we are. There is no more war, and I feel more alive than ever."

"It has been a long time since I had a friend like you," Vice said.

I smiled wide. "And I you."

Epilogue

Arja screamed awake, her eyes staring straight forward as the colour came back to them.

Shock overtook Krix as he watched one of her eyes leak bright red blood. Disbelief squeezed his stomach. He raked his mind of what could have happened to her during the minutes she was in the After. Arja continued to scream, her voice echoing across the battlefield like thunder. The flames were getting closer to them. When Arja's breath finally ran out, she doubled over in Lethaniel's arms gasping for air. The killing blows were still fresh within her belly and skull. Blood and pieces of bone were everywhere.

"Hush, I will fix you," Lethaniel said. Arja started to scream again. Lethaniel put a hand over her belly as he supported her with the other. Krix crawled over to their side, his hand brushing her hair way from her bleeding eye. Lethaniel shooed him like a fly. "Don't touch her while I do this," he said.

Krix moved his hands away, he could feel his heartbeat in his ears.

She was *alive*.

Lethaniel looked back at Arja and smiled though he doubted his presence would lend any reassurance to her. Undoubtedly Arja was unaware of him there. She was unaware of everything going on. She had been pulled back from death, *changed*. That was a lot for a person to go through.

"This will hurt darling, please bare with me."

Arja's screaming paused as Lethaniel's soothing voice hit her ears and she looked at him. Her eyes lost the fear they had held when she first awoke. "Holy shit!" she gasped.

Lethaniel smiled, knowing what she saw in him. "Bare with me." He applied pressure to her form and Arja's pain came back to her, causing her to scream out again. Her body jerked and tensed while the blood around her body, pooled on the ground and staining Lethaniel's pale hands returned into her stomach. Her broken skull reformed, her organs and flesh mended. Below Lethaniel's hands she squirmed less and less and after a few moments, it became bearable, the pain no more than a healing bruise.

Arja's eyes darted around, disoriented, before they landed on Krix. "Krix?" she croaked.

Krix grabbed her hand as she still lay in Lethaniel's arms. "I'm right here," he said, tears running down his face.

He could only focus on the single sharp pupil staring back at him in a pool of red. Beside it he saw Arja's frosty blue eye, now without its pair. Her face was still so beautiful, but he could not be anything but unsettled. This was no ordinary eye looking back at him.

This was a mark of the gods.

Acknowledgements

I am incredibly thankful to everyone who supported and helped me on this writing journey. I've been wanting to be a published author since I was a teenager, now here I am and it's thanks to you folks.

First I would like to thank my husband Matt, who supported and believed in me during this endeavour I could not have finished and published it without you. Even if sometimes your advice was 'you have to chose for yourself'.

Thank you to my darling friend Hollee, who helped me with my website. It looks so much better. I also appreciate you for giving me blunt and honest opinions during my process. I've always, and will continue to, valued your friendship and ability to pick things apart.

Kail, my deepest thank you for working with me on the most beautiful cover art. You absolutely nailed the vision. I still cannot stop looking at it. I hope you create all the art for my future projects.

Dave, thank you for taking my author photos. It was fun to hang out and I look awesome.

Finally, to you reader. Thank you for giving my book a chance. I hope you come along for the rest.

About the Author

Hannah is an indie author who loves of fantasy, food and the fall. Presently she lives in Ontario, Canada with her husband, three cats, grandfather, and loads of magical fae folk who occupy the property and hide her things for fun.

If you would like to stay up to date with Hannah about future books in the series, and a bunch of other random things, please visit www.hannahmanders.com and join her newsletter!

Printed in the USA
CPSIA information can be obtained
at www.ICGtesting.com
LVHW091507221024
794497LV00005B/465

9 781068 899904